Faire Play

Faire Play

REBECCA KOVAR

SSP

Story Spring Publishing
Pekin, Illinois U.S.A.

Story Spring Publishing, LLC
3420 Veterans Drive, #325
Pekin, Il 61554
www.storyspringpublishing.com

Publisher's Note: This is a work of fiction. Names, characters, places, and incidents are a product of the author's imagination. Locales and public names are sometimes used for atmospheric purposes. Any resemblance to actual people, living or dead, or to businesses, companies, events, institutions, or locales is completely coincidental.

Cover Design: Hilary K. Justice
Cover Illustration: "Wild Irish Rose," © 2000, Kevin Dyer, Marietta, GA, U.S.A. www.etsy.com/shop/Castpaper
Cover Image: "Two crossed rapiers with ornate hilt," © sharpner | rfclipart.com (Item #50729). rfclipart.com/user/sharpner
Cover Image: "Vintage Celtic Knot Frame," © Birgit247 | Dreamstime.com Dreamstime.com (File ID#35557636).
http://www.dreamstime.com/birgit247_info
Front Cover/Spine Font: "Gondola SD," © Steve Deffeyes | Fontsquirrel.com. www.deffeyes.com
Back Cover Font: "Gondola SD - Swash," © Steve Deffeyes | Fontsquirrel.com. www.deffeyes.com

Faire Play/Rebecca Kovar. — 1st ed.
ISBN: 978-1-940699-07-3

For Angus, who always believes,

and

In memory of Barbara Burinski – forever my Queen

Acknowledgments

This book would not exist without the support of my critique partner and writing buddy, Danielle Rebisz Fifer, who for years has read my unedited prose and still asks for more. That sort of masochistic devotion deserves a medal, but all she gets is another raw chapter. I am astoundingly lucky she still likes me.

Also instrumental was Dr. Hilary Justice, whose mark-up of a long-ago manuscript—to the point where it appeared the pages were bleeding red ink—changed forever the way I went about writing. She has borne with me on long walks, during which I rambled about character and plot and mental blocks, and offered both solace and good advice. She has also blessed me with the most amazing cover a book could have.

Dr. Rhonda Nicol was always willing to bat around ideas just to see where they went, which is a blessing and a boon. She was my go-to for sharp insight, location of plot holes, and lively discussion on gender tropes and pacing. Any missteps in those arenas are entirely mine, but if I did it right, she deserves credit for her welcome advice.

For years, Colleen Johnson has allowed me to read chapters aloud to her and patiently waited while I scribbled changes, even if it meant putting up with momentary cliff hangers. She has also been a delightful source for double checking my theories of magic and herbal spell craft. For all that and presenting me with food and coffee when I was on a writing jag, I will be forever grateful.

Special thanks to my beta readers. Crow and Lissa; your encouragement was more important than I can ever adequately express. You make me want to keep writing, just to hear what you have to say about it, and you forgive me my trespasses, for which I humbly thank you.

Last, but never least, I am hugely indebted to my family for their love, acceptance, and willingness to put up with me going down the rabbit hole for weeks at a time. Thank you, Morgan and Duncan, for stepping up to the plate and helping with the house, getting homework done without me (sometimes, anyway), and respecting the closed door to my writing space. For Angus, no mere words will suffice. It always comes down to love.

CHAPTER ONE

Heather licked her lips as the hunger began to ease. Feeding left no taste, but she still found it a bitter necessity. She moved through the crowd, trying not to let them touch her, trying not to take more from them, failing at both. They pressed closer to her, practically begging for contact, seeing what they wanted to see—a beautiful, exotic creature that could not exist anywhere but at the faire. Even if she'd wanted to, she could not break the illusion. The presence of so many of the Tribe kept it flowing like gossamer threads, wrapping the audience in shared wonder. She consumed their adulation like normal people drank water. Everyone in the Tribe fed this way, and most of them gave it no thought. She felt it like a sharp needle sliding under her skin, unpleasant but bearable.

Light filtered through red and gold leaves, warming the loamy earth where it had not been trampled hard. Heather slipped through the woods, around the shop with the bright purple trim and the silver amulets. She breathed in the autumn scent—a waft of perfume from the oils booth, the sweetness of cedar from carved boxes, the pungent aroma of warm henna, and underlying it all, the reek of stale beer and overcooked turkey legs.

She quickened her step as trumpets blared to announce the arrival of the Court. The final joust was about to begin, provided nothing went wrong backstage. With men and horses, mishaps were practically guaranteed; the jousters almost made it an art form. At the bottom of the hill leading to the joust field, she slowed. Attendance at the joust fulfilled her duty to be seen on the street, but there was nothing in her contract that said she had to like the venue. She forced herself to watch at least three final jousts at every faire. For an entire year, she had not managed to find them enjoyable, not since the night Sebastian had given her a Kiss and wrecked her life.

Just over the rise, she spotted her roommate. Jezebel's bright red curls and short, round frame were a marked contrast to the ladies-in-waiting who stood on either side. Katie, a petite blond, was always polite but mostly quiet. Paula—tall, dark and lovely—took her role as the Queen's retainer far too seriously and spent her days insisting people bow and scrape. She made no secret of her loathing for Heather, nor had she bothered to explain it. If she had abandoned her post by the Queen's side to spend time with Jezebel, something was definitely not right.

With no cover of trees, the area around the field was always warm. The large audience for the final joust only increased the heat. Heather lifted her braid to let the breeze cool her neck. As she moved to join the ladies, Jez looked up and smiled. Katie tilted her head in greeting. Paula grimaced but did not withdraw as she usually did when Heather showed up.

"What's so interesting?" Heather directed her question to Katie.

"Jocko is going to kiss that girl who's been following him all season."

"Is he going to kiss her or *Kiss* her?" Heather asked, her jaw tight.

"The latter, of course." Paula flicked open her wooden fan and fixed Heather with a withering gaze. "Or we wouldn't bother watching."

Heather turned to Jez. "Did you let him know she's not Tribe?"

Jez nodded, green eyes wide. "He shrugged and said it was what she wanted, so he was going to let her have it."

"Great." Heather kept her hands at her side, balled into fists. "Another victim."

Paula rolled her eyes. "What's the big deal? So she gets the Kiss and spends the next couple of weeks mooning over him and sending him flowers or really bad poetry. It's not a death sentence." The movements of her fan made the edges of her dark hair dance.

"You planning to let her cry on your shoulder?" Jez moved closer to Heather.

"Hell, no." Paula sneered. "She's not one of us. Why should I care if some Mundane bimbo gets what she deserves?" The fan snapped shut.

Heather stood her ground, despite knowing how well Paula used her fan as a weapon. "You don't care even if they are Tribe."

"True enough, but I sure do like the spectacle. Besides, Jezebel has been wrong before. It would be such fun watching that dim little thing get broken in."

"That's cruel." Katie's protest died when Paula turned to her.

Paula shrugged. "That's life. No point in thinking otherwise. Isn't that right, Heather?"

Heather choked down the urge to reply. Everyone knew Sebastian had turned her and then left her to suffer without guidance. Paula was the only one who mentioned it. Regularly. She might be the Queen's handmaiden, but there was nothing of *noblesse oblige* about the woman. How a scathing bitch could be housed in such cool perfection was beyond Heather. Nature itself should rail against the dichotomy.

"Jocko is not Sebastian," Jez whispered.

"I know." Heather turned to watch.

Jocko stroked the girl's hair as he whispered in her ear. He was tall and lean, with smoldering eyes and long, dark hair that curled at his shoulders, the very image of a young girl's roguish dream. His white shirt gapped open at the chest, sleeves slashed from the shoulder and tied at the wrist to show well-muscled arms. Loose pants billowed where they tucked into his boots, yet the drape of the fabric hid almost nothing of his physique. He smiled at the girl as she stared up with awe. That smile was his best weapon, and he knew exactly how to use it.

Heather leaned forward. The Kiss was so beautiful to behold, none of the Tribe could look away. And even from this distance, the ladies would feel its effect.

Jocko wrapped one arm around the girl, drawing her closer as he caressed her cheek. He brushed his lips over hers. She relaxed into him, tilted her head up for more, and closed her eyes. He turned his head to flash a smile up the hill before lowering his mouth to claim his prize. The girl curled her fingers into his shirt as the Kiss took her.

When he broke away, she leaned heavily against him. He pressed gently on the back of her head until she laid her cheek on his chest. His arm remained around her waist, and he stroked her back with his other hand. If he let her go too soon, she would fall, and people would look. The Tribe took care to keep their nature secret.

The Court took care of anyone who failed.

Jocko made sure the girl could stand on her own before untangling her fingers from his shirt. He kissed her hand, bowed, and turned away, disappearing into the growing crowd. She stared in the direction he'd gone long after he was out of sight.

Heather stared, too. They should have felt a surge from the Kiss, even in the midst of the crowd. A Kiss usually bled energy. This one hadn't. She didn't know whether she should be worried or relieved. She still had trouble dealing with what she had turned into. Her turmoil did not stop her from feeding off the patrons, from drinking in their excitement and joy or sometimes their confusion and fear. She regarded the freshly Kissed girl, looking for an answer but finding none.

"Jealous?" Paula asked, standing too close.

Heather thought briefly about punching the other woman, in part because Paula was right, but the last thing she wanted was to admit her attraction to Jocko. "Not jealous at all. Jocko wasn't the one who turned *me*. He just chose me for a partner." Their fight routine had been more of a directive than a choice, but Paula didn't need to know that.

"Don't expect it to last," Paula snapped. "You don't have a good track record for keeping Tribe men interested."

Katie's apology was in her eyes, but she could do nothing to make the situation better. She turned without a word and followed Paula down the hill.

"So," Jezebel said, instantly practical, "do we watch the joust from up here and keep an eye on the girl or swoop down and console her?"

"Neither." Heather turned away. "I'm going to get a drink."

"Ah, then we wait until we stumble across her mooning over Jocko." Jez nodded. "A drink would definitely make that situation easier. At least you're done fighting him today."

Heather shook her head. "Not alcohol. I have the final jam before I get to drown my sorrows."

"You saying you're unhappy here?" Jezebel was clearly alarmed, and for good reason.

Heather's first year had been so bad that people who had never met her were talking about it. It even had a name: The Yarborough Affair. Heather thought that sounded like some drama about Victorian politics rather than the sad tale of a gullible girl. Her last name had become synonymous with tragedy—not the best way to start a new adventure.

"I'm content," she said. "Tired, but content."

Jez patted her arm. "Honey, this late in the season, we're all worn out. Let's go get that drink."

They walked down the hill while trumpets blared. A cloud of dust accompanied the sound of thundering hooves, as the jousters entered the arena. Heather was glad to leave it behind. Carter might pout over her missing his big scene, but if she was lucky, he wouldn't notice her absence. In a crowd of thousands, it was difficult to pick out one person—even the one you were hell-bent on impressing. She could not convince him it was an exercise in futility, despite everyone knowing it had been a jouster who'd turned her without asking if she wanted this life.

A multihued canopy billowed far above the kitchens, hinting at the chill to come. Heather bought warm cider. Jezebel poured beer into her mug and threw away the plastic cup. With most of the patrons watching the joust, finding an empty table was easy. Finding one that was not thoroughly gross proved harder. Heather pushed a half-eaten tray of cheesy fries to the edge of a table and flopped onto the bench.

"It's totally unfair that I have to strap these into steel-boned hell—" Jezebel waved at her ample bosom. "—but Management gets away with selling French fries and nachos, not to mention the plastic cups with brand logos."

"You can't tell me you don't enjoy the attention." Heather sipped her cider.

"Right. Men asking me if my tits are real is a huge thrill." Jez sighed.

"Maybe my lack of cleavage is why the patrons don't bother flirting with me. Never saw that as a blessing before." The audience might be compelled to stare, but it was rare that anyone but children sought to talk to her.

"They're probably afraid to make a move because you're heavily armed."

"Who isn't?" Heather nodded to the hilt of the dagger sticking up from Jezebel's corset.

"You actually use yours, publicly and very well. That can be a little intimidating, especially to Mundanes."

"Jocko only loses to me because the audience gets upset if a guy beats up a woman. Too bad they don't care as much out there." Heather gestured toward the front gate.

Jez shrugged. "I guess they want their fantasy world to be clean, since their daily world is so messed up."

Heather's eyebrows shot up. "Ours isn't?"

"Of course it is, but they don't know that. Mundanes see what we want them to see. We aren't about to air our dirty laundry, even if we do show them everything but that. They wouldn't recognize it anyway. Nothing here is real to them."

Heather scanned the carefully constructed fantasy around her. "I remember."

"So do I, honey, just not well." Jez finished her beer and stood. "Back to the shop for me."

"I'll walk with you," Heather offered.

Jez shook her head. "You'd only have to head back this way. Go shopping, or find a quiet place to rest before the jam. I'll catch you after the show." Jez flounced away, the sway of her wide hips catching more eyes than she would ever believe.

Heather wandered through the faire. The bright banners and sparkling displays of jewelry appeared as a museum exhibit, if a bit gaudier. In the distance, a hammer struck steel with a dull clank. A huge roar erupted from the joust field, telling her one of the men had died. She hoped it wasn't Carter, but only because she liked to see the good guys win.

Sated from her earlier feeding, Heather barely noticed the people around her. Still, she searched for something. It took her several minutes to realize her quarry was the recently Kissed girl. She sighed. It was not her job to look after Mundanes, much less console them for being stupid, but she could not shake the overwhelming desire to find the girl. She'd been that foolish once, and no one had looked for her, even after she'd been turned.

Forcing herself to stop that particular train of thought, she dug into her pouch and found her watch. She had five minutes before all the shows let out at once, flooding the site with stumbling drunks, shrieking teens, hyper children, and exhausted parents. She headed for the music stage to avoid the exodus. She kept her head down and scuffed at leaves, smiling when the wind sent them swirling up. One of the first things Jez had shown her was how to truly feel the ground as she walked, so she could navigate the site after dark.

During the day, there were more people. The thought occurred to her as she ran into someone, apology already coming out as she looked up—straight into Jocko's dark eyes. His hand reached out to steady her. He never stumbled.

"Don't be sorry, darlin'." He didn't bother to hide his southern twang behind what even he admitted was an execrable British accent. "You can slam up against me anytime you want." He turned his smile on her. She resisted the urge to slap it off his face.

"Get your hands off me, Jocko." She jerked back, not waiting for him to comply.

"What's caught in your craw?" He didn't seem offended.

"How's that girl doing? The one whose heart you just broke."

"My dear Miss Yarborough, you can't possibly hold that against me." His voice dripped with charm, a warm honey tone that barely disguised his mockery. "This was her sixth time here. You saw her at our fights, so you know she followed me all day, every time. I tried to convince her I wasn't a nice guy, but she didn't believe me. Said she just wanted me to kiss her, so I did."

"You didn't have to do it like that."

"Why shouldn't I? The worst that's going to happen is she's going to have some very confusing dreams for a few weeks and feel a little empty when they fade. Come winter, she won't think about me at all."

"You don't remember what it was like, do you?" Heather clenched her teeth against her own memories, as if they would come spilling out unbidden.

He leaned over and whispered in her ear, like the barest buzz of a lazy bee on a hot night, "Oh, I remember just fine. I just don't think it was a big tragedy that I ended up here." His breath skittered like silk against her cheek. "And neither do you."

He walked off, whistling.

She stood still, losing focus the way Mundanes did under a glamour. It didn't matter that she was Tribe; he turned her stupid without trying. Even a Kiss shouldn't do what he did with his voice. She hated him for it.

CHAPTER TWO

Heather lost herself in the music, swaying slightly. She had been given the nod to be next up, but it would be a while. Ian and the other musicians tended to get carried away during their jam sessions. Heather tapped her foot in time with the reel, and it took everything she had to not join the dancing. She contented herself with watching the swirl of brightly colored skirts as young women twirled and hopped anywhere they could find space.

After a few more minutes, the musicians took pity and ended the song. The dancers collapsed on the lower level of the stage, panting and laughing. The audience applauded wildly, both for the musical artistry and the plentiful display of heaving bosoms.

Realizing the crowd needed to come down a bit, Heather told Ian she'd changed her chosen tune. He passed the word, and as she stepped up, they began the first strains of *The Blacksmith*. She stepped to the front of the stage. Her face full of joy, she began to sing:

> *A blacksmith courted me, nine months or better*
> *He fairly won my heart, wrote me a letter*
> *With his hammer in his hand, he looked to be so clever*
> *And if I were with my love, I would live forever*
> *Oh where is my love gone, with his cheek like roses,*
> *And his good black billycock on, decked 'round with primroses?*

I'm afraid the scorching sun will shine and burn his beauty,
And if I was with my love, I would do my duty.

The musicians took over for a mini-jam session before Ian nodded to the others and came to whisper in her ear. She reacted with shock and confusion, to let the audience know all was not well.

Strange news is come to town, strange news is carried
Sad news cried up and down, that my love is married
I wish them both much joy, though they can't hear me
And may God reward him well for the slighting of me.

Anger filled her, edged with a bitterness she did not have to feign.

Do you remember when you lay beside me
You said you'd marry me and not deny me

She took a deep breath to finish the verse but was silenced by a rich voice, thick with laughter.

If I said I'd marry you, 'twas only for to try you
So bring your witness, love, and I'll not deny you

People had parted to let Jocko through, his smile full of charm and derision. He sang with no accent at all. Heather glared at him, investing the next lines with vitriol.

Oh, witness I have none, save God Almighty
And may he reward you well for the spiting of me

He interrupted her again, turning to the audience with his arms open, mocking her.

Her lips grew pale and wan; it made her poor heart tremble
For to think she'd loved but one, and I'd proved deceitful

He stepped up to the stage as the audience applauded wildly. As she dropped a curtsy, he took her hand and kissed it. When she snatched it away, the audience laughed. It was all part of the show to them.

Only because they won't see me beat him to a pulp. The thought made her feel better.

She didn't have time to withdraw before the Court approached, so she and Jocko dropped into poses of respect and submission where they were.

"Arise, fair maid and scurrilous rogue. Arise all." The King's voice bounced off the back of the music stage. No one could project like Rodney. He fixed Jocko with a stern look. "What is this I hear about you marrying without consulting the Court?"

"False rumors, your majesty. I assure you, I have not taken such steps."

"Then perhaps we should consider seeing it done." Rodney winked at Heather then turned to the audience. "What say you? Should these young lovers wed?"

The audience roared their approval. The Queen clapped along with them. "I just adore weddings!"

"Then it is settled." The King and Court walked toward the stage.

Heather took her cue to retreat, wanting nothing more than to flee. Jocko grabbed her hand and followed her, then stepped behind her and wrapped his arm around her waist.

"Give the people what they want, sweetheart," he whispered in her ear.

She smiled, leaned into him, and tilted her face up. "You're a dead man."

He laughed and kissed her forehead. She resisted the urge to stomp on his foot, but barely.

She sang the final song with the rest of the cast, the words coming with no thought. She'd lost count of how many 'fare thee wells' she'd given. As the Court descended to lead the parade out, the King motioned to her and Jocko to fall in. Paula stared daggers at them both as they played the celebrated lovers all the way to the front gate. The audience filed out behind the King, rats to his Pied Piper.

The musicians jumped up on the stage outside the gate, drawing the rest of the crowd out. Heather slipped back through the gates unnoticed. As soon as she was back on the deserted site, she untied her bodice. The laces were half undone by the time Jocko caught up with her. She continued walking, but her hands stilled.

"Don't stop undressing on my account," he drawled.

"I wasn't doing it for you."

"So you say. If not for me, then who?"

"For the chance to breathe freely. Get lost."

"You wound me." He clutched his hand to his heart.

"Dare me." She put her hand on her sword and stepped back, but knew better than to draw.

"You don't want to hurt me."

"Oh, I do, more than you know. I might have to prove it to you tomorrow. What were you thinking, interrupting my song?"

"Pleasing the audience, of course."

"Pleasing yourself is more like it. Just like with that girl."

He shook his head. "You gonna continue to gripe about that?"

"It was unkind."

"Let me tell you how her night ended." Jocko grinned. "She wandered around until she met a very nice young man who'd had a crush on her for years. He sweet talked her and her friends into going out to dinner with him and his friends. By the time she left, she was hanging on his arm, smiling and laughing."

"And she's still going to pine for you when she goes home." Heather shook her head. "You don't just shake off a Kiss. It stays with you, haunting your dreams, making you feel horrible and empty."

"How do you know? You're Tribe. It didn't work that way for you."

"Not exactly that way, no. But I've seen it often enough." Heather turned away, unable to continue.

"They live through it," Jocko said softly.

"Of course they do. But they're peculiar until it fades."

"Only sometimes. Maybe it's a good thing."

Heather spun and advanced on him, making him step back. "How is being completely out of it a good thing?"

"It teaches you not to kiss strange men."

"So you give the Kiss out of altruism? I don't buy it."

"No. I do it because it's what I do. What we all do. I don't give a Kiss lightly, but even I have my limits when it comes to being stalked. It's no fun to be harried across the site day after day. If the only way to get them to leave me alone so I can do my job is to give them something they think they desire, then that's what I'll do."

"She'll be back next weekend and the weekend after that."

"Maybe." He shrugged.

"Definitely. I hope she follows you around like a lost puppy. It's the least you deserve."

"Eventually, you'll come off your high horse and give someone a Kiss."

"No, I won't."

"You will. And when you do, you can come talk to me about it. Until then, you only have one side of the story. It isn't always tragic, sugar. Sometimes, it's a blessing." He turned and strode away.

Heather walked slowly, undoing her laces until her bodice hung open. The thin cotton of her shirt stuck to her until she fluffed it out, letting the breeze dry it a little. It was the first time she'd been cool since morning. Her feet took her to the base of the stairs behind Jezebel's shop. She stopped to listen, half-wanting to hear Rascal's voice. Jez thought Rascal was the guy for her. When it came to love, Heather was too accustomed to disappointment to be able to encourage Jezebel's hopes.

The only sound greeting her was the familiar thump of boxes as Jezebel sorted through her stock. Heather climbed the stairs, knocked once, and walked in. The store room was chaotic, as usual. Small, plastic bags spilled out of a crate in one corner. Jezebel kicked boxes out of her way until progress across the room would prove hazardous to anyone not looking out for them. There was some order to the place, mostly around the edges. Pendants hung on dowels on the wall. Disembodied hands covered with tight velvet gloves lined the shelves, rings sparkling on every finger. Trays of earrings were stacked on a table, all the numbers turned out so they could be easily placed in the right spot the next day. Jez seemed to know where everything was at any given moment, so she obviously had a system.

Heather pulled a stool from one corner and perched on it, waiting for Jez to finish. It was always like this on Saturday nights.

"Be right with you, honey," Jez said, not bothering to slow down.

"I have nowhere else to be. I'd hoped you would."

"You and me both." Jez laughed. "Rascal stopped by after closing to see if I liked the rose he sent. I invited him to join us, but he'd made other plans."

"I'm sorry."

"Don't be! He offered me a rain check for tomorrow night. I hope it doesn't actually rain."

"I don't think that will be a problem. I wouldn't mind a quick sprinkle to keep the dust down, but if the temperature drops, it'll freeze overnight."

"I'd rather deal with the dust, thanks."

"You and me both. Fighting is dangerous enough without having to worry about slipping, though it would give me an excuse to accidentally stab Jocko."

Jez straightened, fixing her friend with a stern look. "Don't even joke about it."

"He makes me crazy."

"You need to figure out a way to stop letting him get to you, if only because it makes him so happy when he manages to ruffle your feathers. You don't want to go making a man like that too happy. They find reasons to stick around if you do."

"Just what I need, another person to watch out for."

"What you should do is stop worrying about things you can't control." Jez went back to digging through boxes, stacking them against one wall as she went. By the time she was done, the storeroom was once more navigable.

"I don't know how."

"There's a pretty steep learning curve on that, and you're still fairly new. You'll figure it out. You might start by asking for guidance."

"Not a bad idea. You have anyone in mind?"

"Well, the person most likely to help makes you crazy, so that's out. Let me think about it." Jez straightened up. "In the meantime, let's change and get some dinner. My treat."

"You must have done pretty well today," Heather said.

"Better than usual. Besides, a rose and a promise is reason enough to celebrate, don't you think?"

"Absolutely." Heather hopped off the stool and went to the tiny room she called home during this show. She didn't know why Jez had taken her under her wing, but she was grateful.

CHAPTER THREE

B y the time they got back to the faire site, the parties were in full swing. Heather parked her Jeep in the back lot. It was an impractical vehicle for the road, but she was loath to give it up. Her friend Cami said it was her lodestone, a constant reminder of the Summer of Sebastian. She liked to think of it as proof she had once been free.

She had to give Sebastian credit for one thing; he had told her that summer would be the stuff of dreams, and it was. He was the guy on all the billboards advertising the faire—fifty feet tall, golden hair streaming as he rode, sword aloft—the ultimate renaissance fantasy man, looming over the highway. She had been a lowly apprentice, singing in the streets, leading cheers while keeping idiots off the joust field, doing improv skits that garnered few onlookers. And yet Sebastian, of all people, had noticed her. The Bastard had courted her in the old-fashioned sense, sending flowers and poetry, treating her to dinner, introducing her to the In Crowd, taking her to parties. When she'd watched the joust, the world fell away until all she could see was him—riding, fighting, winning—the most beautiful bad guy in the world. He'd even made dying look good.

She still had no idea what he'd seen in her. She was plain, had no discernible curves, ordinary brown hair, boring brown eyes. He had argued for her beauty so long, she'd begun to believe in it. And all the while, he'd remained a perfect gentleman. Well, mostly. Naturally, she had fallen completely and utterly in love. Like a total idiot.

During the cast party, he had taken her for a walk through town and along the beach. He had said he wanted to give her something to remember him by. She had known their relationship was nothing more than a summer fling, that he would leave with everyone else. She'd told him there was no way she would forget him, so presents weren't necessary. He'd laughed and told her it was important that he leave her with something she could keep forever. They had walked back toward the party, holding hands, the perfect end to a perfect affair.

She hadn't noticed the people on the balcony, though upon reflection, she remembered them leaning over the railing. He'd tilted her face up, the moon a crescent over his shoulder, and had given her the Kiss. Warmth and light had filled her, along with the sense that anything was possible, but underneath it all a terrible ache had formed. Her bones had seemed to turn to liquid as he'd held her up, whispering to her how special she was, just as he'd expected.

His words had haunted her in the months that followed. She sketched and painted him from memory, then went online to find more pictures, hoping she'd stumble across a mention of where he'd be. She imagined flying to see him perform. He would be surprised, thrilled to see her, flattered with her gift of portraits of him. Only he was not performing at any show she could find and never answered the letters she sent. She kept hoping to hear from him long after it became obvious he had no intention of contacting her. Eventually, she succumbed to despair.

Her rapid weight loss had scared her roommates into thinking she had an eating disorder. When her parents insisted she go to counseling, she had numbly agreed. They'd all thought she would be hospitalized. Instead, her amazingly perceptive shrink diagnosed her with a classic case of pining. After a couple of months, during which she managed to find her appetite and get her grades back up, Heather had been pronounced completely normal. Or as normal as she had ever been.

Three months later, the longing had begun. She had known better than to let on, especially since she had no idea how to explain it. She needed to be at a faire, any faire. She needed those people like she needed water and air. It scared the hell out of her. If she went back, she might see the Bastard again, and the very idea sickened her. And yet, it couldn't be worse than the terrible pull that made her feel like her skin no longer fit.

She had tried to stave off the urge to flee by working on a play. They needed set painters, and she needed a fix. Theater was theater, right? Only it turned out to be more like slapping on a nicotine patch, when what she wanted was to smoke a whole pack. At least it had kept her from haring off before the semester was over.

When she got home, she dropped her stuff and headed straight to the faire site. Fewer than a hundred merchants and performers were there to set up, but she felt like she could breathe for the first time in a year. By the end of the day, she'd been given an audition. A week later, she had a contract in hand. On the first day of rehearsal, Jezebel swooped down and claimed her as a friend. Within a month, they were roommates. It had been a whirlwind introduction to a whole new world.

"You planning to spend all night in the truck?" Jez asked.

Heather shook her head. "Sorry. Just remembering the Bastard."

"I figured. You okay?"

"Yeah." Heather hooked the keys to her belt loop and got out.

Jez nodded toward the jouster camp. "Then let's go see what the pony boys are up to."

"Ugh. I was thinking about going to the music pit instead."

"Too early. There was a big dinner for Ian's birthday. They won't be back for a couple of hours, at least." Jez shrugged. "Which leaves Paula's little pseudo-salon or the campfire of the braggarts."

"No choice there. If I beg off, are you going alone?"

"Duh."

"If you're determined to go, I will, too."

Jez laughed. "I can take care of myself, honey. Half those guys are afraid of me and the other half think I'm too fat to waste their pretty attention on."

"That's because they don't have the sense God gave a goat."

"Just the smell," Jez finished for her.

"They'll have showered by now," Heather conceded.

"True, but the residual smell of horse and leather never leaves them."

"And this is a bad thing? Add in the scent of whiskey and you know why I keep going back." It was the absolute truth. She loved the way they smelled, but she would never tell anyone but Jez. The jousters didn't need their egos fed; they were practically glutted by the final joust.

"Here I thought you did it to tease Carter," Jez said.

Heather sighed. "I have never led him to believe I was interested in him. Whatever his deal is, he owns it, not me. I know better than to play in that sandbox again."

"I like their sandbox, even if no one wants to play. Although it's always a pleasure listening to Lewis try out his terrible pick-up lines on me."

"Did it ever occur to you that he might mean them?"

"Not a chance. Have you seen him?" Jez grinned at her. "So, aside from protecting my nonexistent virtue, why are you coming with me to jouster hell?"

"Free booze, good company, and the chance to swat them down a little."

"Any other reason?" Jez prompted.

"I like hanging out with Darius and Lew." Heather huffed. "Why did you make me say that?"

"Because you need to admit to yourself that not everyone is cast from the same mold as Sebastian, and the more you repeat that, the faster you'll get over him."

"The Bastard never brought me to the campfire, so Darius and Lew are clean of his stain, at least in my book. And for the record, I am totally over him."

Jez snorted. "Which is why you just spent five minutes sitting in your car thinking about him."

"They weren't self-deprecating thoughts. Does that count?"

"It's an improvement." Jez led the way.

The parking lot was one of the better lit places at night, making the walk easier. The trail to the jouster camp was off to one side, an invisible line keeping anyone but them from parking nearby. Or maybe it was the increased chance of drunken revelers causing dents when they stumbled away from the frequent parties.

Heather stopped by the stables, waving Jez on. She spent a few minutes stroking the noses of the horses that knew her. There was a new one on the end. Heather reached into her pocket and drew out the cut carrots she had taken from her salad, unwrapped the napkin, and offered them to the hesitant horse. He wuffled at her before taking them, letting her stroke his nose as he ate.

Heather and the horse both moved back as Carter stepped forward. He was exactly the sort of man her mother had hoped she would end up with. Tall and muscular, he had that confident swagger only jousters could manage without looking foolish. His blond hair fell in multiple directions but never looked out of place, for which he was regularly teased. The best thing about him, though, was his smile. He could have done toothpaste commercials, which, considering he lived pretty rough, was saying something. Unfortunately, his pale hair and blue eyes reminded Heather a little too much of Sebastian, so there was no way she could have brought herself to date him.

"Fury likes you." Carter was obviously surprised. "Damn beast doesn't like anyone. He's been a pain since we got him."

"I don't know if it's me he likes, or the carrots."

"I'm thinking it's you. That horse bit the last person who offered him a treat." Carter smiled. "I guess he knows a thing or two about quality."

"Maybe that's why he doesn't like you." There was no sting in her words.

He laughed. "Maybe he feels a kinship with you because you're mean." He pushed his hair out of his eyes. It immediately fell back again.

"Could just be picky about spending time with certain people."

"Who? The horse, or you?"

"Both." Heather smiled.

"I have a surprise for you," he said, reaching for her hand.

Heather drew back. "Last time one of you said that, it didn't work out so well for me."

"Don't be like that." He stuck his hands in his pockets.

"What, cautious? It's an occupational hazard."

"You're a hard woman."

Heather shook her head. "Just a little less naive than most of your girls is all."

"My girls, huh? You act like I have a harem or something." He laughed.

"How many women are sitting on cold benches, waiting for you to notice them?"

"I don't know what they're waiting for. I didn't invite any of them." He turned away. "Come to the fire. Darius has been whining about you standing him up. Again."

Heather followed him. "I didn't make any promises to Darius." She knew she sounded defensive.

"I know. It's just been a while since you came around. He misses you."

They came into a clearing. Rough benches, some stolen from the faire site, were set back from the fire pit. There were more people than she'd expected, including a couple of women she didn't know. She rolled her eyes. The boys should know better than to invite patrons to party. They tended to have fathers—or husbands—who took exception to their absence.

She could almost forgive the squire. Tyler was new to the game and wasn't Tribe. Michael, on the other hand, had no excuse. The woman clinging to him was exactly the sort who brought trouble down on a faire. Drawn by Michael's dark good looks and sweet promises, she would spend the night beneath him and wake up alone. Even if he was beside her, his warm smile would be gone, his dark eyes cold. The man had serious issues with intimacy and no consideration for who got hurt.

Carter followed her gaze. He must have read her mind, too. "Let him be. He's already on edge because the fight went wrong."

"He's a fool," Heather said. "But I won't start any trouble tonight."

Darius rose when he saw her. He was a bear of a man, broad-chested, with a thick waist and tree trunks for legs. If his height had matched his width, he would have needed a Clydesdale to carry him. He would also have stood about seven feet tall. For all his girth, there wasn't any fat on him. She knew for a fact that he was faster than most of his leaner cohorts. Dark hair, shot with grey and pulled into a ponytail, made his sun browned features seem more severe than usual.

He opened his massive arms and bellowed, "Little sister! About time you showed up. Come give us a hug."

She went to him, glad to see his hair still damp from a recent shower. If he'd been fresh from the field, she would have demurred. He wrapped her up and lifted her, tightening his arms. A series of pops drew whistles of approval from Fox, Darius' squire.

"Better than a chiropractor, I swear," she said when he finally released her.

"Cheaper, too." He winked at her. "In case any of you have forgotten, Heather is under my protection. Mess with her and you'll answer to me."

He gave a pointed look at Michael, who responded not at all.

"I can handle myself," Heather said. "But I'll bet your sisters hated it when you did that."

"My parents took one look at me and decided against having another child." Darius winked at her.

"How can I pay you back for that lovely spine realignment?"

"You could get me a beer. I'm fresh out." Darius drank beer like other people drank water, but he never seemed to get drunk.

"Done." Heather turned toward the clubhouse.

"Me, too, honey," Michael called out.

Others followed suit, including Tyler. Fox shook his head. He didn't drink or smoke, and he never brought patron girls to the fire. His biggest sin was a penchant for playing pop ballads on his guitar, and that usually only lasted until someone threw something at him.

Heather turned back and smiled sweetly. "Raise your hand if you joined that chorus." She counted five hands.

"Don't do it, Heather," Darius said, glaring at his companions. "You don't have to do this."

"It's okay. I was going to get one for myself anyway."

"I'll help you," Fox offered, standing.

"No, thanks. I've got it."

She walked over to the cooler, made a basket with her loose shirt, and loaded it up with cans. She carried them back, getting a couple of whistles for her bared midriff. She set her beer down and handed one to Darius.

"Who asked for this?" Five hands shot up. Smile fixed on her face, she grabbed a beer, shook it hard, and threw it across the fire. She repeated the action until the last beer was gone.

"Next time you want something from me, ask politely. I'm not your wench." She flopped down on the bench next to Darius, who had stopped drinking so he wouldn't shoot beer out of his nose.

"I adore you," he finally managed to choke out.

"So do I," Carter whispered. She pretended she hadn't heard.

The camp followers looked scandalized. She had cemented herself as a bitch in their eyes, which was perfectly fine. They were sycophants, and she had no use for any of them. Then again, they weren't there to be used by her.

"Since you can't open those for a few minutes, try this." Darius reached under the bench and pulled out a full bottle of whiskey. He passed it to Carter, who took a bigger slug than usual.

"I'd have brought you a beer if you'd asked," Heather said.

"I'd have asked more politely than they did, if I'd wanted one," Carter replied, handing the bottle to Michael.

"I know." She gave him a real smile, the first one she'd managed since witnessing the Kiss.

"You just about ready for that surprise?" Carter asked.

"Do I get it in public?" Heather countered to the amusement of the men—and some of the women—around the fire.

"I'm an honorable man, Heather." Carter's azure eyes held nothing but sincerity. "Unlike some." He nodded toward Michael, who flipped him off for the slight.

"Okay, then." Heather braced herself. "Bring it on."

CHAPTER FOUR

Carter put two fingers in his mouth and gave a sharp whistle. One of the horses whinnied back, which set off another round of laughter. A low curse came from behind the armory, accompanied by clanging as a bucket flew into the bushes. Lewis stumbled around the corner, still swearing.

"That is a surprise," Darius said. "You can conjure up a black man. I don't know many people with that kind of magic."

"Stuff it, old man," Lew said without malice. "The trick is making a pixie appear." He stepped aside to reveal a small woman with short, spiky black hair, high cheekbones highlighted with a dusting of freckles, and a full mouth tinted with lipstick the color of dried blood. Intricate henna designs covered her hands and disappeared up her sleeve, the red fading into her dark tan.

Heather squealed and launched herself at the newcomer. "Cami! How the hell?"

"Magic, baby. Just like the man said." Cami wrapped her arm around Heather's waist.

"Magic, huh?"

"What else do you call the ability to fly?" Cami turned to Lew. "Don't you dare take credit for this, either."

"Wasn't planning on it." Lew surveyed the benches. "I'm just here for the white women." Several of the patron girls looked nervous. He snorted and pointed at Jez. "That one will do."

"In your dreams, Lewis," Jezebel shot back.

"Let me tell you what those dreams are like, baby, and you might reconsider." He winked at her.

"I might reconsider for something finer than what this lot is drinking. I'm not that cheap." She smiled as he came around the fire to stand behind her.

"Never thought you were." He kissed her on the head and dropped onto the bench beside her. He offered her a flask. "It's warm, just the way you like. I heated it up by keeping it next to my smoking body."

"Smooth, Lew. Real smooth." Jez took a drink, shuddered, and relaxed against his shoulder.

Even sitting down, he dwarfed her. There was nothing small about Lew, a fact he would gladly report if asked, usually accompanied by a wiggle of his eyebrows. He put an arm around her, careful to keep his hand in neutral territory.

Heather looked down at Cami. "Why didn't you tell me you were coming?"

"Because I wasn't. I was going to head home between shows, but Carter e-mailed me and said he'd buy me a ticket if I wanted to come for the last few weeks."

Heather looked at him. "Why did you do that?"

Cami snorted. "It ain't because he likes me, sister."

"I like you well enough," Carter protested.

"I don't," Michael offered.

Cami ignored him. "And it sure as hell isn't because he expects me to sleep with him."

"I've been stabbed once this season," Carter said. "By accident. That's more than enough."

Heather started at the admission. "You didn't tell me that. When?"

"Colorado. No big deal." He shrugged, looking down.

"I have no idea how you can resist that puppy," Cami said. "He's just so damned cute. And he's all noble and shit."

"Bite me," Carter snapped. He walked over to the cooler, grabbed a beer, and leaned against the wall of the armory.

"Hey, I meant that! You're not like these other posers." Cami scanned the bench, flashing her teeth at Michael in a way that could not be mistaken for a smile. Her lip curled at the confused blonde by his side. She shook her head in disgust.

"Cami, you keep insulting us, and I might tell these fine people your real name," Darius warned. "And then you'd lose all your pixie magic and be forced to serve us forever and ever."

"As long as I got to cut you up before I served you that would be okay. You may be big, but even the meat on your bones won't last forever and ever."

"You're a nasty piece of work." Darius laughed. "Come sit by me. If you ask the right way, Heather might even get you a beer."

Everyone dissolved into fits of laughter. Darius relayed the story as Fox found something in the shed that Cami would drink. She said beer was like drinking weasel piss. Heather had never asked how she might know that.

She paused, standing a few feet from Carter. "Did you bring her here just for me?" she asked softly.

"You know I did. You said you missed her like a limb."

"Thank you."

"You're welcome." He hesitated. "I don't want you to think you owe me. That's not why I did it."

"I know." He never demanded anything from her, never asked, never expected. Just hoped, which made it worse. "You're a nice guy." She kissed him on the cheek.

"Around here, they think that means I'm a sucker."

"What they think doesn't matter." She smiled at him then went to give Cami her soda.

"I finally have my two girls in one place," Darius said, patting the bench beside him.

"Please. Like I'm any of yours." Cami snorted. "Now shift over so I can sit by my girl."

Darius complied. Heather sat, and Cami hooked one leg over hers and leaned into her shoulder.

"Are they gay?" The blonde next to Michael whispered, just a bit too loud. He froze. Stunned silence followed, as all heads turned to Cami.

"No, honey, we're not gay. We're just not whores," she said pointedly.

The girl blushed furiously, shoved Michael's arm off her, and stomped away from the fire.

"You are a first-class bitch," Michael snarled.

"Why, thank you!" Cami smiled. "Now you'd best run along and chase that tail like a good dog. Lord only knows what might happen to her out in the dark."

Michael didn't move.

"I think I saw Jocko on the way in," Cami added. "You should get your ass in gear. I hear he's in the mood to give Kisses today. Might steal that girl right out from under you."

Michael glared at her then stalked off.

"Is there some reason you feel compelled to irritate your brother?" Darius asked.

"Old habits die hard. Besides, he's an asshole. That girl would be better off being Kissed by Jocko than spending a night with Mike."

Heather was horrified. "Don't say that!"

"Why not? The Kiss fades, and everyone says Jocko's are the most gentle around. What Michael does to a girl screws her up for life."

"Did you really see Jocko on site?" Heather asked.

Cami sat up. "Why, you chasing that?" Her disapproval was clear.

"No! The opposite, actually. I was hoping to get a bead on his location so I can make sure to avoid him on my way home."

"No worries. He was heading for Miss Paula's snotty soiree, and I don't see you dipping your foot in that rancid pool."

"Not even for a guy I actually like," Heather agreed.

"Like Carter?" Cami teased.

"Don't start," Heather warned.

"What's wrong with him?"

"Nothing. I like him, but as a friend."

"Oh, harsh. That's like a kiss of death to a besotted boy's soul."

"I wish to hell everyone would stop talking about me like I'm deaf," Carter said, coming up behind them. He leaned down and tickled Cami. She was incredibly ticklish, but most people wouldn't use it against her. She wore knives like other girls wore jewelry—only you couldn't see them until they were in her hand.

Heather grabbed the soda before her friend fell off the bench, grateful it was almost empty. Darius caught Cami and swung her around, despite her cursing. She pummeled him with her fists, entirely without effect. He laughed in her face. Part of his enjoyment would come from preventing bloodshed. He was one of the few people Cami was unwilling, or possibly unable, to hurt.

"I'm not besotted." Carter took the seat next to Heather. "I'm just a damned good friend, is all."

"You really are. I've done nothing to deserve that." Heather sighed.

Carter smiled. "Sure you have. You're you."

Lew groaned. "Oh, man! Does that *ever* work? Cuz that line is seriously tired."

"I think it's sweet," Jez said, taking the flask out of his hand.

"You want me to talk sweet to you?" Lew asked.

"No, because you won't mean it. And that definitely isn't your style."

"Baby, that is no style at all. My man is completely sincere when he talks that way. It's unnatural."

"It's called being honest," Carter said. "You should try it sometime."

"I'm honest! I tell everyone I'm a self-involved jerk." Lew's smile shone white in the darkness.

"He does," Jez conceded. "It's refreshing."

Lew looked over at his squire. "You know what would be refreshing, Tyler? If you got off your ass and got us some wood, so the fire doesn't burn out."

"I'm busy," Tyler said. "And I like it dark."

"Get your hands out from under that girl's shirt and get us some firewood. Or are you worried maybe your chippie likes it dark, too?" He leered at the girl.

She had enough sauce, or had drunk enough, that she flipped him off.

He laughed. "That one might be worth keeping around. Too bad you can't give her a real Kiss." It was a cruel shot.

Tyler didn't rise to the bait. "Not my fault. I'm still waiting." He gave the girl a normal kiss and went to load up on firewood. To her credit, she didn't leave.

Lew turned to Jez. "So is he in or not?"

She nodded. "He's a little young, but it will surface sooner or later."

"Good. I don't want to send him packing. That boy's got skills."

"I'll break him in for you," Cami offered, taking the seat Michael had vacated. No one asked how she had escaped Darius. Tyler's date glared at Cami but wisely kept her mouth shut.

Lew shook his head. "If I want him in little pieces, I'll call you. Otherwise, I'd like him to remain whole." He turned back to Jez. "What about Fox?"

Jez looked over at Darius' squire, who had switched to playing something vaguely country or maybe folk. "Definitely. He's obviously one of us and more than old enough to join the party. Why hasn't someone offered him a Kiss?"

"Boy says he's not ready yet. He wants to finish his degree before he comes out on the road with us. After that, I don't think he's got much reason to stick around home, you know what I mean?"

"Too well." Cami frowned. "Way too well."

Heather had marveled at how openly people spoke about becoming Tribe in front of Mundanes. It had taken her a while to realize that people from the outside had no idea what was being said. Tyler came back to the fire, threw in some wood, and whispered to the girl. A few minutes later, they slipped away. Heather smiled. There was nothing to worry about, just a regular boy heading off to make out with a regular girl and take her back to her regular family. At least for now. By the time Tyler got his Kiss, both he and the girl would have forgotten their stolen autumn night.

Lew nudged Jez. "So, you keeping devil-girl at your place, or do we get to hear the fight when she tells Michael she's crashing in his trailer?"

Jez laughed. "Hard decision. The entertainment value of a genuine Rockland fight is hard to beat. All that screaming of creative epithets, lapsing into different languages, and the throwing of things. That's my favorite part. You'd think Michael would have invested in plastic dishes by now."

"Bro's a little slow on the uptake." Cami winked. "And I haven't thrown anything at him in at least six months."

"When was the last time you did a show together?" Lew asked.

Cami, Heather, and Jez all spoke at the same time. "Six months ago."

"A chorus of angels." Carter laughed.

"Fallen angels, anyway." Darius appeared out of the dark. "Straggler alert. Ian's party moved straight from the restaurant to a lake house, and Paula's fete is roving. We should have at least a dozen folks coming by, probably more."

Lew rose. "Then let's put the liquor away. I'm not inclined to fund everyone's hangovers."

"Aw, now I feel special," Heather cooed.

Carter shook his head. "That's all it took, free whiskey? Why have I been beating my head against the wall?"

Cami grinned at him. "Because deep down inside, you are a severely twisted masochist who envisions Heather as your dominatrix, but you haven't yet figured out how to be worthy."

"That must be it." He joined Darius and Lew in hiding the good booze. They left the beer in the cooler so as not to seem cheap.

CHAPTER FIVE

Heather stared at the fire. Tyler had brought just enough wood to fulfill his task. It wouldn't last. She headed for the woodpile on the other side of the shed, enjoying the cool air and the sounds of camaraderie drifting from the camp. She knew it was dangerous to get close to the jousters, but they made her feel like she belonged. She loaded up with wood and returned to the fire just as Paula led a small parade into the circle.

"I see you have a diligent char-woman," she said to Carter. He clenched his jaw and stayed quiet.

Heather dropped the wood next to Jez, kept one piece, and turned to face Paula. The timing would have to be just right. "How was your party?"

Paula settled herself on the bench closest to the fire, ready to hold court. "How kind of you to ask. It was lovely. You should have been there." She smiled, a vicious thing. "Oh, wait, you weren't asked."

"If it was so nice, why are you here?"

"It seemed a perfect night to see how the other half lives." More people had filtered in, keeping their distance, as they sensed drama in progress.

Fox began to play a melody that sounded suspiciously like the soundtrack from a telenovela. Heather grinned, and the cheeky young squire returned her smile.

"Lucky us," Lew said, stepping into the light. He flopped down next to Paula and dropped his arm over her shoulder. She flinched from the weight.

"I was almost out of snacks."

She shoved at him, sliding out from under his arm. "You don't get to touch me."

"Excuse me?" He feigned offense, but there was a hint of anger underneath.

"You heard me. I'm Court. You don't touch me."

Jocko stepped to the edge of the circle. "And you don't pull rank in someone else's place, especially when you haven't earned it."

"Or what?" she challenged.

Darius moved into the light. "Or I will banish you and your attitude from my camp."

"You wouldn't kick me out." Paula looked around for support, but her followers had shuffled back. Carter pointedly looked away.

"I would and see to it that you were censured by the Queen, as well." Darius looked down at her. "When it comes to pulling rank, I win." There was no arguing with that. Darius was the Master at Arms, third only to the Queen and King in the hierarchy.

The wind shifted. Heather tossed the wood into the fire, sending a spray of sparks in a cloud of smoke directly at Paula. She jumped up, checking to see if any cinders had landed on her silk shirt.

"Oops." Heather looked contrite. "Sorry about that."

"You did that on purpose," Paula accused.

"What? You said I should tend the fire, so I did. I can't control how the wind blows."

Several people snickered.

Darius shook his head. "Heather." His tone was mild, but the warning was clear.

"I'm sorry." She smiled at Paula. "Perhaps I'll leave fire building to those better suited to it."

"That would be me." Lew stood up. "Cuz it doesn't get much hotter than this." He turned around slowly, pausing to strike poses that showed everyone the proof of his assertion. Exercise was his religion, and he was very devout. One of the newly arrived guys whistled at him. Everyone cracked up, including Lew. He bowed then went about building up the fire—carefully. People drifted closer, warming their hands.

Heather tapped Jez as she walked by. "I'm heading out. I can't seem to shake the desire to start trouble, and I don't want to cross Darius again."

"I'll come with." Cami materialized at her side.

"Stay for a while. I don't want to be blamed for taking you away just when the party is getting good. There are too many people who'll want to catch up with you."

"You sure? I'm here to see you."

"We'll have plenty of time to hang out. Enjoy tonight." Heather hugged the tiny woman, resulting in several calls to get a room. They both giggled, knowing they would do exactly that, if not in the way the crowd meant.

Heather slipped away quietly. Darius nodded to her but didn't try to stop her. She knew he wouldn't say anything about her bad behavior. She would apologize in private anyway. He might love her like a sister, but he was still Court—real Court, not a hanger-on like Paula—and the last thing anyone wanted to do was piss off the people in charge.

She walked across the site, glad for the darkness and quiet. A few minutes later, the rustle of leaves alerted her that she had company. She stopped walking, waiting for Carter to catch up to her. His chivalry made her tired. She spun on her heel, ready to set him down yet again. Jocko stood in front of her, closer than she'd realized.

She stumbled back. "Are you following me?"

"Yes, ma'am." He grinned at her.

"Why?"

"Because I don't like to see you walking around alone. Something bad could happen."

She crossed her arms. "Just did, apparently."

"Isn't that interesting? When you turned around, you almost looked like you were expecting someone else."

"I was."

"I see. You want me to leave you to whoever you thought would be following you? Because I promise you, there was no one but me."

"You're sure of that?"

"Seeing as how I made sure of that, yes."

"How'd you manage that?"

"I threw Katie into Carter's path. Poor thing is smitten with him in a way you're definitely not. I figured she should find out if she's got a chance before she gets her heart broken."

Heather liked the possibility of Carter being distracted by the little blonde. "She could do worse."

"Not much," he said darkly.

"Carter is a nice guy."

"Could be he just comes across that way."

"You're not one to judge. He's never been anything but kind to me."

He shook his head. "Maybe not. But blood will out."

"Meaning?"

"You, of all people, should know what I mean."

Heather pinched the bridge of her nose to prevent a headache. "Less cryptic, please. I'm tired and not in the mood for games."

He looked at her in surprise. "No one ever told you."

"Told me what?"

"Carter is Sebastian's cousin. Raised side-by-side after Sebastian's mama died. I thought everyone knew."

Heather swallowed hard against the sickness that swept over her. "That doesn't mean anything. They're nothing alike. Look at Mike and Cami. Same family, totally different beliefs."

"I wouldn't bet too much on that, either. In any case, I don't feel comfortable with Carter trying to follow you into the night."

"You did."

Jocko sighed. "One of these days, you're going to figure out who you want looking out for you."

"I didn't ask you to watch over me."

"No, but you need me to."

"You're an arrogant son of a bitch," Heather said.

"Guilty as charged. But that's not what this is about. I just don't want to see you get hurt again."

She couldn't hide her suspicion. "Why do you care?"

"No clue. It just seems the right thing to do." He frowned. "Are you going to let me walk you home or wherever it is you were going?"

"You know I don't like you, right? I mean, I've made that pretty clear."

"Yeah, I know. But you trust me." He shrugged out of his jacket.

Heather blinked. "Stupid as it may seem, I do."

"You're a lot of things, darlin', but stupid is not one of them." He dropped his coat over her shoulders. She hadn't even realized she'd been shivering. "Now, let's take that stroll."

She kept his coat, slipping her arms into it and pulling it closed, strangely comforted by the smell of him surrounding her. It was a mix of amber and moss, complimented by the fading scent of leather and something she could not name. They walked in companionable silence. He made no move to touch her, letting her sink into her thoughts. She wasn't sure if that was a good thing or not.

They emerged in the clearing at the center of the faire, moonlight bathing the site in eldritch light. They stood, looking up at the stars until time stood still. She found herself breathing easily for the first time since Paula and her crowd had interrupted the party.

With an impish grin, he tugged at the end of her hair then raced away. Laughing, she followed him in a reckless dash through the trees. He jumped up on the chessboard stage, spun around, and bowed to an imaginary crowd. She walked up the steps, but didn't come further. He crooked a finger at her, still grinning madly. She shook her head. He dropped into an *en garde* stance. It was the beginning of their fight, but neither was armed. She let his jacket fall and kicked it to the edge of the stage before advancing on him. She could almost feel the weight of her sword in her hand as they circled, maintaining a safe distance. Even in the dark, she knew the boundaries of the stage.

The slow dance of the fight continued. She bared her teeth at him, letting the false enmity fade into a smile. He lunged. She parried, dancing away at the last second. He advanced, his moves languorous, almost liquid.

Insolent dog. Her lines came to her, ringing in her head as if she had spoken.

I would be your pet, love, if you'd but have me. His movement reflected his answer as he flung his arms wide, giving her an open target. She rushed him, seeing her folly a second too late. He side-stepped and grabbed her wrist, wresting the imaginary sword from her hand and tossing it aside as he pulled her to him. He was solid and warm against her.

"You should never drop your guard like that," he whispered into her hair. "A lesser man might take advantage."

"I'd have to find a lesser man, an impossible feat."

They had abandoned the script.

"There are worse things than this." He wrapped his arms around her, his breathing too fast.

She knew she should step away, go home, pretend this game had never started, but she didn't want to. She leaned her head on his chest. It was all wrong, and for once, she didn't care.

"If I tried to kiss you, would you hit me?" he murmured.

"Probably."

"Might be worth the risk." His hands stroked her back.

"Won't know unless you try," she mumbled into his shirt.

"Mmm. Could be hazardous, though."

"You've never shied from trouble before."

"I do every day, sugar. You just don't notice." His fingers slid through her hair until they brushed her neck.

She shivered, but not from the cold. She hadn't been this warm in a long time. "Guess you're too chicken to kiss me, then."

He laughed. "You're the most dangerous girl on this site, you know that?"

She looked up at him. "How so?"

"Because you're the only girl I want. Well, in more than a passing way. But I'm pretty sure that if I kiss you, come tomorrow what you'll want is my liver for breakfast."

"I hate liver."

"Oh, that's all right, then." The hand on her back pressed her closer as he leaned down for a kiss that never came.

"Get your hands off her." Carter's voice rang out.

"I think that's her choice," Jocko said tightly.

"I'm not going to tell you again."

"Walk away, Carter." The warning was clear.

"I don't think so."

Heather pushed away from Jocko and turned to Carter. "How dare you?" she hissed.

Carter stepped back. "I'm just looking out for you."

"Yeah, well, there's a lot of that going around tonight." She put her hands on her hips and glared at him. "I'm going to say this once, so listen up. I am perfectly capable of taking care of myself."

"You don't know him like I do," Carter protested.

"And neither one of you knows me at all, but that doesn't stop you from thinking I'm not smart enough to make my own decisions." She didn't know why she was suddenly angry at Jocko, too. "I am going to walk home. Alone. And if either of you says one word to me or anyone else about this, you will regret it." She jumped off the stage. Carter opened his mouth, but snapped it shut as she drew closer. "Not one word."

She stalked off toward Jezebel's shop, shaking with fury and chilled to the bone. Deep inside her, the empty place opened up and swallowed the night.

CHAPTER SIX

*S*he was curled up tight, warm and comfortable. All around her was the scent of home, of Him. She had nothing else to do, nowhere to go. He stroked his hand over her back in a soothing rhythm, just as He should.

A door opened, letting cold air into the room. She opened one eye to see who had interrupted their perfect evening. A shadow approached, bringing with it the cold of winter, of pain and loss. She hissed to drive it away. The hand on her back stilled, holding her in place, telling her she was safe. She had no way to tell Him she was not. Neither of them would be safe again.

Tendrils of frost emerged from the shadow, snaking toward Him before melting into words. "You have something of mine. I am here to take it back."

Heather wrenched sideways. Heart pounding, she opened her eyes, sure that the shadow would be there, leaning over her. When reason returned, she let out a shaky breath. Cami was wrapped up in the covers. That was why the dream had turned cold. She told herself it was nothing more than that. But she had recognized the shadow's voice.

She found her old, gray sweatpants and dressed quickly. She braided her hair and quietly left the room. Though she usually woke up early, which made her something of a freak at the faire, rarely did she see predawn. There was something strange and heavy about the site, as if it was waiting to fulfill the potential of the day. Fog snaked through the trees, twisting into vaguely menacing shapes. The edges of the buildings were blurred, dreamlike. Heather shuddered. She'd had enough of dreams.

She made her way to the back gate and started her run without stretching. If she took it slow, she would be okay, and starting early meant she would be back in time to join Ricky's morning yoga session.

Her favorite trail led through the woods that surrounded most of the faire site, but the turns and cutbacks made it twice as long as the perimeter fence. She fell into an easy stride, letting her thoughts go in favor of trying to find the newly woken birds that filled the air with a multitude of calls. The fog drifted away, not waiting to be burned off. She slowed when a fox darted into the path, far enough ahead that it had time to stare at her before disappearing into the brush.

She picked up the pace, racing sunrise to see who would get to the front parking lot first. She lost, but only by a few minutes. She streaked past the locked gates and shuttered box office windows, then jumped the low gate by the guardhouse. It was there to stop cars, not people. By the time the patrons arrived, a bored guy in uniform would be checking participant and parking passes, keeping the performers and merchants safe from intruders. She would have giggled at that if she hadn't been breathing so hard.

So much for taking it easy. She passed through the side gate and slowed, taking the time to do a cool-down lap around the site. Gregor waved at her. The blacksmith always got up early to start the forge fire, usually before she left for her run. She waved back but didn't stop. She wasn't in the mood for gossip about who had snuck out of places where they should not have spent the night. At least she wasn't one of them.

The thought gave her pause. Would she have been, if Carter hadn't interfered? She shook her head and decided not to follow that particular line of questioning. It was going to be hard enough just stepping onto the chess stage.

Ricky was already there as she slowed to a walk. Several people were stretching out, including Paula. Heather was suddenly aware of her sweat-soaked clothes. Her braid was coming loose, hair sticking to her face and neck. Paula was perfectly groomed, as usual. Heather took a spot as far from her as possible, firmly putting comparisons out of her mind. The stretching would be good, but what she needed more than anything was the calm that came from finding her center. She closed her eyes and focused on her breathing, the twitch of the muscles in her legs, the muffled sound of shopkeepers opening doors and sweeping off steps.

By the time Ricky finished leading them through the sun salute, Heather had found a measure of peace. She thanked him and headed for the shop.

Jezebel handed her a cup of superb coffee, saying nothing about the obscenely early run. Heather gathered her shower bag and some clean clothes, knowing she would have to watch her time if she was going to make the morning meeting. Cami muttered something incomprehensible, rolled over, and went back to sleep.

"Lucky wench," Heather muttered.

The wait for the showers was fairly short, one advantage to getting up way too early. Most people showered at night. She tended to do both. Heather hung back and sipped her coffee, not wanting to join in the quiet conversations that always arise when people have to stand in line. When it was her turn, she sprayed the entire shower stall with disinfectant and rinsed it down before stepping in, still wearing her flip flops.

She shuddered to think how many people actually put their feet on the floor. It was like asking for athlete's foot—or worse. Lack of decent sanitation was the biggest drawback of living on site. At least twice during each show, she and Jez would rent a hotel room so they could soak in the tub, totally ignoring the fact that thousands of people had probably been in those bathrooms, too.

She ran through singing exercises while she showered, blocking out the laughter that came from those waiting. There was nothing wrong with good time management, and she could always reach higher or lower notes in the steam-filled room. She finished the vocal warm-up and her shower at the same time, wrapped her hair in a towel, and dressed before the residual heat could dissipate.

Clouds of steam came out of the second door as she passed. Jocko stepped out, wearing only a dark blue bathrobe, water dripping from his hair. She kept walking.

"This wasn't what I'd hoped for when I thought about showering with you," he teased. "But it does explain why the hot water started running out." He caught up to her.

"Should have waited a while. A cold shower would do you good." She didn't look at him.

"No need, what with you being so chilly to me and all."

"Business as usual." She kept walking.

"You were a little warmer . . ." he began.

She turned on him. "Don't make me hurt you."

"It's cute when you threaten me. Not talking about it won't change anything. We're back to square one, and I'm okay with that. At some point, you'll admit you're hot for me."

"If that's your idea of courtship, you're wasting your time."

"I got nothing but time, sugar." He bumped her shoulder with his arm.

"Hope you like spending it alone, then."

"That'll do for now." He paused by the cabinet shop, looking up toward his room. "Fight call right after the meeting. I'd hurry if I was you. Don't want to show up without all your equipment."

They had changed the time without telling her. She ground her teeth. "Thanks for letting me know."

"I'll bet that hurt to say." He laughed and walked up the stairs. As soon as he was out of sight, she bolted.

Jez was carrying the last of the boxes down the stairs when Heather arrived. She apologized for not being there to help.

Jez waved it off. "Cami finally got up. I think she brought you some breakfast."

"As long as it's not liver," Heather said without thinking. Jez gave her a puzzled look and disappeared behind the counter.

Heather raced up the stairs, threw her bag in the corner, stripped, and began putting on her costume. Cami watched from her perch on one of the stools, coffee cup in one hand, cigarette in the other. "If I was gay, you'd be my type," she said.

"Damned shame we're not. I'm thinking of swearing off men."

"That won't do a thing to change how straight you are, so I'm not sure why you'd bother." Cami tilted her head. "Of course, it might have something to do with where you went last night."

"I went for a walk. I was back here long before you rolled in."

"I know. You missed Mike's girl freaking out when she saw Paula wrap her skinny leg around him. She got a nice slap in on Paula, too. No real damage though."

"Shame." Heather shrugged into her corset.

"Darius led the Mundane chippie off. I think he ended up taking her home."

"I'm sorry I missed all the fun."

"Don't know about that," Cami drawled.

Heather tensed. "Oh?" If Carter had gone back to the campfire and talked, she would never speak to him again.

"You smelled awful nice last night. Sort of like a guy." Cami winked. "At first, I thought you'd finally let Carter get close to you, but then you started talking in your sleep."

"Did I tell you my darkest secrets?"

Cami hopped off the stool and came over to tighten Heather's corset. "No, honey, but you did mention Jocko." She tugged extra hard, making Heather stand up even straighter. "I thought you weren't chasing that," she said, tying off the laces.

"I'm not." Heather ran a comb through her hair.

"Uh huh. While you're wrestling with denial, you might want to think about how foolish it would be to wind up as Jocko's plaything."

"You make those laces any tighter, I won't live to find out." She twisted her hair into a knot, securing it with pins.

"Maybe I'm just making it harder for him to undo you." Cami picked up the sword bag, holding it out.

"It's under control," Heather said, taking the bag. She walked out the door.

"You keep telling yourself that," Cami called after her.

She was half-way across the site before she realized she'd forgotten breakfast. Despite being two minutes late, she was allowed to check in on time. It had more to do with Rodney arriving on her heels than any grace on the part of the clipboard-clutching secretary. She wasn't about to call out the King for being tardy. Rodney winked at Heather and worked his way around the circle as the first notes were being given. When Bob, their perpetually irritated director, announced there would be a wedding that day, everyone groaned. Weddings were logistical nightmares, but Management loved them. The ten-thousand-dollar fee had a lot to do with that. The free publicity didn't hurt, either.

Heather was tapped to sing wedding-related songs in her second show, because the newlyweds were expected to attend. She made a list in her head and realized it was too short to make a whole set. She preferred tales of love gone wrong, bawdy encounters, and death.

She didn't want to consider what that said about her.

After the meeting, she enticed two apprentice girls to join her. She'd have to split whatever hat she made, but they were decent kids with strong voices and were more enamored of romance.

The invitation to sit in on her set thrilled the apprentices. They were weekend warriors, only flirting with the idea of what it would be like to do this for a living, going home to their parents each night. Jez would know if they were Tribe, but there was no point in asking. The oldest one couldn't be more than eighteen. By this time next year, she'd be safely ensconced in college, all thoughts of going on the road put aside to do what was expected of her. Not that it was a barrier, but it might keep them safe for a little while.

Blood will out. Jocko's words haunted her. People were either Tribe or they weren't. It took the Kiss to flip that switch, but if left to their own devices, even people who had the potential could live normal lives. Looking at the two girls, she hoped they had that chance.

CHAPTER SEVEN

L ew was tapping his foot as Heather joined the fighters. "Timing is everything, Yarborough." This was his first show as fight director, and he took it very seriously.

"I'm not the one who changed up the schedule," she muttered, taking her place opposite Jocko. Others paired off, finding an empty spot.

"Clear!" Lew called, alerting the other performers to the impending rehearsal. "Go through your first fight, quarter speed." He went to check on the apprentices, who were working on hand-to-hand skirmishes. Most of them wouldn't be given weapons this season.

Heather concentrated on her fight with Jocko, walking through it once before taking it to half-speed. They spoke their lines without inflection, more focused on timing than words. She missed a parry and Jocko pulled his sword back. They took it from the top, no banter of words, scripted or otherwise, interrupting the moves. Jocko never gave her grief for missteps, a courtesy she returned. She got it right the second time, and they went back on script.

"Remember your feet," Lew said, timing his critique for a moment when the fight called for separation. "But keep your eyes on your opponent." The last was for the duo behind them.

Heather never took her eyes off Jocko when they fought. He had the reach on her, and the speed. It took a lot of skill to pretend those things didn't matter. In a real fight, she would not win. At the end of their first encounter of the day, she didn't. The harassment he got from patrons until she finally beat him was expected. It was one reason why he got paid more, and why her defeat happened early in the day. By midday, too many guys were drunk and looking for a reason to have fights of their own. She had to win the second time. It made her seem more formidable and him more sympathetic, offering a measure of protection from overenthusiastic patrons.

They finished the run-through and took it up to speed, which, for the purposes of the show, was still a quarter slower than it would be if they were actually dueling. They'd tried it at full once, the audience made up of other performers. Not only was it over far too quickly, but their friends had agreed it had been nearly impossible to see what was happening. Blades swung quickly tended to disappear without a strong background, and the chess stage was open on all sides. Fighting full speed was also incredibly dangerous. She shouldn't have admitted to Jocko how thrilling that had been.

Lew moved back in their direction. "That one's a go. You want to run the second one now, or right before?"

"Both," they said in unison.

Lew cracked up. "Okay then. Quarter speed to start."

"Yes, boss," Jocko drawled.

"Don't sass me, boy, or I'll make you fight Cami next time."

"I'd hardly be able to spot that little girl on stage, much less fight her."

Cami walked through the gate. "Kiss my ass, Jocko. You know I could take you."

"You want to try, cupcake?"

"Not unless they pay me."

"I'd like to play with a woman who knows she can be bought."

"You could have stopped at how you'd like to play with a woman," she retorted, heading for the soda machine. "Not that you could afford me."

"What's your price?" he asked.

"Nothing too valuable. Just your life."

"I got plans for that, so I'll have to pass."

"Figured." Cami lit a cigarette and withdrew to a bench to watch.

Lew crossed his arms over his chest. "If you two are done wasting time, I'd like to see that second fight."

They did a walk-through, both hesitating at the moment he opened his arms. Lew called a halt and told them to start again. Shaking off the memory, they managed to complete the fight. It went better at quarter speed. Imminent danger helped.

Lew held up his hand. "Instead of rushing him, take one step and thrust."

"I don't have the reach for that," Heather protested.

"So slip the blade."

"I haven't done that before."

Lew took her sword and walked through the move. Before the thrust that would lead to Jocko disarming him, he slid his hand down the grip to the pommel. Jocko side-stepped, wrapped his hand around the hilt and pulled it away easily.

"That keeps you from looking like an idiot for walking into him," Lew said.

Where was that advice last night? She pushed the thought away. "It's a risky move for a fighter."

"That's why it will sell better. It can look clever or desperate, depending on how you play it."

"The upshot is that I retain control of the blade, instead of knocking it free, which makes it a little safer for the audience." Jocko regarded Heather, lips pursed. "But I don't want to make that change unless you're comfortable with it."

"Let's run it a few times before I decide." Heather turned to Lew. "Can you get me out of the opening at the front gate? I'm just set dressing there."

"I can do that," Lew said. "I'll want to see you run the fight clean this afternoon, before it goes up." He dismissed the other fighters and walked off to find Bob.

After they had run the disarm a few times, Heather agreed to keep it in. She stepped back to take the fight from the top at performance speed. It went smoothly, but they did it again to be sure.

"I like this change," Jocko said. "It works."

"It's still a little awkward, but I should be able to pull it off. I'll tell you what I think after the next practice."

"Your choice as to whether or not we keep it. I just want you to be comfortable."

"One of the reasons you make a good partner." Heather kissed him on the cheek.

Cami rose, frowning. "Now you really are slipping," she said softly as she passed Heather. "Careful you don't fall."

"I won't," Heather said. She turned back to find Jocko trying to hide a smile. She frowned at him. He put his hands up and backed away. She grabbed her bag and raced across the site to dump it in the booth before the patrons could get to the back of the faire.

The wedding set went fine. The apprentice girls were nervous until the applause rolled in. By the end of the set, they practically glowed. Heather split her hat with them, including the generous tip from the newlyweds, so everyone went away happy. The notoriously hard-to-please Bob even gave them a pat on the back for a job well done. Heather prayed fervently that he would not be watching the chess fight.

The magic show let out, making it difficult to get through the crowd. Heather ducked into a costume shop for a little window shopping. Two women were conferring on possible purchases, each well over $500. When she'd first come to the faire, Heather had marveled at how much money people would spend for things they might not ever use again. Once she'd gotten the Kiss, it had made more sense. Tribe merchants had the same glamour as performers. Sales weren't automatic, any more than getting patrons to put money in her hat was, but they came a little easier. Maybe it was that the products Tribe crafters turned out were just that much finer, or the atmosphere in the shop was more welcoming. Whatever it was, people who perched on the edge of buying could be coaxed to walk away with something they might have denied themselves. Buyer's remorse was rare, which in a way was a gift to people too frequently steeped in guilt.

Marni designed the gorgeous gowns hanging in the windows. Everything about her reflected grace and beauty. She practically glided as she came down the stairs. Her partner, Gina, worked in the next room, selling rogue wear. You could fight all day in her creations then throw them in the wash at night, which was exactly what she'd done before giving up performing.

Rumor had it that Gina had waited patiently for two years before receiving the Kiss. Marni had been afraid that it would destroy their relationship. More than once, a Kiss had become the kiss of death for a couple. Gina had been adamant that nothing could cause her to leave Marni, and she had been right. They were widely regarded as the happiest couple on site. Any site. The flower booth made a mint off them, as evidenced by the numerous roses behind the counter.

"You seem torn between whether you want to be a lady or a fighter," Marni said.

Heather laughed. "As much as I love your work, I don't think I have much choice. I'm not lady material."

"Never say never. You may find it suits you, in years to come."

"Stop trying to convert my customers!" Gina snapped. Her grin belied the rough tone.

"As you wish." Marni walked around Heather, assessing her. "But she does have the right look for the catalog."

Gina nodded. "We're doing a photo shoot next week, for both print and the web. If you want to come play dress-up, we'll pay you to model."

"I'd love to! You don't have to pay me, though."

"Yes, we do. Part of what we'll be selling is you—or the illusion of you. I wouldn't feel right if we didn't compensate you for it. If you don't want cash, we can do it in trade, from whichever line you prefer."

Heather beamed. They had been patient with her drooling over their work, despite the fact that she never let herself buy anything. The glamour didn't work on the Tribe, so she had hesitated in a way the Mundanes did not.

"Does it have to be for me?"

"You can buy whatever you want for whomever you want," Marni said.

"Let me know when and where, and I'll be there."

Both women gave her smiles. For the first time, she realized it was the one thing about them that was identical.

Heather bounded across the site, grinning. The chess game participants were scattered around the edge of the benches, waiting for the Court to arrive. She leaned against a tree, close enough to hear but far enough away that she drew no attention. She ran the fight in her head, remembering to add in the change.

The audience was so large that many of them had to stand. Shows with no hat passing tended to draw larger crowds. The glamour only went so far when it came to cash, and by the middle of the day, most people were tired of being asked for money. It didn't stop them from wanting to be entertained, though.

The King took the stage and gave a little speech. Setting up a real chessboard, he randomly picked an opponent from the crowd. Or so it seemed. Doc took a break from his apothecary shop to come to the chess match every day, dressed in normal clothes. Regular patrons recognized him but didn't let on. The pawns really were chosen from the audience. They would be dispensed with quickly. They never seemed to mind. Just being part of the show was a thrill.

At the King's summons, Heather pushed off the tree and took her place, scanning the crowd for Jocko and silently cursing him for being late.

"Looking for someone?" Paula hissed from her place in the King's retinue.

"I thought I saw Michael's hussy of the week," Heather smiled as Paula looked around sharply. "But I guess I was wrong."

"Bitch," Paula whispered.

"I hear she had claws. How's your face?"

"Prettier marred than yours on a good day."

The first skirmish started, keeping Heather from having to answer. Since Paula was right, a good retort would have been difficult.

Sometime during the catty exchange, Jocko had slipped into position. He caught her eye, waiting for her to give him the signal that she was ready for their fight. She gave the barest nod. They went back to feigning surprise at the outcome of the other conflicts, each one executed as expected. Even the apprentice kids did well. She smiled at the nickname. Some of the apprentices were older than she was, but none of them were Tribe, and it seemed rude to call castmates Mundanes. Plenty of faire participants weren't Tribe, but only the kids worked for free. She didn't fault them for it. She had done the same.

Doc moved Jocko to the center of the stage. Rodney directed her to take him. She saluted him and complied. The audience faded from her mind. Her lines came automatically. Jocko was all that mattered—the ting of his blade striking hers, the grind of metal on metal as she slid into the parry, the dance as they advanced and retreated, the cross-step of a perfect circle.

"I would be your pet, love, if only you would have me." He mocked her with open arms.

"I will, then, but not as you'd like!" she cried, stepping forward and slipping the blade for the final thrust. The disarm took her off balance. Unable to recover, she fell into him, eyes wide. Her blade fell to the ground as he caught her, making it look like part of the choreography. His arm strong under her, he dipped her, his hair forming a curtain as he leaned in for a kiss.

"Groin shot, uppercut to the face," he whispered, lips barely touching hers. "Got it?"

"Yeah."

"Don't follow through on either," he warned.

She was too horrified by her screw-up to laugh.

He pulled her to her feet with a wicked smile for the hoots and catcalls from the audience. She grabbed his forearms and raised her knee. It was a hard move to sell in the round, but she must have managed because a groan arose from the men in the audience, accompanied by a cheer from the women. Jocko doubled over, but not too far, leaving her free to raise clasped hands to his chin. His head snapped up and he stumbled back, wheezing before falling to the ground, knocked out. Heather retrieved both swords and bowed to the King.

"As your majesty wished."

"Oh, well done, my dear!" Rodney meant it. The entire retinue burst into applause, even Paula. "Check and mate," he said to Doc.

"I yield, and ask to remove my knight. The poor man may never mate again, check or otherwise." The audience roared with laughter.

"Let the lady see to him. I vouch for his safety in her hands." Rodney gave her a stern look that did nothing to hide the laughter in his eyes.

"As you command." Heather handed off the swords before kneeling by Jocko.

"I owe you," she whispered, pushing his hair from his face.

"Don't think I won't collect." He let her help him up, leaning too heavily on her shoulder as she led him away.

The adrenaline rush was fading, replaced by the urge to throw up. It took forever to get through the gate. "I can't believe I did that."

Jocko straightened. "At least you still won. That's what matters."

"Well, that and not ruining your chances for procreation." She finally let herself laugh.

He joined her. "Never been too fond of the idea, but not being able to practice would have been rough."

Heather closed her eyes, afraid to speak but needing to know. "What's this going to cost me?"

"Nothing you aren't willing to give. I want dinner."

She sighed. He had expensive taste. "Where?"

"My place."

"I can't cook, Jocko. At least not anything I'd serve you if I want you to live."

He quirked an eyebrow. "You of two minds about that?"

"Not today."

"I'll cook. You'll let me feed you."

"I should bargain with you more often. You stink at it. I screw up, and you serve me dinner?"

"Not serve you, sugar. Feed you." Jocko smiled, slow and wicked. "Your hands will be otherwise occupied."

She blanched. "Doing what?"

"My guess? Trying to untie knots." He walked to the gate, turning back as he opened it. "Eight o'clock. Be on time."

CHAPTER EIGHT

For the remainder of the afternoon, Heather tried to avoid Jocko, so naturally she saw him at every turn. He didn't approach her, just smiled at her until she looked away. His delight in her discomfort irritated her, but she would not back out of the bargain. He'd never let her forget it. What really worried her was how she was going to explain to Cami and Jez why she couldn't go out with them.

She was almost to the final jam when Bob hailed her. She braced herself for his withering comments about the fight. She had hoped he would wait until after closing.

"Nice save on the chessboard," he said.

"The credit's Jocko's," she managed to blurt through her surprise.

"You didn't fall apart, so you get a pass on the screw-up. But work it out or lose the new move."

She nodded, trying to imagine what a world with a nicer Bob would be like. The fantasy didn't last long.

"I know you like mixing it up, but I want you to do the same bit you did with Jocko at the jam yesterday. It will round out this wedding nonsense."

She nodded, because that's what one did when Bob gave an order. "I don't know where he is, though."

"Talked to him already. He's on board for it." Bob headed off to intercept a group of apprentices, leaving Heather to wonder how things had gotten so out of hand.

For some reason, kicking leaves all the way to the stage made her feel better. There was no sign of Jocko. *Of course, because I actually want to talk to him.* She took a moment to lose her frown before joining the musicians. The newlyweds beamed and waved at her.

She couldn't fault Jocko's timing or performance. He arrived at the right moment, sang beautifully, and came up with a new answer for the King. The end result was the same for her. She found herself standing at the edge of the stage, arm and arm with Jocko. The only difference was that today she was resigned instead of angry.

"You've spent all afternoon thinking about tonight," he whispered. She couldn't deny it. "I'm wondering if you're shaking with anxiety or anticipation."

"Neither. I'm just cold."

"That so?" He stepped behind her and wrapped his arm around her waist, covering them both with his cloak. "Better?"

"Yes, actually."

"Don't sound so surprised. I'm not the villain you pretend I am."

"I never thought you were a villain, just a cad."

"I have been," he admitted.

"But you've changed your ways?" She laughed. "I'm not new enough to buy that."

He nuzzled her neck, knowing she couldn't slap him away with everyone watching. "Still smell new," he murmured.

"I'm guessing I smell like sweat and dust and machine oil." She stepped back into him, making him fight for balance. It was entirely the wrong thing to do.

He used the arm around her waist to steady himself, a low growl escaping his lips as she pressed up to him. He hardened against her. He dropped his hands to her hips and moved her forward. "Don't do that again unless you mean it."

She blushed. "I'm sorry."

"I know."

Rodney called the newlyweds to the place of honor behind him as he led the crowd out. Jocko gave Heather a long look before letting the crowd separate them. It was a warning and a promise. If she stood him up tonight, he would raise the price for repaying the debt. She inclined her head in understanding. With uncharacteristic silence, he turned away.

She wondered if Doc would sell her poison as an act of grace then decided telling him why she wanted it would be just as painful as enduring whatever Jocko had planned. She didn't worry about him hurting her, but she knew he found an unhealthy amount of pleasure in watching other people's discomfort. She had never seen him cause it, though. Even when he Kissed a Mundane, he intended no harm. The man was cavalier, but not cruel.

Heather dragged her feet all the way back to her booth. Cami was helping Jez pack up the last of her stock, both of them grinning.

"Good day?" Heather asked.

"Excellent!" Jez laughed. "I had five people come back to buy at the end. Five!"

"And I spent most of the day hanging out with Gregor and helping around the shop. I managed to sell that friggin Claymore so he paid me more than he'd promised. He was so tired of people touching that thing and walking away." Cami did a little dance.

"I am so happy for both of you!"

"Gregor wants to take me out to dinner with the rest of his crew. You're invited, too. Especially since Jezebel here might actually earn her name tonight."

"Rascal came through! Oh, Jez, that's great."

"It's dinner. That's all."

"Let's hope not." Cami wiggled her eyebrows. "Just in case, I'm telling Michael to get his crap out of my bunk."

"Asking Michael," Jez said. "It will go so much better if you don't start from a fighting stance."

"Whatever. Not like he wouldn't give in eventually." Cami turned to Heather. "Are you coming to dinner?"

Heather looked down. "I can't. I have to pay someone back for a favor, so I promised them dinner."

"Favor," Cami said.

"Them," Jez added.

"She's not saying what or who."

"I noticed that."

"Which means that she thinks whatever she's doing is a really bad idea," Cami noted.

"That was my thought," Jez agreed.

"Not too hard to figure out what's going on here."

"Nope." Jez turned to her. "So, what did Jocko do for you that compels you to dine with him?"

"Kept me from face-planting in the middle of the chess fight," Heather admitted.

Cami whistled. "Damn. Not even I can argue with that reason. I heard something went wrong, just didn't know it was you."

"Spectacularly wrong, actually. I need to pay him back for the save, and I'd rather get it over with tonight."

"Just be careful," Cami warned.

"He's not going to do anything she doesn't want him to," Jez protested.

"He has a way of charming folks into doing things that maybe they shouldn't."

"I'm a big girl. I'll be fine. He promised me it's only dinner, and I'll hold him to that." Heather picked up a box and walked up the stairs in an effort to avoid further discussion. There was no way she was going to admit to the conditions of the meal.

She set the box down and went to her room to change, shivering while she waited for the space heater to kick in. Today was the first time the weather had felt like autumn, so she'd had to dig the heater out of the overstuffed hall closet. At least the room was small enough that it only took a few minutes to warm up. She dressed quickly anyway. She'd chosen nothing sexy, which wasn't difficult, as her wardrobe tended more to be more functional than enticing. A hooded sweatshirt completed the dowdy ensemble.

"Nice armor," Cami quipped as she entered the room. "I suggest you keep it on."

"Planned to."

"Good. I don't trust Jocko as far as I can spit."

"Why is that?" Heather asked.

"Because he has Lew's penchant for casual affairs but without Darius to keep him in line."

"Darius keeps us all in line. That's what the Master at Arms is for."

"Yeah, but he's got his hands full at this show, and Jocko tends to fly under the radar, no matter which faire he's at. I don't know why they like him, but every Court does."

Heather shrugged. "He's good at his job."

"There's more to it than that." Cami finished changing. They both walked out into the storeroom. Jez had closed her door, no doubt trying to pick just the right thing to wear. Unlike Heather, most of what Jez had was soft and pretty, so she couldn't really go wrong.

Cami lit a cigarette. "Look, I know you're attracted to him."

"I'm not."

"You suck at lying. And I'm not blind or stupid. Not only is he hot, he's your fight partner. A certain . . . intimacy comes from pointing weapons at each other on a daily basis. There has to be trust. I don't want you to mistake that for love."

"Love?" Heather scoffed. "I know what love looks like, and this is not it."

"I suppose you do. You had real parents."

"Funny, I was thinking more about Marni and Gina." Heather told Cami about the photo shoot. "I'm going to get a new corset for Jez."

"You do so much to make other people feel good. It's disgusting." Cami grinned.

"You don't let me do anything for you, though."

Cami looked at her for a moment. "You make me feel safe. That's enough."

Heather laughed. "You're possibly the most feared person on the faire circuit. When are you not safe?"

"When I'm alone." The admission was out of character for Cami. Heather gave her a quick hug.

"Don't get mushy on me," Cami said brusquely, stepping back. "I have a reputation to uphold."

"You should head over to Gregor's. He hates to be kept waiting, especially when it comes to food."

"Shoving me out the door so you can race off for your own dinner, huh? That doesn't bode well."

"I have time to kill. You're the one with a schedule." Heather paused by the door. "Don't worry about me. I'll be fine. It's just dinner."

"If you aren't home by midnight, I'm coming looking for you," Cami warned.

"I'll be home long before that." Heather closed the door then went to see if Jez needed help.

Jez was trying to tame her hair into a French twist, but curls kept escaping. Her hands shook. Heather took the pins from her and tucked everything into place. The older woman smiled, grateful. The knock on the door made them both jump then giggle.

"Stall him a minute, would you? I need to find my coat."

Heather trotted down the short hall and answered the door. Carter stood there, blowing on his hands. He stepped past her, giving her room to close the door.

"When the weather turns cold, people tend to wear jackets," Heather pointed out.

"Mine's in the back of Darius' truck, and he headed out with Rodney and Ardyth for dinner and a little Court business. I gave my spare to Fox, since he never remembers to bring a decent coat, and he has a long ride home on his bike."

"Bummer. You want my cloak? It'll be short, but at least you'll be warm."

"Thanks, but I'm good. I can layer up when I get back to camp." He paused. "Lew wants to see you."

"I have no doubt about that, but he's going to have to wait until tomorrow. Or Tuesday, depending on what sort of errands Jez has for us tomorrow." Everyone took Mondays off to recover from the weekend. "I know we have a ton of laundry, and she has to make her bank drop."

"Avoiding him isn't going to work."

"I'm not avoiding him. I screwed up, and I'll take my drubbing for it. But I'm not under any obligation to do it tonight, or even tomorrow."

He shook his head. "Suit yourself."

"What did you do that Lew would send you all the way over here to deliver his message?"

"Nothing. I was going to come anyway. I thought you might want to go to dinner with me."

"I'm sorry. I made plans." Heather said softly. "Maybe later in the week."

Carter smiled. "Okay."

Rascal bounded through the door, not bothering to knock. He nodded to Carter before picking up Heather and swinging her around like a child. He set her down on the ground and beamed. Rascal was like a puppy, full of energy, perpetually happy, and easily distracted. His dark hair curled wildly, little pieces sticking to the side of his beard.

"Is Jez ready to go?"

"As soon as she finds her coat," Heather said.

"I warmed up the Beast so she wouldn't get cold." Rascal drove the ugliest van Heather had ever seen. She'd counted sixteen different colors of chipping paint.

"That was good of you."

Carter seemed to relax, obviously thinking Heather was going out with Jez and Rascal. "If you guys are heading out, I'm going to take off. I'll catch you later." He hit the stairs running.

"I notice you didn't set him straight about who was going with me." Rascal was more astute than most people gave him credit for.

Heather shrugged. "It's better that way."

Jez came into the room, smiling hesitantly. Rascal offered her his arm and escorted her down the stairs, leaving Heather to close the door after them. She leaned against it, letting the cold seep through her clothes. With everyone seen off, there was nothing left but to do her duty.

CHAPTER NINE

Heather climbed the stairs to Jocko's room, the cold making her
move more quickly than usual. She took a deep breath and
knocked on his door.

"I wasn't sure you were going to show." He took her coat and hung it
on a peg over the heater.

"I said I'd be here." She looked around the room. Compared to most
living quarters at the faire, it was practically palatial. And very, very clean. A
weapons rack stood against one wall, each slot labeled, the contents well
oiled. His buckler and braces rested on a shelf above it. He had a small
kitchen set up on the counter next to an old, but full-sized, refrigerator.
Pots sat on a double electric burner, one of them already steaming. A tall
lamp dimly lit the makeshift living room. Her gaze fell on a book, open and
face down on an end table. Beyond the couch, it was dark, but she got the
sense that the room held more. She turned her attention back to the
kitchen, not wanting to think about what might be hidden in the darkness.
Jocko chose that moment to pull out a chair. *He actually has a table.* It was
better to focus on that rarity than what he had said earlier.

"Have a seat. Dinner will be ready soon." He turned the chair to face
the kitchen area. "We can talk while I finish."

She walked toward him, fighting fear.

He sighed. "You look like you're walking to the gallows, sugar. Relax. I
won't hurt you."

"I know."

"I've got two heaters going. You might get a little warm in that sweatshirt."

"I like being warm."

"Your choice." He walked over to the electric frying pan, lifted the lid, and stirred. The mouthwatering scent of garlic and something sweeter filled the room.

Heather sat down and watched him move around the kitchen, almost as graceful as he was on stage. He threw herbs into a pot, humming. She recognized the tune as *She Wore a Black Ribbon*. He turned down the heat then rummaged around in a box, still humming.

"Nice set up," she said, desperate for some sort of opening.

"Thanks. After a few years, I got tired of eating out all the time, especially when I knew I could make better food. So, wherever I work, I barter for space with room for a kitchen. Then I find an old fridge at a secondhand store. Every place I stay has one, now."

"What do you barter with?"

"Lots of things. Food, manual labor, leather repair, lessons."

"Ah. Jocko of all trades, huh?" She laughed, relaxing.

"Yes." He turned around, a wide black ribbon in his hand. "And master of some."

She tensed. "You were serious about the knots."

"Did you doubt it?"

She swallowed. "I'm not comfortable with this."

"Does that mean you're backing out?"

"What happens if I do?"

"You miss a good dinner, and I come up with something else."

She swallowed heavily. "Any chance I'd like that something more?"

"Probably not, but you could try me. There's the door."

"You're twisted, you know that?"

"Pretty clear on that score." He grinned. "I told you I'm not going to ask you to do anything you aren't willing to do."

She took a deep breath and nodded. "Fine." She put her hands behind the chair. "Let's get this over with."

He shook his head. "In front."

She offered up her wrists, letting him wrap the ribbon around them. He tied a simple knot in it, leaving the ends free. He had left plenty of play in the binding.

"Work on that while I finish cooking." He returned to the counter and began chopping vegetables. "I don't recommend trying to slip your wrists out. It will only make the knot tighter."

She tested the range of movement, careful not to pull too much. After a few minutes, she was able to reach the knot with the fingers of her right hand, but she still couldn't untie it. She growled in frustration.

He looked over at her and grinned. "You're thinking too much, trying to figure it out with your eyes. See it with your fingers instead." He walked over to her. "In the meantime, taste this."

She let him slip a spoon into her mouth. A cream sauce rolled over her tongue, hints of garlic and something savory filling her mouth. She licked the remainder off her lips. "Wow."

"Didn't expect that, did you?" He went back to cooking.

She managed to loosen the knot a bit. He offered her a small slice of red pepper, sweet and crisp. Her stomach rumbled. She didn't know which maddened her more, the smell of food or the ribbon.

He'd been right about her heavy clothing. Sweat trickled down her back as she managed to twist her left hand so she could reach the knot. It tightened as she did so. A string of low curses followed.

He laughed then fed her a piece of cheese before going back to the stove.

"I'm almost finished. How about you?"

She refused to look at him. "Shut up."

"You get out of that one, and I'll let you feed yourself." The clink of ceramic indicated he was getting ready to serve.

She refused to rush. It was obviously what he wanted. The worst that would happen would be letting him feed her. At least his own dinner would get cold in the process. She held on to that thought as she carefully pushed one end of the ribbon, thrilled when it slipped through the knot. She repeated the action on the other side, but didn't push it all the way.

He set a plate in front of her and pulled out another chair. As he reached for the fork, she undid the knot. She dropped the ribbon in his lap and took the fork from him, smiling.

"Rob me of my fun why don't you?" he huffed.

"You've had entirely too much fun with this already." She reached for the plate. "I assume this one is mine?"

He laughed. "Yes, ma'am. Go ahead and start."

She waited until he got back with his own plate, determined to show she had manners. They quickly fled as she devoured the most amazing pasta she had ever eaten, barely pausing after a few bites to compliment his cooking.

"That was not a meal I'd have expected in the middle of the woods," she said, pushing the plate away to avoid the temptation to lick it clean.

"I told you I'd mastered some skills."

"Where did you learn to cook like that?"

"Culinary school." He cleared the plates. "Close your mouth, sugar, you're gonna catch flies."

"Did you leave because of the Kiss?" she asked.

"No, I left when part of the kitchen blew up and landed me in the hospital for a while."

She didn't know what to say.

He laughed. "You look positively poleaxed."

"I'm sorry. I shouldn't have pried." Most people didn't talk about their lives before becoming Tribe, and it was impolite to ask.

"I don't mind. I've got way too many secrets to be bothered by tales of woe from my youth."

"Couldn't have been all that long ago," she pointed out.

"Only a lifetime." His eyes got darker. "Sometimes I feel like this is the only life I've ever known."

She nodded. "Like what you did before was somehow less real."

"The Kiss is good for that. Makes leaving everything behind a little easier."

"Do you ever go home?" The words were out of her mouth before she could stop them.

"I have a place for the off-season. But this is just as much my home."

"If I had a space like this, I'd be happy to call it home, too."

"All you have to do is make the right deals. You'll figure out something that works for you. It might be a trailer, or a converted school bus, or one of those fine pavilion tents. As long as it's someplace you can call your own, I don't see much difference between this and what's out there."

"I suppose." Heather thought about her parents' split-level house with the garden in the back, surprised to realize she didn't miss it as much as she once had.

"Speaking of deals." He held out the ribbon.

"Oh, no. I did what you asked."

"But there's still dessert," he teased. "I know you have a sweet tooth, and I'd hate to think I went to all the trouble to make you something special just to be refused over a little thing like a ribbon."

"Bastard." She glared at him. "What's for dessert?"

"If you want to find out, you have to play."

She sighed. "Why not? It wasn't that hard."

"That's my girl."

She stomped on the thrill his words gave her. "Give me a minute, okay?"

"I've got all night."

"I don't." She pulled the sweatshirt off and draped it over the back of the chair.

He removed it and hung it under her coat. "It'll be nice and warm for your walk home," he explained.

"How is it that you don't blow a circuit with all this stuff?"

"This is a newer booth. They have their own line."

"Lucky you." The power went out in Jez's booth every time someone used a microwave while they were trying to brew coffee and dry their hair.

"Not luck, skill." He winked at her. "Speaking of which . . ." He picked up the ribbon.

She held her hands out, confident.

"Not this time. Dessert is worth a little more effort." He came around behind her. "Sit forward." He pulled her wrists behind her when she complied. "The binding's a little looser, to make up for the difficulty."

"I'll get out of this one, too," she said, hoping it was true.

"I'll give you a head start. I need to clean up a little to make room for dessert prep." He loaded a plastic dish pan, poured in some hot water from the kettle, and left.

It took longer to figure out how to reach the knot than she'd expected. She found the ends just as he walked back in.

"Did I mention that knot doesn't pull tight?" He made a lot of noise putting away the dishes in an attempt to drown out the insults she hurled at him.

"I'm some of those things, darlin'. But I don't even know what that last thing meant."

"Neither do I. It's something Cami says whenever she argues with Michael, so I'm guessing it's pretty bad."

"She's a wicked little thing." He said it with obvious admiration.

"Did I mention she's going to come for me if I don't get home in time?"

"When might that be?"

"I guess you'll find out if it comes to that. I can't imagine what she'd do if she found me tied up in your room." She pushed at the end of the ribbon. It slid a bit and stopped.

"Clever," he conceded. "But I'm willing to risk it." He went back to cooking.

Her arms were aching by the time he came over with a small strawberry. He popped it in her mouth, wiping her chin with his finger when some of the juice escaped. She rolled the berry around in her mouth as she worked on the other end of the ribbon. She swallowed as he approached with another. He had cut it in half, running it over her lips before letting her take it. She convinced herself that the flood of warmth came from the heater kicking in.

She had almost undone the knot when he came to the table with a plate of strawberries and a bowl. He cut another strawberry in half. Prompting her to open her mouth, he placed it on her tongue. She bit down, reveling in the sweetness. He held up a spoon, just at the edge of her lips. She leaned forward to take it as the knot unraveled. Pudding, unlike any she'd ever tasted, lighter, but richer, too. Her hands stilled, the ribbon wrapped around her wrists. She let him feed her two more bites.

"You aren't having any," she observed.

"This isn't my idea of dessert."

"What is?" Her heart pounded as he gave her a slow smile.

He leaned in and brushed his lips against hers, then pulled back. "That is. But I don't know that you'd like it as well."

"Maybe if your lips tasted like strawberries." Her head swam with the folly of the suggestion.

He ate a strawberry, his eyes locked on hers, then ran his tongue over his lips. "Let's see about that." He kissed her again, still careful. She ran her tongue over his lower lip, nipping at it before pulling away. The ribbon slipped over her hands. She grabbed it before it could hit the floor.

"That was sweet."

"You want more?" He dipped the spoon in the pudding.

"Not of that."

He slid his thumbs over her cheeks as he leaned in. The kiss tasted of strawberry and something much stronger. *Lust.* She lost herself in the texture of his mouth, exploring as she was explored. She let the ribbon fall and reached for him, her fingers gripping his arms as he pulled her closer.

"I was wondering how you were coming along," he said, his breath hot on her neck.

"Piece of cake," she murmured.

"Mmm. For cake I might have to actually tie you to the chair."

"If you did that, I wouldn't be able to do this." She ran her fingers through his hair and kissed him again.

"Wouldn't want to miss that." He pulled her onto his knees. "This either." He stroked her arm, stopping to trace patterns on the inside of her elbow and wrist. She laid her head on his shoulder.

"That would be a shame." She nipped his neck.

"No cake, then."

"No cake," she agreed.

She lost herself in the kiss, the feel of his arms around her. Her hands slid over his chest, exploring planes she looked at every time they fought. The pounding of his heart matched her own. She traced the muscles of his abdomen. He shuddered and kissed her again.

"How long until your defender comes gunning for me?"

"I'm not telling."

"We'd best stop." He gently pushed her back until she had to stand or fall to the floor. Not that he would let her fall.

"Is that what you want?"

"I want all sorts of things, but I know better than to think I'm going to get them."

She straddled him, placing her hands on his shoulders before lowering herself onto his lap. "What sort of things?"

"I told you not to do that unless you mean it." He shifted, not touching her.

"I know." She kissed him.

"Wench."

"That's what the job description says." She wriggled closer.

"Keep that up, and I'm going to forget how to be a gentleman." His body had already forgotten.

She snorted. "Tying me up was your idea of genteel?"

"No, it was my way of teaching you a new skill."

"Ah. So what else are you planning on teaching me?"

"Nothing that involves a chair." He grabbed her around the waist and stood, letting her slide down his body. "You sure you want to take this further? Because now would be the time to leave, if you have a mind to."

She stepped back. "What would you do if I walked away?"

"The rest of the dishes."

She laughed. "And?"

"My level best to see that you owed me another dinner." He grinned at her. "Next time, you can learn how to get out of ropes."

"Oh, that's tempting." She rolled her eyes.

He pulled her close and whispered in her ear, "You know it is."

She shivered, no hint of cold. "So much for being a gentleman."

"If it was a gentleman you wanted, you wouldn't be here." He stroked her back, pressing her to him.

"I had a debt."

"Now you have a choice."

She wrapped her arms around him. "I believe I've already made it."

He took her hand and led her into the living room, pausing to dim the light. They crossed into darkness. She could just make out a door on the opposite wall. Her heart raced. Once she entered that room, there would be no turning back. He reached for the doorknob.

A sharp knock at the front door stopped him. "If that's Cami, I'm going to strangle her," he whispered.

"It's way too early. She said midnight."

"Good to know. If we stay quiet, maybe they'll go away." He pulled her further into the shadows and kissed her.

The knocking changed to pounding. He swore softly. "Stay here. I'll deal with whatever it is and be right back."

She slumped against the wall as he strode across the room, agitation evident. His every movement bordered on violence. It should have made her nervous, but all she could think about was the play of muscles across his back, the feel of his body against hers, the wonder to come.

CHAPTER TEN

J ocko opened the door, letting in a blast of cold air. Paula darted into the room before he could speak. He closed the door, scowling.

"Hello, love," she purred.

"What are you doing here?" he asked.

She pouted. "I thought you'd be glad to see me."

"You were wrong. Go home."

"But you don't even know why I came."

He crossed his arms and looked down at her. "I don't care what your reasons are. I didn't issue an invitation."

"Didn't you?" She smiled sweetly. "How thoughtless of you, especially since I invite you to all my parties." She dipped her finger in the pudding then licked it off.

He growled. "I'm not going to play this game with you."

"But you like playing games." She laughed. "All sorts of games, if I recall correctly."

"Not tonight, Paula." He put his hand on the door.

She didn't move. "Rodney sent me with a message. You should probably answer your phone."

Jocko frowned. "The King wouldn't have sent you. He has his own messengers."

"Ardyth suggested it. We were having a little chat when Rodney came by. For some reason, he thought you might be at my place. It wasn't all that long ago, after all. It makes sense that he turned to me when he wanted to find you."

"So you were convenient. You've delivered the message, now leave."

"That's not all. He needs to see you. Tonight." She gave him a thin smile. "Now, in fact."

He clenched his fist then slowly let it go. "You're lying. Again."

"No, I'm not. They're waiting for you. Darius is with him."

Jocko tensed. "Fine. Message received."

She walked over to him, standing too close. "I'm to escort you." She ran her hand over his chest and down.

He grabbed her wrist. "You need to keep your hands off me."

"Strange, that's not what you said before."

"Don't push me, woman. You wouldn't like the result."

"Oh, I don't know about that. You get wild when you're upset, and I know just what buttons to push to bring out the beast in you."

"Unless you want to see exactly what it is I can do, I suggest you get the hell out of my room." He opened the door.

"Testing your skills was the idea, but we can save that for later. I'm supposed to bring you back, and time is running out, sweetie."

"You can wait for me at the bottom of the stairs." He shoved her through the door, closed it, and flipped the lock.

Heather wrapped her arms around herself in a futile attempt to stop shaking. The warmth of the room did nothing to stave off the chill in her blood. When Jocko approached her, she stepped back. "What was that about?"

"I don't know."

"She expected you to welcome her."

"She expects a lot of things." He reached for her.

She evaded him. "But you are leaving with her."

He sighed. "If the King sent for me, I have to show. You know that, especially if Darius is with him. I'm not stupid enough to take on either one of them when they issue a direct order."

"I guess you should go, then."

"In a minute. For some reason, you seem to be righteously pissed off at me."

"My brain started working."

"Care to explain that?"

She moved past him. "Maybe another time. I'd hate to keep you from your next appointment."

He grabbed her, spun her around, and pushed her up against the wall. "How about we do this now."

She pushed him back. "I don't think so. Paula is waiting for you."

"She can freeze to death for all I care. I want to know why it is that a couple minutes ago you were ready to make love, and now you won't even talk to me."

"Fine. I hate it when I do something stupid, but I own it. I let myself believe that you wanted me. Not just someone, me." She closed her eyes. "And that makes me a fool."

"If you think I don't care who I take to my bed, then you are a fool. And I am, too, for believing you'd see beyond rumors and gossip." He turned away. "Get your coat. I'll walk you home."

"Thanks, but I'd rather avoid Paula."

"You and me both." He gave her a level look. "Despite what you think."

"Do you trust me to lock up?"

"I'm not the one with trust issues. There's an extra key taped under the counter. You can give it back to me tomorrow." He grabbed his coat from the peg by the door. "If you time it right, no one will see you leave, so you won't have to worry about your pristine honor." He closed the door behind him.

She stood in the middle of the room. Her eyes fell on the ribbon. She picked it up, running it through her fingers before using it to tie her hair back. She pushed in the chairs and cleared the table. Anger faded to regret and then to numbness. She took one more look around the kitchen, wishing she could go back in time and refuse dessert. *Liar. Fool.* The two words circled each other in her head all the way home.

The lights were off in the booth, so either Jez had gotten lucky early, or she was still out. Heather tiptoed up the stairs, pausing in the storeroom. She was alone. She opened the notebook they used to remind each other of things and scribbled a quick note. She changed into sweats, put on her headphones, and went to sleep, drowning out thought and the rest of the world.

Despite sleeping later than usual, Heather was up first. She determined to take her time running, just in case Jez had company. She was in no mood to witness the morning-after dance. Even if it was happy, it would be awkward.

The regular route wouldn't give her the distance she needed, so she veered off on one of the smaller paths. The further she went into the woods, the calmer she became, finding her rhythm, until everything fell away except the stretch of her stride and steady, deep breaths. By the time she returned to the site, she remembered what it meant to be strong.

Without the time constraint of the show, she was able to take a long, hot shower with no interruptions. Warmed by the sun, she entered the site feeling more like herself than she had in weeks. Doc laughed when she danced past his shop like a little girl on the first day of summer. She waved at him but didn't stop to chat. She tripped up the stairs and burst into the room. Startled, Jez and Cami looked up.

"That is one freakishly happy girl," Cami drawled.

"Yeah, but she came home last night. Which, I note, you did not." Jez laughed.

"Gregor talked me into drinking some Slavic brandy. Put me in the bed he keeps for when his daughter comes to visit. You have no idea how disorienting it is to wake up in a strange place with stuffed animals staring down at you. I don't know why he keeps the room that way. Antonia isn't a little girl anymore."

Jez nodded. "I don't know that Toni was ever the little girl Gregor thought she was. That is one serious woman."

"Don't I know it. Girl has some mad blade skills and a wit that's almost as deadly." Cami rarely expressed such a level of admiration. "I'm just glad she isn't at this show. She would totally misread my friendship with her dad." Cami shuddered. "Like I'd ever date Gregor."

"Speaking of dates, how was yours?" Heather asked Jez.

"It was nice. I like talking to Rascal."

"Yeah, we know. Was there kissing, at least?"

"Some." Jez smiled. "We're going to take it slow. If all I wanted was to get laid, I'd make Lew follow through on his flirtatious promises."

"Would you, please? I'd like to know if he's as good as he thinks he is." Cami grinned.

"Find out for yourself," Jez snapped.

"Ha! That is never going to happen. For one thing, I don't have enough meat on my bones for Lew to notice me that way. For another, Michael would kill him. And even if both those things were out of the way, Lew says that would be like incest." She turned to Heather. "So how about it? Put on fifteen pounds and take one for the team so my curiosity can be satisfied?"

"Oh, hell no. I love Lew, but I prefer to be his friend, and you know he's no good at maintaining friendships with women after he's slept with them."

Cami nodded. "Speaking of men who don't know how to treat women right, how was *your* date?"

"It wasn't a date. It was dinner. And it was fine."

"Details," Jez demanded.

"He's a really good cook." Heather shrugged.

"Wait." Cami straightened. "You had dinner in his room?"

"Yeah. It's more like an apartment than a room."

"You failed to mention that part of the arrangement." Cami looked at her, suspicion growing.

"It was no big deal. He made me dinner and dessert. Then I came home."

Jez looked over at Cami. "Notice how she's leaving out the part where he kissed her?"

"Big gaping hole in the story. Makes me wonder what else she's not telling us."

"There was kissing, okay? And then he got word that Rodney and Darius wanted him and that was that." Heather looked down at the floor, determined to keep the rest of the details to herself. Her humiliation was bad enough without sharing it with her best friends.

"Damn it!" Cami stubbed out her cigarette.

Heather's head snapped up. "What? You were the one who didn't want me to fall for him."

"Too bad you didn't take my advice."

"Trust me. There is nothing going on between me and Jocko. And there won't be."

Cami glared at her. "I'd feel better if you weren't so unhappy about that."

"I'm fine with it," Heather said. "I'm going to get my laundry together. Let me know when you're ready to head out." She went to her room, ignoring the discussion that began as soon as she shut the door. By the time she came out, Cami was gone.

Jez handed Heather a cup of coffee. They sat in companionable silence while Jez did her books. The Monday routine was comforting. Heather paid the few bills she had and took inventory of their pantry. It didn't take long.

Jez closed her computer and looked up. "Don't mind Cami. She just doesn't want you to get hurt again."

"You can both stop worrying about that happening."

"Because it already has." Jez sighed. "It's written all over you, honey. You don't have to tell me what happened. I'm here for you either way."

"Why do you love me so much?" Heather asked.

"I just do. When you're around, I have a purpose."

"Besides being an incredible jeweler?"

"The Kiss heightened my creativity and my confidence. You make this place feel like home." Jez looked around. "Such as it is."

"Don't knock it. It's the only home I've got at the moment." It might not be that comfortable, but it served its purpose.

"I'm glad you stay with me. It's nice to know I've got someone to watch my back and share my secrets with."

Heather sipped her coffee. Jez was right. Trust held them together. "Paula was the one who brought the summons last night."

"Ouch." Jez winced. "Was she awful to you?"

"She didn't see me."

"Neat trick."

"It was dark where I was," Heather admitted.

Jez squeezed her shoulder. "Oh, honey. I'm sorry."

"I still had my clothes on."

"Were you planning to keep them on before that?" Jez refilled their cups.

"No," Heather admitted. "So I guess I owe Paula for rescuing me from another bad decision."

Jez raised one eyebrow. "I wouldn't tell her that."

"Wasn't planning to."

"So, what now?"

Heather shrugged. "I leave him to his own devices and get on with my life." She didn't see any other option.

"If you think he's going to let it go at that, you don't know Jocko."

"No," Heather said softly, "I really don't."

CHAPTER ELEVEN

The Monday errands went quickly, mostly because Jezebel insisted they drop off their laundry instead of hanging out to do it themselves. After checking their post office box and making the bank deposit, they went to the thrift store. Jezebel found a smart, navy dress with a classic 1940s cut, perfect for the Funky Formal. It was the best party at the faire, essentially the prom everyone in the Tribe wished they'd had. Attire ranged from black tie to exotic, the only rule being that faire costumes were not allowed. Heather tried on a series of dresses, but none of them were quite right.

Jez swung across the shop, holding up a crimson gown and grinning madly. "They just got this in."

Heather looked skeptical but agreed to at least try it on. She stepped into it, sure that it wouldn't fit. She had an impossibly long waist and small breasts, so most dresses were either too short-waisted or too low-cut for her to look good in them. Not having hips to speak of didn't help. She pulled the thin straps over her shoulders and let Jez zip her up, waiting for the inevitable gaps. The top fit her perfectly. When she stepped out to look in the mirror, her eyes grew wide. The heart-shaped neckline made the most of her minimal cleavage. The skirt dragged on the floor, but it wouldn't take much to shorten it. It was gathered into the bodice in a straight line that ran just below her waist, making her look taller. When she moved, the skirt swirled with a satisfying swish.

"Yes!" Jez squealed. "With the right shoes, it wouldn't even need hemming."

"Heels, on me?" Heather shook her head. "I don't think so."

"Come on. You must have worn heels before."

"Not for years."

"Then it's high time we got you some. You'll need to practice if you're going to dance in them."

Jezebel's luck held. She found the perfect shoes in the thrift store. Heather found a man's suit jacket that fit her broad shoulders and was just roomy enough to allow wearing a light sweater underneath. For a wonder, Jez approved of it, telling her it looked like she was wearing her boyfriend's coat. She clapped her hands to her mouth, horrified.

Heather laughed. "It does look like a boyfriend jacket. Sort of the point of the style."

"Did you just use the word 'style' in a complete sentence not having anything to do with fighting?" Jez teased.

"Very funny. For your information, I used to have a very distinct style."

"Which was?"

"Artist chic. A lot like what I wear now, but with more scarves and fewer sweats."

"When did that change?"

"When I started hanging out with actual artists," Heather said. "Besides, being surrounded by gorgeous women allowed me to stop trying so hard. I can't compete with the likes of Paula."

Jez waved off the idea. "Artifice is not style, honey."

"You can't tell me she's not beautiful."

The clerk looked up from the register. "I don't know who Paula is, but I know beauty, and you've got it in spades." He blushed and went back to ringing up the purchases.

"That is the nicest thing I've heard all day," Heather said. "Thank you."

"There's a rack of scarves over there, if you're interested." He waved to the corner. "Some of them are hideous, but there's a couple of really cool ones. There's no one else here, so I can wait to check you out again." His mouth formed an 'o' in horror and he blushed again. "I . . . I meant . . . Oh, hell."

Jez patted his hand. "It's okay, dear. She has that effect on people."

Heather rolled her eyes and went to the scarf rack. He was right about most of them being awful. Cami would love them. She picked out two with jarring patterns and uncovered a large, thin shawl, shot through with gold thread. When she pulled it off the rack, a woven scarf fell to the floor. The work was finer than she expected to find in a thrift store. She picked it up. *Cashmere and silk.* The grey was the same color as the hounds-tooth jacket. She brought them over to the counter and thanked the clerk. He wouldn't meet her eyes, but when they got in the car, Jez said he'd been watching Heather as they'd walked out.

They bought groceries, Heather thinking wistfully how nice it would be to have a full-sized fridge, then picked up the laundry and went home. They spent the rest of the morning rearranging the storage space. Jez went to find Rascal and convince him to go back to the thrift store to help her bring back a couch. His ugly van had to be good for something.

Cami came in, looked around, and left again. While Jez was gone, she harassed Lew and Michael into building shelves. Heather painted labels on them so Jez would know where everything was.

"Hey, hotrod." Michael nudged Cami with his shoulder. "We have some extra lumber, and there's a board left over from the shed repair. You want me to build you a target?"

Cami narrowed her eyes. "Why are you being nice to me?"

"Mom asked me to take care of you," he admitted. "We both know I won't do that, but I have to tell her I did. I figured you'd let me do this much."

Cami paled. "When did you talk to her?"

"Last night. She said to tell you to call her. Now you can't blame me for not passing on the message."

"I can't believe you ratted me out." Cami advanced on him.

"She knew already." Michael backed away. "Darius sent her an e-mail letting her know where you were. I had nothing to do with it."

"He'd make a fine target," Cami snarled.

"Good luck with that." Michael laughed. "So, you want me to give you something to practice on, little engine?"

"Keep it up," she warned.

"Not my fault dad named you after his car."

There was a moment of silence before Lew burst out laughing. "Your full name is Camaro?"

"You tell anyone else that, and I will gut you in your sleep." Cami turned to Michael, obviously struggling to calm down. "If you make me a nice target, I will call mom and tell her that you are taking very good care of me."

"Done." Michael dragged Lew away before he could do anything more to enrage Cami.

"I thought you got along with your mom," Heather said. "Why don't you want to call?"

"When Michael calls, she tells him all about the house and garden and my Aunt Rosa. When I call, she tells me how much she wants grandchildren." Cami snorted. "I would happily get sterilized to make the request moot, but I can't find a doctor who will do it, no matter how vitriolic I get about the evils of procreation. This keeps up, I'm going to find a way to remove my own uterus."

"That's a bit extreme," Heather said. "But I have to agree that you should be no one's mother. Ever."

"The voice of reason. Want to call my mom for me?"

"I have my own family to avoid, so I'll pass on that."

Cami shot her a quizzical look. "Your family is totally supportive."

"Yes, and no. They think this is a phase, something I need to get out of my system. I don't know what it would take for them to stop believing I'm going to come back and finish college."

"Try taking Jocko home for the holidays."

Heather gaped at her. "I cannot believe you just said that!"

"Sorry. It was the most outrageous and unlikely thing I could think of." Cami pursed her lips. "Unless you weren't being straight about there being no chance of you two hooking up."

"As far as I know, we have no future together."

"Which is not at all the same thing as saying you have no desire to jump his bones. How close did you come to that last night?"

Heather shoved her hands in her pockets and looked away. Her hand closed on something hard and cold. "Oh, crap! His key."

"He gave you his key?" Cami narrowed her eyes. "This is supposed to convince me that nothing is going on how?"

"I locked up after he left. With Paula." Heather found Cami's shock satisfying.

"Ballsy. She's going to hate you for being there."

"She hates me anyway. I have no idea why. But she didn't know I was there, and no one is going to tell her."

"I cross paths with the psychotic bitch, I'm more likely to cut her than talk to her, so you've got nothing to worry about from me. If she does find out he wants you, it's going to get ugly. She's never stopped chasing him." Cami shook her head.

"Whether he wants me or not is just as moot as your mom's desire for grandchildren. But I do have to return his key. He's probably pissed about the fact that I've taken this long to get it back to him."

"I doubt that. He's gone."

"How do you know?"

"Doc told me. Jocko up and left in the middle of the night. Par for the course. Dude is always disappearing without notice."

Heather shrugged. "Then I'll give the key to Jasper. It's his shop. He can give it to Jocko when he gets back."

"Take it to Doc. Jasper is out with Tansy," Cami said. "I will never understand that woman. I can barely tolerate one man at a time. No idea how she manages being married to two."

"It seems to work for them, so I don't question it."

"Good policy. If you're going to see Doc, I'll head to jouster hell and oversee the construction of my new target. Maybe they'll work faster if I throw knives at them."

"Darius would be pissed if you nicked one of his boys, even your brother."

"I don't miss," Cami said over her shoulder. "Ever."

"Hence, the warning," Heather called.

She ran up the stairs to leave a note for Jez before heading for the apothecary. Doc would be working. The man was as dedicated to his craft as he was to his wife. Their love affair was the stuff of legend, and the sudden appearance and assimilation of Jasper into the relationship was still a topic of quiet conversation. Heather never joined in the speculation. It seemed rude.

Doc sat at a table at the back of his workshop, mixing tinctures. His blond hair was short, threaded with gray, and thinning at the top. If she had to guess, she would put his age around sixty. He was thick around the middle, like her dad, but without the love handles. His glasses perched on his nose, always seeming about to fall off but never actually slipping. When he looked up at her, his blue eyes shone.

"Hello, sweetheart. Come to keep an old man company?"

"I don't want to interrupt your work."

Doc smiled. "One of the many things I admire about you. I'm all finished with this batch."

"Love potions?" she teased. He frequently grumbled about the fools who requested those.

"Why? Are you in the market?"

"Hah! I know better than that." She fingered the key in her pocket. "You'd probably give me something to settle my stomach and put me to sleep."

"Best cure for love sickness."

"No need. I'm immune."

"Ah, the folly of youth." Doc shook his head. "You all think you're immortal and immune to love, as if the former was desirable and the latter was not."

"I was looking for Jasper."

"The lad is out with our wife, picking up a shipment of cedar and looking for a decent bottle of port. I suspect they won't find one, but the tale of the hunt will be good to hear over a glass of the wine they bring back as a sop. You may leave whatever you've brought in the box over there." He waved vaguely toward the counter. "And join me for lunch, if you've not yet eaten."

"I will, if you'll let me help you restock."

"Gracious lass. I will take advantage of that offer." He retreated to his living quarters, widely acknowledged as the most luxurious place on site. Tansy had taken ill at one show while Doc was visiting his son. She had been rushed to the hospital and barely survived. After that, he had resolved that she would never be subject to the unsanitary conditions of a show again. She wouldn't hear of leaving the faire circuit, so he built a real apartment, complete with running water, on every site. The apothecary was his passion, but everyone knew he'd been rich before becoming Tribe.

Heather wrapped the key in a piece of paper, wrote Jocko's name on it, and placed it in a finely made box with Jasper's name carved in it. There were three boxes, side by side. They only ever opened their own. That was legend, too.

Doc bustled around the kitchen—a real one—making sandwiches and brewing tea. Heather sat at the teak table and placed the cloth napkin in her lap. Sun shone through the large windows, warming her face. She closed her eyes and let her tension unravel.

"You make me wish I could paint." Doc placed a plate in front of her. "There is a classic beauty about you."

Heather blushed. "You flatter me."

"Pish tosh. I tell the truth as I see it." He pulled up a chair. "It's a shame Anthony chooses not to be Tribe, or I'd try to play matchmaker for you two."

"I thought everyone who could be Tribe got turned eventually."

"Most of us have already made the decision to live our lives as nomads, so we look forward to finding out if we will be Tribe. Offspring are almost guaranteed to turn, but they can decide against it. Anthony has other passions. They do as much to sustain him as being Tribe does for us. He just finished his internship in Seattle." Doc smiled. "He stubbornly refused to do it at the hospital where I practiced."

"Why?"

"Because he wishes to make it on his own. When a wing is named after your father—or grandfather, in his case—it is difficult to convince people you are not being favored over your coworkers. I did not have his sense."

They fell silent as they ate. Heather sipped the tea, trying to determine what was in it. Doc wouldn't test her, but he always appreciated it when she figured out his recipes. She identified chamomile, lemon balm, lemongrass, and peppermint.

"Well done!" Doc clapped. "But there's one more thing."

Heather took another sip, trying to separate the flavors. "I can't place it."

He smiled at her. "Catmint."

"Is that like catnip?"

"The very same thing, in fact. It has soothing properties for humans, as well."

"As long as it doesn't make me chase stuffed mice around and then fall asleep, I'm all for it."

"If it has that effect on you, let me know. I'll want video." He cleaned up and turned to her. "Now, I shall put you to work."

"You know I'll pester you with questions, right?"

"I count on it, my dear. It is why you are a joy to have around. You ask for nothing but knowledge and actually listen when I impart it. That is a rare pleasure for me."

Heather filled small bags with herbs while Doc informed her of their uses. He mixed teas. When the light began to fade, he called an end to the work day. Heather tidied up the counter while Doc stocked the shelves.

"Can I ask you a question?"

"Have you not been doing that?" he teased.

"This is different." She hesitated. "I want to know more about the Kiss, if you don't mind talking about it."

"It does not bother me to speak of it."

Heather frowned. "Why don't we talk about it more?"

"Even normal people don't look too closely at their lives for fear of what they might find. For us, it is a bit more fraught. The Kiss makes us more of what we already were, and that is enough for most. They use their enhanced creativity to craft objects of beauty or entertain, but they do not want to consider the price."

"I live with a merchant. They think a lot about prices."

"That is business. I am talking about something quite different." He pursed his lips. "Are you sure you want to know the rest? It may be better to accept that we are what we are."

"Parasites who feed off our crowds?" She was only half-joking.

"That is not entirely true. What we do allows them to feel those emotions at higher levels than they normally allow themselves. We simply skim off the top, so to speak. Only in one instance do we take directly."

"Giving the Kiss."

"Lust is the most powerful raw emotion save grief. But it is an individual thing and therefore must be taken directly. Even then, the Kiss has some benefits for those who receive it."

"I fail to see what they get out of it."

"Satisfaction."

"No offense, Doc, but if my experience is any indication, it's not that satisfying."

He grimaced. "What was done to you was inexcusable, especially because you are Tribe. Trust me when I say that the circumstances of your receiving the Kiss are not the norm. The physical effects of the Kiss fade quickly for Mundanes. The aftermath is often a burst of creative energy, the confidence to try new things, or the decision to follow a path they had not thought possible."

"So it's just me who's a freak," she muttered.

"You are not responsible for that," Doc snapped. He took a deep breath. "There are rules about bringing someone into the Tribe. It is only to be done when there is sufficient time for the adjustments to be made and the longing explained. If one is lucky enough to know someone with a Talent like Jezebel's, becoming Tribe can be an informed decision."

"That might have helped. I still don't understand why I felt compelled to get to a faire."

"Gifts come with a price. We may feed off the patrons, but we need each other for sustenance, too. You performers, especially, provide us with enough residuals to keep us going for weeks."

"How so?"

"You draw the largest crowds, incite the biggest reactions. Think about how you feel when your audience is greater than seating allows. They spill over, as does their energy. The final joust is a massive swirl of emotions, like sitting down at a banquet and knowing you can eat as much as you want and still leave a full table when you're sated."

"What would happen if we didn't seek out the Tribe?"

"We can feed off any emotion if it's large enough, but if there is no Tribe, the effects fade too quickly to be of any use. We become agitated. Those who go too long without Tribe contact become desperately unhappy."

"So it's a life sentence." She had known that, but never admitted it out loud.

"I prefer to see it as a way of life. It is possible to leave."

"Sure, if you don't mind being miserable."

"Having another passion mitigates the longing. Plenty of Tribe members drop off the circuit to pursue other careers, have a family, get a degree— whatever other thing makes them happy."

"And that works?"

"To some extent. They can hold the hunger at bay for a while but will need to find Tribe to sustain themselves. Working a single faire can give them enough to ride out the rest of the year, or most of it. The longing returns, usually about six months after the last contact. Small pockets of Tribe who are also making their way in normal lives can be found anywhere an audience comes to watch live performances. The symphony is particularly nice, providing it's not being broadcast."

Heather frowned. "Why would that make a difference?"

"The waves seem to interfere with feeding. Running water can do the same thing on a much smaller scale. Apparently, it caused an entire Tribe to become violently ill at the premiere of Handel's *Water Music*." Doc chuckled.

Heather stared at him. "There was Tribe back then?"

"We have always existed. The early Tribe was much stronger, of course. Intermarrying with normal humans weakened the blood lines. The original Tribes had multiple Talents, many of them closer to active magic than we can now manage. Their need to feed was greater, as was their influence on the audience. I doubt any of us could handle the strength of emotion generated by a fight at the Coliseum. Not that I have any desire to watch some poor unfortunate battle to the death! Nor, for that matter, attend an actual joust to the death. Our poor specter of that is enough for my old heart."

Heather shuddered. "I can't imagine what it would be like if we were even stronger. We're scary enough as it is."

"There were not so many then, and they stayed together. Fewer entertainment venues were available to provide cover. It would be difficult enough if people were to find out now. Imagine what it must have been like in ancient times or the actual Renaissance."

Heather shuddered. "The Inquisition would have had a field day with us."

"Why do you think it was formed?" He was deadly serious. "It did succeed. The Tribe was forced to scatter. The only thing of similar magnitude was Cromwell's reign in England. You'll find more Tribe in Wales and the Highlands, simply because it was harder to reach them in those places. Some returned to England, but London was never the same after the Puritans drove out the Tribe. Migration to America proved particularly disruptive, since everyone was hiding what they were and coming from different cultures. It's a wonder any of us were able to find each other, considering how often we had to flee."

"How did they recognize each other? It's not like we have marks or a secret handshake."

"Did you ever get the feeling, upon meeting someone for the first time, that you had known them all your life?"

Heather nodded, thinking about her first introduction to Cami and her instant friendship with Jez.

"Those people are your tribe."

"But I don't feel that way about everyone who's Tribe."

"We are still human, my dear. More human than our forbearers, certainly. There are always people toward whom we feel ambivalent and others whom we dislike upon meeting. Just as there are those who spark instant love, or something more carnal. The world would be much less interesting if that were not true." He winked at her.

"But those feelings can change," she protested. "People who started out disliking each other can become friends. Lovers can drift apart or have a bad breakup and wind up hating each other."

"To know that we are not locked into anything, no matter how sure we are of our paths at the beginning, is one of the best things about life. If we don't like the story we're in, we can rewrite it to suit us."

"You make it sound easy."

"Not easy, possible. If you desire something badly enough, it is worth the effort to pursue it, much in the same way that you put effort into avoiding something when you do not want it." He looked up and smiled. "Tansy and Jasper have returned."

Heather looked out of the shop. There was no one in sight. "Do you have some sort of psychic connection?"

"No, I have very good hearing, and Jasper's truck has a rather loud engine." Doc laughed.

"I'll go. Thanks for everything. Sorry I'm such a pest."

"Not at all. I found it a pleasant diversion. It reminded me of when I used to lecture." He gave her a hug. "You are welcome to stop by anytime."

"Thank you."

Her thoughts swirled as she walked across the site. The Tribe was both more and less than she had thought. Was it biology or magic? And why was Sebastian's Kiss so terrible? She wondered if things would be different if it had been Jocko who had Kissed her. Or even Carter. Speculation was pointless. She would never know what it was like to be glad of the Kiss. She added it to the list of things the Bastard had taken from her.

One thing was certain; she would never bring someone into the Tribe, dooming them to a life of constant travel or perpetual dissatisfaction. No matter what Doc said, no benefit could be worth robbing another person of their choices. Kissing a Mundane was completely out of the question. Maybe it did give them that nudge to do something great. It didn't matter; it was more than she was willing to bear.

CHAPTER TWELVE

Laughter came from the booth as Heather drew near. She hesitated but climbed the stairs. She had nowhere else to go. Rascal and Jez were sitting on the new couch, which was surprisingly not ugly.

"Damn, woman, you look like someone just kicked your puppy," Cami said, hopping off a stool.

"Nothing like that. I was just thinking."

"Dangerous thing, deep thoughts," Rascal said with a grin. "I try to avoid them."

"That explains so much about you," Cami drawled.

"Is she always this harsh?" Rascal asked.

"Yeah, but don't let it bug you," Jez replied. "She only insults people she likes. She doesn't bother talking to the rest."

"That's not true. I insult Paula all the time. That's more out of a sense of duty, though."

"That woman is not right," Rascal proclaimed. They all nodded in agreement.

"You hungry, honey?" Jez asked. "I bought Chinese."

"Starving." Heather grabbed a container and a set of chopsticks, fully intending to finish the contents. "What's the occasion?"

"I wanted to thank Rascal for helping me get the couch, but I can pretend it was to thank you for the shelves. They're wonderful." Jez smiled at her. "See? You do make this more of a home."

"Least I could do. Besides, Cami beat the boys into building them. I just painted."

"How was your visit with Doc?" Jez asked.

"Illuminating."

"By which she means the old man talked her ear off, and she did everything but take notes and ask when the test would be." Cami grinned at her.

"Pretty much. I helped him restock, and he answered some questions for me. Doc knows so much."

"Did you ask him how to avoid rogues and scoundrels?" Cami quipped.

"So I could spend the rest of my days at faire alone?" Heather laughed. "I don't think so. I could ask him how to make tincture to help a friend be less caustic. That might be useful."

"You wish. No herbal mixture is going to turn me sweet. I have snake venom for blood." Cami flicked her tongue out and hissed.

"Nothing wrong with being sweet," Rascal said, putting his arm around Jez.

Cami made a gagging noise. "Please. Heather's still eating."

Jez stuck her tongue out and snuggled into Rascal. "Hey, do you think Doc has a potion that would turn Paula into a decent human being? Maybe an antipsychotic. He was a real doctor. He should know how to do that."

"It's a lost cause. She's no more changeable than Cami is," Heather said.

"Mention me and her in the same sentence again, and we're going to take this outside," Cami threatened. "I suppose I could preserve our friendship by making the bitch disappear."

"Someone might notice," Heather said. "And disposing of the body is bound to be a hassle."

Cami spun a knife through her fingers. "Not if I do it right."

"You'll have to wait for that," Rascal said. "She's gone."

"That's good news!" Jez said. "When did she leave? And, more important, is she gone for good?"

"I don't know about that. She was gone this morning. I heard Katie talking about it at breakfast. I guess Paula disappeared in the middle of the night without a word to anyone. Probably went on an extended shopping spree. That woman has way more money than sense."

Heather set down the container, feeling suddenly ill. "I need to use the privies. I'll be right back." She bolted for the door. Maybe she'd make it before she threw up.

"I'm going with her." Cami followed fast on her heels, grabbing their jackets from the newly hung pegs over the space heater.

Fresh air helped alleviate the urge to vomit but did nothing for the acid sting of humiliation. Jocko and Paula had gone off together, were probably laughing at Heather's naiveté. The only thing that kept her from breaking down was Cami's presence, quiet, accepting, mad as hell—whether for her or at her, Heather didn't know.

They walked in silence for a while. It wasn't as cold as it had been the night before, but despite the warm jacket, Heather shivered. Cami took the lead, heading into the woods behind the jouster camp. She continued until they came out into a clearing. Cami's target stood in the center, the white and red circles shining in the light of the almost full moon. Cami drew throwing knives from her pocket, keeping three and handing the rest to Heather.

Cami held up the knife, demonstrating the proper grip, then let it fly. It landed dead-center with a satisfying thunk. She repeated the action then stepped aside. Heather concentrated and whipped the knife across the clearing. It hit the target and fell to the ground. Her second try stuck, but barely, about as far from center as it was possible to get. Cami demonstrated again and tossed her last knife without looking. It hit the target, landing right next to her first two knives. Heather's final try landed two rings from the edge. Cami trotted out and retrieved the knives.

"Go again, but relax. Think of the target as the back of Paula's head." Cami handed off all six knives.

"Or Jocko's," Heather muttered.

"We'll get to him in a minute. One target at a time. This round is for the skank ho."

Five knives landed solidly in various outer rings. Heather took a deep breath and let her shoulders drop, weighing the knife in her hand. She held it up, ready.

"Bitch stole your man," Cami whispered.

Heather let the knife fly. It landed at the edge of the bulls-eye.

She turned to Cami. "What the hell was that?"

"The truth as you see it."

"He's not my man," Heather protested. "She can have him, and good riddance."

Cami sighed. "Get the knives."

Heather walked out and yanked them off the target. The one near the center had sunk deep. She brought them back to Cami.

"God save me for saying this, but you need to cut Jocko some slack."

"Excuse me?"

"He's not with Paula."

"Right. She comes by his place, expecting him to follow like a dog, and he does. They both disappear in the middle of the night, and neither one of them comes back. What does that tell you?"

"Nothing," Cami said.

"That's a bit too much of a coincidence for me to overlook."

"Then she just won." Cami tucked the knives in her pocket.

"I think she did that when he left me in his room to chase after her. I may not have your experience, but I'm not stupid."

"Yeah, you are." Cami lit a cigarette. "You draw a conclusion without having all the information."

Heather crossed her arms over her chest. "I know what I saw."

"Exactly what she wanted you to see. If you think she didn't know you were there, you're wrong. She watches his place. When she can't, she has Katie or one of her other toadies do it for her. Paula is stalking him, and he knows it. You can bet she volunteered to go get him for Rodney, knowing it would upset you."

"None of which explains why he took off with her in the middle of the night."

"Are you really that thick? He didn't leave with her. The Court sent him to do something. Paula knew he was going and took off on her own to make it look like they'd gone together. So far, that's working out well for her."

"Why are you defending him?"

"Because, as much as I dislike the guy, he's not such an asshole that he'd leave you hot and bothered in his room without a good reason. Chasing after a woman he hates would be right off the list."

"He's the one who brought her into the Tribe. He must have had a reason."

"He was really young when he did that. He's been paying for it ever since."

"He's not that old," Heather countered. "And neither is she."

"Older than she looks. Way older than she acts, especially around you. I've seen teenagers handle competition better."

"She hated me before Jocko ever noticed me."

"Sure she did. You're everything she pretended to be when she got him to Kiss her. If he liked the act, it was a pretty good bet he'd fall for the real thing. When you became his fight partner, she lost what little grip she had."

Heather stared at the target, trying to think and avoid thinking at the same time. It almost worked. Cami stubbed out her cigarette and pulled out another one. Heather snatched it from her and held out her hand.

"You don't smoke."

"Shut up and give me a light."

Cami slapped a lighter into her hand. "That was a pretty nice move. I didn't think you were that quick."

"Apparently, I'm pretty friggin' slow."

"That's what you get for being above listening to gossip."

"I guess that will have to change." Heather took a drag and barely managed to release it without choking. "In the meantime, what am I supposed to do?"

"Watch your back around Paula and give me back my damned lighter."

"I meant what should I do about Jocko? We didn't part on the best of terms."

Cami rolled her eyes. "I'm willing to tell you about his stalker. That doesn't mean I'm going to help you hook up with him."

"That ship has sailed, but I still have to work with him."

"You'll figure something out. Now stop pretending you know how to smoke and come back to the booth with me. It's getting cold."

By the time they got back to the shop, Rascal was gone. Jez had cleaned up and gone to bed, leaving a note to remind Heather she'd agreed to help with inventory. Even with the new organization system, it was likely to take up most of the next two days.

"Well, at least you'll be too busy to get into any trouble," Cami quipped as she walked to their room.

"Trouble is out of town," Heather muttered, following her.

Gina came by Wednesday afternoon to remind Heather of the catalog shoot. "We're starting ungodly early, so don't party all night."

"No one gets up before Heather," Jez said, looking up from her laptop. It was her one concession to modern business. "She runs every morning."

"I guess that explains your tight little bod."

"I'm telling Marni!" Jez said.

"If you think my girlfriend hasn't noticed how pretty Heather is, you're sadly mistaken. Marni did invite her to model for us, after all. Maybe I'm the one who should be jealous."

"As if," Heather scoffed. "That woman worships you."

"What can I say? I'm a goddess." Gina cackled. "You're going to have to find someone else to venerate you." Gina winked at them and strode off, still every inch the fighter.

"Carter worships you, Heather," Jez teased. "If he's lucky, they'll let him grovel at your feet in a couple of the pictures instead of standing around and looking all noble and hot."

"Very funny." Heather laid down her clipboard. "Look at the time! I'd better go take a shower if I'm going to give my hair time enough to dry in braids. Have to get pretty for the photo shoot, after all. You can finish up, right?"

"Vain wench," Jez chided.

Heather laughed. "That's high holy vain wench to you."

Jez snorted. "Off with you then. I'll meet you upstairs afterward. You have to practice dancing in those shoes, so you don't face-plant at the Formal and give Jocko another chance to rescue you."

"If he doesn't get back here by tomorrow night, he'll be the one who needs rescuing. We have to perfect the fight or take it back to the old routine, which we'll still need to practice. Lew will have a fit if we screw it up again." She still smarted from having to take his criticism alone. He hadn't been terribly harsh, but it had been embarrassing. Despite her mixed feelings about Jocko, it would have been nice to have him back her up.

The showers were abandoned when she got there. She took her time, running through a good portion of her repertoire. *Might as well practice something.* She toweled her hair as dry as it would get then twisted it into French braids on either side of her head. It was as close as she would come to curling her hair. By morning, it would have a nice wave, much better than her perfectly straight hair, at least for the sort of romance novel cover shots the photographer was likely to insist on shooting. It occurred to her that she would have to put on full makeup, not the quick dash she did at the beginning of a faire day that always faded before her second fight. She had never cared for the stuff, but for Marni and Gina, she'd make the effort.

As she walked past Jasper's shop, she couldn't help looking up at Jocko's room. The windows were dark. She shook her head. Walking across the site, she devised numerous scenarios in which she accidentally eviscerated him. *Inconsiderate bastard.*

As if summoned, a shadow stepped into her path. "Hello, Heather. I've been looking for you."

She froze, dropping her shower bag. "Sebastian."

She couldn't breathe, couldn't move. Cold snaked around her, sinking into her bones. She drew a shaky breath. Then another. He was still beautiful, no sign of the monster he'd become in her head.

"No welcome? I'd thought better of you," he chided.

"Wh . . . what are you doing here?"

"I have business with Darius. But when I heard you were here, I decided to seek you out." He made it sound like an honor, as if she should welcome his attention.

Blood returned to her veins, heated by raw anger. "For what?"

"I thought we should talk." He towered over her, as he always had, but now she saw menace where once she'd seen protective strength.

She picked up her bag. He moved closer, and she and instinctively dropped into a fighting stance. "I have nothing to say to you."

"Then don't speak." His words lashed across her.

She backed up. "Let me rephrase. There is nothing you can say that I wish to hear."

"I came to apologize." Nothing in their history could convince her he spoke with sincerity.

She moved past him. "Stuff your apology. It's too little, too late, and I'm not really interested in your bullshit excuses for why you ruined my life and then ran away."

His hand shot out, catching her arm. "You will hear me out."

"The hell you say," she snarled. Her attempt to wrench her arm away failed.

"Doesn't sound like she's interested in what you have to say, Sebastian." The lazy drawl came from between two booths. "And I don't much care for the way you're manhandling her."

"Jocko." The name was a curse on Sebastian's lips.

"Might want to take your hand off my partner."

Sebastian released her. She stepped back, fighting the urge to run, not knowing which direction to take. She watched as two wary shadows faced off.

"If you've got business with Darius, see to it. Then get the hell off my faire site."

Sebastian arched an eyebrow. "Your faire, is it? I hadn't realized you were made King."

"No, but you know how I'm regarded by the Court. Hell, your own boss likes me more than he likes you, and Darius' opinion seems to matter to the Queen."

"They don't see you for the scum you are," Sebastian spat.

"And yet, he's still a better man than you will ever be," Heather countered.

"This is a discussion best left to morning. Perhaps by then you will have found some measure of self-control," Sebastian said to her.

"I won't have any more reason to hear you out tomorrow."

"We shall see." He turned and disappeared back into the shadows.

"You okay, darlin'?" Jocko asked.

"I'm pissed right the hell off is what I am."

"I'll make sure he doesn't bother you. Tomorrow or any other day." He laid a hand on her arm.

She shook him off. "You're on my list, too."

"Okay. You can explain that to me when you're ready. Unless you're not talking to me, either."

"Oh, we'll talk. And then we'll fight. But right now, I'm going home and getting into bed."

"Let me escort you," Jocko said. "Please."

Fine. Just keep your mouth shut."

"I can do that." He fell in beside her and did not leave until she had closed the door and thrown the bolt.

Heather flopped onto the couch. She covered her face with her hands and let herself cry. After a few minutes, she remembered the photo shoot and reined in her emotions. No amount of eye drops would undo the damage of a serious crying jag. She would have to wait. At least Paula seemed to be blowing off the shoot. It was going to be difficult enough to feign happiness with Sebastian on site.

Cami hit the door and cursed. Heather jumped up and let her in.

"So, you've heard." Cami hung up her jacket.

"More than that, I've seen."

"Shit, shit, shit! I told Darius not to let the son of a bitch out of his sight. He said it wouldn't be an issue. It seems he was wrong." Cami paced. "How bad was it?"

"Not as bad as it could have been. He scared the hell out of me and then we argued a little."

"And he left it at that?"

"Jocko showed up."

Cami tapped her finger on her lips. "That explains why he backed down."

"I guess Sebastian didn't want witnesses." Heather shrugged, hoping she was a good enough actress to seem nonchalant.

"That might be part of it. But not wanting to tangle with Jocko would be foremost."

"I'd put my money on Sebastian, if it came to a fight." The admission made her feel disloyal.

"I wouldn't. You don't know what Jocko is capable of doing."

"I fight him all the time. I'm pretty clear on his ability. Sebastian has forty pounds and two inches on him. His reach is a lot longer."

"Not what I was talking about. I wouldn't mess with him."

Heather looked at Cami, stunned. "That is the first time I have ever heard you admit someone might be able to take you."

Cami turned away. "Break me is more like it," she muttered.

"With any luck, Sebastian will finish his deal with Darius and leave before the weekend."

"I sure as hell hope so. I'm going to be too busy to watch your back all day."

"Not that I want you following me around all the time, but you're on vacation," Heather reminded her.

"Not anymore. Bob gave me two shows a day."

Heather clapped. "Excellent!"

"Stuck it to him on the contract, too. The man can't abide an empty stage, and we both knew it." Cami grinned. Getting their way in a contract was a rare treat for any performer.

"No wonder you're so happy."

"I'd be happier if the Bastard would leave town so we could get back to our normal routine of irritating Paula and pretending you aren't falling for Jocko."

"Don't start," Heather warned. "Not tonight."

"Sorry, I didn't think." Cami gave Heather a one-armed hug. It was the most that could ever be expected of her.

"At least he came back in time to work out the fight. And I can't fault his timing."

"The man has a funny way of being where he's needed, whether you want him there or not."

"Tonight, I can honestly say I wanted him there." Heather shuddered. "Sebastian is not at all who I thought he was. I figured out he was a rat bastard after the whole Kiss thing, but I swear he felt . . ." She couldn't find the right word.

"Evil?" Cami supplied.

"That sounds melodramatic, but yeah."

"Trust your gut about things like that. Stay away from him."

"You think?" Heather stared at Cami. "I'm going to be a paranoid wreck until he leaves."

"Just don't show it. His kind feeds on that sort of fear."

Cami's words echoed what Doc had said on Monday. Heather nodded. "This day is officially over. I am going to bed early. Tomorrow has to be an improvement." She walked into her room.

Cami followed. "Sounds like a good plan. I'm going to go torment my brother, unless you want me to stay."

"No need. Jez will be back soon, and I can lock the bedroom door, if you don't mind sleeping on the couch."

"Beats listening to you snore."

"I do not snore!" Heather threw a pillow at Cami then closed the door on her laughter.

She opened one eye, arching her back and stretching, wondering why she was alone in the bed. He was standing at the window, looking out, just as he had after he'd tucked her into the blankets. She called for him, and He turned, smiling at her. He motioned for her to stay where she was before returning to his watch. She sighed, wrapped the blankets around her and wondered when she would feel warm again.

Whispered conversation, too low to make out at first. Heather blinked in the darkness, trying to clear her head.

"You don't have to do this." A woman's voice, quiet and soft.

"You know I do." A man's voice, low and strained.

"I'm here now. You can go home."

"Don't fail me. Keep her safe."

"Always have, always will."

Such strange dreams. Heather drifted off, trying to escape them.

CHAPTER THIRTEEN

Cami didn't stir when Heather walked into the living area. Jez sat at her workbench, steam rising from the cup beside her.

"It's early for you." Heather yawned and poured herself some coffee.

"I woke up a couple of hours ago with a new design in my head. Couldn't get back to sleep, so I figured I should at least sketch it." Jez slid a drawing across the counter.

Heather looked at the intricate spiral. "Oh, that's nice!"

"Thanks. You running this morning?"

"No. I can miss a day."

Jez relaxed, a sense of sad resignation coming from her.

"I wasn't planning on running anyway. I have the photo shoot this morning. I'd be a lot happier if my friends wouldn't assume I'm so fragile that the Bastard showing up is going to break me."

"Don't say it like that," Cami mumbled. "Find a different word." She rolled over and went back to sleep.

"I'm sorry." Jez sighed. "I just hate that he's here."

"You're in good company." Heather refilled her cup and drank enough to keep it from sloshing as she walked toward Rogue & Tailor's.

When Heather arrived, Katie was helping Marni rack the gowns for the photo shoot. Her blond hair hung loose around her shoulders, making her look younger than she did on a faire day. Or maybe it was the Hello Kitty T-shirt. Heather smiled.

"If you want coffee, step next door." Gina pushed off the counter. "These two are refusing help."

Heather took her up on the offer. They sorted through the stock of wench wear then pulled out simple bodices and skirts in bright colors before moving on to the selection of menswear.

Heather held up a deep blue doublet. "I think this would look good on Carter."

Gina matched it with a pair of blue pants with silvery gray trim, added a white shirt, and racked the outfit. "That boy is far too pretty. It's a wonder some girl hasn't snatched him up." She thought for a moment. "Or some boy."

A clatter came from the next room. Katie blushed as she righted the stool she'd knocked over. The photographer strolled in and pulled Gina and Marni aside to discuss locations. Katie and Heather withdrew.

"Who else is coming besides us and Carter?" Heather asked.

"Paula said she'd be here. She got back last night, so she's probably sleeping in." Katie smiled.

Heather tried to ignore the knot forming in her stomach. "At least you and she will be used to wearing gowns. I think Marni would be better off leaving me to model wench wear."

"Oh, no. She pulled out a couple of pieces specifically for you. The blue dress is to die for. She'd be disappointed if you didn't want to wear it."

"It's not that I don't want to. I just don't really know how to carry off a gown."

"It's easy. You keep your upper body really straight and pretend that there isn't ten pounds of fabric sitting on your hips." Katie giggled. "Good thing I know where all the local chiropractors are or I'd be totally crippled. It's one of the first things I look up when I get into town."

"Ouch. And I thought it was rough getting thrown all over the place by Jocko."

"You guys look good together." Katie looked up, eyes wide. "On stage, I mean. I bet they'll have you pose with him for some of the shots."

"I didn't realize he was going to be part of this." Heather hid her surprise in her now-cold coffee.

"I overheard Paula mention it to someone last night. It makes sense, though. If it was your catalog, wouldn't you want pictures of him in it? He's awfully good looking."

"Can't argue with you there. Too bad beauty isn't always reflected in character."

"Nope. Paula proves that." Katie covered her mouth.

"You won't get an argument from me," Heather assured her. "Why do you hang out with Paula anyway?"

"Honestly? It makes life easier. For me, attending the Court is just a job. She takes it very seriously. I have to spend all day with her, so it doesn't make sense to fight her on the little things."

"I don't envy you. You couldn't pay me to be Court. Too much hassle."

"That's only for the real Court. The rest of us are just there for show. It's not so bad. The view from the reviewing stand is amazing."

"Especially when Carter jousts," Heather said.

Katie sighed. "I've never been any good at hiding things."

"No need to. But you might have to hit him over the head to get him to recognize genuine interest. Boys are slow like that."

"Not all of them." Katie nodded at the window, smiling.

Heather turned to see Jocko strolling across the site, looking more rumpled than usual. He stared at the ground as he walked, hands jammed in the pockets of his leather jacket. As if feeling her gaze on him, he looked up and smiled. Without thinking, she took a step toward the door. He whipped his head to the side, smile fading to a grim line. He turned his eyes back to her and quickened his stride. His entire body screamed a warning that no words could match. She stumbled back from the ferocity of it, clutching the counter for balance, his message clear. He was not the only one watching her.

Heather straightened, bolstered by anger, most of it directed at herself. "I should be stronger than this."

"Even strong people have weaknesses." Katie moved to the doorway between the shops. "Which is why you have friends to protect you."

Heather steadied herself. "You should come by the shop and hang out with us sometimes. It's sort of a ratty place, but we have a good time."

"I'd like that." Katie shifted position, making it impossible for anyone to get through without pushing her aside. She raised her voice a bit. "You can't get into gowns alone. I'll help you out."

"Thanks. I can use all the help I can get."

Paula stepped into the shop. "Admitting you need help is the first step." She eyed Heather. "And by the look of you, it's way past time you got some."

Heather smiled sweetly. "Funny, I didn't think I was the one not getting any."

Paula glared at her. Katie stayed still, her body a wall between them.

"You get some while I was gone, darlin'?" Jocko had entered the shop from the opposite side.

"Is it your business?" Heather shot.

"It might be." His laugh was a bit hollow. "They say it's bad for the knees, and we have a fight to work through."

"I knew you had only one thing on your mind." She gave an exaggerated sigh. "You're all about the fight."

"So are you." The warning look remained through the banter.

"Rehearsal will wait. Today we are glorified mannequins." She struck a pose and let her eyes lose focus.

He chuckled. "I've been worse things."

"Past tense, Jocko? Do tell." Sebastian stepped up behind Paula.

Jocko's hand dropped to his hip, where his sword should be. He flexed his fingers. "Why don't we go someplace private, so I can explain everything to you? Won't take but a minute."

Sebastian took half a step back but recovered before it could be interpreted as retreat. "There is no time for that. I believe you have business." He turned to Gina. "Carter sends his apologies for being tardy. He's tending to one of the horses and asked me to tell you to start without him. He should arrive shortly, providing Fury does not kill him in the stall."

Gina looked up at him, lips pursed. "We'll start with the ladies, then. The paired shots will have to come later."

"If you wish, I could stand in his stead, at least until he arrives. We are not so dissimilar. Carter wouldn't want the schedule changed on his account."

"It would go faster if we could have both the men and women dressed at the same time," Marni said. "Sebastian and Carter are close enough in looks that it won't mess up the composition to use him as a place holder."

She turned to him. "Unless you want to take part. No such thing as too many pretty men in a catalog, especially when it's mostly women who will be shopping from it."

"I would be honored."

"Okay, ladies on the left, gentlemen on the right!" Gina handed gowns to the women as they passed then followed the men into her side of the shop. "I hope you two aren't shy. You're going to need some help, and even if you stripped down naked, I wouldn't be interested." She paused. "Or impressed."

The women left the men to banter with Gina. Their own dressing area erupted in chaos. Marni laced Katie into a velveteen gown of forest green, the front split to reveal an underskirt in autumn colors that on close inspection had the pattern of swirling leaves. It was a simple dress, befitting a young woman not yet on the marriage market. Katie wore it as easily as she had her jeans, but she moved with a great deal more grace.

As she explained the physics of movement in a hoop skirt—which included warnings to not run for any reason—Katie laced Heather into her first gown. The blue brocade was embroidered with silver thread, a single pearl sewn at each crossing. Fit through the waist, it came to a point in the front. Steel boning created a clean line from neck to hip. The sleeves were slashed to reveal a sheer silver fabric and fell open from the elbow. The neckline was entirely too low.

"I'm not made for these things," Heather grumbled, trying to adjust the dress for some semblance of modesty.

"Stop tugging at it!" Katie commanded.

Heather blushed when shown how to stoop and scoop—a move that involved lifting her breasts while Katie pulled the laces even tighter. When she straightened and turned to the mirror, she barely recognized herself. Katie reached into a box filled with jewelry and pulled out a string of pearls with a large sapphire hanging from it. She fastened it around Heather's neck.

Heather swallowed, putting her hand to her chest. The jewel hung just above impossible cleavage. "Are you sure?"

"They aren't real," Katie said.

"These breasts or the jewels?" Heather tried to take a deep breath but found it difficult. She was bound in finery from which she could not escape without help.

Katie laughed. "Welcome to my world. The right gown can give anyone cleavage. It's like magic."

"Thank goodness for that," Paula said, turning to assess the other women. She was a vision in crimson and gold. "Without magic, there's hardly a pair of breasts between you two." She didn't need the dress to help her in that area. Her gown highlighted the deep curve of her waist, lush breasts, and softly rounded hips.

"You look amazing," Heather said. There was no harm in telling the truth, and if it would make the photo shoot more pleasant, she would compliment Paula all morning.

"Of course I do," Paula replied.

Marni frowned.

"How could I not in such a gorgeous gown?" Paula amended.

"You are all stunning." Marni smiled. "Now go remind the men why they volunteered for this."

Gina laughed and peeked through the curtain. "You sound like a pimp, sweetie."

Marni threw a roll of ribbon at her partner then hustled the women out for the first session. The men had already left; the ability to dress quickly being one of the many benefits of freedom from corsetry.

The swing of the hoop skirt required adjustment in the way Heather walked. Following Katie's advice, she managed not to trip over the thing as they walked to the Fairy stage. It was used mostly by storytellers during the faire day. A cottage formed the back of the stage, built around a large tree. Sunlight filtered through leaves just beginning to turn, creating a warm glow. As the women approached, their partners for the first photos were obvious.

Carter had apparently shown up while the women were dressing. He stood in the center of the stage, dressed in a black doublet slashed with red and trimmed in gold. His hair brushed the high collar, a gold circlet keeping it from falling in his eyes. He smiled when he saw them but did not move.

Jocko lounged against the cottage, seemingly at ease. Heather knew better. He was coiled as if to strike. Tight brown pants outlined the muscles in his legs, set off by a huntsman's tunic in dark green. He lacked only a bow to perfect the image of Robin Hood. His hair was pulled back, secured with a leather tie. A sword hung on his belt—his long sword, not a stage weapon but a real, heavy blade. It went well with the costume. She was sure that wasn't why he'd retrieved it.

A slow smile spread across Sebastian's face when he saw them. His dark blue surcoat was shot through with silver, highlighted by the heavy silver chain around his neck. Heather's mouth went dry as she recognized the piece she had picked out for Carter. Sebastian's blue eyes glittered as he noted her discomfort. He opened his arms, welcoming her. With great care, she managed to walk up the ramp without stumbling. She kissed Carter on the cheek.

"I'm sorry," he whispered. "I didn't know."

"Thank you for holding the dogs at bay," she said loud enough for everyone to hear.

He shrugged. "It's what I do."

The photographer shooed everyone but Jocko and Katie off the stage. Paula pulled Carter aside, fussing with his collar. Heather watched the photographer, admiring his eye for composition and the way he used the natural light. He created a story for the models, letting them improvise as they played it out.

"That blonde is a pretty little thing," Sebastian whispered. Heather tensed as he stepped up behind her. "But I don't think there's much to her. She's perfect for him."

"You're not a very good judge of people," Heather said.

"I know quality when I see it." He leaned down and dropped a kiss on her neck. "And when I taste it."

"Back off," she growled.

"I expected a warmer welcome."

"How could you?" The words came out strangled.

"Did I not treat you well? You seemed to enjoy my company."

"Right up until you put my soul in a blender and hit pulse."

"I had heard you hold the Kiss against me. I did not mean to hurt you. I am sorry if I did." His honeyed words seemed to settle on her skin, as unwelcome as his touch but harder to shake off.

"Considering you made no effort to contact me after that, I doubt your sincerity."

"I apologize for that, as well. I had family and business matters that took me out of the country for a while." His fingers found hers and intertwined. She hardly noticed.

"I should have at least written." He'd have done better to stay quiet.

She snorted. "And what would you have said? Sorry I upended everything you had planned for your life and then left without a word of explanation?" She pulled her hand away.

"It was ill-done, I admit. And selfish. I wanted you to join the Tribe. Memories of that Kiss still haunt me." He lifted a strand of her hair. "Never have I tasted anything so sweet—or had such a powerful reaction." The back of his hand brushed her shoulder.

"For me, it was nothing but bitter." The words came softer than she'd intended, sadder.

He put his hand on her waist, leaning in to whisper. "Can you lie to yourself so easily? I remember your response."

Her body remembered as well. Heat flooded her, burning, shameful. She drew a shaky breath. "You used me."

"Not as well as you deserved," he murmured.

"No. It was terrible." Her words were as much to convince herself as him.

"I truly am sorry." He turned her, tilting her chin until she looked into his eyes. Languor settled over her as his arms went around her. She was lost, drowning. He lowered his head to kiss her.

Without warning, he jerked back.

"I told you it wouldn't take but a minute," Jocko said, low and dangerous. "You want to do this now?"

Sebastian held up his hands. "I was merely apologizing."

"Is that what you call it? Because I think there's a different word for it, and I might just have to explain to the lady what that is. The Court might be interested, too."

"No need. I will act in accordance with the rules." Sebastian stepped to the side.

Jocko lowered his sword. "See that you do."

The photographer was snapping madly. "I don't even have to pose you! This is excellent!" He turned to Carter and Paula. "You're up next, but I don't know if you can beat that."

"Try me," Paula walked onto the stage. Carter didn't move until she hissed his name.

Jocko took Heather's arm gently and led her to a bench. "I need you to look at me, sugar."

She blinked then met his gaze. "I don't feel so good."

"I know. It will pass." He might have been talking to her from across a room.

"I think the corset's too tight."

"That could be it. Why don't I walk you back to the shop so Marni can help you out of the dress?"

"You're being very good to me." She frowned.

"I'm always good to you, darlin'. You just don't always know it." He helped her up and led her back to the shop.

Heather leaned her head against the wall as Marni unlaced the gown. She didn't remember how she'd gotten there. Marni handed her a robe and ducked out. She returned a few moments later with a cup of coffee and a cranberry-orange muffin. Heather's hand shook, so she set the cup down. She sat in the chair, staring at nothing.

"Eat," Marni prompted. "You should know better than to try to flounce around in five pounds of costume on an empty stomach."

"Katie says it's ten pounds."

"Court ladies always complain." Marni laughed. "Except the Queen. She handles everything with grace, whether Tribe squabbles or drunk patrons."

Heather nodded. "It must be tiring."

"All Queens do the same. I think they get more from it than it takes out of them."

"Sort of like a Kiss but with perpetual feedback?"

"Perhaps. I've never been bold enough to ask." Marni looked at her. "If you want to back out of the rest of the shoot, I'll understand."

"No. I feel better now." Heather finished her coffee. The muffin had disappeared, though she had no memory of eating it.

"Then let's get you into the next gown. It won't be as tight as the last one."

"I'm sorry I was so foolish." Heather stood and dropped the robe onto the chair.

"You just didn't know what you were getting into."

"That happens to me a lot."

Marni nodded. "It happens to all of us."

The other ladies came in as Marni finished lacing Heather into a russet gown, as comfortable as a nightgown, if a bit clingy. The scoop neckline was more modest, but still showed a bit of cleavage. Heather stepped out of the dressing room and went in search of coffee. She couldn't seem to get enough of it.

Gina turned and assessed Heather. "I see Marni has shifted tactics in trying to lure you to the noble side. She should have known you'd prefer comfort to extravagance. That dress looks like it was made for you."

Jocko stepped up, his gaze hungry. "I think it was made for me."

"I don't think you'd look as good in it." Gina chuckled and went to help the other men dress.

Jocko approached with reverence. He lifted his hand but let it fall, uncertain.

"It's okay to touch me. I won't break." She smiled at him.

He flinched. "You're too strong for that."

"Not strong enough," she whispered, afraid to speak the truth too loudly.

He wrapped his arms around her. "Then I'll be strong for you."

During the next two sessions, Heather posed with Carter and Jocko. Sebastian kept his distance, but his eyes never left her for long. Without guile, Carter found good reasons to keep the other men apart. Katie did the same whenever Paula and Heather seemed ready to snipe at each other. Cami showed up near the end. She sat in the back row, flipping her knives and catching them, her focus alternately on Sebastian and Paula. They both pretended not to notice her, but their manners improved.

It was well past noon when they finished modeling Marni's finery. Sebastian and Paula led the procession back to the shop, heads together in quiet conversation. Katie accepted Carter's proffered arm with blushing grace. Jocko and Heather brought up the rear, staying close but not touching.

Cami sprinted up, dancing backward in front of Heather. "There's a pair." She nodded toward Paula.

"Maybe they'll hook up and leave the rest of us alone," Heather said.

"Looks more like conspiracy than love. You two should be careful around them."

"Concern for me, Cami?" Jocko laughed. "I think that's one of the signs of the apocalypse."

"It's not so much that I care, but if the four of you go at it, the clean-up is going to be hell."

"Don't worry. We can handle whatever they throw at us."

"Cocky son of a bitch." Cami shook her head. She turned and raced toward the shop to warn the costumers of the impending invasion.

Marni insisted on feeding everyone before they switched to modeling rogue wear. Gina dashed around putting together outfits until Marni forced her to stop and eat. She wolfed down a sandwich then went right back to it.

Sebastian rose. "I am afraid I must leave. This has been a delightful experience. I do hope you will forgive me." He inclined his head to Marni and Gina. "Ladies."

"Thank you for helping out," Marni said.

"My pleasure." He glanced at Heather then walked out.

"If anyone else is too tired to continue, don't feel obligated to stay," Gina said. "I don't need as many photos of my stuff. It's pretty basic."

Paula hesitated before making her decision. "As long as you don't need me. I haven't checked in with Ardyth on the weekend schedule. I hear there are some changes." She seemed contrite, but Heather suspected it was just that she didn't want to lower herself to wear peasant clothes.

"You should come, too, Katie," Paula suggested.

"No way. I don't have a meeting with the Queen, and this may be the only chance I get to play wench this season. I've been waiting all day for this." She looked at Marni. "No offense."

"None taken." Marni smiled.

"Excellent! I finally get a chance to woo someone to the rogue side." Gina crowed.

"Just make sure she's back where she belongs this weekend." Paula's tone was light, but there was no mistaking her ire.

"I've never failed to do the right thing," Katie said pointedly.

"Now would not be the time to start." Paula turned and left.

Gina shook her head. "I'm glad she's gone. I'd hate to see what you folks might do to her when armed."

Heather perked up. "We get to fight?"

"I figured it was the best way to show off what I do best. And what you do." Gina smiled.

"I don't know how to fight," Katie said softly.

"We'll let the masters of mayhem go first," Carter offered. "That way I can show you some basic moves."

"Masters of mayhem? I like that." Jocko winked at Heather. "Maybe we could contract out as an act."

"It has potential." She thought about the benefits of working with him at every show. Her mind went places it should not. "In the meantime, why don't we get changed?" She walked away, ignoring Cami's skeptical look.

"I'll head out." Cami rose.

"If you want to join the party, I wouldn't mind," Gina said. "I could use pictures of a murderous pixie wearing my designs."

"You're aware I'm armed, right?" Cami glared at her but couldn't project any malice.

"Sort of the point, short stuff." Gina grinned.

"Can I have copies for my portfolio?"

"Absolutely. That goes for everyone."

"What the hell. It beats watching these guys pretend they know what they're doing."

"Make her wear fuchsia," Heather suggested. "She's so pretty in pink."

Cami growled in response and stalked off to pick out some pieces. Nothing Gina had pulled out earlier would be small enough. She joined the ladies in the dressing room just as Katie expressed delight over the ability to dress herself.

"You're not what I thought," Cami said grudgingly.

"A sycophant?" Katie offered.

"Basically."

"It's a role. We're more than the parts we play."

Cami snorted. "Maybe you are. I'm a violent, sarcastic person all the time. And I know for a fact that Paula is always a stuck-up bitch."

"I don't know what's wrong with her," Katie said. "She has everything. You'd think she'd be nicer."

"I met her parents once. They're just like her," Cami said. "Blood will out."

Heather looked up sharply. "Her folks came to a show?" Heather's parents had yet to see her perform.

"They believe she's in line to be Queen," Katie added. "They think it's fitting."

Cami shook her head. "Because they don't know how it works. Queen isn't a role; it's something they are."

Heather nodded, remembering Marni's earlier comment. "I know the King is more interested in keeping order in the Tribe than anything else, but where does the Master at Arms fit in?"

"He cares more about the Queen than anyone else," Katie offered. "Including himself."

"I thought he looked out for both the royals."

"Kings take care of themselves," Katie said. "Queens are vulnerable because they care about everyone, Tribe or not. Some people see that as weakness."

"I want a handbook," Heather grumbled.

"What for? We just explained it all to you. Everyone except the top of the Court is selected for their performance skills. Just be happy we're peons."

"What you are is late," Gina said, poking her head into the dressing room. "Get a move on."

The photographer let them arrange themselves for the action shots. Heather and Jocko used the opportunity to run through their fight. By the time the photographer had finished with them, they could run the fight smoothly every time.

Carter led Katie through rudimentary fight stances. Once he explained it as a dance, she gained confidence, though she admitted it would be a long time before she'd feel safe picking up a weapon.

"I'm patient," Carter said. "And we have a few weeks left at this show, so if you want to come by during the week, I'd be happy to train you."

Katie blushed, but agreed she'd like to try.

The photographer kept snapping, probably waiting for at least one couple to kiss, but none of them indulged him. They finally wrapped up the session as the light began to fade. "I'm afraid we worked up a sweat," Heather apologized to Gina as she entered the shop.

"Don't worry about it. I was going to let you all have the outfits from the shoot anyway." They whooped with appreciation and swarmed Gina with hugs until she shooed them away to find their regular clothes.

"What a perfect day." Heather pulled her shirt over her head.

"If you say so," Cami muttered. She and Katie exchanged a puzzled look.

"I can't wait to see the pictures." Heather smiled.

"Neither can I." Cami twirled a knife as she stepped out of the dressing room. "A thousand words isn't even going to cover it."

CHAPTER FOURTEEN

Jocko and Carter had already left when the women emerged. Katie reluctantly took her leave. Cami and Heather walked across the site in comfortable silence, taking the long way to enjoy the last warmth of late afternoon. The nights were getting colder. They came around the corner of a potter's shop, still wrapped in their own thoughts.

Cami stopped and grabbed Heather's arm, turning her back. "I left a knife at the shop. Walk me back?"

Heather frowned. Cami did not forget her knives. Ever. The panicked look on her friend's face exposed the lie. Heather turned around slowly.

Paula had her hands on Jocko's chest. He was looking down at her. They were too far away to be heard, but Heather knew that intense look. He took Paula's wrists and pulled them behind her back until she arched. She pressed herself against him. He lowered his head, speaking quickly. She stood on tiptoe and kissed him.

Heather dropped her new costume and ran, not caring where she went as long as it was away from the lovers. Cami called after her. Heather outran her friend, not wanting to hear explanations or apologies. She passed through a gate and continued into the woods, waiting for her feet to match the pounding of her heart. She forgot her form and her breathing. She wanted to forget to breathe altogether.

After a while, she hit her stride, muscle memory taking over as her feet took her deeper and deeper into the forest. The path narrowed, twisted, widened again. Branches whipped against her, the sting a welcome reminder of her folly. Finally, she outran the words, the thoughts, and became nothing but a body in motion, practically floating, lost.

When she finally slowed, she had no idea where she was. It was exactly what she had hoped for. She wandered down the dark path, enjoying the cold air on sweat-drenched skin. A small voice in her head expressed worry. She smacked it down, choosing to embrace discomfort. She drew the night around her, letting it fill her until she was blackness, void of stars.

And still, she could not stop the thoughts from returning. Once again, she had allowed herself to be deceived by the attentions of a beautiful man. She had heard the tales of conquest and distance, knew he was unlikely to change. Her desire to believe that he would be different with her—because of her—had been stupid.

Am I so desperate to be loved? She knew the answer and hated it. She wondered if she should walk away, go home, finish school. If other people could find a way to deal with the longing for the Tribe, she could.

Jez would be heartbroken. The thought made her stop. Jez must be insane with worry. Cami would be freaking and taking it out on anyone in her path. Not for one moment had Heather considered their feelings. Shame washed over her. She had love, fierce and constant. She hardly deserved it. At some point, she would have to go back and face them. Best to spare them more distress.

She turned around, following the path, trying to remember which turns she had taken. Exhaustion swept through her. Hours of running stacked on the exertion of the day made her legs weak. She stumbled, wanting nothing more than to find a soft place to curl up and sleep. The voice of reason returned, miffed at having been ignored, and harried her on, aided by the specter of humiliation that would accompany being found, dirty and wretched, asleep in the woods. *Providing, of course, that anyone is looking for me.* She shoved the thought aside. Wallowing really was pathetic. She trudged on.

Rounding a bend, she saw the lights from the parking lot in the distance and sobbed with relief. She wiped her face with her shirt and ran her fingers through her tangled hair, then sat down on a log, drawing steady breaths to gather fortitude for the walk back. Unfortunately, determination did nothing to bolster her muscles. She took a few wobbly steps and fell, tearing her jeans. Blood wet the fabric. She cursed and rose again.

Voices came from the woods behind her. Her gut twisted as she recognized Sebastian's deep rumble. She stepped off the path and leaned against a tree, hidden from anyone who did not look carefully.

"Stop complaining. We will keep looking until we find her. I am not going to lose her again."

At least someone wants me. The thought horrified her. His voice was full of anger. He might want to find her, but he did not want her. *Not the way Jocko* . . . she choked, covering her mouth to keep from crying out. Jocko didn't want her that way, either. She kept still until the searchers disappeared along the path she had just left. At least it was too dark for them to notice the blood.

She did not see anyone else as she crept back to the site. She stopped at a faucet outside the showers and washed her face, looking up every few seconds. It reminded her of the deer by the pond near her parents' house. The ache of memory caused more tears. She washed them away. Going home wasn't an option, and she knew it. She was Tribe and would have to make the best of it.

Light spilled from the windows of Jezebel's shop. Heather leaned on the banister as she climbed the stairs. Blood trickled down her leg. She opened the door with every intention of collapsing on the couch while Jez fussed over her the way her mother might, but the room was empty. Heather poured herself a glass of water, hands shaking. She turned as the door opened then clutched the counter to keep from falling over.

Tansy walked in, carrying a leather satchel. "You need to sit down."

"How did you know I'd be here?" Heather asked.

Tansy smiled. "Just a hunch." She steered Heather to the couch. "Take off your jeans so I can see to your wound."

"It's not bad," Heather protested, despite not having looked at it herself.

"I've been married to a doctor for twenty years. Arguing with me serves no purpose." Tansy pulled her auburn hair into a ponytail. "Unless you prefer that I get Doc?"

Heather shook her head. She struggled out of her jeans, wincing as the fabric scraped across her wound, then sat on the couch as ordered. Tansy laid her wide shawl over Heather's lap then pulled out a first aid kit and set to work. The single bulb in the overhead light made the silver streaks in

Tansy's hair shine like filigree. Her touch was gentle and sure. Heather sat back and closed her eyes, silently accepting the pain.

"You won't need stitches, but it's going to ache for days. Be careful when you fight this weekend."

"Maybe if I'm lucky, I'll slip and Jocko can finish me off," Heather muttered.

"Is self-pity working for you? If so, go ahead and steep yourself in it." Tansy's soft voice reduced the sting of the words. "But I'm fairly sure there are better ways to deal with what you're feeling." She finished bandaging the cut.

"Like what?"

"Hard drugs." The sarcasm was evident—and welcome.

Heather opened one eye. "Bring any?"

"You know Doc. He's all about natural remedies for what ails you."

"I'm open to suggestions for those, too."

"I find it helps to speak." The first aid kit in order, Tansy returned it to her bag.

"Thanks, but I'm not sure I can talk about this right now."

"You misunderstand. Speaking is not conversing. You need to say what's bothering you, out loud."

"I don't have the words."

"Of course you do. You're just afraid to say them. That's always the way. It's easier to get twisted up in thoughts than clearly state the reason behind those thoughts."

"You sound like my shrink."

"There's a correlation between therapy and reading tarot cards. In both cases, we get people to look at things from a different angle, present possibilities, prompt them to recognize the patterns in their lives. Fools think I tell their future. What I do is identify potential paths."

"What I do is make mistakes."

"That's a good start." Tansy crossed her legs and leaned forward, palms on the floor, stretching.

"I fall for the wrong men."

"Nothing unusual about that. I spent most of my twenties dating the wrong men." Tansy quirked a smile, green eyes sparkling. "It was a lot of fun. Until it wasn't."

"Did they break your heart?"

"When I let them. Sometimes I was the one who called it off. I almost walked away from Doc." She went back to stretching.

"I can't imagine that. He loves you so much."

"Yes, and at the time, that scared the heck out of me."

"Love shouldn't be scary."

"Of course it should. It's an incredibly powerful force." Tansy unfolded and looked up at Heather. "Who are you in love with, and why does it scare you?"

Heather shook her head, throat constricted.

"Words." It was a command.

"I'm not in love. I thought I might be falling in love, but I was wrong."

"If you believed that, you wouldn't have taken off. So who are you in love with?"

"It doesn't matter. He doesn't feel the same way."

"Did he say so? Because I'm fairly sure that Jocko is still out in the woods, frantically searching for you," Tansy said. "Unless I'm wrong about the object of your affection."

"No." The word was so small, her voice just above a whisper, but the pain was enormous. "But it still doesn't matter."

"If his fear for your safety is any indication, it matters to him."

"He's not interested in love. I need to let it go."

"So you get to decide how he feels about you. Based on what?"

"I don't know. Maybe on the fact that the last time I saw him he had his arms around Paula and was kissing her?" Anger chased away the tears that had threatened. "That's good enough for me."

"Really." Tansy's voice was hard. "Did you consider asking him what that was about?"

"It was sort of obvious."

"That's what Cami thought when she threatened to slice open his stomach and strangle him with his own entrails."

Heather laughed despite herself. That was so like Cami.

"Things aren't always what they seem, honey. You might want to give him a chance to explain. Then, if you don't like what he has to say, at least you'll be making an informed decision."

"I don't want to talk to him."

"That's your choice." Tansy stood. "But you may want to go into your room and close the door, because he's heading this way."

"How do you know?"

"It's a Talent I have. I don't question it anymore."

"I'm not wearing any pants." Heather squeaked. She tried to stand but her legs wouldn't hold her.

"I'll get some." Tansy headed for her room. "Someday, you should let me take you shopping for real clothes."

"I like my comfy clothes!"

"You might try some that fit. You spend too much time hiding yourself from the world." She came back with a pair of black sweatpants, a pillow, and a blanket. "I'll set you up to sleep here. It doesn't look like you have much chance of making it to your bedroom." She helped Heather into her sweats.

Heather flinched as footsteps pounded up the stairs. "Will you send him away?"

Tansy shook her head. "You'll have to do that." She walked across the room and let Jocko in. "Do you want me to stay?"

"No," they said in unison. Heather glared at him.

"Okay. No killing each other. Doc will be pissed if he has to get out of bed. And so will I."

"Thank you," Heather said, "for everything."

"No problem, honey. You know where to find me if you need me." She wrapped the shawl around her and left.

Heather and Jocko stared at each other, the silence stretching until it filled the room. He was waiting for her to speak. She could not.

After a few minutes, he pulled out a cell phone and walked to the window. "She's home. Hers. No, she was here when I got here. No. No. Can you take care of that? Yeah, that works. Thanks." He flipped the phone closed and turned back to her. "Darius is calling off the search."

She nodded, sliding further down on the couch.

"Are you okay?"

She nodded again.

"You want to tell me what you were thinking, going off into the woods at night alone?" He sounded like her father.

"It wasn't night when I left."

"Heather," he half-growled.

"I felt like running, so I did."

"That would be a whole lot easier to sell if the effect of your sudden desire to run hadn't resulted in short, dark, and maniacal tracking me down and issuing death threats."

Heather shrugged. "That's between you and her, I guess."

"No, sugar. Whatever set you off was obviously between you and me. Only now it's between you, me, and half the damned people on this site. Since it's impossible to keep rumors from spreading, I figured I should get the story from you."

"I just told you." She wouldn't meet his eyes.

"Lies won't do."

"They seem to work just fine for you."

"Any minute now, you're going to tell me what that means."

She said nothing.

He pulled out a stool and sat. "Take your time. I'm not going anywhere."

"Jez and Cami will be back soon. I doubt they'll put up with you sitting here all night."

"Darius is hosting a last-minute pizza party. Everyone who went looking for you is going to be hanging out at his place tonight."

"Bastard," she spat.

"That covers my parentage. I'm still waiting for the rest." He crossed his arms.

"I don't owe you an explanation."

"No, I don't suppose you do. But it sure would help to know what I did to set you off," he said.

"You made me think you cared about me."

"If I didn't care, why would I have spent most of my day trying to protect you?" he asked.

"You know, I'm still confused about that. If you aren't interested in me, why would you bother to keep Sebastian away from me?"

"I'm not sure why you think I'm not interested in you, all things considered."

"Huh. Let's see. Leaving with Paula on Sunday night? Disappearing with her for three days? Making out with her this afternoon? Yeah, I think that will do for a start."

"Whoa. You seriously think I'm hooking up with Paula?" He ran his fingers through his hair.

"Looks that way."

"Only if you want it to."

"It's none of my business what you do. I'm a little slow, but I get why you might be interested in her. She's beautiful and talented and in with the Court. I'd just appreciate it if you'd stop flirting with me. I can't play that game without meaning it."

"I want you to hear this, loud and clear. There is nothing on this earth that would make me want that woman."

"Again, you mean."

He winced. "Yeah."

"So why would you run off with her?"

"I don't know where Paula went when I was gone, but she wasn't with me. If you doubt that, check with Darius. But watch what questions you ask. He doesn't like people poking into Court business."

"Even if I accept that, there's still the kissing. Sort of hard to deny that when Cami and I both saw it."

"You think that's what I was doing, but you're wrong."

"Which part of her lips on yours did I misinterpret? Because I'm pretty sure that's the definition of kissing. At least I thought it was when we were in your room."

"The difference being that what passed between you and me was mutual and desired."

"Are you trying to tell me that she took advantage of you?" Heather laughed. "Damn. You must think I'm an idiot."

"I'm beginning to."

"Well, maybe you're right. I was stupid enough to fall for your tricks, after all. No need to worry about that in the future."

"No matter what I say, you aren't going to hear me. But I'm a glutton for punishment, so I'm going to keep trying to get through to you. What you saw today was me taking Paula's hands off my shirt and telling her to stay the hell away from me. She tried to kiss me. You took off after seeing that, so you missed the part where I damned near knocked her on her ass and told her that if she comes near me again, I will Break her."

"I never took you for the sort to beat up a woman. Without choreography anyway."

"I'm not. That was break with a capital B. If she continues to stalk me, I will make sure that she is no longer Tribe."

"It's not like you can vote her out," Heather scoffed. "Tribe is forever."

"There are ways." He went back to the window and leaned his head against it. "I shouldn't have told you that. Now, you'll try to find out how you can undo what Sebastian did to you and go back to your old life."

It had been her first thought. "That wouldn't be such a bad thing."

"Trust me, it would be." He turned to her, eyes haunted. "The Kiss you got was not right, not normal. Most of the time it's a gentle thing or a joyful rush."

"That's what I hear. I wouldn't know."

"What you suffered is nothing compared to the Breaking. It's horrible. That's why it doesn't happen very often. Only the Court can order it."

"And you'd ask them to do that just to make sure she leaves you alone? How is that better than beating her up? I'm hardly her biggest fan, but I'd hate to see anyone lose a life they obviously love, even if it means I have to put up with a complete bitch."

"She's more dangerous than you know. I'm only one of her targets. For some reason, she's gunning for you, but I don't know why."

"Because of you."

"Is that what you think? That this is just about a fight over a man? She might harbor delusions about getting me back, but that's frosting on her little cake. If I had enough on her to send her to the Court for judgment, I would have done it yesterday. All I can do is bide my time and hope no one gets hurt."

"You're scaring me, and I really don't need that tonight."

He knelt down beside her. "I'm scared for you. When you disappeared, I thought I would lose my mind. I sent everyone I could after you."

"Even Sebastian," she said.

He started. "What?"

"I heard him when I was on my way back. He said he would keep looking until he found me. I wouldn't have thought you'd send him out for me, but I guess everyone was searching. I feel like such a fool. I'm going to spend forever thanking and apologizing to people."

"I didn't send him. Darius told him to stay put. Neither one of us wanted him near you." He regarded her intently. "After the convoluted steps I took to keep him away from you today, why would you think I'd send him out to find you in the dark?"

"I don't know. Everything I thought I knew has turned out to be wrong."

"Not everything." He took her hand, threading his fingers through hers. "You were right about me being interested in you." When she didn't pull away, he reached out to stroke her cheek. "Fascinated is more like."

She looked into his eyes, trying to find the lie. "Don't play with me," she warned.

"No games, sugar. I told you the truth when I said you're the only girl I want."

"I believe you followed that with 'in more than passing, anyway,' so my questions about your sincerity don't just revolve around Paula."

"I need to learn to watch what I say around you."

"You need to learn a lot of things," she said.

"I'm a pretty quick study." He leaned in to kiss her. She let him.

CHAPTER FIFTEEN

eather took Jocko's gentle kiss, an offer of peace. The tightness in her chest unraveled for the first time since she had become Tribe. She wondered why it hadn't happened when she'd kissed him before. The kiss deepened, and she realized she had been the one to push for it. He groaned into her mouth. In a rush, hunger consumed her. She threaded her fingers in his hair, pulling him closer, drawing in his rising lust and . . . confusion? She released him, closed her eyes, and let her head fall back on the pillow. Her breath came in ragged gasps that matched his.

"What did you just do?" His voice shook.

She opened her eyes. He sat back, regarding her, wary.

"I kissed you."

"Yeah." He released his breath in a whoosh. "It's just . . ."

"Just what?"

"That was damn close to the Kiss. And not the same at all."

She looked at him as if he'd sprouted wings. "You can't give a Kiss to someone who's already Tribe."

"Yes, you can." He swallowed hard. "It's just a really bad idea."

"Why?"

"Because the results are completely unpredictable, except in a couple of instances, and this wasn't one of those."

She turned her head so she wouldn't have to see his fear. "Maybe you should stay away from me. I have no idea what I'm doing when it comes to this stuff."

"The Kiss or relationships?"

"Both." She sighed. "Shouldn't there be some initiation rite or class? Something to help the newbies figure out what the hell is going on?"

"New Tribe members usually get filled in a little faster than you," he said.

"Am I just that slow?"

He shook his head. "No, you were that hurt. People have no idea how to deal with someone else's pain. The most they can do is offer sympathy. The least they can do is ignore it. Your friends didn't want to open up fresh wounds, and you adjusted okay, so they figured you had it under control."

"I did. Or I thought I did. At least until you." She met his gaze. "And now you're afraid of me."

He shook his head. "I'm afraid of my reaction to you. Totally different animal."

She raised one eyebrow. "I might be relying on gossip and rumor here, but I'm having a hard time believing you're afraid to give in to desire."

"You just fed off me," he pointed out. "No one does that."

She pulled the blanket up and sank deeper into the couch. "I didn't mean to."

"I know." He moved closer and took her hand in his. "Don't look so horrified. I enjoyed the living hell out of it. More than I should have. I pulled back because it was the only way I could keep myself from jumping you."

"And you don't want to." She had projected what she wanted onto him. That was the only reason he'd responded. She stared up at the ceiling, cursing herself for idiocy.

He ran a finger down her cheek, turning her face so she met his eyes. "Oh, I want to, but this isn't the time."

"There's a schedule we're supposed to follow?" Her brow furrowed.

"First of all, you had a crappy night that resulted in you being hurt. I'm not going to make that worse or take advantage of your emotional reaction to finally being home safe. Second, this isn't exactly an ideal location. It might be a little awkward to have your friends walk in, don't you think? I'd like to keep my internal organs where they are, if you don't mind. At least for a while longer."

"If you are playing with me, I will remove them myself," she growled.

He leaned in and whispered, "When I play with you, you'll know it. And if you don't like it, you can gut me."

"Don't think I won't." She tried desperately to ignore the heat that spread through her at his words.

"You need to rest, and I need to make a call." He tucked the blankets around her and walked to the window for a better cell signal. She felt herself slip toward sleep, missing entirely whatever he said into the phone.

His arm wrapped around her side, keeping her close. She dug her nails into his forearm, just enough to let him know he belonged to her. He laughed and stroked her arm before gently prodding her fingers from his flesh. She wriggled until she was as tight against him as she could be. His fingers found the tender spot on her neck, rubbing until closed her eyes with a sigh. She drifted off, warm, wanted, safe, home.

Dreams faded with the smell of coffee. The sun shone through the window, too bright for morning. Heather groaned as she tried to sit up. Her legs cramped, making it difficult. She blinked and looked around. Jez leaned over her workbench, concentrating.

Cami sat on a stool, smoking, and staring at Heather. "The slug's awake."

"Good morning to you, too," Heather mumbled. She concentrated on standing up.

"Would be if it was morning." Cami hopped off the stool. She caught Heather's arm and lowered her back to the couch.

"Oh, god." Heather waited for the dizziness to pass. "How long did I sleep?"

"Long enough to make us wonder if you were ever going to wake up." Jez set down her tools and swiveled to regard Heather. Dark circles accented her tired eyes. "You scared the shit out of us."

Heather cringed. "I'm really sorry." It went so much deeper than that, but she didn't know how to say it.

"You should be sorry," Cami said. "Though some crimes are their own punishment. You missed a hell of a party at Darius' house."

"At least some good came of my rampant stupidity." Heather scrubbed her hands through her hair and winced when her fingers caught on tangles.

She paled as she thought about what she must have looked like last night.

"Want to try standing again?" Cami offered her a hand. "I was told to get you to Doc's place when you woke up, but I can't carry you there."

Heather made it to the counter with more help than should have been necessary. She held on to it while she stretched. The cut on her knee opened up, but the pain was second to the protestations of her legs. She had to find a way to work out the kinks, or she would never be able to fight.

Jez rose. "We're going to help you across the site so Doc can see to you."

"I hate to ask, but can't he come here?" It sounded like whining, even to her.

"He could, but my guess is he wants to get you into his therapy tub. And by the looks of you, that's a damned fine idea." Cami regarded her. "I don't think I've ever seen you this messed up and dirty."

"Don't think I've ever been." Heather pushed the stretch further, determined to walk into Doc's place on her own power.

Jez helped work out the worst of the tangles in her hair. Cami brought her clean clothes. Heather hoped desperately that she would not run into anyone as she staggered across site then dismissed the idea. She had already been seen at her worst by the one person who mattered. Strangely, that made her smile. With her ratted hair and dirty face, dressed in the least flattering clothes imaginable, Jocko had still wanted to kiss her.

Heather spent over an hour in Doc's tub. Whatever he'd thrown into the water had worked. Disregarding the cut on her knee, she felt as good as new. Doc had sat near the hot tub for a while, reading to her from Anthony's favorite story book. Even though his son was grown, Doc admitted he carried it with him from show to show. Heather felt no embarrassment about sitting up to her neck in water while he read to her. It might have been because he was a doctor, but she suspected it had more to do with him being Doc. Making people better is what he did, and if that meant lulling a bruised woman into feeling like a kid again, he would do that. When she finally got out, skin wrinkled like old prunes, he fixed up her knee with some paper stitches so it would be less likely to give her trouble while fighting. He gave her a bag of tea with instructions to drink at least three cups before bed and another before the show began. She knew better than to ignore his instructions.

Her stomach growled as she walked home. She hadn't eaten since lunch the day before. More than anything, she wanted to go by Jocko's place and ask him to make her something good, but she couldn't bring herself to do it. She knew he would feed her. She didn't know if she could avoid feeding off of him. That hunger frightened her more than anything ever had.

Jez was still working when she got back. Cami shoved a sandwich at her and set about brewing tea. Heather ate, stunned. Cami didn't take care of people. Not like that. It wasn't in her nature. Threatening the life of your would-be boyfriend? That she could do with relish. Heather smiled. She had such good friends.

Lew stopped by that afternoon to remind her that he would need to see the fight before opening. Heather knew he was really checking up on her. The act reeked of a command from Darius. She was glad for it anyway. Katie popped in, honest about being concerned and adamant that no one had sent her. They convinced her to stay for a while. When Jasper showed up just before dusk, it became obvious that Heather was being monitored very carefully. After he left, Cami and Jez looked at each other, nodded, and locked the door. They made Heather eat again, tempting her with the fresh fruit salad Jasper had brought. She had no doubt about who had made it. It was loaded with exotic fruits she couldn't identify, and it tasted like heaven. After her final cup of tea, Heather crawled into her bed and passed out.

Neither Jez nor Cami would let her run on Saturday morning. Jez shoved a box at her and told her if she needed a workout she could haul stock up and down the stairs. She did just that, albeit slowly, and found it helped relieve the stiffness.

Considering how strange her week had been, Heather was looking forward to the faire day more than usual. Paula's hostility could not touch that mood, especially when Katie was standing behind her making faces every time she caught Heather's eye. Even Bob was nice to her, which meant he didn't bring up her humiliating flight into the woods in front of the entire cast. He usually relished those moments.

Lew had his director face on as he called the fighters to the run-through. Not until he asked her where her weapon was did she realize she'd left her fight bag in the shop. She blushed.

"I promised her she could use my sword whenever she wants." Jocko winked at her and handed her his spare. His hand brushed hers, sending a jolt up her arm. By his startled look, he'd felt it, too. They shook it off and ran through the fight until Lew was satisfied.

"Whenever I want, huh?" She handed the sword to Jocko.

His dark gaze held promises as yet unfulfilled. "You know where I live."

"I also know better than to show up without an invitation."

"Guess I'll have to see to that, then." He walked off, whistling.

Opening gate felt surreal, as if she were experiencing it for the first time. The sensation lasted through her first set. The crowd didn't seem to mind. They were generous in their applause. She drank it in, growing stronger. They were just as giving when she passed the hat. She practically danced to the hill to watch the first joust. Okay, so it was a little bit like a marionette jerking on strings, but it still felt good.

The joust crowd was always smaller in the morning, but they were sober, so their excitement felt more pure. Carter shone like the sun as he won the test of skills. He bowed to the Queen and blew a kiss at Katie. Ardyth turned to look at her lady in waiting, arms crossed and lips pursed. That got a laugh. Katie's blush could be seen across the field.

As the crowd thinned out, Heather spotted Jocko speaking with a young woman. She wore one of Marni's gowns, a plum and blue confection that made the girl's skin glow. Or maybe Jocko was doing that. Jez shot a look at Heather. She searched herself for the expected jealousy and found only calm. Wooing patrons was part of his job, and he was very good at it. The little blonde smiled at him, and the women on the hill realized she was the girl he had Kissed the previous weekend.

"She doesn't look at all besotted," Heather mused.

"Maybe she found out what he's really like," Cami quipped. Heather shoved her playfully.

"Or maybe he was telling the truth about that Kiss."

The girl kissed his cheek, dropped a curtsy, and walked away. The handsome young man who joined her gave Jocko a thumbs up when she wasn't looking. Jocko watched them go, a huge smile lighting up his face.

"I still don't like him," Cami grumbled.

"You don't have to." Heather grinned and walked down the hill.

The first red rose was delivered to Jezebel's shop. The next two were handed to Heather directly. The rose girl refused to say who had sent them. Three more were waiting at the shop when she stopped in for lunch. Still no attribution. She put them in a vase behind Jez's counter. After her first fight with Jocko—the one she lost—the rose total stood at ten. Cami had been unable to get the manager of the rose shop to divulge the identity of the sender.

"Could be Jocko, upping his game," Jez offered.

"Why would he do that, when all he has to do is smile at her?" Cami teased.

"Bite me."

"Maybe it's Carter," Jez said. "He's a romantic, even if achieving his desire is hopeless."

"He'd be smarter to send them to Katie," Heather said. "I wish I could redirect them. She's nice once you get her away from Paula."

"I hate to summon the devil, but did you consider Sebastian?" Jez asked.

"Briefly. Then I came to my senses. The gesture is big enough for him, but the Bastard doesn't do dramatic without taking credit. Besides, he should have figured out by now that his attention is unwanted." Heather frowned. She remembered telling him to stay away from her at the photo shoot, but she couldn't remember what else they'd said.

Cami snorted. "Like being shut down ever stopped a man from trying."

"For all we know, this is some patron's way of getting my attention. I always feel bad turning down the inevitable dinner invitation."

"Why? They don't know you. They watch you perform and think that's who you are. At the end of the day, we turn into real people." Cami regarded her. "With questionable fashion sense."

"Says the woman who owns more black clothing than you could find at a Goth convention."

"Yeah, but on me, it looks cool." Cami walked off, flipping her knives.

When a full dozen red roses had been delivered, Heather was sure curiosity would kill her. Maybe she was a cat. She laughed as the thirteenth rose was delivered. She tossed it at Jez and waved as she headed for the rose booth.

"White for gratitude," she told the girl behind the counter, "and yellow for friendship. Could you wrap the stems with this?" She handed the girl the black ribbon. She would have to thank whoever was sending her flowers for the idea, and on the off chance Jocko was behind them, this might make him come forward.

Her second singing set went almost as well as the first. She got the same surge of satisfaction, if a bit less money. She raced back to the shop to see if she'd gotten more flowers. Jez pointed to two roses, bound together with wire. The attached card was sealed. She broke it with her dagger. There was one word on the card. *Destiny.* Underneath, in gold ink, was the letter S. Fifteen roses symbolized sincere apology. She threw the roses and card on the counter, and clapped her hand to her mouth so she wouldn't vomit on Jezebel's jewelry.

Jez read the card. "Son of a bitch!"

"Give them away," Heather ground out. "One with each purchase, or the whole lot to the first happy couple you see. I don't care. I don't want them here when I get back."

Jez nodded, pale.

Heather picked up the last two roses. "Except these. I have plans for these." Two bound roses for two people in mutual love. So much for sincere apology. She wanted to shove the flowers down his throat, thorns and all. She marched over to the kitchen and hailed Grady. The big man laughed at her suggestion but took the roses from her. She stomped off to the chess match, the embodiment of high dudgeon.

Jocko slid up beside her as she waited for the King's summons. "Please tell me that I am not the cause for the murderous look in your eyes."

"Sebastian," she growled.

"Did he hurt you?" Anger spilled off him. She tried to feed off it but got nothing.

"No. He irritated the hell out of me."

"I can't stop him from doing that," he said. "But if I get him alone, I'll gladly beat the shit out of him for you."

"Feel free."

"In the meantime, you need to calm down. I don't want that much hellfire directed at me when you have a sword in your hand."

"I'm not mad at you."

"No, but strong emotion has a way of coming out in a fight."

She took a deep breath then another. "Sorry. I'll get it together. You don't have to worry about me."

"Good to know." He brushed her hand with his, the most contact he could manage with the crowd around. In a few minutes, they would have to pretend to be adversaries. Breaking the illusion before it began would not please anyone. He disappeared into the crowd.

When their match started, she moved too fast, hit too hard. Jocko began to fight her for real, parrying with full strength to give both her and himself enough time to recover for the next shot. When she had him at her mercy and the King cried hold, she stepped in, grabbed him and kissed him until his knees buckled. She let him slide to the ground. The crowd screamed their approval. She stood still, absorbing it all, strong and terrified at the same time. His wink released her to bow to the King. Doc whistled. Rodney's eyebrows climbed almost into his crown. She jumped off the stage and fled as fast as her bum knee could carry her. She'd hardly noticed it during the fight.

Grady had done as promised. Heather spotted one of the flower delivery boys. She hadn't bothered to learn his name. They were mostly local kids. She gave him a ten dollar tip to deliver her roses, took a card and wrote one word. *Never.*

"There's another five bucks in it if you deliver these to him personally."

The boy held up the dead roses, baked to a somewhat greasy brown. "Right away." He could make a name for himself with a delivery bound to spark drama.

By the time she returned to the shop, Jezebel had given away the rest of the flowers. Heather grabbed the whiskey from under the counter and took a slug. The burning sensation in her throat helped. She leaned against the wall as the shudder took her.

"Honey? You have the final jam to do." Jezebel pried the flask out of her hands.

"I don't fucking care," Heather spat.

"Wow. You really are pissed. You never use that word."

"Times change."

"Just so long as you don't let the Bastard change you," Jez said.

"He did that once. Never again. I'm stronger now." She pushed off the wall and strode out into the crowd, drawing power from the audience as she passed each stage.

She headed for Doc's shop, seeking answers she knew he could not give with patrons present. Being near him would be enough.

A little girl stepped onto the path. Huge brown eyes stared from under brown curls framed by a precariously tilted flower garland. "Lady?"

Heather stopped, struck by the purity of the girl's awe. She squatted down and, despite the pain of her wound cracking open, smiled at the girl. "What is it, honey?"

The girl took a moment to answer. "I want to be just like you when I grow up." Her determination hit Heather with more force than should have been possible.

"You can be whatever you want, baby." She reached out and straightened the garland. "And I can't wait to see the great things you're going to do."

The little girl beamed at her then raced back to her parents. When Heather stood, Sebastian was looking right at her. A grim set to his mouth, he headed for her. She stood her ground, hand automatically going to the hilt of her sword.

Darius swooped down on her and grabbed her by the elbow. "You are going to be the death of me," he snarled. Sebastian changed directions.

Heather smiled up at Darius. "Good afternoon, Your Lordship."

"Stuff it, little sister. I am doing everything in my power to see you safe, yet you insist on spitting into the dragon's face." Despite the admonishment, she felt his pride in her.

"What have I done to displease you?"

"Dead roses?" He laughed in spite of himself. "I knew you were feisty, but that was brilliant. Or would have been if Sebastian were not seriously unstable when it comes to you."

"Fuck him."

Darius' eyes widened, just as Jezebel's had. "Watch your mouth. And your back. I've got everyone available helping with that. If you could try not to provoke Sebastian it would be a great help."

"Tell him to stop trying to manipulate me, and I'll happily leave him alone. Forever."

"I'm doing my best to get him off site after tomorrow. Could you please try to behave yourself until then?"

"I'll see what I can do." She shrugged.

"You'll promise to stop being so damned reckless, or I will lock you in Jezebel's shop and post guards, performance schedule be damned."

"Yes, Your Lordship." She dropped a curtsy and hissed at the cost.

"Don't mess with me, girl."

"I'm sorry I'm such a pain in your butt. I will endeavor to be a better subject."

"See that you do. I'm not above taking you over my knee."

"Dirty old man." She stood on tiptoe and kissed his cheek.

"Hoyden."

"That's Cami's job description. I'm more of a rogue."

"Well, rein it in when you aren't on stage." He walked her to Doc's shop. The two men exchanged a long look before Darius left to prepare for the final joust.

Heather waited until Doc was busy with a customer before slipping out of his booth. He looked up and shook his head, resigned to letting her go. She gave him a little bow and walked back to Jezebel's shop. The crowd drifting toward the joust gave her cover. Sebastian would likely be a guest of honor on the reviewing stand, but it didn't hurt to be careful. Defying Darius never worked out well for anyone.

She offered to help Jez in the shop. A rush turned Jez into a dervish. Heather packaged the sales, glad for the excuse to remain quiet while Jez poured on the charm. The customers provided a low hum of energy, different from the pulse of an audience but satisfying in its own way.

The horn called for the final joust, drawing away the last of the customers. Heather and Jez pulled stools from under the counter and sat. They listened to the pound of hooves and the roar of the crowd, far enough away to keep from being intrusive. They closed their eyes and let the excitement wash over them.

"Pardon me?"

Heather opened her eyes. A young woman stood at the counter, dressed in costume. A lot of patrons did that. Maybe taking part fed something in them, too.

She smiled and hopped off the stool. "See anything you like?"

"Oh, everything!" The girl gushed. "But I can't shop. I have to save for books. Lit classes kill you with multiple texts."

"I remember." She didn't miss the beginning of semester bank drain.

"You're Heather, right? I have something for you." The girl stepped back and lifted a basket of roses.

A chill went up Heather's spine, followed by the rush of anger. She stomped it down. The rose girl wasn't to blame. "Keep it."

"I can't do that! I need the money and he said that he'd give me a big tip when I reported the delivery. He said I had to give it to you alone."

"He can get stuffed."

"Please. I just started. If people find out I can't make good deliveries, no one is going to buy my flowers."

Jez came over. "Let her make the delivery. Maybe you can top what you did with the last ones."

"Fine." Heather looked at the floor.

The girl looked perplexed as she reached into her basket. "He seemed really nice," she said by way of apology.

"They all do, honey," Jez replied.

Heather looked up, steeling herself.

The girl drew out a bouquet of brilliant orange roses. "He looked all over. I was the only one who had any of these left. Orange, for fascination." She handed the flowers to Heather. "He said you'll understand the message, but he didn't write one."

Heather's heart raced. Holding the bouquet together was the black ribbon. A small pouch hung from it. She peeked inside and blinked several times. Before Jez could look, she cinched it shut.

"Thank you. I'm sorry I was harsh. It's been a long day for me. I'll bet it's been hard on you, too."

The girl gave a tentative smile. "No problem. Thanks for helping me out."

"What's your name?" Jez asked.

"Celeste."

"Nice to meet you. I'm Jezebel, which you probably figured out. I give employee discounts, so if you change your mind about wanting to buy something, come on by when it's slow, and we can talk."

"Really?" The girl perked up. "Thanks!" She turned away.

Heather called after her. "For the record, he is a good guy, but he wouldn't appreciate you spreading that around."

Celeste turned and smiled. "I'll keep it to myself."

"A bit of advice," Jez said. "Be careful who you kiss around here."

"I'm always careful about who I kiss. My older sisters taught me that." Celeste walked off, humming.

Heather arched an eyebrow at Jez. "Tribe?"

"Seems like."

"How do you know?"

Jez shrugged. "No idea, but I'm never wrong."

"Paula said you have been."

"That's because I lie if I think the person will be more trouble than the Tribe deserves." Jez winked at her. "I'm guessing those flowers aren't from the Bastard."

"Definitely not."

"You're not going to tell me what's in that bag." It wasn't a question.

"Definitely not."

"I respect that. Now, you need to head off to the jam. The joust is almost over. Thanks for keeping me company."

Heather gave her a hug. "Thank you for putting up with me."

She unwrapped the ribbon and tied her hair back with it. Jez put the flowers in a vase and shoved her out of the shop.

Heather waited until she was almost to the music stage before looking in the small purse again. She tucked it in her belt pouch and tied it with a double knot. There was no way she was going to risk losing that key.

CHAPTER SIXTEEN

Jocko leaned against a tree beyond the last of the benches in front of the music stage. He made no move to join the jam. She fixed him with a wicked smile and began to sing.

Me hat is frozen to me head,
me feet are like two lumps o'lead,
with the cold I'm nearly dead
from standing at your window.

Let me come in the soldier cried,
cold blow and the rainy night,
let me come in the soldier cried,
I'll never come back again—oh.

Jocko's lips curved in a slow smile.

Me father's working down the street,
me mother the bedroom keys does keep,
me doors and windows all do creak,
I cannot let you in—oh.

He shook his head and glanced heavenward as she repeated the chorus.

The crowd began to clap in time.

> *Then she let the soldier in*
> *kissed his ruby lips and chin,*
> *they went back to bed again*
> *and the soldier, he won her favor.*

> *Then she blessed the rainy night,*
> *cold blow and the rainy night.*
> *Then she blessed the rainy night,*
> *that ever she let him in—oh.*

Jocko laughed. He knew what came next. She inclined her head to him and continued to sing.

> *Now you've had your way with me,*
> *soldier will you marry me?*
> *No me love, that ne'er can be,*
> *so fare thee well forever.*

> *The soldier got up off the bed*
> *put his hat upon his head.*
> *She had lost her maidenhead*
> *and her mummy had heard the jingle.*

He waited for the killing blow. His eyes never left her.

> *Then she cursed the rainy night,*
> *cold blow and the rainy night.*
> *Then she cursed the rainy night,*
> *that ever she let him in—oh.*

He clutched his chest and fell back against the tree, feigning distress. Applause washed over her. She dropped a low curtsy, flashing more cleavage than usual. She would have to thank Katie for that bit of advice. When she stood, he bowed to her, knowing the tease had been meant for him. She returned to her place at the edge of the stage as Ian stepped forward. When she looked out past the audience, Jocko was nowhere to be seen. It didn't bother her at all.

It was not often Ardyth made it to the jam early enough to sing. Heather provided quiet harmonies beneath the Queen's melody while the crowd sat, rapt. Rodney arrived with the rest of the Court. Darius had won the joust and was covered in grit and blood to show it. For some reason, women thought this was hot. Heather felt the lust roll off them, drank it in until she felt like a chalice overflowing. Doc had been right about it being heady. She spilled the power back over the audience with the final song. It had been too much to hold and seemed a good way to send them home. Darius stared at her for a moment then shook his head as if trying to clear it. He offered her his arm and she smiled. Being at the head of the procession was a new experience.

"Do you have plans for this evening?" Darius asked.

"Are you asking me on a date?" she teased. "I think Ardyth might object."

"I have but one Queen." He laughed. "I was just curious."

She tilted her head and eyed him with suspicion. "I haven't spoken to Jez or Cami yet, but I can tell you I think coming to your fire tonight would be a really bad idea."

"We'll make up for it next weekend. I was merely wondering if you're staying on site or going out for dinner."

"So you know whether or not you have to dispatch someone to keep an eye on me?"

He grunted in answer.

"I'll be in good company. We can deal with whatever comes our way."

"I am trusting you to behave," he growled.

She smiled up at him. "Never said I'd behave. But I won't start trouble, if that helps."

"It will do." He gave her a stern look. "Don't make me come after you."

"No, sir."

Without seeming to do so, Darius handed her off to Fox, who offered to walk back across site with her. She agreed rather than subject the squire to Darius' displeasure. He was shy and remained quiet until she asked him what classes he was taking. Fox knew he was Tribe and wanted to go on the road with the jousters, but he had decided he could put up with living in his parents' house until he was finished with school. She admired that. Most nights, he went home and studied. He deposited her at her booth and thanked her for the conversation. He was still standing at the bottom of the stairs when she got to the door. She smiled at his dedication to duty.

Jez and Cami had already changed and were discussing dinner when she walked in. She went to her room to shed her costume. She dressed in jeans, a sweater, and her new jacket. She slipped the little pouch into her pocket.

Cami narrowed her eyes. "That's a little nicer than what you usually wear after a show."

"You're the one who ragged on me for having no sense of style. I thought I'd take your advice and clean up a bit."

"Doesn't have anything to do with those, then?" Cami gestured toward the orange roses.

"Good lord." Heather rolled her eyes. "Does Darius have everyone watching me?"

The dodge worked. Jez and Cami both blushed.

"If I promise that I will not run off, or let Sebastian anywhere near me, will you let it go?"

"You can control the first part, not the second," Cami said.

"Sure I can. I'm going to dinner now, and I guarantee Sebastian will not be there. Since it hasn't come to the point where I have to tell Darius where I am every waking moment, and you two just made plans, I expect no objections." She looked at them in turn, willing them to trust her.

They nodded, clearly unhappy but unwilling to push. She walked out into the night, knowing Cami would be on the phone to Darius the second the door closed. She calculated a five minute window before he released the hounds. She trotted across the site, laughing. Merchants still trying to close their shops looked up and shook their heads at the crazy actor.

She slowed as she approached Jocko's booth. The light from the window was dim. She fingered the pouch as she mounted the stairs and wondered if she should turn around and join her friends. Before she could lose her nerve, she put her hand on the doorknob and turned. It wasn't locked.

She stepped inside, letting the warmth spread over her. The kettle was whistling on the burner. She turned it off then called out to let Jocko know she was there. He didn't answer. She shrugged and made a cup of tea. Wrapping her hands around the cup, she went to satisfy curiosity. She picked up the book that still lay on the end table. *The Dancing Wu Li Masters.* She blinked then read the back cover. It wasn't at all what she'd expected.

"Interested in physics?" Jocko walked toward her, pulling a shirt over his head. It showed his muscle definition almost as much as his bare skin had. She still preferred him without it.

"I don't know much about it," she answered.

"You should read that book. It's more philosophy than science. I think you'd like it."

She looked at him skeptically. "If you say so."

"Trust me." He walked into the kitchen.

The view from behind was as good as the front. She took a deep breath, trying to focus on something else. She set down the book, followed him, and leaned against the half-wall that separated the kitchen from the living area.

"I like the way you're wearing your hair," he said over his shoulder.

Her hand went to the ribbon. She'd meant to take it out. "Thank you for the flowers."

"I heard what happened to you. Getting a rose shouldn't be a bad experience."

"Ah, so it was pity that motivated you."

He stopped moving. "Oh, no, darlin'. I don't feel pity." The words were light but there was a ring of hard truth in them.

"No mercy, huh?" she prodded.

"Pity and mercy are not the same thing." When he turned to face her, his eyes were dark and dangerous. "But I'm not known for mercy, either."

"I'll keep that in mind." She pulled the pouch out of her pocket and held it out to him. "I didn't need to use this."

"Hold on to it. You never know when it might come in handy."

"Why would I want to keep it?" she asked.

He took a step toward her. "You might find reason."

"Think a lot of yourself, do you?"

He chuckled. "I think you're standing in my room."

"Maybe I was just hungry. The rose girl said I'd understand the message. I understood it to mean you were offering me dinner."

Another step. "Are you hungry?"

She swallowed and nodded. "Very."

"I could feed you." His smile was wicked.

"Do you want to?"

"More than you know." He closed the distance between them, kissed her lightly, and slipped her jacket off her shoulders. He dropped it over the back of a chair before pulling her to him and giving her a proper kiss. She held herself still, not knowing what to expect.

"Now who's afraid?" he murmured in her ear.

"What if I lose control again?"

He lifted her chin with a finger. "I'm counting on it." He kissed away her fear, hands sliding from her back to her waist.

He lifted his head. "Still hungry?"

"Starving," she whispered.

"So, do I feed you?" His eyes glittered. "Or take you out to dinner?"

"I . . ." She couldn't find words.

"You have between now and the time I get to the door to make a choice." He walked slowly across the kitchen. Hand on the doorknob, he turned to her. "Open it or lock it?"

"Lock it." The sound of the bolt turning made her heart pound.

He moved toward her with predatory grace. She stepped away from the wall, turning her head as he circled her. His arm wrapped around her hips, and he pulled her back to him. He locked her in place, letting her feel his desire. A shudder ran through her when he bent down and kissed her neck. His free hand slid under her sweater, over her stomach and up, tracing lazy circles.

"Last chance," he murmured.

No going back. She dug her fingers into his thighs and pressed back against him. His hand continued to explore, gently cupping each breast in turn, his thumb sliding over her nipples until she thought they would tear through the lace that bound them. He turned her around and planted a searing kiss on her lips. She gave as good as she got. She sagged against him, relieved that she hadn't drawn from him. He might say he was okay with it, but it still frightened her.

They continued to kiss as he moved her through the living room. Her back hit the wall. He pressed his hips against her as he devoured her mouth.

She pulled up his shirt, wanting to feel the warmth of his flesh under her hands, needing to know this was real. They stumbled through the door into his bedroom.

He whipped off his shirt and threw it in the corner. She managed to get her sweater over her head with a stunning lack of grace. She sat on the bed to remove her boots.

He was there before she could reach down. "Let me."

She dropped back on her elbows for balance as he pulled off each boot and stood it next to the bed. He dropped her socks into them. She shot him a questioning look.

"Figured I'd put them where you could get to them, in case you change your mind and want to leave in a hurry."

"Mighty kind of you."

"Yet another thing I'm not. But I am considerate." He leaned over her, hands on the bed by her head. "Thorough, too." His kiss was tantalizing and slow. She ran her hands over his chest then around to his back to pull him closer. He tensed and broke the kiss.

Her eyes grew wide as her fingers felt ridges of scar tissue. "What happened?"

"Kitchen fires do some serious damage." He tried to pull away, but she tightened her grip on him.

"Don't," she whispered.

"This is the part where you ask to see them and then decide you have to leave, because you don't know how to deal with it."

"If I get up off this bed, it won't be to put my clothes on," she said. She let her fingers explore his back. "Does it still hurt?"

"No. It was a long time ago." He pulled her to her feet. "Might as well have a look. It's all part of the package."

"You don't have to show me anything you don't want to."

"Gotta give you the opportunity to bolt." He turned around. Scars twisted in ropes between his shoulder blades, stopping just above his waist. He drew a sharp breath when she traced one.

"They look like rivulets of water." She stepped back.

His shoulders dropped. Resigned to rejection, he turned away.

She shimmied out of her jeans, dropped her bra on top of them, and got back on the bed. "Your turn."

He turned around slowly and raked his eyes over her before stripping. Getting out of jeans rarely involved grace, but he managed it.

She sighed softly. "Like watching my Christmas present unwrap itself."

He joined her on the bed. "Mine stopped part way." He slid her panties off and tossed them aside. "Much better when you finally get to hold it." He stroked her from ankles to thighs.

She shuddered and sank into the soft comforter as his hands continued to explore. Warmth coiled and swirled wherever he touched her. He brushed her breasts with the back of his fingers then lowered his head to kiss them in turn. She moaned and clutched his arm.

"That's a pretty little sound, almost musical. I wonder if I can make you sing?"

He trailed kisses over her ribs and down her stomach. His hair fell like a soft blanket over her leg as he rubbed his cheek against it. Hot breath caressed her as he moved to nuzzle her other thigh, nudging it until she was open to him. When he tasted her, she bit down on a scream, not wanting him to think it was so easy. But it was.

Her head dropped on the pillow as she arched to meet his mouth. He cupped her bottom and held her up as he licked and probed. She was unable to hold back the moan. He began to hum, the vibrations heightening the near-unbearable sensations. He brought her to the edge. And stopped. She collapsed on the bed, panting.

"Please, please don't," she cried.

He chuckled. "No mercy, remember?" He reached over and pulled a condom from a carved box and slipped it on. "But I am considerate." He rose up on his knees, pressing against her, holding her hips still as she struggled to take him in. A strangled mewl escaped her lips as he rubbed slowly against her.

"Not yet." He took her taut nipple into his mouth, sucking as she ground against him, desperate. He was rewarded with a frustrated groan.

"That's it, sugar, sing for me." He entered her and held still as she lifted her hips to draw him deeper. She dug her fingers into his arm as he drew back, trembling as each move brought her closer to completion.

"Open your eyes," he demanded. She blinked then held his gaze. He smiled, a wicked thing, and drove into her.

She cried out, arching to meet him again and again, sure she would find release. The wave crested then receded as he pinned her to the bed with his hips and kissed her, long and slow, resisting her struggle for more. He rolled over so she was on top of him. She took his hands from her hips and raised them over his head, leaning down to kiss him as she began rocking. Her nipples brushed against his hard chest, spreading a fire she was sure would consume them both.

He pushed against her grip, driving her back. He broke free, grabbed her wrists, and held them out, pulling her arms taut and forcing her upright. Releasing her, he dropped his hands to her waist. She lowered herself, letting her fists support her as she rode him. There was nothing but this, nothing but need, nothing but him. She kissed him. Filled to bursting, she finally let go, the hunger pouring out of her.

His snarl was that of a caged animal, desperate and mad. He thrust into her as she writhed against him, demanding, needing more. He fought the pull, breath ragged. She captured his mouth, drawing the song forth as she finally found release. He wrapped his arms around her and rolled until he was over her. She trembled as he moved inside her, finding rhythm in the vibration wherever their skin met, heart pounding in time to his. As the tempo increased, she opened herself and gave back what she had taken from him. He roared as he joined her bliss.

She stroked his ruined back as he tried to regain his breath. "I'm not the only one who can sing," she murmured.

"Definitely the most dangerous woman on site." He kissed her neck.

She laughed. "You may want to keep that in mind."

"Trust me. I'm not likely to forget it."

She woke with him curled around her, arm over her waist. The breath of sleep, warm and steady, flowed over her neck. It was both strange and completely comfortable to be snuggled up in his bed. *I am a complete fool.* She had no illusions of love—on his part, anyway. She would keep her feelings safely guarded. For now, it was enough to have affection. *And lust.* She knew that had not been spent. For good or ill, they wanted each other.

Forever was for other people.

He stirred. "You're awake."

"Sorry. I didn't mean to wake you."

"Don't think so loud." He nuzzled the back of her neck.

"You can read minds now?"

"No, but I'm pretty good at reading bodies. You tensed up."

"It took me a minute to figure out where I was when I woke up." The lie came out smoothly.

"I could remind you." He stroked her ribs then traced circles on her stomach.

"Mmmm. I figured it out. For one thing, you have a real bed."

"Came with the place." He kissed her shoulder. "One of the perks of renting from Jasper."

"Remind me to thank him."

"You planning on making this public?" The question held surprise.

Alarm bells went off in her head. "Would it bother you?"

"There you go, freezing up again." He pressed against her. "I've got no problem with folks knowing. I'm surprised you'd suggest it, all things considered."

"Because of your reputation." She sighed. "I don't really care what other people think."

"That makes two of us. I'm not inclined to talk about my love life, but you can tell whoever you want. I hear women discuss these things."

"As opposed to the locker room talk men engage in?"

"No lockers here. And there's no one I feel the need to impress by trotting out conquests."

"So this was a conquest?"

He sighed. "No, sugar. This was a decision made by two people who like each other. I'm not going to let you turn this into something it wasn't."

"You don't have to worry about that," she assured him. "I'm fine with things as they are."

"Shame. I was hoping to explore a little further."

The specifics of how became very clear to her. "Oh! I suppose that would be okay."

"I think we can manage more than okay." He set out to test his theory, and all discussion ceased.

In the darkness of early morning, they sneaked off to the showers. She was delighted to discover he was even more fanatic about disinfecting them than she was. Having someone to wash her back was lovely, but neither one of them was inclined to do much more than that.

She declined his offer of breakfast, determined not to feed the rumor mill. Leaving before Gregor awoke to start his forge was vital. She braided her hair, and a lock of his, before slipping out into the pre-dawn. Despite the chill in the air, she remained warm all the way home.

She cleaned the coffee pot and set it to brewing. Serenaded by the soft snores of her roommates, she sat down to repair her costume and figure out what she would say when they awoke. The sounds of a faire morning drifted up to her. Merchants opened doors and called greetings to others doing the same. She thought briefly about running but decided against it. Her knee still hurt—more after last night, though she hadn't noticed at the time—and she'd had enough exercise to warrant another day off. She was on her third cup of coffee by the time Jez stumbled out.

"If Cami sees you in the same clothes you were wearing last night, there's going to be hell to pay." Jez yawned. "There's a sweatshirt on top of my laundry basket."

"Thanks." Heather retrieved it and returned to the living room.

"Not the best subterfuge, merely the best I could devise." Jez handed her a muffin. "You look hungry."

Heather twitched. "Not really."

"Smiling like the Cheshire Cat will do nothing to hide your activities," Jez pointed out.

"I'm not really that worried about it."

"Careful on site. If both of you are smiling like that, Paula will be apoplectic."

"I don't care, and my guess is that you won't see anything out of the ordinary from Jocko. I get the feeling he's good at hiding things." Heather tilted her head. "You seem to be taking this well."

"It's your life, honey. None of my business if you choose to live it dangerously. Just be careful of your heart, okay?"

"My heart is fine. I know the score when it comes to him."

Jez grinned. "I'm going to guess it was worth it, then."

"Quite."

"Good," Cami said from the door. "Because you seriously needed to get laid."

Heather snapped her head to regard her friend. "Who said I got laid?"

Cami snorted. "No one had to say it. Considering where you were last night, it's not hard to figure out."

"And yet you didn't come by to flay the flesh from his bones."

"Nah. I figured you had it covered." Cami winked.

A horrifying scenario presented itself, fully formed, in Heather's mind. "How many people knew where I was?"

"Me and Jez." Cami poured herself a cup of coffee. "And Darius." She smiled as Heather paled.

Heather set down her cup, a little harder than she'd meant to. "He's going to kill me."

"No he's not. You're a big girl. Besides, since he knew you were safe, he got to party for a change."

Jez shot Cami a hard look.

Heather narrowed her eyes. "What do you mean?"

"He's had a watch over you since you took off," Cami admitted. "Everyone got a good night's sleep last night."

His words from the previous day came back to her. "He's protecting me from Sebastian."

Cami nodded. "Maybe now he'll back off."

"I'm not shouting this from the rooftops in order to make the Bastard leave me alone."

"Embarrassed?" Cami shot.

"No, just not interested in throwing meat to the rabid gossips."

"Wise choice." Cami sipped her coffee. "Might want to lose the shit-eating grin, though."

"Not going to happen," Jez piped up. Heather whipped a throw pillow at her head and marched into her room to change into costume.

CHAPTER SEVENTEEN

H er friends were right; losing the smile proved impossible. When asked, Heather attributed it to a perfect fall day, excellent tips in her hat, Bob's rare praise at morning meeting for their fight improvisation, or pleasure at how well the proofs from the photo shoot had come out. None of those things were lies, and they hid the real reason well enough. She and Jocko avoided each other except when they fought. Since they were supposed to be happy for the chance to try to kill each other, that worked out well, too. They did not miss a beat. Rodney and Doc looked a bit disappointed when the fighters stayed on script for the chess fight.

Katie escaped from Paula and the Court, with the Queen's tacit approval, so she could watch the final joust with Heather. She showed up in the wench attire Gina had given her, and her smile was almost as big as Heather's. Fox whipped up the crowd for Carter who was, as always, playing the good guy. Michael's squire, Brock, did the same at the other end of the field.

Heather and Katie ducked under the ropes that kept the audience from getting too close to the jousting field then raced around the enclosure to the gate, annoying several intern kids in the process. Fox ran over to them, skidding to a halt in front of Katie.

"I'm glad they freed you." He pulled out a favor—a long string of ribbons in Carter's blue and white. "My lord would be honored if you would favor him. For luck, I mean."

Katie took the ribbon. "I'd like that. I've never had the chance before."

"Stand here. When they call for favors, wave it in the air, and he'll come to you," Fox instructed.

"Tie it tight," Heather advised, loudly. "They hate it when it slides down their pole too soon." The crowd laughed. A good portion of them were drunk. It didn't change the energy they gave off.

"The view from the chute is best," Fox said. "As long as you stay out of it when the gates are open, you can watch from there." He raced back across the field to remind the audience of the cheers he had taught them.

The knights entered moments later, a more stately procession than in earlier shows, befitting the gravity of a fight to the death. Heather frowned when she realized Carter was riding Fury. Just days ago, Lew had said the new horse wasn't battle ready.

Carter's eyes shone as he spotted Katie. He nodded to her and smiled, the brightness rivaling the afternoon sun. She blushed.

Michael looked over at her and sneered. "I look forward to receiving my opponent's chattel after I end his miserable life."

"We'll die before we come to you," Heather spat.

"No, my dear, but soon after, if only a little." The meaning was not lost on the audience. His crowd roared approval, while Carter's crowd hissed and booed. Michael might be difficult to deal with, but he was superb at his job. Being the bad guy suited him well.

Carter rode over to Katie to receive his favor. "You honor me, my lady. I will win this fight for you."

Katie blushed and dropped him a curtsy. From his angle, her cleavage must have been spectacular. He tore his gaze away and paraded his favor around the field. The King commanded the presentation of arms. The Archbishop stepped forward to give the blessing, quieting even the drunks. Prayer was prayer, whether real or for show.

The knights bowed to each other and retreated to opposite ends of the field. Michael began his charge before the signal. Carter's horse reared as he kicked it then launched toward the center of the field. A roar of approval went up from the crowd. Heather and Katie looked at each other, eyes wide. That was not how it was supposed to happen.

The first pass ended in two shattered lances. The knights raced to the end of the field, rearmed, and bore down on each other. Michael's lance shattered on Carter's shield, the pieces flying almost to the reviewing stand. The King and Queen held position, but most of the Court and guests stepped back. Except Sebastian. He narrowed his eyes, calculating. For all his faults, he knew his profession. Something about that pass had been wrong.

On the third pass, Michael changed the angle of his lance. When he struck, Carter was lifted up and back off the horse. Katie grabbed Heather's hand as Carter fell to the ground. No matter how many times they had seen it, the danger of the move scared everyone watching. Lew caught the horse and pulled him to the edge of the field.

Carter gained his feet quickly and threw off his helm. Michael bore down on him, lance lowered. Carter dodged and fell again. On the next pass, Carter grabbed the lance and pulled, unseating Michael. It was the beginning of the end.

Fox tossed a sword to Carter while Brock did the same for Michael. They circled each other. Swords slammed against shields. Carter disarmed Michael and rushed him. Michael dodged and bashed him with his shield. He threw it aside as he dove for his sword, bringing it up to parry Carter's blow. He planted his feet on Carter's stomach and heaved him to the side. Carter rolled, losing the shield and coming up with the sword held two-handed. Michael sliced Carter's arm. Carter slashed him across the middle in return. They slowed, exhausted by the weight of the armor as much as the fight. Michael swung at Carter, his grip on the sword too loose. Carter flung it away, spun past him and sliced the back of his leg. Hamstrung, Michael dropped to his knees. Carter stepped in, grabbed Michael by the hair, and pulled his head back. He looked to the King for approval. The audience screamed for the evil knight's death.

"May God have mercy on your soul!" Carter cried. "For I surely will not." He raised his sword.

Fury reared and broke free from Lew, snorting and wild. Fox raced to catch the beast. Darius cursed for the ruined moment. Carter turned his head and released Michael, who had not seen the commotion behind him. Michael scrambled for his sword, the only way to sell the mishap as a planned event. The audience roared with delight at the unexpected turn. The horse picked up speed and pounded down the field, straight at Michael. He turned at the last minute and stumbled back. Carter threw himself in front of the horse and grabbed the reins. Fury reared and pulled his head up until Carter's feet barely touched the ground. Carter let his weight hang on the reins, drawing the horse down. One hoof came down squarely on his foot. Fury surged forward, knocking Carter back. Another hoof struck his side. The horse bolted.

Free of the armor that slowed the combatants, Brock launched himself at the horse, grabbed the pommel of the saddle and swung up. He let Fury take a few steps before shortening the reins and pulling his head sharply to the right until he was forced to turn in circles. In a few seconds, it was all over. The horse stood, shaking and blowing. Carter lay still on the field. The audience was eerily silent. Darius nodded to Michael, who picked up his sword, limped over to Carter, and drove it into him. The audience got the death they had come to see. They cheered and booed and applauded wildly.

Heather tugged at Katie, who was pale and trembling. It was entirely possible that Katie would throw up. Heather dragged her to the side and helped her step over the rope. Seconds later, the gates flew open and the horses pounded out. Darius' face was a twisted mask of anger, more frightening than what had happened on the field. The squires ran over to Carter with a stretcher. They carefully lifted him and carried him off as the audience filtered out, completely unaware of the real tragedy.

"Oh, God!" Katie repeated the cry over and over.

Heather put her arm around Katie's shoulder. "It's going to be okay. He's probably on his way to the hospital already." There was always an ambulance waiting, though it was usually a patron who got whisked away in it.

Katie wiped her eyes with her sleeve. "Sorry. I should have handled that better."

"What, seeing the guy you have a massive crush on taken down by a crazed animal? I'd say your reaction is pretty normal."

"Does everyone know?" Katie sniffled.

"Anyone who knows what to look for. At least you can be sure he feels the same about you."

"How would I know that?"

"The favor. Usually Carter asks for a little girl to favor him, with the help of her mother. He's never given it to just anyone." Heather knew if she could keep Katie talking, she'd remain calm.

"He never asked you?"

Heather sighed. "He did, a few times, and I turned him down politely. My experience with favoring a jouster didn't turn out so well."

Katie laughed then blushed. "Forgive me. That was rude."

"Not at all. It's common knowledge that Sebastian set me on fire and left me to burn."

"It seemed like you might be getting back together at the photo shoot."

Heather frowned, trying to remember. "That will never happen."

"I'm glad. He's charming, but I don't think he's very nice."

"Cami says trust your gut about things like that. She's usually right." Katie looked at the ground. "You've got really good friends."

"And now you're one of them," Heather stated firmly.

Katie smiled. "I can't tell you how much that means to me."

Heather cocked her head. "Are you going to the Formal?"

"Of course. I never miss the opportunity to dance all night with hot men." Katie sighed. "I was looking forward to dancing with Carter. He's been so patient, teaching me to fight. I wanted to have a real dance with him, not one where we're pretending to try to hurt each other."

"If he's not completely racked up, I expect he'll be there anyway. He's not going to miss the chance to tell the story of what happened today. You know how they like to embellish."

"I don't think it could get much more intense," Katie protested.

"Just wait." Heather laughed. "Why don't you come by the booth and get ready with us? I've got enough room in the Jeep for four. It's not a limo, but the company will be good."

"I would love that! If nothing else, the fact that I'm not around to serve her will make Paula nuts." Katie came to a halt. "That's not why I want to go with you guys."

"I didn't think so. But it's a definite perk." Heather winked at her. "Pretty soon, we'll have tempted you over to the dark side. Next thing you know, you'll be wenched out and wielding weapons."

"That would be awesome. The lady thing is getting old." They walked in silence for a few minutes. "It's strange, but since I met you, I'm more willing to take risks and stand up for what I want. It's like knowing you has made me as brave as I've always wished I was." Katie shook her head. "That sounds totally stupid."

"Not really. It could just be that seeing how the other half lives opened your eyes to a few things. I don't think I deserve any credit for that."

"I don't know. I've been doing this for a while, so it's not like I didn't know people outside the Court. It's different when I'm around you." Katie shrugged.

"It's my awesome powers," Heather quipped. "I wake up the dreams people keep hidden."

Katie laughed. "How cool would it be if that were true?"

"Cooler than I'm ever going to be. So far, the only thing the Kiss has given me is a nomadic lifestyle and a penchant for getting into trouble."

"I think that may be the very definition of cool." Katie gave her a sly look. "For teenage boys, anyway."

Heather cackled. "See, already you're learning how to cut your friends to the quick. You're going to fit in just fine."

They raced each other across the site, arriving at the jam out of breath. Ian nodded to Heather from the stage. She shook her head to indicate that she was not going to join the musicians. The run across the site had been enough for her still-tender knee. She and Katie hung out at the back of the audience, just waiting for the day to be over.

Michael excused himself from a group of patrons. The winner of the joust was always surrounded and peppered with questions. For once, she felt bad for him. He looked drawn and tired as he approached them.

"I promise to be nice to you for the rest of the year if either of you has a can opener," he begged.

"I'm afraid you're stuck until closing, Tin Man," Heather apologized.

"Bummer. I wanted to let you know that Carter is going to be okay. They took him for x-rays, which he bitched about like a little girl. No offense intended."

"How bad do you think it is?" Heather asked.

"He probably has broken bones in his foot, so he'll be out for the rest of the season." Jousters always judged their injuries by how soon they'd be able to ride again. "No idea about the ribs, but the bruise is huge."

Katie looked stricken. For the first time since Heather had met him, Michael showed concern for another person. Well, as much as he could manage.

"Don't sweat it, babe. He'll be fine. And he'll milk the sympathy for that bruise for all its worth. If you were looking to get in good with him, there's your opening." He walked off to join the Court.

Heather gave Katie a tight hug. "Told you he'd be all right."

"Thanks." Katie stepped back. "I wish there was something I could do for him."

"There is. Make him a new favor for next season. The old one is getting ratty."

"Oh! That's a great idea."

"I'm skipping out on the procession. You should go dance while you have light enough skirts for it," Heather suggested.

Katie beamed and raced after the crowd pouring out the front gate. Heather walked home, tired but satisfied. As she was about to round the corner by the kitchen, she heard voices.

"I need to stay here," Jocko growled.

"You need to do as the Court orders. That is not negotiable." There was no denying Darius when he used that tone. At least not that she'd ever witnessed.

"You know as well as I do that it's not safe for me to leave now."

"Are you implying I can't handle the situation?" Darius asked.

"That's not what I meant, and you know it."

"Then I suggest you do your job and leave mine to me." Darius kept his voice steady, but he was agitated.

"This is twice in two weeks." Jocko switched to pleading. "There has to be someone else who can go."

"If there were, we'd have sent them. I'm no more pleased with this turn of events than you."

"And if it turns out you need me here?" Jocko asked.

"You'll be back by Wednesday," Darius assured him. "I can handle whatever comes up between now and then."

"You'd better hope you're right." Jocko said fiercely.

Heather blanched. No one talked that way to Darius. What made Jocko think he could?

"Did you just call me out, boy?" Anger rolled off Darius, so strong that Heather stepped back, glad they could not see her.

"Not yet."

Heather crept away. Something told her that neither man would be happy to realize they had been overheard. Not that she had any idea what it was she had heard, except Darius sending Jocko away. She sighed. So much for a repeat of the previous night. She consoled herself that he would be back in time for the Funky Formal. If nothing else, she wanted to see his reaction to her in the red dress.

Cami caught up with her as she neared Jezebel's booth. "Glad I found you. Let's help Jez so we can get to dinner faster."

"How do you know I don't have other plans?" Heather asked.

"Simple. I'm not letting you make other plans. You're spending the night with me and Jez. We're going out to eat, and then we're coming back here and drinking a little too much."

Something unraveled inside Heather. "That sounds divine."

There were no last-minute shoppers, so breaking down the display went quickly. Jezebel said she wasn't even going to bother doing her books until morning, at which both Cami and Heather expressed shock. Costumes tossed into various corners, they changed and practically ran to the parking lot, overtaken by the normal hunger brought on by a day of performance and sales. They picked up supplies after dinner and headed back to the shop to make hot cider with rum.

They were well into their second cup when Cami stood up and faced Heather. "Here's the thing."

"Oh, damn," Heather groaned. "I hate it when you start with that. It means I'm not going to like what comes next. If you're planning to lecture me about Jocko, don't worry about it. He's going away again."

Cami drew back. "Say what?"

"I overheard him talking to Darius. The Court sent him off again. He didn't sound happy about it."

"He wouldn't be," Cami muttered. "But that wasn't the thing."

"Good, because I don't want to hear it."

"You don't want to hear this, either," Jez said.

"I know you heard about Carter." Cami's jaw was set, and Heather knew she was thinking that it could have been Michael injured on the field. For all their animosity, they did love each other.

"Worse, I witnessed it. Katie was completely freaked out. Mike says Carter's going to be fine, but he's out for the rest of the show."

"Which brings me to the thing." Cami took a deep breath then spoke in a rush. "They needed someone to ride in his place, and Sebastian offered, and Darius couldn't find a reason to refuse, so he's here for the rest of the show."

Heather froze. The room kept moving. Jez gently took her cup away and set it on the counter. Cami bolted the door.

"Honey?" Jez crouched down. "You okay?"

Was she? She didn't know. A terrible sense of foreboding filled her. At the same time, she was relieved to have a better understanding of the conversation by the kitchens. Jocko had wanted to stay to protect her. Darius would do it instead. Guilt chased out fear. So much concern, just because she couldn't stand up to Sebastian and make him leave her alone. Why did he even bother pursuing her? He obviously didn't care about her. He never had. She had been sad about that once, but that had faded. More in the past few days. She wanted to talk to Jocko, to have him hold her and tell her it was okay, to make love and forget the pain of betrayal. But he was leaving. He might already be gone. Maybe she could use the key and sleep in his bed, surround herself with his scent and warmth until he got back. She imagined days of sleep. If he'd left the book, she could read it and then they could talk about it when he got back. Would Sebastian look for her in Jocko's room? The thought chilled her. She didn't want him there. He would ruin everything. He would ruin her.

Cami swore softly. Heather looked up at her, puzzled. "What's wrong?"

"You've been catatonic for the past twenty minutes."

"No I haven't. I just took a minute to think."

"She's right, honey." Jez was paler than usual. "Your eyes went blank and you didn't respond to anything we said."

Heather blinked. "That cider must have been stronger than I thought."

"I like that explanation better than others I could think of," Cami said.

"Like what?"

"Like the Bastard still has some hold on your mind and snapped it like a twig, for starters."

"Cami!" Jez snapped. "That is totally uncool."

"No, it's totally possible," Cami argued. "She needs to know that. Something about Sebastian has changed. I don't know how or why, but he can do things he shouldn't be able to do—like make a woman who hates his guts turn around and kiss him."

Heather was having trouble following. "Who hates him as much as I do, and when did he do that to her?"

Cami clenched her fists. "He did that to you, Heather. The day of the photo shoot, right before I showed up."

"No, he didn't. We talked. I told him to leave me alone. Then I felt sick and had to sit down, and Jocko took me back to Marni's to eat something. I sure as hell didn't kiss the Bastard."

Cami dug into her bag and pulled out a sheet of proofs Heather hadn't seen before. In several of the pictures, she was looking up at Sebastian with adoration. In the last two, Jocko stood with his sword pressed into Sebastian's back. She dropped the page as memory rushed in, sickening in detail.

"I . . . I don't understand." Tears filled her eyes.

"Neither do I," Cami said. "But we need to keep you away from that son of a bitch until someone figures out what the hell is going on."

CHAPTER EIGHTEEN

voiding Sebastian proved easier than they'd expected. Darius kept
him busy in rehearsal during the day. Heather stayed home at
night, always with company. She cleaned up the booth then put
hooks on earrings and strung pendants for Jezebel. The Formal generally
required an extended period of recovery before the next faire day, so
Jezebel was doing all her prep early.

Heather used the key only once. She lay on Jocko's bed, staring at the
wall and remembering. Indulgence led to desire that threatened to awaken
the hunger. She forced herself to get up then made the bed. Continuing
along the anti-Goldilocks path, she went through the refrigerator and
tossed anything that had gone bad. Then she straightened the counter.
Darius must have insisted that Jocko leave right away. She tied a series of
complex knots in the ribbon and attached it to the back of the chair.
Escalation might prove interesting.

Tuesday afternoon, they began preparing for the Formal. Tansy came by
to see if Jezebel had a wrap that would go with her dress, a flowing white
gown reminiscent of those worn by Ginger Rogers. In exchange for the
shawl, Tansy loaned Heather a necklace made of fine, black chain in a lace
pattern. Tiny red jewels glittered wherever the chains met. Cami refused to
say what she would be wearing, much less show it to anyone. Katie came by
to get their opinion of her dress. It was a simple design, dark green moiré

with a tulle petticoat.

"It's just . . . blah," she complained.

"We could lower the neckline a little," Jez suggested.

Heather nodded. "And shorten the skirt to tea length so you can show a little leg."

Cami threw her head back and stared at the ceiling. "Do you want to stand out?"

"That would be nice. I spend a lot of time in Paula's shadow."

"Then ignore the advice of your wicked stepsisters here and trust your fairy godmother." Cami grabbed a pair of scissors and steered a suddenly pale Katie toward Jezebel's room.

"Was the fairy godmother on crack?" Heather asked Jez.

"I'm not sure, but I do know Cinderella was tripping when she agreed to the whole pumpkin thing. So that's consistent."

The door closed. Heather and Jez looked at each other and burst out laughing. Heather put on the strappy, black heels for one more practice session and danced around the room. Jez pulled a bag from under the counter and advanced with a fiendish grin.

"You know what's in here?"

"No, but you're already scaring me."

Jez shook the bag. "Big, fat curlers."

Heather backed up. "No way."

"Oh yeah. You're going to shower after your run—which, by the way, you are doing entirely on the faire site—then I am going to curl your hair."

Heather shrieked as Jez chased her around the room, brandishing curlers. They collapsed on the couch right before Cami and Katie emerged, the dress hidden in a bag.

"We don't get to see?" Heather asked.

"Nope. Ms. Katie and I are saving ourselves."

Jez snorted. "As if."

"In fact, we're going in Katie's car so no one gets to see either of us until we make our debut."

"This is mutiny," Heather muttered.

"Yeah, but you'll like the new world order." Cami smiled. "I promise."

Katie beamed. "She's amazing with scissors."

"Okay, beauty rest for everyone," Jez commanded.

Katie left, still smiling, and they all fell into much needed sleep.

Heather followed orders and chose a route to run where she could be seen. It irritated her that Sebastian had stolen her freedom—again. She shook off the anger. As she reached the place where running became all, she fed the endorphin rush into her excitement about the Formal. She hadn't been this eager for her prom. Either of them. Not even the prospect of spending the afternoon in curlers could dent her enthusiasm.

Katie came over to help with makeup. She set out pots, powders, brushes, and various other tools. Heather groaned. Inquisitors hadn't had that much equipment. She said as much.

"I don't question you when you show me how to use a sword, so I expect you to accede graciously to my wishes when it comes to my specialty."

"I can't believe you cart all that stuff around with you," Heather said.

"Oh, this is nothing. You should have seen my set-up when I did pageants. It was almost obscene."

Cami howled. "You're a beauty queen?"

"Please. I won a handful of regional pageants. I started when I was six. As you can imagine, it was not my idea. It was sort of fun, though. And it has come in handy when navigating various Courts." Katie set to work on Heather. Forty-five minutes later, she stood back, pleased with her work.

Heather braced herself before turning to the mirror. Her eyes were wide. Really, really wide and not just from the surprise. There was no denying that she was wearing makeup, but it was not at all the tragedy she'd expected.

"I still look like me," she said.

Katie laughed. "Well of course you do. Only more so. That's what good makeup does. What did you expect?"

"Tammy Faye," Cami drawled. Katie threw a sponge at her.

"Keep it up, and I'll go after you, too." She glanced at her case. "I don't know that I have the right base, but a little cosmetic alchemy and I could work something out."

"I've got it covered," Cami said, backing away.

"Have it your way." Katie shrugged. "I'll just see to Jezebel, here."

"That's okay," Jez said. "There's not a lot you can do to hide the freckles."

"I'm not going to hide them, silly. But I'll make you a deal. If you don't like what I do, you can always take it off. We have time."

Jezebel relented. By the time Katie was done, even Cami had to agree she was brilliant with cosmetics.

"See?" Katie winked at Heather. "I have a little magic of my own."

"Wait'll the boys see you in your dress," Cami said. "That's going to be some serious mojo."

"Speaking of which, I think it's time we went back to my place and got ready." Katie packed up her case while Cami got her outfit.

"I'm going to pull the Jeep up to the shop. Bob can bite me, if he even notices." Heather stopped at the door, hand flying to her head.

Jez looked at her and laughed. "I'll get the car. You take those out. But don't do anything else."

"You put me in curlers so I wouldn't leave," Heather accused.

"I was wondering how long it would take before you figured that out. You're getting slow." Jez dodged the pillow Heather whipped at her. It hit the door and fell to the floor.

Night had fallen by the time Heather and Jezebel were ready. They grabbed their cloaks, the one piece of faire costume that would not get them turned away at the door, and a bag with a change of clothes, in case something went horribly awry. Better to change into street clothes than miss a minute of the highlight of the season.

The Formal was held at an old inn. They'd had to rent it for the night to keep the locals out. Too many fights had broken out in the past. The community might like the money the faire brought to the area, but they still regarded faire folk as freaks.

If only they knew how true that is. Heather dismissed the thought. This was a night to revel in their strangeness, even more than they did during faire days. Over the top did not begin to describe the outfits she'd seen at some Formals. Of course, it was easier to pull off when it wasn't so cold. She drew her cloak around her as she and Jez walked from the parking lot to the inn.

Strings of tiny lights wrapped around the balusters leading up to the door. Heather clutched the railing, wondering again if the shoes had been a bad idea. There was nothing for it but to go forward. She could always take them off if they proved difficult. At least they weren't glass slippers.

The place was decorated to the hilt, but it paled in comparison to the beauty of the guests. Gregor greeted them at the door, his stove pipe hat making him seem even taller. It should have been incongruous with his crisp western shirt and black jeans, but he managed to pull off the look. He grinned at them, took their money, and handed them dance cards. A stamp on their hands proved they were old enough to drink.

Jez snorted at that. "Anyone looking at me can tell I'm hell and gone from twenty-one."

"Your beauty, it is eternal," Gregor said, completely sincere. Jez blushed.

"Why can't I find one of those?" she asked under her breath.

"That one's available," Heather replied.

"Nice try, but Gregor and I have never clicked that way."

They found an empty booth near the back of the room and dropped their cloaks. Within seconds, Jez was lost in the crowd, intent on not missing a single dance. Heather surveyed the guests, disappointed when she couldn't find Jocko. Darius must have been wrong about his being back in time. She grabbed her pencil and set out to find dance partners.

As if summoned by her random thought, Darius stepped into her path. "Oh, my. You have outdone yourself, Heather." The fact that he hadn't called her *little sister* made the comment even more remarkable.

She twirled. "Do you like it?"

"You are stunning. And I am in for a very long night."

"You don't have to watch out for me. There are at least a hundred people here already, and the night is young."

"A good portion of those people are male." He smiled at her.

"That makes dancing more fun."

He plucked her card from her fingers. "Then let me be first to sign, if not first to dance with you. I like to let the young men attempt to impress you before I fail utterly at it."

"I'm not exactly the belle of the ball type," she protested.

"Tonight, that's likely to change."

She grinned up at him. "Change is good."

"The death of me," he muttered and disappeared into the throng.

Heather drew a line through several of the slots on her card. She liked having time to catch her breath once in a while. Ricky approached her, sporting a perfectly tailored, silver grey suit. The man knew how to dress, that was for sure. They signed each other's cards and moved on. Rascal approached next, a tie-dyed linen jacket making her blink. Jezebel's name was down for three dances.

Heather made her way to the bar, stopping to fill up her card on the way. Carter sat in the last booth, his leg up on the bench. She put him down for one of her breather slots. He didn't have many free spaces. She told him to keep one open for Katie before slipping off for a drink.

Paula walked in on Sebastian's arm. There was no denying the beauty of the pair. Sebastian sported an Armani suit, perfectly cut. Cufflinks flashed when he unbuttoned the coat. *A button-down shirt should not reveal that much about a man's form.* Knowing who and what he was ought to have rendered him unattractive. Heather swallowed and focused on Paula instead. Her black gown clung to her body, parting to reveal ample thigh as she moved. Diamonds sparkled in her ears, almost unnoticeable compared to the wealth at her throat. There was no doubt they were real. Several cameras flashed as the couple stopped. Heather looked away and ordered a double scotch, glad she'd remembered to eat.

"Excess is delightful, in its place." Ardyth sipped her wine. Her rich auburn hair fell in soft waves, free, for once, from the confines of a crown. She wore a simple knit dress in forest green. Her bare feet were tucked under the rail of the bar stool, shoes forgotten under it. Heather still had the urge to curtsy. As if she understood, Ardyth laid a hand on her arm and shook her head slightly.

"This is, of course, just such a place. I think they're well suited, don't you?" She winked.

"More than you know."

"My dear, nothing goes on at faire that I don't know." The words rang of truth. "I am also a connoisseur of quality. While the packaging can be quite lovely at a party like this, I do not always care to see what is underneath."

Heather smiled into her drink. "Your majesty is wise."

"Never doubt it."

"I don't suppose it rubs off," Heather said hopefully.

"You might be surprised."

The DJ announced that they had five minutes before the first dance was called, sparking an increased frenzy of card swapping. A ripple went through the crowd, followed by a dead halt, when Katie walked in on Cami's arm. Cameras flashed madly. Those without pulled out cell phones to capture the scene. Paula clenched her teeth at the stolen spotlight.

Cami wore a black catsuit with a dangerously deep V neck, covered, barely, by a plum-colored bolero jacket. Spike-heeled boots came up to her thighs, a crop tucked into the holster on the side of one. Her hair was spiked up, flecks of glitter catching the light as she turned her head slowly to survey the crowd. Thick black eyeliner curled into a tribal pattern at the edge of each eye. Her purple lips parted in a wicked smile as she presented her date.

Katie's dress had been utterly transformed. The scoop neckline had been dropped precipitously yet still managed not to reveal too much. The sleeves of the gown had been removed entirely. Black satin gloves stopped just above her elbow, highlighting a complex Celtic tattoo on her bicep. Heather blinked. It was obviously not fake. The skirt fell to mid-thigh, slashed to reveal layers of black tulle. Sheer black stockings kept it from being too revealing. Her heels laced up to the ankle with ribbons made from the excess fabric of the gown.

They ignored everyone as Cami led the way to the dance floor. Cami nodded to the DJ. He grinned and put on a salsa. Everyone stared as the two women danced. Michael stepped onto the floor, holding his hand out to one of the rose girls. He wrapped his arm around her, holding her gaze as he led her through the steps. Had she been half the dancer Cami was, it would have rivaled the previous show. The spell broken, the dance floor filled up.

Heather took the long way back to her table to avoid being jostled by dancers. Wasting good scotch was a sin, especially because she'd discovered Ardyth had paid for it. She normally started with something lighter, but she could nurse the double shot for a good, long time. She had purposely left the first dance open, so she could assess her future partners. From what she could see, she had made good choices.

Jasper claimed her for the second dance, a classic disco tune. He was dressed, as always, in neat, well-fitted clothing that still managed to keep him from standing out. They shimmied with the other dancers until he gave her a sly look and went into full Saturday Night Fever mode. She threw back her head and laughed, then joined him in outrageous antics. They received a round of applause, even from those they had accidentally slammed into during their spins.

Bob shocked Heather by being a stellar swing dancer. At one point, he scooped her up and swung her around. Unlike Jasper, he made sure they had clearance first. He threatened to throw her, until she mentioned that she was likely to put out an eye with her shoe. At the very end of the number, he dipped her almost to the floor. He kissed her hand and deposited her on the arm of her next partner, a shy gamer named Danny. She was glad it was a pop tune. The poor boy would have died if it had been a slow dance.

When her first free dance came up, Heather stepped onto the veranda to cool down. She was not alone, though most of the people around her were out there to smoke. She moved away from them and leaned back against the railing. A few local boys lounged against their car across the street. She ignored the catcalls, convinced they were not for her. The suggestions stopped abruptly, and by the time she turned her head, they were back in their car, pulling away. She smiled. She hadn't seen which of the large men at the Formal had shut down the boys, but the freaks had won the round. She checked her card and went back in.

The DJ occasionally called out free dances. A good thing, or Heather would never have caught up with her friends. Katie promised to tell her the story of the tattoo another time—and to show her the other one, definitely in private. Jezebel bemoaned Rascal's attire, but it was obvious she enjoyed his quirkiness. Cami had intimidated almost all her dance partners, which hadn't stopped them from asking her out. The world was full of fools.

Heather, out of breath and happy to escape the slow dance, dropped onto the bench across from Carter. He bought her a soda and thanked her for helping Katie.

"She's not at all who I thought she was," Heather admitted.

"Me either. I'm glad you told me to leave a dance open for her. Not that I'm much for dancing tonight." He grinned.

"How are you holding up?"

"I'll be fine." He shrugged. "But don't let on. I've gotten more attention tonight than I've seen in four seasons on the road."

"As you cannot dance, cousin, perhaps you would loan me your date?"

Words like finest silk wrapped around Heather.

She shook off the sensation and looked up at Sebastian. "Perhaps you'd like to ask me rather than assume I'm to be handed off at your whim."

"If you prefer. Would you dance with me if I promise to behave like a gentleman?"

"Break that vow, and I'll see you suffer for it," she warned.

He tilted his head in accession. "I would not dream of it."

She glanced at Carter.

"Go ahead," he said. "We can catch up at that lunch you promised me." He looked at Sebastian and narrowed his eyes. "Treat her right this time, or no broken bones will stop me from taking you down."

"Tsk. Such doubt does not become near-brothers like us. I will treat her as well as you would, given the chance."

Carter's eyes flashed at the barb. "See that you do. And stay where I can watch. It is my dance, after all."

Sebastian led her onto the dance floor. His arm went around her, but he didn't try to pull her closer. "Time was, I wouldn't have had to fight for a dance with you."

"Time was, I would have been fool enough to be flattered by your attention. I know better now. What do you want?"

"Just a dance, as I said."

Heather snorted. "I don't trust you. I don't like you."

"Yet you agreed to the dance. There must be something you like about me."

"Your absence, mostly. But I wasn't going to let you cause a scene, so shut up and dance, so I can get back to having fun."

"That was the idea," he murmured. "Let us begin the dance."

She was pressed against him with no memory of how it had happened. She knew she should pull away but didn't know why she thought that. His hand stroked her back as they swayed to the music. The feel of his chest brushing over her nipples sent shivers of anticipation through her.

This is all wrong.

His desire rose to meet hers, rolling off him in delicious waves. She drank it in, wondering what it would be like to run her fingers over his hard stomach. They had never made love, though it seemed they ought to have. She licked her lips—and tasted anger. It did not come from him. She craved it more than the lust. Savoring the strength of the heady emotion, she turned her head, seeking the source. The man in her arms was forgotten as she met dark eyes full of fury. She blinked, trying to figure out who he was and why he was so angry.

Her head began to clear. Horror replaced false desire as she realized what had happened. The Bastard had done it again, and she hadn't noticed. She shoved him away from her and stormed off the dance floor. His laughter rang in her head, louder than the music. Determined not to stumble, she slowed. A soft hand touched her wrist, shattering his pull on her. She turned to find Ardyth beside her.

"I was about to step out for some fresh air. Will you join me?"

"Of course. I . . . I think I need that, too." She turned and followed the Queen onto the veranda. The breeze sent shivers down her spine, but she was glad for it. The cold was real.

Ardyth reached into her purse and pulled out a pack of cigarettes. She lit one and regarded Heather with curiosity. "That was interesting."

"I don't even know what that was."

"No, I don't imagine you do." Ardyth sighed, blowing smoke into the night. "It seems there are some developments I do not know enough about. That will change." She took another drag. "Might I suggest that you avoid Sebastian for the rest of the evening?"

"Gladly. He creeps me out."

"That will not be the general assessment of your encounter on the dance floor, but it is a valid reaction."

Recognition returned, and with it total embarrassment. "I might want to avoid Jocko, too."

"He poses an entirely different threat."

"You mean the fact that he just shot daggers at me from across the room?"

"I do not think they were meant for you in the way you believe."

"All the same, I'm pretty sure he's not going to want to come near me." A pang of regret caused her stomach to clench.

Ardyth sighed and stubbed out her cigarette. "We need to have a long talk, and soon. Come by the perfumery tomorrow afternoon at three o'clock. My suite is upstairs. I will let Darius know you plan to join me for tea, so he doesn't get upset when he can't find you."

"Why is he so intent on keeping an eye on me?"

A small smile tugged at the corner of her mouth. "Darius takes his job very seriously, one of the many things I love about him."

Heather looked down. "I should go home."

"Stay. Dance. Drink. Flirt. Laugh with your friends. It will be the best revenge."

"Thank you," Heather said softly.

"Don't thank me. It's not just for you that I make these suggestions. I would imagine that the rest of the evening will be much more entertaining if you don't let Sebastian ruin it for you. He so loves to have his way, and I rather delight in denying it to him." Ardyth laughed. "Terrible of me, I know. Hardly befitting a Queen."

"Just because you're Queen doesn't mean you can't be human."

"You see? Wisdom does rub off." Ardyth hooked her arm in Heather's. "Now let's go in and show . . . the Bastard, I believe you call him? . . . what a good time looks like."

Determined to do just that, Heather accompanied her Queen back to the ball.

Lewis came to claim his dance. Heather stepped back.

He turned slowly. "Like what you see?" He wore a long sleeved, silk crew neck shirt, the color of new cream, tucked into black jeans. Both molded to his outrageously ripped body.

"Can I draw you sometime?" Heather blurted.

Lew laughed. "That's second only to 'come upstairs and see my etchings' in the cheesy pick-up lines department. I expected better of you, babe."

"I'm serious. I haven't done a portrait since I left college, but I think you'd be fun to draw. Clothes on, of course."

"What fun is that?" He teased. "I tell you what, next time we end up at a show together, you can put me in whatever position you want. But right now, I want to take you out on the dance floor and show you how well I can move."

It turned out to be an impressive show. She ought to have slapped him at least a dozen times for the way he touched her, and if there had been anything behind those caresses, she would have. It was just Lew, giving in to the music and intent on showing her a good time.

She had just enough time to drink a glass of water before Rascal found her and tugged her onto the dance floor. They thrashed to a Goth metal tune, his enthusiasm infectious. She handed him off to Jezebel, who gave her a long look before heading off with him. Heather returned to her table and downed the rest of the scotch. The burn satisfied something primal.

"You been drinking like that all night? Because it might explain a few things."

Heather turned to Jocko. He was resplendent in a turn-of-the-century tuxedo, complete with tails. His white shirt set off a dark red vest. He even had a pocket watch attached with a gold chain. Desire flooded her—and came up against a wall of anger. At least the emotions were real.

"That was my first drink. But I could use another." She glanced at her dance card. Darius was nowhere to be seen. She could make it up to him later.

"I'll get it," Jocko said. "Stay here. Right here, so I know where you are."

"No. I'm not going to let the Bastard keep me from enjoying myself. Queen's orders. If you want to join me in that, you're welcome to come along for the ride, but I'm driving." She strode off toward the bar. He followed.

She let him fume while she ordered their drinks. Darius did not surface to claim her for his dance, which was somewhat of a relief. She'd seen him dancing. It wasn't pretty.

She handed Jocko his drink and sipped at her own, waiting for him to speak. He said nothing.

"I like the outfit." Sticking to small talk seemed a good idea. "Where did you get it?"

"My granddad was a riverboat gambler. I'm the only one in the family who can fit into it."

"Too big for the others?"

"Too small." He smiled despite himself. "I'm the runt of the litter."

"Good lord! You're hardly a small man."

"Remember that, do you?" There was a hard edge to his voice.

"I remember a lot of things."

"For a minute there, I'd say you'd forgotten me entirely. Right about the time you forgot yourself."

She set down her drink. "Are you spoiling for a fight right now, or can we talk about that later?"

"We need to talk about a lot of things, apparently."

"Get in line," she muttered.

He stiffened. "Pardon?"

"The Queen asked me to tea. Doc says he has some things he needs to tell me. Cami is chomping at the bit to get me alone. I'm pretty sure Jez is planning a chat along the lines of the ones my mom used to give me when I stayed out past curfew. That enough for you?"

He blew out a long breath. "Sorry. I'm a little wound up."

"You?" Heather sputtered. "I'm so tense I could explode at any minute. Dancing only does so much."

"I wish I'd been here in time to get on your dance card."

It was more of an opening than she'd expected him to give her. "It's not too late."

"No?" He regarded her skeptically. "You'd still dance with me after I was a jackass?"

"If I held that against you, we'd never spend any time together."

"Now, that's my girl."

They downed their drinks, slammed them on the bar, and headed for the dance floor.

She groaned when the country number began. He grinned at her then grabbed her by the waist, leading her with confidence. As they spun around, he swept her off her feet. Literally. His hands never left her as they moved across the floor, but he didn't press his advantage. She wished he would. His lean body was tantalizing, close. She wanted to explore his long lines, touch his hair, kiss him.

The difference from her dance with Sebastian could not have been more stark. This desire was genuine and all hers. She just hoped she wasn't the only one feeling it. Jocko gave off nothing until the last measure. He spun her out, pulled her back, and locked her to him. As the last note faded, he captured her mouth in a searing kiss. This time, the catcalls were definitely for her.

The only thing more satisfying than Jocko's kiss was the frustration sluicing off of Sebastian as he witnessed it. Perversely, Heather used it to strengthen herself. Sebastian jerked as she pulled from him. His eyes grew wide as he realized what she'd done, and he shut himself off from her. She smiled at him like a cat that'd eaten his pet hamster. Within minutes, he headed for the door, dragging Paula with him. She shot Heather a murderous look as she left. Heather wiggled her fingers as she waved goodbye.

"Taunting them was both cruel and dangerous," Jocko whispered as they retreated to a corner. "But really fun to watch."

"I've had enough of being jerked around by them."

"Glad to hear it. Because if I ever catch him with his hands on you again, I will kill him."

"As long as I get to watch, I'm all for that. When can you start? I could catch up to them, and we could do it tonight."

Jocko chuckled. "I think Cami is rubbing off on you."

"Maybe it's not her influence at all and I really am that vicious. There's a lot you don't know about me."

"I reckon you're right. Maybe I should find out a little more." His hand slid down to her hip.

"Keep that up, I might show you a thing or two. But you may not like it."

"I'll take my chances." He trailed his fingers over the back of her thigh and up.

"I wouldn't be so sure you'll get that chance. We're not in your room now. Neutral territory demands better negotiation."

"We're not in my room *yet*. Wouldn't take but a few seconds to remedy that, and I'm inclined to negotiate from a position of power."

"Mere seconds, huh? You really must have some powerful magic."

He pulled her back to him and whispered in her ear. "What I have is a room at the inn."

She swallowed. "It's not that easy. I gave Jezebel a ride."

"There's a big, deep, claw-foot tub in the bathroom."

"That's fighting dirty," she groaned.

"I told you I'm not kind." He played with a long curl that had come free. "Why don't you see if Jezebel can catch a ride home? Maybe she can convince Cami how much fun it would be to have a sleepover with her new girlfriend. That way, Paula can't torture Katie. Everyone wins."

"You're a little too clever for your own good."

"Oh, it's all for my own good, sugar, but it could be for yours, too, if you want."

She wanted. Badly. He made her crazy in ways she could handle. She tore herself away from him and set out to find Jez, grateful that she wouldn't have to explain herself to Cami, too. Jez agreed to the plan and sent Rascal to retrieve the bag with Heather's spare clothes while she hunted down Cami.

The Formal was winding down, but enough partiers remained that Heather and Jocko had to weave through a crowd to get to the stairway. Most people didn't realize they were together. From the corner of the dance floor, Ardyth smiled at Heather before returning her gaze to Darius. She must have said something to him, because he looked sharply at Jocko. The younger man only smiled and stepped into the hallway, Heather on his heels.

CHAPTER NINETEEN

Jocko unlocked the door and pulled Heather into the room. As soon as it was closed, her back was against it, his body pressed to hers as he put to shame the kiss on the dance floor.

She pushed him back. "Skipped right over the negotiation part, did you?"

"Nope, just thought I'd open it right."

"Interesting gambit. Not sure how I should counter that."

He handed her the black ribbon, kinked where he had untied the knots. "Try this."

"What should I do with it?" she mused aloud.

He hung up his coat and turned to her. "Whatever you want."

She put her arms around him, grabbed the ends of the ribbon, and pulled him close. "This will do." She kissed him. "For a start."

"Good choice." He kissed her bare shoulders.

She draped the ribbon around her neck and unbuttoned his vest. He reached for the zipper of her dress, but she stepped out of reach.

"Stay right there." She handed his words back to him. "So I know where you are."

He shook his head and smiled. She laid the vest carefully on the back of a brocaded armchair then returned to unbutton his shirt. It hung open while she ran her hands over his stomach and up to his chest. His breathing quickened, but he did not move. She slipped the shirt over his shoulders and laid it over the vest. She took his hand and placed it flat against her shoulder, his fingers splayed over her collarbone.

"Don't let that fall." She pressed into his hand, took the ribbon, and tied it around his wrist.

"What do you plan on doing with that?" he asked.

"Whatever I want, remember?" She stepped behind him, keeping hold of the other end of the ribbon. She kissed his back, just below the scars. He hissed as her mouth moved up, tongue tracing along the edge of one twisted ridge.

"If you don't like that, I'll stop," she said.

"No. It's just . . . surprising."

"I'm full of surprises." She reached for his other hand, pulled it back, and tied the ribbon around it, leaving ample play between the tight knots. With a last kiss for the worst of his scars, she came around to face him.

"What now?" he asked.

"Now, I have a very good time." She traced the line of hair from his chest down, sliding one finger under his waistband. His breath caught when she leaned in and flicked her tongue over his nipple. She liked his reaction so well that she did it again then switched to the other one. Her finger toyed with the top button of his pants.

"You wanted to talk." She ran her palm over the placket that hid the buttons, surprised to find that he could, in fact, get harder. "I'm not inclined to speak right now, so why don't you tell me something you want me to know."

"If I'd had my way, you'd have been up here an hour ago."

"So you lust after me. I knew that." Hands on his hips, she lowered herself to the floor, the dress puddling around her. She toyed with the first button, looking up at him.

"That's not it."

"No?" She flicked open the button. "Seems like lust to me." She rubbed her cheek on his hip.

He struggled for words. "Okay, yes, but that's not all."

Another button. "Not love, surely."

"I . . ." He could not finish.

Two more and he was free. "Shhh. I don't need what you can't offer." She wrapped her hand around him. "But I will take suggestions about what you want."

"Anything you're willing to give." He jerked when she tightened her grip.

"I'm a very giving person." She wrapped her mouth around his desire in proof. She pulled back a moment later. "You're supposed to be telling me things. Anything at all. Talk about physics if you want. While you speak, and stay still, this continues."

"You are a wicked woman," he groaned.

Her answer was not verbal.

"I like your voice. I'd forgotten what it was to want to sing, not just to have to." He gasped as she began humming. He caught his breath, barely. "That may be the best payback I've ever gotten." The trembling in his legs spoke of his fight to remain motionless. "When I first saw you, I couldn't believe they'd assigned you to fight me." His voice broke as she took him deeper. "I didn't think you'd be able to keep up." She increased the pace. His breath became ragged as words failed him. She stopped.

"Damn it, I can't do this."

"Yes, you can." She wasn't sure he'd understood the words.

"You did surprise me, in a lot of ways." A deep groan followed the admission. "I've never had that kind of rhythm and flow with a partner." She demonstrated the possibilities of the statement. "Even when we don't get it right, it works."

He writhed. She allowed it.

"You make me care more about the fight, the show . . ." He choked, fighting for more, fighting against it. ". . . everything."

She pulled back as words finally failed him. "That wasn't so hard, was it?"

He reached down and lifted her to her feet, the ribbon hanging from one wrist. "You want to try it?"

"Maybe another time."

He spun her around and unzipped the dress. She let it fall to the floor and stepped out of it, then bent down to pick it up. When she straightened, there was a feral glint in his eyes. She walked over to the chair and laid the dress across it. He dropped the pants on top of it as he pulled her back to him.

"This is a nice look for you." His hands cupped her breasts, nearly spilling them out of the strapless demi-bra. He steered her toward the bed, continuing to explore. He especially liked the thin patch of lace that masqueraded as underwear. "If you wore this during the day, I could sneak you up to my room and pleasure you between fights and we wouldn't even have to get undressed."

"There is no way we could get away with that."

"No," he admitted, "but now you're going to think about it all during the show."

"So are you," she pointed out.

"I already do." He turned her around and kissed her. "Even more now that I know what it's like to be inside you."

She put her foot on the edge of the bed and bent over to remove her shoe.

"Aw, I like those."

"Do you? Well then, I guess I'll leave them on." She put her hands on the bed for balance as she lowered her foot. When she started to straighten, he put his hand on her back to stop her.

"Good idea." He slipped the thong over her hips and let it fall as his fingers played. She shuddered when he slipped them inside her. She writhed as his thumb stroked her in time with each thrust. His cock rubbed against her ass, maddening in its closeness.

"More," she whispered. He held her tight against him and curled his fingers. Spots of light danced in front of her as she came. He lowered her to the bed, stroking her back as the tremors subsided.

He pulled the pins out of her hair, letting it fall in waves over her shoulders. Then he rolled her over and knelt down. His tongue flicked over her, setting off another wave of sensation.

"I can't," she gasped.

"Yes, you can." He refused to let her recover.

She arched against his mouth until she was sure she could bear no more. He released her and removed her shoes. She curled up in the middle of the bed, shaking. He unfastened her bra and dropped it on the floor.

"There's a lot of things you can do that you didn't think possible." He ran his hand over her side.

Under his touch, her body calmed. He rolled her onto her back, stroking her stomach, her thighs, her arms. His kisses were long and sweet, filling her with a heavy warmth. She relaxed into the bed, staring up at him in wonder. He pulled back and ran his hand over his erection. Like a magician, he produced a condom, and slid it on, obviously enjoying her reaction. He lowered his head for another kiss as he entered her, not breaking away until they were fully joined.

"Yes." She sighed and closed her eyes.

"No rest for the wicked," he whispered, pulling back and then thrusting into her. Her eyes flew open. He did it again. "You didn't think I'd let you sleep tonight, did you?"

"I . . ." Her reply was stolen by the increase in tempo.

"Not so easy to talk, is it?" He grinned at her, slowing.

She tossed her head back and forth, whether in answer or pure pleasure, she didn't know. It didn't matter. She gave herself to the feel of him, their mingled scent, his intoxicating kisses. She felt the tension build inside her as she twisted to meet him.

"That's it, sugar, let me feel you come around me. Give it up to me. Give me everything."

"Take it," she moaned, pushing her hips against him and releasing her magic.

He met it with his own. The two forces coiled and slammed back into them. The orgasm took them in concert, one sensation, one emotion, one song that would not end. They shook uncontrollably, dissolving into tears as they were finally released.

Sleep did not follow as they'd expected. They lay stunned, occasionally looking at each other but mostly staring at the ceiling. The swirled plaster followed very precise lines instead of twisting randomly. She wondered who would go to the trouble to do that in a hotel. Thoughts drifted in but left just as quickly, refusing to be tied down. From his puzzled silence, she figured the same thing was happening to Jocko. Or maybe she had dreamt the whole thing. Nerves still twitched and jumped whenever she moved, denying that possibility.

"Never did that before." Jocko's voice drifted to her.

"Um. You did that before with me."

He chuckled. "Not the love making part."

"Oh. The magic." She still wasn't sure any of this was real.

"Magic." He thought for a minute. "Yeah, I guess you could call it that. I sure would like to know how you do it."

She let her head fall to the side. He was pretty in profile. "You did the same thing."

"No, sugar, I reacted to it without thinking." He licked his swollen lips. "Which also shouldn't happen."

"You said that when you kissed me, up in my booth."

"Apparently, you got even stronger since then. I just don't know how."

"You know way more about it than I do."

"Not about this." He turned to meet her gaze. "This is way beyond me."

"Then let's start with what you do know. I'm so new, this is all a mystery. I just found out that some people have different powers."

"Talents, really. It's something you build up, not wield." He looked back at the ceiling. "Not in most cases."

"Terminology aside, there are people who can do things other people can't. Like Tansy knowing when someone is getting closer."

"I think those things were always in them, even before they became Tribe. Doc knew how to heal before he became Tribe."

"Sure, but he was trained to be a doctor."

"He became a doctor because he knew how to heal, not the other way around. The same way that metal always sang to Gregor, did things for him that it wouldn't do for other people, long before he became Tribe."

"Maybe we all have something we could do before that we just got better at, the same way my singing improved."

"Sure, but that's basic, like what everyone gets when the switch is thrown."

"How does that work, anyway? Why are there some people who become Tribe and others who don't?"

"No idea. It just happens. Maybe it's biological, like Doc says, or metaphysical, as Tansy believes." He laughed. "Take my advice and walk away if they ever start that discussion in front of you. It's been going on for years, and as far as I know, they haven't gotten any closer to agreement."

"Which leaves us back where we started, with no idea what just happened." She threaded her fingers through his. "Except for really great sex."

He smiled. "No doubt about that."

She thought for a while. "Why shouldn't it have happened?"

"No reason to deny ourselves really great sex, least none that I can think of."

"Nice dodge. Now, answer the question."

"I can't."

"Can't, or won't?" She tried to pull her hand away but he locked her fingers in his.

"Both."

"Considering what just happened to us, and how freaked out I know you are, despite trying to hide it now, what would keep you from telling me what you do know?"

He sighed. "I already told you what I can. You shouldn't be able to feed off me, or feed me like that. What I did just now was a defensive move. I've only ever done that on purpose."

She lay perfectly still. "You were trying to push me away?"

"Not me. The . . . magic." He shook his head. "I don't know if I can get used to thinking about it that way. It just is what it is."

"So it acted on its own to protect you." She swallowed heavily. "What kind of monster am I?"

"You aren't the monster," he whispered, turning away. "I am."

"No, you aren't." It was easier to believe it of herself than him.

He flinched when she touched him. "You give back. It's different for me. I can't take from the crowd, only individuals. And I can't give off what I take, unless I pour it back into the audience."

"Why not?"

"I don't know. I'm immune to anything thrown at me by the Tribe."

"That's not true. Tansy knew you were coming."

"I just set off her radar." He tensed. "Which also shouldn't happen. Shit."

"But it happens with me."

"All the time."

"You don't like that." She rolled away from him.

He pulled her back, wrapping himself around her. "No, sugar, I like it too much. Knowing where you are, constantly aware of the energy you give off like a battery that never runs dry, all I want to do is fill myself with you."

"I'm not objecting." She snuggled back into him.

"You would, if you knew how dangerous that is. For both of us."

"Why?"

"Because I shouldn't be able to feel it at all. There are a lot of people out there who don't like my particular Talent. Or mutation, whatever the hell it is. As soon as someone figures out you can reach through it, they're going to come for you to get to me."

"Someone else, you mean. I've already got one obsessed, psycho ex-almost-boyfriend." She knew instantly she should not have said that.

He locked his arms around her as his whole body went rigid. "Oh, hell. He knows."

"About us? I'm pretty sure he was clueless before tonight. Unless Paula told him. She knew I was in your room that first night."

"I swear to God, I am going to Break that bitch."

"Let it go. Even if she hadn't told him, our lip lock on the dance floor would have clued him in. You may remember his frustration when he saw it. Well, before I fixed that for him."

"Which would have clued him in about what you can do. While we're trying to figure stuff out, how did you manage that?"

"No idea. It just seemed like whatever he was putting off was dangerous. I took it and used it against him. So maybe I am a monster, after all."

"Or a god." Nothing in his voice indicated teasing.

"Yeah, that's it. I'm an all-powerful, omniscient deity who can tell exactly what you're feeling right now."

"Which is what?"

"Really, really scared."

He pushed away from her. "How do you know that?"

"Because, jackass, everyone fears what they don't understand, and you've been working yourself into a tizzy over stuff even I don't understand, and I'm the one doing it." She gave an exasperated sigh. "I liked it better when we were having casual sex."

"Casual?"

"You professing your undying love?"

He remained silent.

"Right. Then casual sex it is. Which, for the record, is just fine with me. We are what we are, Jocko. We can't do anything about it. We aren't likely to answer the great mysteries of the universe tonight. The best we can do is indulge in them or try to get some sleep."

"That's or, not and?"

"Are you telling me that you still want me, now that you know I'm some sort of scary monster-god?"

"Maybe I just get turned on when you're pissed off at me."

"You must walk around horny a lot."

"Constantly." He set out to prove it.

Heather soaked in the tub, morning light playing across the water. Jocko hadn't lied about the bathtub. She'd have made his life hell if he had. More than she already did, anyway. He came in with a cup of coffee and set it on the little stool next to the tub.

"Now who's the god?" she quipped.

"I'm just an acolyte, darlin'." He let her take a couple of sips of coffee before washing her hair.

She leaned back into his hands as he massaged her scalp. "I could get used to being worshipped this way."

"Just this way?" he asked.

"I'm fairly sure I could come up with a few other things." She dunked her head to rinse off the shampoo.

"I have faith in your powers of creative suggestion. But I doubt we'll have time to explore those before we have to check out." He worked conditioner through her hair. "We could go back to my place and see what you come up with."

"I wish. Everyone would know where to find me, now that our secret's out, and they all seem hell-bent on talking to me today. Might be a bit awkward if they decided to show up while we were involved in some elaborate ritual."

"That's what locks are for."

She snorted. "You willing to explain to Ardyth that I missed tea with her because I was too busy having sex?"

"No, ma'am. That woman is a brand of scary all her own."

"Is that any way to talk about your Queen?" she chastised.

"It's the only way to regard any Queen," he replied. "Trust me. The Court are dangerous people."

"Good thing this one likes us, then."

"A very good thing."

She finished bathing and insisted that he take a turn while she braided her hair and gathered their things. She missed her chance to wash his hair. He stood dripping on the bathmat. She took a towel and dried him off, reveling in the chance to run her hands over him one last time before returning to the complications of their world. Their scheduled departure was delayed by the distraction of his growing hard while she dried his legs. She relished making it worse then ran when he realized she intended to leave him that way. All plans for going home clean were thereby spoiled.

CHAPTER TWENTY

Jocko insisted they stop at a grocery store before heading back to the site. Since he also invited her to dinner, she didn't object. Heather called Jez and discovered their fridge was almost empty, too. On the way back, Jocko gave her advice for dealing with the Queen. By the time he was done, she knew she was out of her element where the Court was concerned, but at least she wouldn't be going in blind. He reminded her that they needed to run through their fights. She groaned and added it to her schedule. She dropped him at the gate by Jasper's shop then parked her Jeep in the back lot.

When Heather walked into the booth, Cami was on the couch, sharpening her knives. She looked up, lips set in a thin line, but said nothing. Metal scraped over stone. Heather put away the groceries then took her bag and gown into her room.

"So, you went and did it." Cami folded her arms over her chest.

"What, had sex?"

"If it was just that, I'd have no problem with it. You had to go and fall in love."

Heather shrugged. "He's not the sort."

"Maybe not, but that's not stopping you."

"And you got that from the way I put food in the fridge?" Heather started a pot of coffee.

"No. I figured it out last night, when you got away from one dangerous man and headed right off with another."

"You're reading too much into it. He tempted me with the prospect of awesome sex, followed by a long soak in a big bathtub. I had both and regret neither."

"At least the bath won't come back to haunt you."

Heather glared at her friend. "What is your problem?"

"I'm scared for you." The simple admission was so unlike Cami that Heather gaped.

"Why? It's a faire fling. People have them all the time."

"I don't know why, and it pisses me off, okay? There's something happening around here that is not right, and Jocko falling in love is so far outside the natural order it sets off every alarm I have. Considering that I'm loaded with them, that's starting to get on my damned nerves."

"He's not in love with me," Heather said. "He just likes how we are together."

"If you say so. But I've never seen him slip like he did last night when he saw you with Sebastian."

"Slip how?"

"Control. Jocko is all about it. He was so furious last night, I thought he was going to take down Sebastian right there, in front of God, the King, and everyone. Hell, I could almost feel his anger. That's never happened before."

"I've been hearing that a lot lately." Heather could not keep from smiling.

"I'll bet."

"His being angry at Sebastian is what made it possible for me to break away, so I'm grateful for it. But it doesn't mean he loves me. He just wants to keep me safe from the Bastard. And bang me silly."

"Maybe you're right. I sure hope so."

"You hope I don't find love." Heather frowned. "Which part of that says best friend to you?"

"The part that knows how it will turn out if you think you can find it with him."

"You don't know what will happen. No one gets to know that. We can hope, plan, dream, but when it comes down to it, we're just stumbling toward a future that can change at any second."

"I'm not sure if that's the most optimistic thing I've ever heard, or the most cynical."

"I don't even know what shows I'm doing next season. I'm not sure where I'm spending the winter. Two years ago, I was thinking about whether or not I should change my major – a memory so distant it feels like it happened to someone else. One moment altered the entire direction of my life. It was terrible, but sometimes I think it was the best thing that ever happened to me. So, as far as I can see, optimism and pessimism are just two sides of the same coin. Everything is going to be fine, and everything will suck, but only sometimes."

"Oh, hell," Cami groaned. "He didn't make you fall in love with him. He infected you with philosophy. I may have to kill him."

Heather laughed. "Can you wait until the end of the show? Because I'm sort of liking having regular sex for a change."

"Fine. But no promises after that."

"Deal."

Cami accompanied Heather across the site, ostensibly on her way to practice. They both knew that wasn't the real reason. Whether she wanted it or not, Heather was going to have some sort of bodyguard, especially after last night. She added Darius to the list of people she needed to talk to, though she doubted he would lift the order. She was beginning to think they should just slap an ankle bracelet on her and track her like an ex-convict. At least then she wouldn't be messing up everyone else's schedule.

Doc was puttering in his shop. He offered her breakfast, but she refused, opting to help him organize his shelves instead. They worked in silence for a little while, which was unusual enough to make her jumpy. Doc always had something to say.

Grasping for something to start the conversation, she blurted out the first thing that came to her. "How does one dress for an audience with the Queen?"

Doc looked at her over his shoulder. "That would depend on the reason for it, and whether or not it was to happen during a faire day."

"Nothing like that. She invited me for tea this afternoon."

"Then it's a social visit, and you are dressed just fine."

"I'm kind of nervous," she admitted.

"No need for that. Ardyth is a lovely woman."

"All this Court stuff is way over my head."

"So it is for most of us. But as her interest in you at this point is most likely personal rather than political, I suggest you simply enjoy the conversation."

Heather nodded and went back to arranging vials. "Last night, you said you had something to tell me."

He looked sheepish. "I'm afraid I was not being entirely honest."

"Is this just another one of Darius' ploys to make sure I'm never alone?"

"We cannot help it if we are concerned for you, but if it makes you feel any better, this idea is entirely my own. I wish to show you how to do something, if you'll allow it."

"You know I like it when you teach me things," she said. "It makes me feel like leaving school wasn't such a bad idea."

"You can go back, you know," he said gently.

"I know." She thought back to her last semester and shuddered. "I'm just not sure I should."

"Perhaps in time, you'll find a way."

"If I had professors like you, it would be a lot easier." She smiled at him. "So maybe I should just let you teach me whatever it is you think I need to know."

"Go to the herbs. You will need betony, celadine, comfrey, fern, mullein, pennyroyal, and rosemary."

She pulled the jars from the shelves and brought them to the work bench.

"And heather, of course." He smiled at her.

She laughed and brought him the last ingredient. "What is all this for?"

"You are going to make an amulet for protection."

"You don't believe in magic potions."

"Not true. I don't believe in love potions or things that purport to attract money. I have never found either to be particularly effective. And when they do work, the result is rarely what the person asking for them wanted."

"So what is this supposed to do?"

"Keep you safe from unwanted attention." He left it at that.

She didn't. "Does everyone know Sebastian is attacking me?"

"No, most people think he is trying to woo you back."

"Having him invade my mind isn't my idea of romance. How does he do that?"

"We don't know."

"But you've been discussing it."

"I cannot let a puzzle go, as you know. But I would not have you believe I was indulging in idle gossip."

"No, of course not." Heather looked down at the workbench. "Tell me what to do."

She followed Doc's instructions, adding ingredients in precise amounts and specific order. He stressed the importance of intention. That wasn't a problem. She wanted to keep Sebastian at bay. When she finished, Doc handed her three tiny pouches. She filled them with the fragrant herbs and strung each pouch on a silk cord.

"Wear one next to your skin whenever you go out."

"To heck with that. I'm never going to take them off."

Doc laughed. "Do not wear them in your sleep."

"Why not?"

"Just trust me."

"You're going to make me figure out why on my own, aren't you?"

"What kind of teacher would I be if I gave you all the answers?"

"The kind whose classes were always full," she quipped.

"And whose students left having learned nothing," he countered.

She slipped one of the cords over her head before taking the others back to the booth. For a wonder, Jez did not lecture her about her foolish choices. Maybe she was too busy setting up for the weekend. Heather headed over to Jocko's place and let herself in when he didn't answer.

She found a notebook in the living room and tore off a sheet to leave him a note. *Off to see the Queen. Rehearsal at 4:30?* She paused, wondering if she should say anything else. She decided against it and signed the note with an H. She left it on the table, locked the door after her, and headed out. She ought to have asked Doc for a tincture to soothe nerves.

She found the stairs behind the gate by the perfumery. Brock looked up from his graphic novel, nodded to her, and trotted off to assure Darius that she was where she was expected. Not that the hulking blond said as much. Brock almost never spoke. Lew joked that the squire's tombstone would read Played Well Alone.

She paused at the top of the stairs. Ardyth opened the door wearing jeans and a pullover sweater, still every inch the Queen. She led the way into what she lightly referred to as the solar. Tapestries hung on three walls. Sunlight from a south-facing window fell across two overstuffed arm chairs. On the table between them was a large bowl filled with balls of yarn. More yarn spilled from a bag on the floor. Ardyth told her to have a seat then retreated to fetch some tea. She returned moments later, handed Heather a cup, and settled into the other chair.

"You look like a cat in a room full of rocking chairs." Ardyth laughed.

"I'm sorry. I guess I don't know what to expect."

"Tea, of course, and conversation." Ardyth tilted her head. "Though I suppose even that might cause a bit of anxiety, if you've been listening to any of the tales about how terribly frightening we Queens are."

Heather blushed.

"Ah, that explains it. Relax and enjoy your tea. I asked you here to apologize for a failing on my part, not to take you to task for anything you may have done."

"I don't understand."

"That is why I am apologizing. No one ever explained things to you, though Doc says you sought to remedy that on your own. You chose your mentor well. He knows more than anyone about being Tribe, with the possible exception of the Court, and I believe he may know more about some aspects than any of us. All the same, I am sorry it took so long for you to be properly educated about your new life."

"It's not your fault," Heather protested. "This is the first show we've done together."

"The Court is not confined to where we are currently performing. Someone ought to have noticed, and their failure to do so reflects badly on us all. Rest assured, that will be addressed." Ardyth's green eyes flashed with irritation.

"I don't want anyone to get in trouble because of me. I muddled through okay." Heather looked out the window. "Until now."

"Your compassion for people who have failed you is admirable."

"I don't like conflict. Which is sort of funny, considering that I love to fight."

"Choreographed fighting is a dance. Since it requires a determination to not injure your partner, merely make it seem as if you wish to, it is more an act of trust than anything else."

"That's what Cami said."

Ardyth's eyebrows raised. "Is it? Then she is coming along faster than I'd suspected. Thank you for telling me. I'm relieved to know she's mellowing a bit."

"I wouldn't go that far. She still wants to kill or maim most people she meets."

Ardyth laughed. "I doubt that will ever change, nor would I want it to. She is a rare individual, honest about her feelings regardless of how they are received."

"I have no idea why she decided to make friends with me," Heather admitted.

"Because you don't ask her to be anything she is not. That, too, is rare. I see it wherever you go. You are kind even to people who annoy you."

Heather shrugged. "I figure there must be a reason people are the way they are, so it seems unfair to judge them just because I don't know their story. Most people mean well."

"But not all." Ardyth's eyes narrowed. "Which, as you already suspect, is part of the reason I invited you here."

"Sebastian." Heather sighed. "Why won't he just leave me alone, so I can get on with my life?"

"Because he can't. Whatever he did to you when he gave you the Kiss, he did to himself. I suspect he enjoyed it a great deal more than you."

"That wouldn't be hard. It wasn't one of the better experiences I've had."

"I am going to guess it was the absolute worst." Ardyth's eyes darkened. "Which is another thing that must be addressed."

"I won't object if *he* gets in trouble," Heather said.

"I would imagine not. Until that can be arranged, however, we need to ensure that he does you no more harm."

"Darius is already having me shadowed. Short of locking me in a tower, I don't know what else you can do."

"We are, sadly, fresh out of towers." Ardyth smiled at her. "So I am afraid you will have to put up with guards of one sort or another until the end of the show."

"It's two weeks. I can deal with that. I just feel bad that people are taking time away from their own lives to watch over me."

"You get used to it. Eventually, you come to treasure their desire to see you safe."

"No offense, but I'd rather not have to discover that for myself." Heather sipped her tea. "What does Sebastian want from me, anyway? And how did you know what he's been doing?"

"The simple answer to the first question is that Sebastian wants power."

"Then he's going after the wrong girl. I am about as far down on the totem pole as a person can get. Heck, I don't even belong to any really popular clique. Aside from this meeting, and hanging out with Darius by the campfire, I haven't spent much time with, or even around, the Court. What could he possibly think I could do for him?"

"That brings us to the second question." Ardyth set down her cup. "Bear with me while I figure out how to answer it." She picked up her knitting.

Heather was not about to push. Well, any more than she had already. Jocko had been wrong about the Queen. She was just a really nice woman who wanted to make things right. Heather put her head back and closed her eyes.

Contentment washed over her, through her. This was the perfect place to sit and think. Or not think. She wished she didn't have to leave it. There was so much demanded of her out there. She didn't mind. It was part and parcel of who she was, but she sometimes longed for the freedom to do whatever she wanted without people wondering what it meant. Without having to explain it to the rest of the Court.

Heather's eyes flew open.

Ardyth was looking at her intently. "I love to knit. It gives me time to think."

"What just happened?"

"A cruel experiment. It seems I am going to spend a great deal of time apologizing to you."

"I did not just hear your thoughts." Heather shook her head. "That's not possible."

"No, you did not, and no, it is not. What you felt was a taste of what I feel. It's not so different from what we get from our audience."

"Yes, it was. That was way more intense. It was personal. How did you do that?"

"I didn't. You did." Ardyth finished the row and set aside her knitting.

Heather stared at her, unable to find the words for all the questions she had.

"You, my dear, awaken desire."

"I don't understand."

"What did you get from me?"

"That you want to be free," Heather answered as if compelled, "but not really. I don't know how to explain it."

"You don't have to. I know my own desires. What I didn't know, until now, was how your Talent works. It is one thing to know how to read what a person wants. It is another thing entirely to fulfill it."

"Still lost, here."

"The Kiss makes us more of what we are. You grant people more of what we need."

"But I didn't do anything for you."

"Oh, dear." Ardyth reached for her hand. "You don't know when you're doing it, do you? Because you do it all the time."

"Do what?"

"Try to make people happy. You give us what we need to feel better. For me, it was a sense of purpose and the realization of how strong I am. You didn't try to do that, because you didn't know it was what I needed. You just supplied it without thinking."

"That's a good thing, right?"

"A wonderful thing. I suspect most people don't realize you've done it. They just feel better after being with you."

Heather slumped with relief. "Okay. I can deal with that. I'm like the bluebird of happiness."

Ardyth laughed. "What a lovely way to put it."

"It's going to take me a while to wrap my head around this."

"Quite a long time, I should think. I wish I could give you that time."

Heather looked up. "I hear a 'but' in that statement."

"Indeed. If I am correct in my assessment of your Talent, you are in more danger from Sebastian than we believed."

The pieces fit together in Heather's mind with a horrifying click.

"Because what he wants more than anything else is power, and I give it to him without knowing it." She followed that thought down a darker path. "He can't be the only one who wants things that aren't necessarily good for other people."

"No."

"Great, from bluebird of happiness to demon summoner in less than thirty seconds." Panic threatened to overwhelm her. "What am I going to do? Can you tell me how to stop?"

"I don't think you can, nor do I think you should."

"I try to keep a positive outlook, but I know the world is full of terrible people. I don't think I can deal with knowing I made their twisted desires come true."

"It is not quite that powerful a Talent. But you do need to learn to control it."

"I can't very well stay away from people I don't know are good until that happens. We have a show tomorrow. The law of averages tells me some of the people who show up won't be very nice."

"You have lived for over a year with this Talent. Can you think of anything truly awful that has come of it?" Ardyth asked.

"Besides Sebastian stalking me? Not that I know of."

"Can you think of anyone whom you suspect has benefited from it?"

Heather thought instantly of the little girl with the fierce determination to become a warrior. And how safe Cami felt around her, Jezebel's finding a sense of home, Katie's new bravery. She nodded.

"Then I see no reason to lock yourself away. Be the bluebird. We will deal with any demons you may summon by accident. In the meantime, I believe you have a fight to rehearse."

Heather flinched. What did Jocko need from her? Was he like Sebastian, only interested in her for what she could bring him?

"Stop that!" The Queen's voice broke her reverie. "You are not to use the knowledge you have gained here to destroy the friendships you've built." It was a command, not a suggestion.

"I thought you said reading thoughts was impossible."

"Reading the fears of a young woman who suddenly has reason to doubt the world around her does not require clairvoyance. The wisdom that comes from watching people over many years suffices. There are only so many emotions, after all, and suspicion is a fairly common one."

"I'm sorry."

"No need to apologize. I've given you the second biggest shock of your young life and am now sending you out to do your job with no time at all to process the new information. It's a wonder you haven't been swearing at me for the past few minutes."

"I would never do that!" Heather protested. "Okay, I might do that to someone else, but not you."

Ardyth smiled. "Sometimes, it is good to be Queen."

Darius was coming up the stairs as Heather went down. He nodded to her but did not stop. Heather walked through the gate and turned to latch it.

"I have news, my love," Ardyth said. "Test results indicate a first blood situation. I thought you should know before I speak to anyone else."

"Please tell me it's not the old world strain."

Ardyth laid her hand on his cheek. "No, we'd have known sooner. You would have sensed it."

Heather frowned, hoping Ardyth wasn't sick. She decided to keep the conversation to herself, since it wasn't her business anyway. Besides, her life was messed up enough without being called out for eavesdropping on the Court.

CHAPTER TWENTY-ONE

The third time Heather missed a parry, Jocko took the sword out of her hand. "What's wrong with you?"

"Nothing." She reached for her sword.

He held it away from her. "We aren't going to run this again 'til I'm sure you're okay."

"I'm fine."

"No, you aren't. You don't make simple mistakes."

She glared at him. "Just spectacular ones, apparently."

"You planning on telling me what's up so we can get back to the fight, or are we going to run it cold for Lew in the morning?"

She shook her head. "That's not an option, and you know it."

"Then get it together."

"What do you want from me?" she asked.

"I want you to concentrate, so neither of us gets hurt."

"Fine. Give me back my sword and we'll do this right." Anger, more at herself than him, helped her focus. They ran the fight three times without error. He was willing to stop at two, but she wanted to prove to herself she could shove her problems to the back of her head and do the job. She pushed for a fourth run, but he refused.

"We'll do it again tomorrow, before meeting. Right now, I want to make you dinner."

"Why?"

"What kind of question is that? I want to feed you because I'm guessing you haven't eaten today. Your hands are shaking, and you're pale. I don't know what else might've caused it, and you don't have to tell me. But seeing as how you accepted that offer earlier today, I'd be obliged if you'd let me cook for you, so I can feel like I was of some use."

"Sorry. My manners are slipping. I'd love some dinner."

"You have nothing to apologize for." He put his arm around her shoulders and led her to his room.

Hunger hit with the warmth. She stumbled to the table and dropped into a chair. He put away the weapons, went to the fridge, and returned with a slice of cheese.

"Eat that. It'll bring your blood sugar up."

She forced herself to comply. He was right about it making her feel a little better, though taking the edge off her hunger brought back the ability to think. Better to watch him cook. He moved almost as fast as he did when they fought, a sure sign of worry.

He put a plate in front of her—spaghetti with meat sauce. She laughed.

"I know it's not fancy, but it was the quickest thing to make."

"It's perfect. This is one of my comfort foods." She finished half of it before she remembered to thank him.

"That's what friends are for," he said.

"Is that all we are?"

"It's a good place to start."

She set down her fork. "I think we moved beyond that, don't you?"

"We did, but I'm not going to assume that'll continue unless you tell me it's what you want."

"I have no idea what I want. Except sleep. A lot of sleep. And for this show to be over, so I can figure out what I'm going to do next."

He looked down. "You could sleep here. I'd keep you safe."

"Jez and Cami might have a fit if I don't check in."

"I could take care of that for you."

"I'm not sending you out in the cold when I'm perfectly capable of going myself."

He reached into his pocket, drew out his phone, and flipped it open. "Technology, darlin'. You should try it."

"Funny. Jez doesn't turn on her phone until the weekend, and I don't have Cami's new number."

"Got that covered, too." He dialed. "I've got her . . . yeah, all night."

She went to the door and turned the lock.

Jocko listened for a moment, the line of his jaw clenching along with his free hand. "You ever say anything like that again, we're going to dance."

The reply was loud enough for Heather to hear, if not the exact words.

"Don't know which part of that wasn't clear." He flipped the phone closed. It rang immediately. He shut it off.

"That was Darius." She wasn't asking. "And you just pissed him off. Again."

"Seems like."

"Most people avoid making him mad. He's not the kind of guy you want as an enemy."

"Neither am I," he stated flatly.

"Are you going to tell me what he said?"

"Best if I don't."

She didn't push. He cleared the table and cleaned up the dishes. When he got back, she was stretched out on the couch. He sat down, put her legs over his, took off her boots, and began rubbing her feet.

"Don't suppose you want to talk about your afternoon."

She shrugged. "The Queen wanted to warn me about Sebastian."

"Not like you needed much warning. I'm guessing that wasn't all she had to say."

"No, but I'm not ready to talk about the rest of it. I'm sorry. I don't even know what to think, much less what to say."

"You apologize too much." He smiled at her. "I don't need to know your business."

"What do you need?" she asked.

"To know you're safe."

"No, I meant what do you need in your life?"

"Nothing I don't have."

"That must be nice."

"Most of the time, it is. I'm a pretty simple guy."

She laughed. "Not buying that for a minute."

"It's true." He looked at her. "Always has been. Other people add complications, and I deal with those. Then I go back to being happy to fight, cook, travel, and meet people."

"And steal Kisses," she added.

"I don't steal them, sugar. I give them. It's not the same thing."

"I wish I'd met you before . . ." She looked away.

"So do I. But since we can't undo the past, only choice is to go forward." He pushed her feet off him. "Which tonight means getting you to bed."

"Very seductive." She grinned at him.

"You said you wanted to sleep. I have every intention of honoring your wishes."

"So you say."

He stood. "Trust me. I can control my desires. Even around you."

"I don't know whether to be impressed or disappointed."

"Why choose between them?" He picked her up and carried her to his room.

She tested his resolve by stripping down to her underwear before getting into bed. He watched with appreciation but didn't move. He undressed and joined her, put his hands behind his head, and closed his eyes.

"You could have stayed up," she said.

"I plan to. But I feel better knowing you're safe beside me, in case I do fall asleep."

"You're going to stay awake to watch over me?"

"Won't be the first time." He opened one eye and looked over at her. "But it's a lot more comfortable than huddling outside your booth."

"Sounds a little bit like stalking to me."

He chuckled. "Seemed a lot more like following orders from where I was standing."

She rolled onto her side and put her arm over his stomach, then traced the cut of his muscles.

He took one sharp breath, then breathed normally. "That doesn't count as sleeping, sugar."

She ran her hand over his hip. "I just want to see how much control you really have."

"Keep it up."

"I plan to." She proved her point. He showed remarkable restraint. She kissed her way from his chest to his stomach. He kept his hands under his head. She stripped off her underwear then straddled him.

"I know you want me," she purred. "It's hard to hide."

His eyes darkened as she rubbed against him. "Very hard."

"But you aren't going to make a move?"

"Nope."

"Very noble of you."

"I try."

She raised up on her knees, supporting her weight as she licked his nipples. He bit his lip to keep from making a sound. She flicked her tongue over his lips then lowered her mouth to his. As he opened to receive her kiss, she slid down on his swollen cock. He groaned into her mouth. She pulled back and grinned at him.

"I admire your control." She wriggled until he was as deep inside her as he could get.

"That's it," he growled. His hands went to her hips as he pushed up against her. He rolled her under him. "You are the most maddening woman I've ever known."

"That's working out well for me."

"But you aren't thinking straight." He grabbed a condom. "Sort of important, unless you want to stop and have a conversation right now."

She snatched it away from him and tore it open. "Talking is not what I want to do." She slid the condom over him, taking time to elicit a groan.

"I truly was going to let you sleep."

"Shut up and love me."

"Since you insist." He thrust into her. She wrapped her legs around him, taking him deeper. He captured her mouth, slowing until the rhythm of their bodies mirrored the languid exploration of the kiss. She reveled in his weight on top of her, the way he filled her, the small sounds he made. His jaw clenched, a sign he was holding back.

"Come for me," she whispered.

"Not yet." His response was strangled as she clenched around him.

"Let go," she coaxed. "Fill me. I want it."

He gave in, throwing his head back with a roar. She held him to her as her release followed, gentle, satisfying.

"Now I'm ready to sleep," she said. "And you can, too. I'm not going anywhere tonight. I promise."

"So do I." He locked his arm over her as they fell asleep.

After a quick breakfast, Jocko walked Heather home. They were past the point where gossip was a concern. It surprised her to discover she no longer cared what other people thought of their relationship, despite the fact that she wasn't sure of its parameters herself. They walked to the showers together. She refused to let him come in with her. They didn't need to be that public about it. Besides, there was nothing remotely romantic about shivering while the other person rinsed off. He was waiting for her when she got out, so he could walk her back to the shop and hand her off to Jezebel. She was beginning to understand the Queen's desire for freedom.

When she got to the morning meeting, Heather joined Cami at the edge of the circle.

"Darius is spitting nails," Cami whispered, ignoring whatever Bob was droning on about.

"What for?"

"He thinks Jocko's taking you for a ride." Cami looked up at her. "Which probably isn't far from the truth, if your smile is any indication."

"I'm the one who bought the express-ticket to damnation. And it's none of Darius' business."

"No, but that doesn't change anything. If you were smart, you'd smooth things over with him instead of digging in your heels."

It was sound advice. Unfortunately, Darius left as soon as the meeting was over, and Lew pulled her aside to run the fight. Satisfied, he sent her off to the front gate. At least during faire day, she didn't need bodyguards. During fights, she had Jocko and some of the Court. When she sang, the audience provided too many witnesses for Sebastian to attempt anything. She kept an eye out for him anyway.

The Queen showed up at Heather's final singing set. Her presence unraveled some of the fear Heather had carried all day. When Ardyth joined her for the last two songs, her spirit soared. She took from the crowd and gave back with joy. There would be no way to repay the Queen, but a single look from her said it would not be necessary.

Free for the rest of the afternoon, Heather decided to help Jezebel in the shop. Business was good, precluding conversation. Heather didn't mind.

Being with Jez was comforting, no matter what they were doing.

When the shop finally cleared out, Jez pulled out the stools and plopped down on one. "How has your day been?"

"Mostly good. You?"

"Profitable." Jez grinned.

"Excellent! Can we do dinner tonight or do you have plans with Rascal?"

"Dinner would be good. I have no idea what's up with Rascal."

Heather frowned. "Everything okay?"

"As far as I know. I told you it wasn't anything serious." Jez shrugged. "As opposed to what's going on with you and Jocko."

"I don't know if it counts as serious," Heather said. "I know better than to put too much stock in a faire fling."

"He's a decent guy," Jez said.

"I agree with you, obviously, but that's not what most people think."

"Gossips don't think. And he doesn't waste his time combating the rumors."

"You seem to know him pretty well, but I've never seen you hang out with him," Heather said.

"We don't cross paths that often. He was really nice to me when I was getting the business up and running. And when I got sick at one show, he took care of me. I wasn't supposed to tell anyone that. He doesn't want people to think he's nice."

"Why not?" Heather asked.

"Because he isn't always a nice guy, and it's easier if folks don't expect him to be."

"He's been nice enough to me."

Jez raised one eyebrow.

Heather blushed. "I meant before."

"I'm glad. I'd hate to have to change my opinion of him." Jez looked at her watch. "Aren't you going to the joust?"

"Nope. If I was sure that Darius would win, I might go to watch him run Sebastian through, but I don't think I could deal with watching Darius die at the Bastard's hand, even if it's fake."

"Fair enough. You can stay here with me and my nonexistent customers."

"I like the real ones better. They increase the chances you'll buy dinner." Heather laughed.

"Damn. Trouble approaching." Jez nodded to the side of the shop. Paula was headed their way, obviously in a hurry. She carried a dress over one arm.

"Jezebel." Paula nodded to her before turning to Heather. "I can't believe I'm saying this, but I need your help."

Heather's eyes narrowed. "With what?"

"Katie's not feeling well. She promised to be at the joust to give a favor. There's a bit that's supposed to happen at the end."

"Can't you do it?"

"No. Darius won't like it." Paula looked at her, pleading. "Please. I know we aren't friends, and I have no right to ask this of you, but I thought you might do it for Katie."

"I'll do it because you need help and said please."

Paula looked startled. "Oh."

"You can use the upstairs to change," Jez offered. "Heather's going to need assistance getting into the dress."

"Thank you." Paula led the way.

Heather looked back at Jez, who held up her hands and shrugged.

A few moments later, Heather came down the stairs wearing Katie's dress. It fit fairly well, but she still felt awkward. She had never realized how naked she felt without her weapons. She walked beside Paula, both of them suppressing giggles at the stunned looks they received from other participants.

When Heather lined up with the Court, the King frowned but said nothing. The Queen arched one eyebrow and inclined her head. There was no doubt in Heather's mind that another talk was coming. She glanced at Paula, who stared straight ahead. The Court took the dais. As the King and Queen sat, the trumpet blared. Heather jumped. She had never heard it so close.

Tyler raced up to the edge of the dais and held up a favor. Paula stepped forward to receive it. She turned, holding it out. Heather flinched back as if looking at a live snake. The favor was blue and white—Carter's colors. Except Carter was not riding.

"Take it," Paula hissed.

"You said Darius . . ."

Paula cut her off. "I said he wouldn't let me do it. It's no big deal. At the end of the joust, Sebastian will ask you to go with him. You can tell him to get stuffed. It was supposed to be Carter's bit with Katie and be all lovey, but do whatever feels right to you."

Sebastian was going to win. Bile rose in Heather's throat. "You do realize I'm going to kick your ass when no one is looking, right?"

"I'm just the messenger. Please, just do this so we don't screw up the show."

Heather snatched the favor out of Paula's hand. "Fine, but you owe me. Huge."

"I know. I'll make it up to you."

The knights rode in. Heather's stomach clenched when she saw Sebastian. He was, as always, the picture of nobility. The crowd cheered for him, fooled by his beauty into thinking he was the good guy he portrayed. She wanted nothing more than to wipe that charming smile from his face.

The King stood to read out the charges to be settled by a joust to the death. He didn't have to fake his irritation. He had not missed the favor being handed to Heather. Rodney looked at Paula when he read the charge of "conduct unbefitting a member of the nobility." She shrank back. He finished his proclamation and called for the knights to seek the favor of a lady. They rode to their ends of the field to receive favors from patrons then both returned to the dais.

The Queen stood, holding out a favor in green and black. Darius lowered his lance to receive it.

"I am surprised you allowed this," she said, smiling for the crowd.

"It was not my doing, your Majesty," Darius replied.

"It may yet be your undoing," she warned.

Heather stepped forward to tie the favor on Sebastian's lance. She kept her gaze on her hands.

"May this be the first of many favors," he said.

She smiled sweetly. "Drop dead, you rotten bastard." She didn't care if the audience nearby heard.

"Not today, love. I will come for you after I dispatch Lord Darius. Be ready."

"You'll be disappointed."

"With you? Impossible."

The King spoke softly so the crowd could not hear. "I will see you both about this, as soon as the show closes." The knights nodded and withdrew.

The knights bowed their heads as the blessing was given. Darius could have burned holes in the ground with his eyes. His jaw was set, nostrils flaring. He wheeled his horse around and headed for Fox, who backed away with his hands in the air. Darius snarled, and the squire snapped back into place and handed him a lance.

Both lances shattered on the first pass. By the way it snapped, Heather knew that Darius' lance had not been scored to break. He snatched the second lance and had it lowered before Sebastian reached mid-field. That one broke, too. Sebastian rocked back but didn't lose his seat. As he rode down on Darius for the final pass, he slipped his feet from the stirrups. Darius' blow sent him flying further than usual. Sebastian hit the ground hard. Heather hoped the fall bruised him to the bone. She was disappointed when he proved hale enough to rise quickly.

Darius rode down on Sebastian, lance lowered. He practically threw himself from his horse when Sebastian grabbed the lance. Darius held his hand up for his sword and caught it without bothering to turn. Sebastian barely had time to receive his own sword before Darius was upon him.

"You will suffer!" Darius did not hold back on his swing.

"Not today!" Sebastian answered as he parried. His laughter sent a chill through Heather.

The fight was more real than anyone in the audience realized. Sparks flew as they traded blows, a sure sign they were dangerously close to losing control. Neither would abandon the choreography, but it was a near thing. Darius' eyes held murder, and if thousands of people had not been watching, the end of the fight would likely have been much different. Sebastian's killing blow left a line on Darius' neck. Blood dripped between his fingers as he fell to the ground, body still trembling. Only those on the reviewing stand knew it was due to his effort to restrain himself.

Sebastian called for his horse, his crowd on their feet, cheering. He rode to the dais. Heather stepped back.

Paula shoved her forward. "It's almost over. Just play along, and everything will be fine."

"There won't be enough makeup to cover what I'm going to do to you,"

Heather promised.

Sebastian brought his mount alongside the dais. "A kiss, my lady?" he called. The crowd roared.

Heather leaned over so he could hear her. "I'd rather kiss a pig."

"So I observed." His arm shot out and wrapped around her. He pulled her onto the saddle in front of him. She struggled, but he locked his arm around her. "Play nice, sweetheart. Give the audience what they want."

She felt sick, hearing Jocko's words coming from his lips.

The King and Queen had risen to their feet but were powerless to stop Sebastian as he rode around the field, holding Heather tightly to him. The squires opened the gate, and the horse made a bee-line for home. Sebastian smiled broadly for the crowd as he raced up the chute.

"Let me go," Heather snapped. "Now!"

"Soon. It wouldn't be safe here." He pulled her closer. "We wouldn't want anything bad to happen to you."

"You should be more worried about your own safety," she ground out. "Jocko is going to freak when he hears about this."

"Do you think he actually cares for you? I thought you had more sense than that."

"Like you're any judge of quality. Besides, you're the one who left me to suffer, remember? So if you'll just let me down—again—I'll be on my way."

"You don't want me to do that." His voice was soothing, rich. She felt the pull of it, but it didn't sway her.

"I really do."

"As you wish, my lady. Here we are." He lowered her to the ground by the stables.

Carter stood and limped toward them. His blue eyes were wide and full of suspicion. "Where's Katie?"

"She couldn't make it, cousin. Heather graciously agreed to take her place. I'm afraid she was not as pleased as that slip of a girl with the terrible crush on you might have been." Sebastian dismounted and tossed his reins to Brock. "I must go work the crowd." He turned to Heather. "May I walk you out?"

"You can die in a pit," she said.

"Perhaps another day." He gave her a mocking bow and went out to meet the inevitable bevy of women who waited by the gate after the final joust.

Carter unclenched his fist and turned to Heather. "I'm so sorry. I worked out that bit before I got hurt. I was hoping . . . never mind what I hoped."

"It wasn't your fault. Nothing came of it." Heather sighed. "But I really want to get out of this dress. I'm going to check on Katie and give her back her clothes."

"Tell her if there's anything she needs, I've got the truck keys, and I'll be glad to run into town for her."

"I'll do that." Heather turned away.

Carter laid a hand on her arm. "You sure you aren't mad at me?"

"Not even a little. To prove it, I'll take you out to lunch this week, my treat. If Katie's feeling better, I'll ask her to come along."

"I'd really like that." Carter smiled at her and for once, there was nothing in it but friendship.

CHAPTER TWENTY-TWO

Heather stopped by the booth to grab a change of clothes. She promised Jez a full run down of what had happened at the joust then headed over to the shop where Katie was staying. The heavy gown dragged at her.

The ladies in the henna booth waved at Heather as she walked past. She slipped around the back of the shop and went up the stairs. A muffled sound greeted her knock, which she took as permission to enter. She followed the sound down a hall and found Katie in a small room. She was in bed, with the covers pulled up to her neck.

"Hey, girl. You okay? I came to return the dress. I think I can get out of it myself, so you can stay in bed if you aren't feeling good."

"Heather, please, go." Katie cried.

"I'm not going to catch whatever it is from over here. Besides, there's no way I can make it across site again in this dress. I don't know how you do it." She reached behind her and untied the laces. The dress was a little large, so she was able to shimmy out of the top without much problem.

"Go, now!" Katie begged.

"That would hardly do." Sebastian stepped into the room and closed the door. "I went to so much trouble to arrange this."

Heather whirled and almost tripped over the skirt. "What the hell are you doing here?"

"Getting back what is mine." He looked at her as if she were a horse at auction.

"Piss off."

"Your manners reflect the company you've been keeping. That will have to change." He reached for her.

She stumbled back. "Don't touch me."

"Oh, I plan to do more than touch you, and the beauty of it is, you will ask me to. Beg me, in fact."

"Fat chance."

In one stride, he closed the distance between them. He grabbed her arm, spun her around, and pushed her against the wall. The rough wood scratched her cheek. He pulled her wrists behind her and bound them, then stepped away from her.

"Would you like to see how it works?" he asked. "It only seems fair, since it was you who gave me this gift."

Katie cowered on the bed, tears forming. Heather blinked. Katie hadn't moved the whole time. Her stomach turned as she realized that Katie, too, was a prisoner.

"Leave her alone," Heather spat.

"Why? She's fond of me." He stroked Katie's cheek. She relaxed and rubbed against his hand. "Tell me, sweet girl, what do you want?"

"You." Katie looked up at him with adoration.

"And how will you prove that to me?"

"However you want." She licked her lips.

"Good girl. I may keep you as a pet. You like it when I stroke you, don't you?" He ran his hands over the blankets covering her.

She wriggled, straining against her bonds. "Yes."

"See how easy that is?" Sebastian turned to Heather. "I expect the same from you. I may keep the two of you, so there is a witness to how completely you each consent."

"You son of a bitch." It came out weaker than expected.

"I don't like that title nearly as much as Master." He pushed her back against the wall. "Say it for me." He stroked her injured cheek.

Again, the pull of his voice settled over Heather. She closed her eyes. It didn't work as it had at the dance. She took a shaky breath. "Master," she whispered.

"That does wonderful things to me," he murmured, pressing against her.

She was grateful the gown hanging from her hips kept their bodies apart.

"Giving you the Kiss awoke such things in me, created a hunger only you can sate. I cannot wait to see what I can take when I'm inside you."

She fought against the terror of that image, grasping for something to distract him. "I don't want to share you," she said in a rush.

He chuckled. "But you will. You will do whatever I wish you to and gladly."

"Yes."

Released from his spell, Katie stared at her, pale and shaking. Heather hoped she would stay quiet.

"Good girl. How delightful it will be when the Sword-Breaker realizes you've thrown him over for me. There won't be a thing he can do about it, once you tell him it was all your idea. I look forward to his impotent anger. It's a shame I won't be able to taste it." He thought for a moment. "Unless, of course, Paula is right and his vaunted immunity slips when he's around you. Breaking him with the help of his lover would be delicious irony, don't you think?" He rubbed his hand over her breasts. They responded despite her revulsion.

"I'm going to leave, now that I know you will be safe here, waiting for me to return. The weakling who stands for a King wants to chastise me for ill-using you. Poor fool." Sebastian locked eyes with her, his voice taking on the edge of power. "Don't call out. Don't try to leave. I will find you and punish you." His smile chilled her blood. "You will like that, as well, but only during."

"I'll wait for you." She returned the kiss he gave her but imagined biting off his tongue.

"Of course you will." He laughed. "Soon, I won't need to use my Talent. You will come to me freely. With you in thrall, the Court will be forced to remember what we truly are. Then we can feed with abandon." He stroked her cheek, smiling when she flinched in pain. He kissed her again and left.

Heather began working at the knot before Sebastian's footsteps had faded. She explored the shape, imagining it flat, like the ribbon. It proved quite a bit tighter than Jocko's playful bindings.

"What are we going to do?" Katie's panic filled the room.

Heather closed her eyes and drank it in, stuffing her guilt firmly in the back of her mind. "We're going to get the hell out of here. Can you move your hands at all?"

"No. He tied them down tight. I can hardly feel them."

"Damn." Heather twisted her wrist. She winced as the rope scraped against her skin. She looked at Katie. The woman needed a distraction or her panic would choke them both. "What did Sebastian mean when he called Jocko a Sword-Breaker?"

"Sword-Breakers are the people who dispense Court justice. They break the bond to the Tribe."

"How?"

"I don't know. There are only a handful of them, and only the Court knows who they are. The Broken never remember who did the Breaking."

"Then Sebastian could be wrong." Heather worked the end of the rope back and forth.

"I hope so," Katie said.

"If he's doing what the Court asks, I don't see the problem."

"If it gets out that Jocko is a Sword-Breaker, a lot of people would go after him."

"And do what?" One loop loosened, but not enough.

"Kill him," Katie whispered. "Or try, anyway. You have to figure Sword-Breakers are good enough to overcome whatever Talent is thrown their way, so removing them isn't easy."

"What does someone have to do to get the Court to send a Sword-Breaker after them?" Heather ignored the pain, focusing on moving the rope back and forth.

"It has to be pretty bad. Theft will get you banished, and no one will hire you ever again, but that's basic justice. Hurting children is a Breaking offense. Rape or the giving of a Kiss to an unwilling Tribe member, which is pretty much the same thing, will get you Broken."

Something Jocko had said came back to her. "What happens if you give a Kiss to someone who's already Tribe?"

"Lots of things can happen. You could both end up being stronger. You could bond for life. One or the other could be drained beyond repair. Or go crazy. Not that I see much difference between the two. It's one of the few rules for being Tribe. You don't give the Kiss to another Tribe member.

You're not even supposed to Kiss Mundanes more than once, though it has happened, if someone didn't realize the person had been Kissed before."

"What happens to the Mundanes?" Skin tore from her wrist as she tried to keep the end of the rope from slipping out of her grip.

"They get addicted to it. Their mark becomes masked, so we don't recognize them. Then they seek out Tribe for Kisses over and over until they're so weak they can hardly stand. Sometimes, they pass the addiction back to one of us. That's when it gets really ugly. The hunger becomes insatiable."

"How are we supposed to know who has been Kissed and who hasn't?" The end of the rope slipped through the loop, but the knot still did not give.

"There's just something about Mundanes who have already been tagged. Like a low-level hum. Haven't you noticed?"

"I've never done it," Heather admitted.

"You're kidding! Why not?"

"My experience being on the receiving end was horrible. Why would I do that to someone else? Did you actually like it?" Heather asked.

"There are no words sufficient to describe how amazing it was." Katie looked away. "I'm sorry. That was thoughtless."

"Don't be. I'm relieved to know you didn't suffer what I did." The other end of the rope refused to move.

"It's supposed to be a gift, whether the person turns Tribe or not. We give first then take. It's not supposed to hurt."

"I don't know that the Tribe can control it as well as they'd like us to believe. Then again, since Sebastian has proven to be a sadistic megalomaniac who enjoys rape, I guess we do put who we are into it."

As the idea sank in, Katie's fear rose. Heather let it build then siphoned it off. Katie didn't notice. *Great, use her like the monster I am.* She decided to wrestle with her conscience after they were free.

"I hope Jocko is a Sword-Breaker so he can snap Sebastian in two. Come to think of it, he might just kill him." Heather liked that idea a little too much.

"That would not be good," Katie said.

A push at the end of the rope, just enough to give her hope. "I'm thinking it would be just fine."

"No, because then the Court would have to Break him, too," Katie explained. "And considering how rare Sword-Breakers are and how difficult to fight off, it would be a total mess."

"Then there's the whole prison thing." Blood welled up from one of the raw spots.

Katie shook her head. "I don't think that would be an issue."

"They tend to put people away for murder."

"They need a live body for that. The Court doesn't screw around when it comes to murder. They'll turn someone over for rape, after they have them Broken, but murder is dealt with in very . . . medieval ways."

She couldn't tell Jocko what had happened. Someone would, though. Her head pounded. She clenched her teeth and concentrated on the knot. It was coming undone, but she didn't know if she would be free before Sebastian returned. The thought of him touching her again made her ill, but better her than Katie. No matter what happened afterward, she had to get them out of the room. She prayed that Rodney kept Sebastian and Darius talking for a long time. Long enough for Jezebel to worry about where she was, just in case she proved unable to defeat her bindings. Of course, Jez would probably go straight to Jocko. It seemed there was no way out of her predicament that did not saddle her with another one. Given the choice, she would opt for the lesser of two evils. Much lesser.

The knot finally gave. Heather pushed the ends of the rope through until it was loose enough for her to shake free. She stripped out of the dress, pulled her knife from her boot and went to free Katie. When she pulled back the covers, Katie flinched. She was completely naked.

"Did he . . ." Heather couldn't finish. She cut the rope.

"No. Well, yes, what you saw, which isn't as bad, but it's bad enough." Tears fell. "I let him strip me without protesting. I would have . . . I couldn't fight . . ." Katie couldn't finish either.

"Jocko may not have the chance to kill him. If I see him first, I'll do it myself." Heather released the drawstring on the neck of the under-dress and stepped out of it. She grabbed her clothes and got dressed.

"Don't go near him!" Katie's voice was muffled by the shirt she was pulling over her head.

"Not without heavy weapons and back up." Heather jammed her feet into her boots.

"You saw what he could do. You wouldn't have a chance. He'd make you want him."

"It didn't work on me. I was pretending."

Katie stared at her, then shook herself and finished getting dressed. "How did you manage that?"

Heather took off the amulet and handed it to Katie. "Put this on. I have others. I'm taking you straight to Doc. Tell him what happened."

"I don't think I can." Katie looked at the floor.

"He's a doctor. You can't shock him, and he won't shame you. He'll know what to do. You can stay in the sick room tonight. You'll be safe there."

"Where are you going?"

"Home." Heather led the way down the stairs, pausing to make sure Sebastian was not lurking. The ladies in the Henna booth looked up then went back to cleaning their shop, completely unaware of the trauma above the stairs.

Heather escorted Katie to Doc's. "Tell him everything." She shoved Katie into the shop. Doc looked up, startled, and came around the counter. "Listen to her. Do what you have to. I'll be at Jezebel's."

Heather ran full out across the site. People called to her, but she didn't look to see who they were. As fast as she ran, it still felt like she was pushing through a wall of gelatin. Nightmares had nothing on the events of the afternoon.

She burst into the shop, slammed the door shut, and slid the bolt home. Jezebel came running from her room. Heather took one look at her and burst into tears. Jez wrapped her in a hug and did not let go until she had stopped shaking.

"Do you want to tell me what happened?"

Heather hiccupped. "Sebastian."

"Well, yeah, honey, I figured. But what, exactly?"

"He planned to rape me. He kidnapped Katie." Heather wasn't going to say more than that.

"What?" Jezebel yelled. "Does Darius know?"

"I doubt it. They're currently meeting with the King. Or I hope they are."

Jez paced across the room. "You have to tell someone."

"I left Katie with Doc. I figure he knows the proper channels."

"You should tell Jocko."

"No!" Heather clenched her fists until her nails bit into her hand. "If I tell him, he'll go after Sebastian and then he'll be the one in trouble, and the Bastard will walk free."

"He's going to find out."

"I know, but if the Court is already dealing with it, then he won't interfere." She hoped that was true.

Jez put her hands on her hips. "And when he realizes you didn't tell him yourself? What then?"

"I guess we have a fight."

"You need to go to him."

"I told you I can't tell him."

"Then don't. But I can't protect you, honey. Not against Sebastian." The pain of the admission was clear in Jezebel's tone.

"I don't even know if Jocko is on site."

Jezebel pulled out her cell phone, turned it on, and shook her head as she dialed. "I'm buying you a phone on Monday. Your stubborn refusal to have one has to end."

Heather went to pack a bag. She looked around her room with sorrow. Even this little bit of home had been taken from her. She wanted to stay, to sleep in her own bed and wake up with everything back to normal. She slipped another amulet over her neck and tucked it in under her shirt.

"Jocko is coming over, so you don't have to walk there alone." Jezebel stood in the doorway. "I'm sorry. I wish I could keep you safe."

"So do I. But I'm not going to put you in danger."

"The danger doesn't end because you aren't here," Jez said softly. "I'll call Rascal and see if he's willing to camp out on the couch." Her reluctance was obvious. "Cami went to dinner with Gregor and his staff. I don't know when, or if, she's coming home."

"Call Lew. He would stay, and he wouldn't expect anything in return. Except maybe dinner."

Jez swore. "I was going to take you to dinner. Maybe Jocko would come along."

Heather shook her head. "I'm not hungry. I just want to go to sleep."

Jez cocked her head. "Why do you think Lew would come?"

"Because he doesn't have that many women who just want to hang out with him. It would make him happy to be your hero. And he's pretty sure you'd kick his ass if he tried anything." Heather smiled for the first time since she'd left the shop that afternoon. "He's a good guy, despite his swagger."

"Yeah, but he'd die a little inside to hear you say that."

"I wouldn't do that to him. He's my friend, too." Heather thought for a moment. "Don't tell him about Sebastian, okay? I don't know how Lew feels about him, and I'd rather this stay quiet for as long as possible."

"Don't worry. I'll make up a reason for him to come over."

The knock on the door made Heather jump. She swore under her breath as Jezebel went to answer it. She let Jocko in. Heather walked out carrying her bag and costume.

"I hope you don't mind me inviting myself over."

"Of course not. I'd have asked you myself, but I couldn't find you after the show."

"I went to check on Katie. I took her to Doc's because she wasn't feeling well."

"That was good of you." Jocko reached for her bag.

Heather flinched when the strap scraped against her wrist. She tugged the cuffs of her sweatshirt further down and followed him out with one last look at Jez. The sadness in her smile was heartbreaking.

They didn't speak as they walked across site. Jocko let her into his room, took one look around outside, then closed and locked the door. He put her bag by the couch and hung her costume on a peg next to his. She stood in the kitchen, not knowing what to do. He pulled out a chair for her and went to the fridge.

"I'm not hungry." The words were hollow, lifeless.

"Then you don't have to eat. Won't stop me from cooking." He prepared a meal with none of the usual light banter. She stared at the table, not seeing it. The scene in Katie's room played in her head with endless variations of "what if?" appended. Closing her eyes did not help. Every sound from the kitchen made her jump.

Jocko put a plate in front of her. She looked up at him and frowned.

"I said I wasn't hungry."

"Thought you might have changed your mind. I'm not going to force you to eat, but it doesn't seem right to eat in front of you without at least offering you something."

"Thanks." The smell of garlic and ginger wafted up from the plate. If her stomach weren't tied in knots, she would gladly eat.

He ate half his dinner before pushing the plate away. "So, I heard about this afternoon."

Her eyes widened, breath coming too fast. She struggled to calm down. "What did you hear?"

"That Sebastian kidnapped you from the joust field. Carter assured me that he let you go by the stable, but I'm still considering kicking his ass."

"Let it go. He didn't get what he wanted from me. I'm pretty sure Rodney is reading him the riot act right now."

"Doesn't change the fact that he upset you."

"I'm fine," she lied.

"Is that why you've lost your appetite?"

"Part of it. I just wasn't expecting to have to come in contact with him, considering how hard Darius has tried to keep that from happening."

"Come to that, Darius might take Sebastian out before I get the chance."

"Let him. Let the Court deal with it." She picked at the food in an effort to mollify him.

"I will, for now. Not going to make any promises for the long run."

"Please." She looked at him. "I don't want to cause trouble."

"Darlin', you are nothing but trouble," he said.

She nodded and looked down at the table. "I know, and I'm sorry."

"Why are you sorry?" He tilted her head up. "I like trouble, especially the sort you bring. Just not the kind that's come down on you lately."

She gasped when he laid his hand on her wrist. His eyes narrowed. She tried to pull away, but he grabbed her hand and shoved the sweatshirt back. A low growl came from deep in his throat.

"What is this?"

She searched for a suitable lie, cursing herself for not having thought up something sooner. "I got my hand caught in the reins."

"I see." He cleared his plate and came back for hers. When he reached for it, he took her other hand and pulled back the sleeve. "Both of them?"

"I . . ." She had nothing.

"Those aren't leather burns, sugar. Those are rope burns. So why don't you tell me why it was I couldn't find you after the joust?"

"Leave it alone." She pulled her cuffs down.

"Like hell." He paced across the kitchen, fists clenched. "I'm going to kill him."

"No, you aren't."

He stopped, glaring at her. "What's to stop me? Why do you want to?"

"Because if you leave to find him, I'm going to be alone, and he knows just where to look for me. Knowing him, it's exactly what he's waiting for."

"What did he do to you?" He braced himself, afraid to hear her answer.

"Not what he wanted to. I got away when he left to see the King." She looked up at him. "Thank you for making that possible."

"What did I do?"

"You taught me how to untie knots."

He began pacing again. "Oh, yeah. I'm definitely going to kill him."

"Since I obviously can't stop you, would you at least be willing to wait until morning? I'm really tired, and I'm freaked out, and I don't think I can take any more drama tonight." She wiped away her tears with the back of her hand and hissed as her shirt rubbed on her wrist.

"Stay put." He went to the back of the shop. She kept her eyes on the door, terrified Sebastian would appear.

Jocko came back a few minutes later with a first aid kit. "Take off the sweatshirt."

She struggled out of it, biting back a curse whenever the fabric touched a raw spot. He applied an ointment and wrapped gauze around her wrists, securing it with tape. Then he put a salve on her cheek without asking for further details.

"We'll cancel the fights tomorrow if you can't do them."

"No way," she protested. "He doesn't get to take that from me, too."

"What did he take?"

She laughed, bitter. "What didn't he take? First, he takes my plans for my life. Then he rides back in and takes this one, too. I was finally beginning to feel like I belonged here. Like I was home. And now there's nowhere I can go where I feel safe."

"You're safe with me," Jocko said softly. "You always have been."

"I know, and I appreciate that." She put her hand over his. "But I don't think you're safe with me around."

"How do you figure?"

"He thinks he can use me to get to you. He said when I'm near you, you're vulnerable, and it won't matter that you're a Sword-Breaker."

Jocko pulled away from her, his chair falling over as he stood. "What did you just say?" he hissed. His face was a rigid mask as he regarded her, all warmth gone from his eyes.

"I . . . it was just something he said. I didn't mean—"

"What you meant doesn't matter," he snapped. "Just saying it was enough."

Anger flooded her. "I'm not the one who came up with it, so getting mad at me seems sort of pointless, don't you think?"

"If you know what I am, why did you come here?"

"What kind of a question is that? Is knowing—which , by the way, I didn't until just now—supposed to change how I feel about you?"

"Yes."

"Sorry to disappoint you, but I don't really care all that much. What you do for the Court is none of my business. If I were you, I'd be a lot more concerned about the fact that both Sebastian and Paula have figured it out. I'm not a threat to you. They are."

"Everyone is now. Everyone."

CHAPTER TWENTY-THREE

Heather hadn't thought she could feel any lower. Jocko didn't trust her to keep his secret. She stood and put her sweatshirt back on. If he could cut ties that easily, she would have to do the same. She just wished it didn't hurt so much. She retrieved her bag and set it on the table. He watched her without a word. When she shrugged into her coat, his eyes narrowed. She left her costume where it hung. It was no longer important. Nothing was, but a change of underwear would come in handy. She picked up her bag and headed for the door.

"What do you think you're doing?" he asked.

"Leaving," she said. "I thought that would be obvious."

"You can't."

"Watch me." She walked past him.

"I won't let you." He grabbed her arm.

She whirled on him, breaking free. "You'd damn well better. Being stuck in a room with a guy who expects me to do what he says, just because he says it, should only happen once per day."

"Don't you dare compare me to him!"

"Then stop acting like you can control me," she snapped. "I've had as much of that as I can take."

"What I want is to keep you safe."

"Really. Considering you just made it clear that you think I'm a threat to you, I don't see why you'd bother."

"Where would you go?" he asked.

She put her hand on the doorknob. "Home."

"You'd put Jezebel in danger just because you're mad at me?"

She looked over her shoulder at him. "No. I'm going to get in my truck, drive until I find an all-night coffee shop, get the biggest espresso they have, and hop on the highway. I'm not going to stop until my mom opens the door and asks me why I'm there. Along the way, I'm going to come up with an explanation that won't freak her out entirely or land me in the nuthouse." She opened the door.

His hand shot out and closed it. "Wait."

He was too close, too fast. She couldn't win. Her heart pounded, and she fought the urge to vomit. Fear brought rage. She seized it and held on.

"Wait for what? For Sebastian to stake out my truck? For you to talk me out of it?" She glared at him.

"For me to get my coat on so I can walk you to your car." Resignation covered his anger but didn't hide it.

"Fine."

"Just one question before you go. Does Sebastian have your parents' address?"

She paled. She had sent the Bastard a Christmas card out of spite. "Yes." It was barely a whisper. She dropped her bag and covered her face with her hands.

"Then that won't work." He pulled a pencil from a drawer and began writing. He tore off the page and handed it to her.

"What is this?"

"My sister's address in New Orleans. I'll call her to let her know you're coming. You can figure out what to do from there."

"Why would you do this? And why would she take me in? She doesn't know me."

"I told you, I want you to be safe. Gabrielle will take care of you until you find your feet. She's good people. So good she won't even tell me where you decide to go next. You'll like her. She thinks I'm a jackass, too."

"Is she Tribe?"

"Of a different sort." He shrugged. "But there's plenty of Tribe in New Orleans, even now. You'd do okay there if you decided to stay."

She sighed. "I'd like to meet your sister, if only so she can tell me embarrassing stories about you as a kid."

He snorted. "She will, guaranteed."

"It would be so much more satisfying if you were there. I don't think I've ever seen you blush."

"Now, that's just cruel." He sobered. "I can't come with you. For one thing, Darius would hunt me down and kill me. Well, try anyway."

"Don't say that!"

"Relax, the old man's got nothing on me." It was a suicidal notion. No one beat Darius unless it was choreographed that way.

Heather frowned. "He's going to be really mad if I take off."

"I'd worry more about the Queen, if I were you. She won't be happy to know Sebastian won, even if you are out of his reach."

"Sebastian wins either way. If I stay, you and I are both in danger."

"I'm going to have to deal with him whether you're here or not. Once I tell the Court what happened to you—"

She cut him off. "Katie took care of that."

"What does Katie have to do with this?" he asked.

"She was there. Sebastian used her as bait. I'm guessing it was Paula's idea, since she's the one who set me up at the joust." Heather sighed, resigned. "I can't leave yet. I have to beat the crap out of Paula, or I won't be able to live with myself."

"I'll gladly do that for you," he said darkly.

"Oh, no. That's one fight I get to handle on my own. Her, I can take."

"I'd put money on you against just about anyone."

"Except you," she pointed out.

"I don't know. You could probably take me if you had a mind to."

She snorted. "Please, I can't even win an argument with you."

"Were we arguing?"

She shoved him. "How do you do that?"

"Do what?"

"Get me to stop hating you."

"Aw, you never hate me, darlin'. I just piss you off."

"Constantly," she agreed.

"Since it seems you're not running off into the night, we might as well get to bed."

She shook her head. "I'm sleeping on the couch."

"If you sleep on the couch, I have to sleep on the floor. I'm not letting you out of my sight."

"Guess it's a good thing you have a rug then, huh?"

"Have some pity, woman."

"Fine, I'll sleep in your bed." She met his gaze. "But that's all I'm doing."

"Whatever my lady wishes." He bowed to her.

She slapped him on the back of the head, picked up her bag, and went to bed. She lay there, listening to the clank of dishes as he cleaned up the dinner she hadn't eaten. When he walked into the room, she tensed. He took off his shoes, then sat at the foot of the bed and regarded her.

She sat up and crossed her arms over her chest. "You planning to stare at me all night? Because it could get a little creepy."

"When I was a kid, I took in a lot of stray dogs. Made my momma crazy with it, but we had the space to keep them out back, so she let me."

She sucked in a breath. "If you're comparing me to a dog, I'm leaving."

"Best get up, then." He smiled at her. "But I'd rather you hear me out. See, there were some dogs that came along fine, happy to have someone to look after them. They were easy to keep, but we found them good homes. There were lots more that were hurt, or scared, or downright mean. Now, I knew they couldn't have started out that way. Something bad had happened to them. Maybe a lot of people hurt them, or maybe it was just one person over a long time. Whatever it was, they were broken inside. Might seem strange, but I liked those dogs better. They needed me. No matter how many times they tried to bite me, I didn't strike back. They expected pain or neglect. That was just about the saddest thing I could imagine, so I did everything I could to convince them that life didn't have to be that way." He paused. "When I first met you, you were like those dogs—cautious and a little mean. I figured with a bit of time, we could get to be friends."

"I thought we were," she said.

"Me, too. But when I walked in here just now, you flinched like those dogs used to. I need you to know that I won't lift a hand to hurt you, but I don't know if anything I say will convince you right now."

"Right back at you," she said.

He looked startled.

"You got those dogs to come around because you showed them that you were a good guy. Eventually, you trusted them not to bite you. I don't get the benefit of the doubt, apparently, so it shouldn't come as a surprise that I'm a little reluctant to lick your hand just because you fed me and gave me a warm place to stay. There's more than one way to hurt someone."

He winced. "I deserved that."

"Tell you what, you get over the fact that I know what you do with your Talent and accept that I have no intention of telling anyone else about it. I'll try to remember that not all men are manipulative assholes. How's that for a start?"

"Pretty good, except that most men are manipulative, especially when it comes to women, and I can't claim to be noble in that regard. But I can promise that I will never touch you if you don't want me to."

"No, you can't. If our recent history is any indication, we're going to poke, and prod, and shove, and grab each other when we fight. And we are going to fight. I will accept a promise that you won't force or coerce me to do anything I don't want to do, even if you think it's for my own good."

He sighed. "Had to add that last part in there, didn't you?"

"Yep. Just because you think something is good for me, doesn't mean it is. I may not know all the dangers inherent in this life—or in hanging out with you, for that matter—but I will not tolerate being expected to go along with anything just because you say so."

"I suppose there's nothing for it but to agree to your terms."

"Sure there is. We can go back to being no more than fight partners. I don't want to give that up. It's the one thing that works right most of the time."

"Maybe you could do that," he said. "I'm not sure I could. I'm always going to want to protect you, to talk to you, hold you, make you crazy."

"The last is sort of a given," she said wryly.

"Works both ways, sugar."

"Since we've reached détente, at least, and possibly approached some sort of accord, can I please go to sleep?"

"Go ahead. I'll stay here and make sure nothing happens to you."

"Don't be an idiot. You aren't a dog, and I don't expect you to curl up at my feet and pretend you are one. Go read a book or whatever it is you do when I'm not here."

"Mostly what I do is try not to think about what I would do if you were here," he admitted.

She rolled her eyes. "If that was supposed to be sweet, you missed."

"Don't I get points for honesty?"

"Yes, you do. Now, go about your business so I can sleep."

He stretched out next to her, on top of the blankets. "Keeping you safe is my business now. So if you don't mind, I'll just lay here and think of ways to do that."

"Suit yourself," she said, snuggling down under the covers.

His low whisper came as sleep claimed her. "Would if I could, sugar."

They woke up early, determined to get hot showers. As a mark of how deep her paranoia had set in, she let him come in and wait while she showered, then did the same for him. He was good enough to turn his head while she stripped and got dressed. She wasn't so good.

"Hardly fair, darlin'," he said, stepping into the shower.

"Never said I played fair, did I?" She twisted her hair into a knot. "Besides, I figure it's my obligation to womankind to admire your ass whenever possible."

"So it's duty?"

"Well, yeah. What else would it be?"

"I was sort of hoping for raw lust," he said.

"Oh, there's some of that, but I can control myself."

"That so?"

"Yes, sir. You just watch and see."

He rinsed the lather off his body. "Since I have no intention of taking my eyes off you today, that should work out just fine."

"You, on the other hand, might have a problem."

"Why's that?" he asked.

"Lace," she said.

He laughed. "You're one seriously mean woman."

"You'll note I didn't correct that assessment."

He shut off the water. She turned around to give him some privacy. He grabbed her around the waist and kissed the back of her neck.

"Hey! You're still wet," she protested.

He cupped her breasts and ran his thumbs over her nipples. They hardened instantly. "And now, so are you," he whispered in her ear. "Game on, sugar."

"You are so going to pay for making me shiver in the cold."

"That's not the only way I could make you shiver." He released her and dried off.

"It's not that easy, you know."

"Nothing worthwhile ever is." He finished dressing, smiling when she turned to watch him.

"Do you run?" she asked.

He shook his head. "Not since I stopped being a delinquent."

"Then you're going to have a heck of a time keeping up with me this week."

"Didn't say I couldn't, just that I don't make a habit of it."

"I guess we'll have to test your ability."

"Test away. I plan to." He grinned at her and led her back to his place to get into costume.

Jasper met them at the bottom of the stairs. "I let Katie into your room. Seemed safer than keeping her in the shop until you got back. I hope you don't mind."

"No, that was good." Jocko sighed. "How am I going to watch out for two of you?"

Heather slapped him in the back of the head.

"Ow! I'm not liking your new habit."

"Then quit being an ass. You aren't the only one capable of defending us."

"Listen to the lady," Jasper said, unable to hide his smile.

"You are wise, Jasper," Heather said.

"No, ma'am, just married." He turned to Jocko. "Darius says it's under control, whatever it is, and that Katie will fill you in." He looked at his watch. "Darius expects to talk to you before the meeting, so you'd better hurry up."

"Thanks," Jocko called over his shoulder as they ran up the stairs.

"Anytime, man." Jasper retreated into his shop.

Katie jumped to her feet when they burst through the door. She put her hand over her mouth, color draining from her face.

Jocko skidded to a halt. "Sorry. Didn't mean to startle you."

"No, it's not you," Katie said.

"I know." He headed to his room to change.

Heather took her costume off the peg and reveled in the warmth as she quickly dressed. "You going to be okay?" she asked.

"Probably not," Katie admitted.

"You'll be close to the Queen all day. Nothing will happen to you."

"Yeah, but I'll be close to Paula, too, and I'm really not looking forward to that."

"Leave her to me," Heather said. She reached into her bag and handed Katie a small dagger in a velvet sheath. "But tuck this in your cleavage, just in case."

"I can't do that!" Katie protested. "Ardyth would have a fit."

"I'll bet she has a weapon on her somewhere," Heather said. "But if it makes you feel better, put it in your basket and make sure you keep that close to hand. And don't take off the amulet today, no matter what."

"Okay."

Jocko emerged, dressed in soft leather pants that laced up the side. Heather was glad to see a placket under the lacings. He belted his shirt and pulled his weapons from the rack. He tucked a dagger into his boot sheath then turned up the cuffs so it was hidden.

Heather raised one eyebrow. "That's new."

"No, it isn't. I just don't bother to carry it most days." He looked over at her. "You need a sword?"

"I expect Cami will bring mine to the meeting. I don't like your grip."

"Not what I heard," Katie quipped. A look of horror crossed her face. "Oh, hell. I didn't mean to say that out loud."

Jocko chuckled. "Not to worry, darlin'. Jasper says you have something to tell me."

"Darius said there's nothing they can do about what happened yesterday." She looked at Heather, who nodded. "After the joust, I mean."

"Maybe they can't, but I can." There was no mistaking his meaning.

"Darius said you wouldn't be happy about it. He promised to keep us safe. Both of us."

"Yeah, he did such a good job of that yesterday," Heather said.

"Cut him some slack," Jocko warned. "There wasn't a hell of a lot he could do when he was supposed to be dead on the field. And he couldn't very well show up on site after that. He sent word to me, but by the time I got it, you had already disappeared. I went looking for you, but neither of you were at Katie's place when I got there." His frustration roiled across his features.

"He'd better win the final joust from now on, then." Heather wrapped her cloak around her shoulders. "And keep the Bastard away from me. Darius might not think I can handle myself, but I'd be happy to prove him wrong."

"Oh, I think he's got a better handle on your ability than you think," Katie argued. "If I understand him right, he's going to ask you to be bait."

"The hell he is!" Jocko scowled.

"Back down, dog boy," Heather snapped. "I'll hear him out. If I don't feel confident I can do what they ask of me, then I won't do it. But either way, it's my decision."

"You can't not do what the Court says," Katie protested.

"Watch me."

Jocko chuckled. "Like I said, my money's on you, every time."

Katie looked at the two of them like they were insane. "Jasper says there's another way into his shop. We're supposed to take that and go to the meeting together." She turned to Jocko. "You go out the main stairs. We're not to be seen with you."

"This is already aggravating," he growled.

Heather sighed. "Nothing is going to happen between here and the meeting. We'll just have to hope that Sebastian doesn't realize we're immune to his talent now."

"I'm not a big fan of hope," Jocko said.

"I am," Katie said. "It's the only thing keeping me from running away right now."

"Who would you be running from?" Jocko asked, his voice low. "Sebastian or me?"

"Sebastian, of course. You've never done anything to hurt me." She tilted her head. "I'm not afraid of you, Jocko. And you don't have to be afraid of me, either."

He froze. "Excuse me?"

"I heard the same thing Heather did last night. I don't believe Sebastian, and even if I did, I wouldn't be stupid enough to spread that around. I gossip as much as the next person, but not about stuff like that." She looked him up and down. "I'm not above talking about those pants, though."

"Is that good or bad?" he asked.

"Ha! That's for you to discover on your own." She glanced at Heather. "We should go."

"One second." Heather walked up to Jocko and kissed him on the cheek. "Do something about your hair."

He pulled the black ribbon out of his pouch and tied his hair back, keeping his eyes on her the entire time.

She laughed. "I don't care what the Court wants me to do today, it is SO on."

"I'm gonna hold you to that, you know."

"You are going to lose." She turned away.

"Shows what you know, sugar. When it comes to this, I can't lose."

Katie waited until they were in Jasper's shop. "What was that about?"

"Just a little game." Heather smiled.

"How can you play when you know they're going to ask you to do something dangerous?"

"If I focus on that, the Bastard wins. I'm done giving him power over me. The bet with Jocko is a good way to start. One way or another, I'm coming out on top."

"If I had a man like that, I'd want to be on top, too," Katie said. "Better view."

Heather turned to her, feigning shock. "Why, Miss Katrina, I do believe you just said something raunchy!"

"It's hardly the first time." Katie laughed.

"Aw, and here I thought I was a bad influence on you. Now I'm disappointed."

"Don't worry. I suspect I'll become a hellion in no time if I keep hanging out with you guys."

"Glad to hear it." Heather hooked her arm in Katie's as they approached the meeting. "Hold on tight. This might be a bumpy ride."

They positioned themselves with their backs to the pole barn so no one could sneak up on them. Katie reached into her basket and pulled out a pack of cigarettes. One look told Heather to stay quiet about it. She wisely obliged, but she did move upwind. Katie nodded her head toward the gate.

Paula was headed their way. Heather moved closer to Katie.

"Good morning, ladies," Paula said. "Though I use the term loosely."

"Get the hell away from me," Katie hissed.

"Is that any way to talk to your betters?" Paula's smile was vicious. "Ah, well. You must be tired after last night."

"Why would I be tired?" Katie turned to Heather. "Are you tired?"

"I am, actually. I guess it's to be expected." Heather yawned.

Paula smirked. "Oh?"

"Yeah. It was sort of a rough night, but then, you knew that."

"I don't know what you mean." Paula feigned innocence.

"Huh. I thought you knew exactly what I was doing. Guess I was wrong."

"Why would I even care what you did?"

Heather smiled. "Because I figured with all your spies, you'd have been informed that I spent almost the whole night fucking your ex-boyfriend."

Katie choked out a cloud of smoke.

Paula turned bright red. She snarled and swung her fan. Heather turned so the blow glanced off her shoulder, then came back with a right cross that landed squarely on Paula's jaw and laid her on the ground. The morning chatter stopped as everyone stared, mouths hanging open.

"Oh, damn. I'm so sorry. Fighter's instinct, you know." Heather offered Paula her hand.

Paula refused and struggled to her feet, teeth clenched. "I am going to end you."

"Take your best shot, if you want to go again," Heather said. "Next time, I won't be so gentle."

"That is quite enough." The Queen stepped forward. "Paula, you are relieved for the day. I'd suggest getting some ice on that. It's likely to bruise." She turned to Heather. "You and I need to have a little talk."

"Yes, your majesty," they said in concert.

"Katie, you will attend me today. You can start by getting me a cup of coffee."

Katie stood rooted to the spot.

"Go, child," the Queen said softly.

Katie shook herself and went. Paula glared at Heather.

"You, too, Paula. Stop and see the medic, then head over to Doc's place. I expect you to remain there until I come to check up on you."

Paula dropped the barest curtsy before stalking off to the first aid shack.

The Queen guided Heather away from the crowd. "Not the most subtle way to handle that," she chided. "But it must have been terribly satisfying."

"A bit." Heather kept her face down so those who still watched would not see her smile.

"I must admit, you solved the problem of how to contain Paula today, so I am grateful for that. I will keep Katie with me. But you, my dear, must go about your day as scheduled."

"I'd planned to. Jocko intends to be my shadow, and I don't think anyone can stop him once he decides to do something."

"A man can have worse qualities."

Heather glanced over at him. "Noticed that."

"Yes, I suppose you did. You know we cannot move against Sebastian on your word alone."

"So I hear. As long as he stays away from me, you won't have to move against me, or Jocko, either. But I wouldn't bet on Sebastian's ability to restrain himself."

"We are counting on him being rash. He doesn't like to be denied."

"I noticed that, too."

"If you can manage to hold back your desire to commit murder, and if Darius can talk sense into your young man, we will find a way to remove the threat."

"He's not my anything," Heather protested.

Ardyth frowned. "It is extremely foolish to lie to me, Heather. I can always tell."

"I wasn't lying. Whatever else he is, Jocko is entirely his own man."

"Ah. I misunderstood. For a moment there, I thought you were trying to convince me that you don't love him."

"I . . ." Heather struggled but couldn't find any words.

"If nothing else, dear, you shouldn't lie to yourself." The Queen turned away, stern look in place for her audience.

Heather waited a few moments, trying to look suitably chastised, before joining the rest of the performers for morning meeting.

Cami stood at the edge of the circle. "You couldn't wait until I got here to lay out the bitch? I'm going to have to rethink our friendship."

"Don't worry. You'll hear the story a hundred times today."

"Already half-way there, sister." Cami grinned at her. "But I still wish I'd seen it."

"Me, too." Heather laughed.

Bob glared at them then began a long lecture on professionalism, staring straight at Heather the entire time.

CHAPTER TWENTY-FOUR

Darius must have kept Sebastian busy backstage, because Heather didn't see him until the first joust. She stood in Darius' corner, the Court's only concession to her. At least on that end, she could taunt Sebastian openly. She took special delight in leading the crowd in booing him.

Jocko watched from the top of the hill, the only concession the Court would grant him. Heather hoped Jezebel could keep him calm enough to let her do what she needed to do.

Sebastian smiled at her as he rode by. There was nothing friendly about it. She cheerfully called him the son of a pox-ridden whore, among other things. She leaned on the fence as he rode down the field, surreptitiously loosening her bodice. Fox tossed the ring in the air at precisely the right moment, but Sebastian's lance went wide as she bent to flash him, her breasts almost spilling from the bodice. She tugged up her laces, turned to the crowd, and raised both arms, as if conducting an orchestra.

As instructed, they shouted, "What's the matter, can't keep it up?"

"The wench will find out soon enough," he retorted.

Heather rolled her eyes, and her whole head along with them. "Promises, promises, and not a one kept," she sang.

The crowd howled.

She gave an exaggerated sigh. "A good man is hard to find. A hard knight is damned near impossible."

The next time he got back to her side of the field, she let the crowd shout out their own taunts. Their creativity impressed her. By the time they got drunk, they'd be totally out of hand. With any luck, she wouldn't have to witness it.

Sebastian looked down at her, his eyes dark with the promise of things she was certain she would not like. "I cannot wait to bend you to my will, wench."

"Get bent yourself, you overstuffed meat puppet. I'll see your guts on the ground before you touch me."

"Don't make threats you know you can't carry out," he chided.

"Try me," she spat.

"Oh, I plan to. At least twice." He smiled at the crowd. "Tonight."

They liked that. Crowds were fickle; this one could turn on her in a second. Heather wrapped her fingers around her wrist and squeezed until the pain defeated fear.

"You aren't even good for half a night," she called, "and your squire is twice the knight you are!"

Fox stared at her as if she had gone completely mad. She winked at him. He threw his hands up in the air and shook his head.

"Poor boy. He's going to be mucking out stables for a week for that." She beamed at the crowd. "But I doubt he's sorry." She relaxed when they laughed. She'd gotten them back on her side.

Darius rode up to her before his final run. "You've a sharp tongue on you, lass. Keep it up and I won't have to take that puffed up sot down myself."

The crowd hooted. They were hers for the rest of the show. She let them surround her as they pushed their way back onto the site proper.

Within seconds, Jocko was at her side. "A bit extreme, don't you think?"

"Just doing my part for King and country," she said, laughing.

He shook his head. "Now I know why Darius says you'll be the death of him."

"Don't blame me. It was his idea."

"Tell me again how I'm supposed to keep from killing the Bastard when he comes after you?"

"Who says I'll let you do the honors?"

He lowered his voice. "Speaking of letting me do things, rumor is you told a terrible lie to goad Paula into hitting you."

"Do you object?" she murmured.

"Only to it being a lie," he said.

"You're going to have to work on that."

"I think I could manage a little hard work." He pulled her to him, dropping his hands to cup her rear. "Don't you?"

She raised her voice as she shoved him away from her. "I'm not your wench." The people around her laughed.

"Maybe not yet," he conceded. "But the day is young." He let her walk off with the crowd, but he didn't take his eyes off her.

Heather went to her singing set thinking the day might have potential after all. Cami perched on the balcony above the stage. Heather nodded to her, glad Darius had arranged for someone to be around when Jocko had other obligations. She sang a ballad, but changed to bawdier tunes when the crowd seemed restless. Luckily, Ian could switch gears without missing a beat. The audience perked up and sang along when she taught them a drinking song.

Cami whistled to her at the end of the next tune. Heather flicked her eyes over the audience. Sebastian stood to one side, watching her. She nodded to him.

"And now, my friends, I'll sing you a little song about a woman as was wronged by the man who claimed to love her. Don't you worry, though. It ends well." She stepped back and whispered to Ian, who nodded. She folded her hands and assumed an innocent air.

> *Soldier, soldier would you marry me,*
> *You claim no pike nor spear?*
> *How could I marry such a pretty girl as you,*
> *Without no boots to put on?*
> *Off to the cobbler she did go, as fast as she could run,*
> *Brought him back the finest that was there.*
> *The soldier put them on.*

She mimed pulling on boots, clomping around the stage with a manly swagger. The audience laughed.

> *Soldier, soldier would you marry me,*
> *You claim no pike nor spear?*
> *How could I marry such a pretty girl as you,*
> *Without no cloak to put on?*
> *Off to the tailor she did go, as fast as she could run,*
> *Brought him back the finest that was there.*
> *The soldier put it on.*

She swirled her own cloak over her shoulders and showed it off with an exaggerated runway strut. The next chorus found the soldier lacking a hat. She stole Ian's hat and plopped it on her head. It came down over her eyes. She pushed it back and continued.

> *Soldier, soldier would you marry me,*
> *You claim no pike nor spear?*
> *How could I marry such a pretty girl as you,*

She drew out the last word, took a deep, exaggerated breath then rushed the last line.

> *With a wife and child at home?*
> *The audience groaned. A few people laughed, mostly men.*
> *Off to the blacksmith she did go, as fast as she could run*
> *Brought him back the finest that was there,*

Her eyes locked on Sebastian.

> *And pierced him through the heart.*

She beamed with the satisfaction of a woman who was most capable of taking matters into her own hands. The audience rewarded her with thunderous applause. She dropped a little curtsy. Sebastian clapped loudly—and slowly. He bowed to her then slipped away. Above her, Heather heard the distinct thunk of a knife hitting wood. When the crowd had cleared out, Heather collected the money from her hat.

Cami walked with her until they could see the main stage. "You should be fine from here. I can see the Queen's entourage approaching. I've got a set to do while you and the boy muck about on stage."

"Not my fault we spend most of the scene glaring at each other. I didn't write the script."

"Try not to moon too much," Cami said over her shoulder.

"Try not to gut anyone," Heather called. Trading barbs served as thanks. Cami didn't like debt, no matter which way it went.

Heather made her way toward the stage, running the fight in her head. When she felt a hand on her elbow, she turned to tell Jocko how well her set had gone. And found herself looking up at Sebastian.

"I like how your confidence has grown," he said, locking her arm in his.

"No thanks to you." She had no choice but to walk with him, at least until she could figure out what to do next. Her other hand went into her pocket. Technically, she shouldn't have those, but she'd always thought sticking strictly to period clothing was ridiculous. She sent up a prayer of thanks to whatever deity had blessed her with a practical streak.

He shook his head and sighed. "Hand where I can see it, please."

She took her hand out of her pocket and showed him that it was empty.

"There's a good girl." He looked down at her. "If I hadn't left you to find your own way, you'd be just like the rest of the sheep, blindly following orders. But you aren't very good at that, are you?"

"Depends on whether or not I respect the person giving them, I suppose."

"We shall have to work on that."

"We aren't going to work on anything," she said. "You are going to release my arm and slink back into whatever hole you were hiding in before you decided it was time to annoy me with your presence."

"I don't take orders well, either." His hand came down on her wrist. "Nor do I like it when mine are ignored."

"Then give them to someone else," she hissed through her teeth.

"There is no one else for me. I was in no way ambiguous about that."

"Was that right around the time you were telling me how much fun I'd have watching you rape my friend? Because I'm not clear on how that works, exactly. Me being the only one for you, that is. I'm pretty clear on what kind of scum-sucking pig would force himself on a woman."

"I liked you better when you were biddable," he said.

"I liked you better when you weren't a psychopath, so we're even."

"It is a shame your friend got away. I'd begun to change my mind about her. It's more fun to break a girl with spirit. Mundanes are no challenge, though I will admit that I have a fondness for the ones who keep coming back to be Kissed. Right up to the point where they collapse. Pity about the last one. I thought she'd pull through."

"Guess you're zero for two on the Tribe girls, because I have no intention of letting you break me, whatever the hell that means." Heather didn't want him to elaborate.

"That was never my plan. You are too precious a resource for that."

"Is comparing me to a commodity supposed to endear you to me?"

"Commodities are to be traded. You, my dear, are too rare a gem for that. Or haven't they told you yet?"

"Told me what?" She scanned the crowd.

"Don't bother looking for your lover. He's . . . otherwise engaged at the moment. Something about a lost child. I would imagine they'll find her eventually. I didn't leave her that far out."

"You're serious." She shook her head in disgust. "Is there nothing you won't do?"

"Not much, if it serves my purpose." He shrugged.

"Which is what?"

"Destroying the Court system."

She gaped at him. "You have completely lost your mind."

"I assure you, I am quite sane."

"All evidence to the contrary?" She snorted. "So tell me how you plan to take down an entire system run by some of the scariest people the Tribe can produce."

"The way all systems are taken down. From the inside."

She laughed. "Right. You're going to become a King. I don't see it happening. That's not something you just announce."

"Oh, no, my sweet. I am going to do it by controlling a Queen. Much as they like to hide it, they are the real power here."

"What makes you think I'll help you get to Ardyth?"

He frowned. "You really don't know, do you?"

"Know what?"

"I don't need that tired husk of a woman. I have you."

Heather pulled back. He stopped but didn't release her.

"I can't believe I ever thought you were smart. Look at me." She spoke as though he were a slow child. "I am not a Queen."

"Not yet, but you will be."

She stared at him for a moment, as the weight of what he'd said hit her. It tasted of truth. Everything made sense now—Doc's lessons, Ardyth's sudden interest, Darius' over-the-top protection. And not one of them had been willing to tell her directly. For the third time in two years, her life had been taken from her. She took one shaky breath, then opened her mouth and screamed.

The sound filled her until there was nothing else. Eyes open, she still did not register the effects of her pain and horror as it rolled over the crowd. Numb to everything but the purity of the note, she didn't realize Sebastian had released her. Lack of breath did not stop her. The scream was all.

A hard slap snapped her head sideways. The sound stopped. She blinked several times, tried to swallow, tried to breathe.

Nothing.

Another slap. She struggled to focus.

Green eyes, full of fear and warmth and love. And something else, almost hidden. A terrible longing for home or something more than home. Children? *No, that can't be right.* But it was. She felt the desire as if it were her own.

"You'd be a good mom," Heather croaked.

Jezebel cocked her head. "I think I hit you too hard."

"I'm still standing."

"Not by much, honey." Jez wrapped her arm around Heather's waist. "I need to get you to Doc."

"No." Heather gently removed Jez's arm, but kept her hand. "I have a scene. I'm late."

"I think they've delayed a bit."

Heather looked around. No one met her eyes. Patrons sat on benches or leaned against each other, some holding their heads, others staring sickly at the ground. Ardyth moved from one to another, touching them, speaking softly. Further back, Rodney was drawing people to him, shaking hands or clapping them on the back as he spoke to each one. They still looked dazed, but one by one they drifted away, drawn by the sound of Ian's rich voice.

He glanced at her then focused on his growing audience.

"I don't want to know what you did," Jez said. "But I'd really appreciate it if you never did it again."

"Okay." Heather winced at the pain of speaking. "I broke my voice."

Jez handed her a flask. "Don't think about it. Just drink."

Warmth spread through her as the thick liquid coated her throat. She tasted honey and some sort of berry. "Mead?"

"Magpie Mead, the absolute finest." Jez smiled at her. "You're going to buy me another bottle, because I'm giving the rest to you when the day is over."

"Okay." Her vocabulary seemed stuck.

"You ready to go see Doc now?"

"No. The schedule. Bob." She couldn't put the words in the right order. Her ears were still ringing, the regular sounds of the faire barely getting through.

She tried again. "Tell Doc I need the throat thing—sage, honey, lemon, but no whiskey. He'll know. I need a big cup." She reached into her pocket and pulled out a micro recorder. "Ask him to put this in his box."

Jez took the device and tucked it in her pouch. "Are you sure you're okay?"

"Not really, but I don't have time to think about that. If I don't make it to the fight, everything is going to fall apart. I can do this. I have to." Heather looked down at Jez. "Thank you."

"No problem, honey. You go do what you need to do. I'll bring you the drink when the scene is over, okay?"

Heather nodded. Walking to the stage, she realized she had no idea what had happened to Sebastian.

For once, the thought of him caused no alarm. In fact, she could not identify a single emotion of her own. She recognized sadness, confusion, joy, wonder, even fear, but they did not come from her. They popped up and faded as she passed people. She tried to find some reaction within her, to no avail. The vague desires of the crowd were surreal bubbles that burst when she reached for them.

Without knowing how, she shut down her sense of them. By the time she made it to the stage, she had retreated into a void. The only thing that mattered was getting through the scene.

Jocko arrived just after she did. She glanced at him but felt nothing. She jumped up onto the stage and took her place, immersing herself in the scene. Muscle memory got her through the dance that evolved into a fight. Jocko disarmed her, and she dropped to her knees with his sword at her throat. His hand shook. It had never done that before. She looked up at him and noted the fright hidden behind his stage smile.

The Queen called for truce. The King announced that the combatants would meet again, to settle their differences in a civilized game of chess. Jocko withdrew, as required, his reluctance to leave her clearly outlined in his stiff carriage.

The captain of the Queen's Guard reached down to help Heather to her feet. "Her majesty wishes to speak with you." His grey eyes were completely neutral. Everything about Ash was. Despite being handsome and almost as broad-shouldered as Darius, he tended to blend into the background. She wondered how he managed it. He retrieved her sword and handed it to her.

"Thank you." She sheathed the weapon and followed him off the stage.

Calm washed over her as he led her across the site. She opened herself up, just a little, to confirm that it came from him. She frowned. There was no doubt he was doing it on purpose.

"How do you do that?" she asked, coming alongside him.

The barest smile touched his lips. "Do what?"

"Don't mess with me today. I'm not stable."

"So I gathered." His deep voice slipped around her like a cloak. "It's a Talent, like any other. I had it long before I was turned. It came in handy for soothing cows."

"Cows?" She laughed then choked on the pain of her raw throat.

"They tend to panic when in labor, especially if they're out in the field. I was very good at calming their nerves. Now, I do it for people." He looked down at her. "I guard the Queen. She is far safer when people are calm. The more they've had to drink, the more necessary it becomes to quiet them."

Heather frowned. "Do you think I'm a threat to her?"

"I think you are a threat to us all." There was no accusation in his tone, just statement of fact.

"Then why are you taking me to her?"

"Only a fool disregards the wishes of his Queen. I am not a fool."

"You don't like me very much," she said.

"I don't know you well enough to like or dislike you. Until today, I had no reason to form an opinion."

"And now?"

"Now, you've given me reason to notice you." He glanced at her. "But I do not base my assessments of people on a single incident."

"I'm glad," she said.

"Most people are," he replied.

She got a brief flash of what lay beneath his calm before he closed it off. If Ash ever stopped blending into the background, he would be a very dangerous man. She had no desire to see that.

He led her to the Queen's garden. Ardyth sat on a bench, the skirts of her heavy gown spread around her. Flowers grew along the path, a riot of color even this late into autumn. Posts formed a circle around the garden, a rope keeping the audience from approaching. Ash unhooked one of the ropes to let them in. He nodded to the Queen and stayed where he was, letting Heather approach alone.

"It's a bit like a zoo," Ardyth whispered.

Heather had thought the same thing but was not about to admit it.

Ardyth handed her a cup. The smell of sage was overwhelming. "I intercepted Jezebel. I hope you don't mind. I thought it best to have Ash bring you here, where we might talk in private."

"As you wish, your majesty." Heather sipped the warm brew. It tasted of earth, new trees, bitter rain, and flowers.

"If you thought to hide your distrust and anger from me, you have sorely underestimated my Talents." Ardyth gave her a wry smile. She moved her skirts and motioned to the bench. "Sit, we haven't much time."

"For what?"

"Explanations and apologies."

"I suppose I owe you that." Heather sat.

"No, my dear, I am the one who must apologize. I should have told you as soon as I suspected."

Heather stared into her cup, afraid to speak. The pain had receded a bit, and she wondered what else Doc had added.

"Did you think I wouldn't know what made you scream?" Ardyth asked. "I must admit, I was not prepared for your reaction. It was . . . impressive."

"I made those people sick, didn't I?"

"You made them feel too much. The average person is not capable of handling the level of emotions you uncovered. They did not feel what you did, for which we should both be grateful, but you opened them in ways they could not handle."

"I am such a freak," Heather muttered.

"As are all Queens."

The confirmation sparked renewed panic. Heather struggled to contain it before it escaped. She jumped as it was snuffed out, like a thick blanket had been thrown over a fire. She glanced up at Ash. He shook his head and turned away.

"He's really good at that."

"And a number of other things," Ardyth agreed. "I won't be able to keep him much longer if the other Queens find out. He would be a good Master at Arms, though he's not likely to follow that path. That takes love, and he is quite unprepared to give it."

"How do you deal with knowing so much about people?"

"You do it all the time. You simply don't realize it. With a bit of training, it becomes easier."

"I don't want it to be easy. I don't want it at all." Heather shuddered.

"No one does. That is why we learn to turn it off. Which it seems you have discovered how to do on your own, a bit too effectively. You cannot live that way."

"It's working just fine for me, thanks."

"Is it? When you looked at Jocko, what did you feel?"

"Nothing."

"That would explain his distress."

"I didn't mean to upset him. I didn't mean for any of this to happen. When Sebastian told me . . ." Heather's eyes grew wide. "Where is he? Oh, God, the little girl. He put her in the woods." Panic returned.

Ash took a step toward them, but Ardyth waved him away. "The child is fine. Sebastian is gone, as is Carter. I don't know where they went, but they took the truck."

"Then it was all for nothing!" Heather cried. "What I did . . ." She choked, unable to continue.

"No." Ardyth's voice cracked like a whip. "It was not what we'd hoped for, but I assure you, he will not escape my wrath. What you did today will seem like child's play compared to how he will suffer."

"Doc has the recording. You have what you need. Can I just go back to being a girl with a sword who sings sometimes?"

"You are that, Heather. We can train you to handle your Talents, but no one will make you do anything you don't want to do. Not ever again."

"Right. Like people aren't going to treat me differently when they find out I'm a Queen."

"It won't come to light unless you reveal it yourself. I suggest you not do that unless and until you are willing to take the role. Some Queens are not as sanguine about having others around as they pretend to be. Masters at Arms are even less inclined to be in company. You will have more peace if you keep this to yourself."

"Um." Heather struggled with how to approach her next question. "How am I supposed to explain what happened today?"

"Extreme distress brought on by an attempted kidnapping by a rapist will be enough for most people, and it has the added advantage of bringing to light Sebastian's true nature. Of course, he may not live long enough to suffer the consequences, but that is no longer your concern. I doubt he will come near you again. He was, after all, the first person you took down with your scream. He barely managed to keep his feet long enough to run away."

"I'm really sorry I missed that," Heather said.

"As am I." Ardyth sighed. "It is time to go. We both have roles to play. I have told Bob you will not be able to sing this afternoon and made him promise you won't suffer for that."

"Give my set to the intern girls. They're good, and they could use the money. Tell him to let them pass the hat. They deserve it." The realization that she had just given orders to the Queen shocked her.

Ardyth laughed and patted her on the knee. "You may have a harder time hiding your nature than I'd thought."

"What am I going to do?" Heather cried.

"Learn. Live. Decide what you want to be when you grow up. Or decide you don't have to grow up. All options are open to you, including a few you didn't know about before. Just don't panic. Ash has a hard enough job." Ardyth smiled at her.

"Okay. I'm going to go back out there and pretend there's nothing wrong with me. Good thing I'm an actress, huh?"

"There is nothing wrong with you, dear. Nothing at all."

Heather watched Ardyth change into the Queen as she rose. They really were two completely different personas. Ash waited for her to pass beyond the posts, then attached the rope and escorted them both onto site.

Cami appeared to take her turn as guard dog, apparently unaware that Sebastian had fled. She looked up at Ash, who nodded to her before stepping out to clear a path for the Queen. People parted before him without his speaking a word.

"That is one mountain of a man," Cami said. "I wonder what it would be like to climb him."

Heather burst out laughing. "I adore you."

"Get all mushy on me and we're through," Cami threatened.

"Wouldn't dream of it. I'm counting on you to keep me grounded." She smiled, feeling happy for what seemed like the first time. "Now let's go get into trouble."

Cami grinned wickedly. "Let's do."

Telling Cami about the ordeal was easy. She expressed regret that she hadn't been around to take Sebastian down, but mostly she just listened and nodded. There were definite advantages to Cami's emotional distance from, as she put it, all the damned monkeys who populate the world. She made no distinction between Tribe and Mundanes when it came down to stupidity, though she did allow that a new category should be made for the particular depth of Sebastian's asinine plan to destroy the Court. Heather didn't bother to mention how he'd thought to do that, and Cami didn't ask for details.

"The important thing is that you managed to chase him off with your astounding vocal technique," Cami said. "If he's stupid enough to show up anywhere I am, I'll peg him for you and watch him bleed out. Now I have a good reason."

"Providing you can take him down," Heather said.

Cami looked at her evenly. "I told you. I always hit my target. You've never seen me miss, have you?"

"No, but . . ."

"We all have our Talents, babe. Accuracy is mine. Now run along and play with your overgrown toothpick and leave the real edged weapons to the professionals. I think I see your boy lurking. For some reason, he doesn't seem too keen on coming over while I'm here." She gave Heather a little shove then walked off, juggling her knives.

CHAPTER TWENTY-FIVE

The chess stage stood empty. Heather wondered how Bob had let it happen. At least that was something for which she couldn't be blamed. Jocko leaned against the tree where she usually waited. His emotions were so tangled that she shut them away from her. He would have to tell her what he felt, if he wanted her to know.

"So." It was as good a beginning as any. "Who found the girl?"

"James."

"Storyteller James or intern James or the James who owns the pottery shop by the mud pit?"

"Intern James, if you can believe it." He shook his head. "That kid has some mad tracking skills, especially for someone who isn't Tribe yet."

"Jez say he will be?"

"He's got all the marks. Why, you looking for someone to Kiss?" The teasing was light, tentative.

"Don't even joke about it. You know how I feel about that." She shuddered. That was one more thing she'd have to ask Ardyth about. She hadn't heard of a Queen giving a Kiss.

"The little girl is gonna be fine. She thought it was a big adventure. The nice man let her pet the ponies." Jocko brushed her hand with his. "How are you doing?"

"I've been better. I blew out my voice screaming." As if he couldn't tell from the way she croaked.

"Heard that."

"Who told you?" From what she'd seen, the Court had tamped everything down quickly. Their ability to do that frightened her, despite having benefited from it.

"No one told me, sugar. I heard you all the way in the woods. Don't think I've ever moved that fast in my life."

"I guess you can run," she said.

"When I have a good reason. By the time I got back, Sebastian was already gone. I'm sorry."

"For what I went through or because you didn't get to kill him?"

"Both." He sighed. "I promised to protect you."

"Apparently, I'm better at protecting myself than anyone believed, including me." Despite having stumbled her way to safety, she realized she was proud of herself.

"I guess you won't need me to look after you anymore."

She drew back and looked at him. His shoulders drooped and he appeared to be trying to sink into the tree.

"Are you feeling sorry for yourself?"

"Maybe I am, a little," he admitted. "I liked keeping you safe. At least those times I didn't suck at it."

She gaped at him. "You have got to be kidding me! Come over here so I can smack you in the head again."

"I'll pass."

"Man, do you have a lot to make up for."

He looked at his feet. "I know. I should have been there when you needed me."

"You don't have to make up for being where you were told to be, doing what you were told to be doing. But you damned well better figure out how to make amends for throwing yourself a pity party in the middle of one of the worst days of my life." She crossed her arms over her chest. "Unbelievable."

His head jerked up. "And here I thought I was being open and honest."

"I think I liked you better when you were a swaggering cad."

"I'll work on that." He gave her a cautious smile.

"If nothing else, you'd better shake off your angst before the fight, or I swear I will purposely miss and run your sorry ass through."

The threat brought him back to himself. "You could try, darlin', but it won't be easy."

"Like anything with you is," she huffed.

He grinned at her. "Some things are."

"Not anymore. You're back to square one, buddy."

He sighed. "Damn. I was sort of looking forward to finding out if you were serious about that lace."

"Looks like today isn't working out so well for either of us." She shoved off the tree. "I'm going shopping, blissfully alone for once. I'll be back in time for the fight. Be ready. I have a lot of things to work out, and you're a convenient target."

"Just like old times," he said.

"Square one," she repeated. He wisely stayed put as she walked away.

She lost herself in the beauty of fabric, the chatter of customers, and the charm exuded by Marni and Gina. They let her wander through the racks without offering assistance. It was nice to have someone sense her needs. She frowned at the thought. A lot of people did that for her. When had she stopped noticing? Jocko wasn't the only one who needed to make amends. Heather picked out a brocade bodice, green leaves on a pale blue background with tiny, dark pink flowers. It would make Jezebel's eyes stand out. She found a long skirt in the same green as the leaves.

Marni raised an eyebrow when she laid down the outfit. "That's it? All these sparkly things and you opt for something so modest?"

"Jez likes things simple. A gown wouldn't work in her shop."

"Ah, wise choice, then. I'm adding a shirt, though. And you still have credit here. Maybe you'll find something for yourself."

"If I ever need a gown, you're the only one to make it." Heather smiled at her. "For now, I'm still in Gina's camp, and she already gave me a costume."

"Told you the girl was a fighter," Gina called from her end of the shop.

Marni rolled her eyes, but she laughed. "Incorrigible, the both of you. You aren't going to want to lug these around. I'll send them over to Jezebel's at the end of the day in a nice package, so you can watch her open it."

Heather leaned over the counter and kissed Marni on the cheek. Gina protested at being left out and strode over to get her own peck.

"Now, head on out and teach that boy a lesson or two." Gina winked at her.

"Trust me, I've already started." Heather grinned. She left the shop lighter in spirit.

Ardyth stopped Heather before she got to the chess stage. Ash stepped aside but didn't go far.

"You're flagging, dear. You didn't draw anything from the audience this morning."

Heather opened her mouth but was not given a chance to speak.

"Yes, I will explain that. Later. If you don't open up very soon, you're going to drop. I would hate for that to happen in the middle of the chess match."

"I don't know how anymore," she whispered.

"Nothing has changed since this morning, Heather. Do as you have always done. It will be fine."

"Yes, Your Majesty." Heather curtsied.

As the pawns fell in the first moves of the chess match, Heather opened herself up to the crowd, taking sorely needed energy. It was easier when she didn't focus on one person. She sailed through her fight with Jocko, not missing a beat. She didn't even come down hard on him. He seemed a bit disappointed, so she decided to help him out. The man obviously needed to be slapped back into his old self.

When he finally yielded, she leaned in and whispered, "Lace, and not much of it."

A slow smile spread across his face. "Utterly cruel," he murmured. "Welcome back."

With her singing sets canceled and no desire to see the final joust, Heather bounded over to Jezebel's shop. It was awash in roses. She drew back.

"They aren't all for you." Jez smiled. "But most of them are. And they're numbered, so you read the notes in order."

"Do I even want to know?" Heather asked.

"Couldn't tell you. I didn't read any of them. Start with the white ones."

Jezebel took the note, her hands shaking. *One last apology.* It was signed

"Jackass." She laughed and picked the card off the yellow ones. *Step one, friendship, maybe?* She smiled. The note on the lavender roses simply read: *It's rare.* She moved to the vase that held a single peach rose. *And sweet.* Two orange roses were tied together with a white ribbon. *This is where I run out of poetry. Told you I was a simple guy.* She snickered. He might pretend to be uncultured, but he knew the meaning of each rose.

When she reached for the single red rose, Jezebel slapped her hand. "That one's not for you."

"Rascal?" Heather asked.

"Hasn't been seen around these parts in a while, honey." Jez didn't seem disappointed.

"Are you going to tell me who, then?"

"Lewis." Jezebel snorted. "Like I'm buying what he's selling. Still pleasant to get a flower, though."

"Yeah, I feel no need to bake any of these."

"That's a nice change."

"Amen to that." Heather pulled out a stool. "You want to hear the dirt now or later?"

"Well, I assume Sebastian accosted you, and you dispatched him by breaking his eardrum, since he was gone before I got there and slapped you silly. How's your jaw?"

"Not bad. You hit like a girl."

"Good thing, huh?" Jez sobered. "Katie's a bit broken up that Carter took off, too. She'd thought better of him than that."

"I guess Jocko was right when he said blood will out." Heather shook her head. "I feel bad for Katie."

"We could be judging Carter unfairly. He might have had good reason to go with Sebastian."

"You're a better person than I am. Guilt by association works for me." Heather sighed. "But I'm disappointed in him, too."

"The story will come out, whether he returns to this show or not. Darius will be furious if he doesn't get the truck back before we close. So will Michael. There's no way he wants to haul horses with his shiny, new SUV. I guess we'll just have to wait for the gossip to filter down before we find out what happened."

"I'm not a big fan of gossip."

Jez snickered. "Why would you be? You've been the topic of it for weeks."

"These people seriously need new hobbies."

"Honey, we make our living with our hobbies. Gossip is all that's left when the work is done. Well, that and hooking up, and not everyone is as successful at that as you."

Heather groaned. "The gossips are going to have to find someone else to talk about. I called a halt to extracurricular activities."

"The rose shop will be glad to hear that. We've still got one weekend left for floral apologies."

"Speaking of which, I owe you one. An apology, I mean."

"For what?" Jez asked.

"Everything I put you through during this whole debacle with Sebastian. And not being around because I was too busy hiding out at Jocko's place."

"Eating great food and having even greater sex," Jez said, "is not anything to apologize for. That man is smoking hot."

Heather rolled her eyes. "That man is a giant pain in my ass."

"Too bad you fell in love with him, then."

"I am not in love with him," Heather protested. "I wish people would stop assuming I am."

"The hell you say." Jez put her hands on her hips. "You have many skills, but you can't lie worth a damn."

Heather waved it off. "Doesn't matter. He likes me just fine, and you're right about the great sex, but that's all it was. Jocko doesn't fall in love. I don't expect that will ever change."

Jez threw her hands in the air. "I look forward to the day when you both pull your heads out of your butts and confront your feelings for each other."

"Don't hold your breath. The best I can hope for is that we'll find a way to stay friends."

"It's a start," Jez said.

"Speaking of friendship," Heather said as one of the interns approached, "I got a little something for you." She took the package and thanked the girl.

"What did you do?" Jez asked.

"Open it." Heather sat back and reveled in Jezebel's squeals over her new costume. She couldn't have asked for a better end to the day.

Heather found the routine of Monday errands soothing. She convinced Jez to leave her to do the laundry. Something about the smell of soap and the steam-covered windows made her happy. They met Tansy for lunch and the promised shopping trip. Heather couldn't remember the last time she'd been in a mall. She found it surreal but vaguely amusing. Trying to set up cell phone service when she had no permanent address was fun. They finally gave up and went with a pay-as-you-go program. She assured Jezebel that she would, in fact, remember to pay.

Tansy insisted they go to a salon to round out the indulgent afternoon. Heather let go of her fear of scissors and allowed the stylist to cut two inches from her hair. She adamantly refused suggestions of layers and highlights. Fancy hair required upkeep, and she knew she wouldn't see to it. One of the things she liked best about life with the Tribe was the lack of expectation regarding fashion and beauty trends. Everyone did their own thing, and that was just fine.

They rode home full of the satisfaction only a mad shopping spree could bring. To keep Jez from throwing out her sweats, Heather promised to wear them only when running or sleeping. As silly as it seemed, the new clothes bolstered her decision to take control of her life. She even managed to dissuade her father from trying to convince her to come home. Or maybe he was just glad she finally had a phone. Either way, she was pleased with the result.

It took only two days of staying apart for the rumor mill to decide that she and Jocko had had a terrible falling out. She sniggered when she heard it then went back to helping Jez with inventory. The rumors would change when they were seen practicing their fight on Thursday, and she expected to find those just as amusing. No one would believe he was leaving her alone simply because she'd asked him to.

Carter returned on Tuesday and remained sequestered with Darius for most of the day. No rumors circulated about it, either because no one knew enough to speculate or because they were too afraid of what Darius would do if he heard them. Not a word was spoken about the events of the previous weekend, at least not where Heather could hear. She was quite sure it was discussed elsewhere. It didn't matter.

Michael showed up at their door on Wednesday morning. "I come in peace," he said when they let him in. Three sets of eyebrows went up.

"That's a first," Cami drawled.

"Says the homicidal maniac. Don't shoot the messenger." He glanced at Cami. "Or let her throw anything at me."

"Oh, this should be good," Jez said.

He turned to Heather. "Carter would like to speak with you."

She snorted. "I'll just bet."

"He thought you'd be reluctant, so he said you can choose when and where and have whomever else you want present."

"You know that's an exact quote, because my brother just used 'whomever' properly," Cami quipped.

"Stuff it, little engine." He shot her an exasperated look. "You don't have to give me an answer right now. You can send word to the camp."

"As long as no one expects me to do it under a white flag." Heather looked up at the ceiling and sighed. "He can come here, if the ladies have no objection."

"None at all," Jez said. "It'll be refreshing to get a firsthand account for a change."

Cami shook her head. "Count me out. I'm not sure I could keep from beating the crap out of him long enough to listen to his lame excuses, and attacking someone who's already been crippled won't do anything for my image."

Michael snorted but refrained from further comment.

"Send him now," Heather said. "We might as well get this over with."

Cami walked out with Michael. Jez went back to working on her latest design. For lack of anything better to do, Heather cleaned the room. It had the desired calming effect. When Carter arrived, she let him in and told him to sit. The last thing she needed was a man towering over her, especially one who looked so much like Sebastian.

"Speak," she commanded, crossing her arms.

"Thank you for agreeing to talk to me. I'm surprised, actually."

"So am I."

He sighed. "You must think I'm pretty awful, and I don't expect you to forgive me, but I want to explain." His blue eyes pleaded for understanding.

She was in no mood to give it. "Get to it, then."

"I didn't know what happened on Sunday. I swear I didn't. When Sebastian came to see me, he looked really sick."

"Good," Heather spat.

"He told me he'd had some bad news and needed to go home. He said Darius knew about it, so it would be okay if we just left. I had no reason to doubt him. He's always put the job first. Anyway, I left Darius a note and took Sebastian home. I didn't find out what he'd done, or tried to do, until I got back."

"I find it very hard to believe that he said nothing about me during the entire trip," Heather said.

"He did. He was worried about you. He said you didn't seem like yourself, and asked me to look out for you."

"Get out!" Heather yelled.

Carter held up his hands. "Wait. I'm not here to spy on you. I told him that you're my friend. Well, I guess you were my friend, but I don't expect that to continue. Anyway, I told him that you seemed just fine to me, and being with Jocko obviously made you happy, so I was happy for you. He hit me pretty hard when he heard that. Good thing we were pulled over at a rest stop. I guess being on the sideline for the past week or so, I missed a lot of what went on around here. I really didn't know he was trying to hurt you, or I would have done something about it."

"And now that you do know, what do you plan to do?" she asked.

"I've already done what I can. I told Darius where Sebastian is and the places he'd be likely to go. If he manages to elude the Court, he won't find sanctuary with me. He may be blood, but he's also crazy and more dangerous than I'd ever imagined. I want no part of him."

"And you expect me to believe you. Why?"

"I don't expect anything." He looked up at her. "But I have never lied to you, Heather. Not about anything."

She stared at him for a moment. "Say that again." She took a deep breath and opened up all her senses.

"I haven't lied to you. I had no idea Sebastian was obsessed with you, much less what he'd planned to do. I would have stopped him, somehow, if I'd known. I am really, really sorry, but I don't expect you to forgive me. I just wanted you to know, so maybe you won't hate me."

She took a step back as the force of his emotions struck her—sincerity, humility, sorrow, and a tinge of hope, but no guile anywhere. That should not be possible. Everyone had ulterior motives, even when they meant well. Carter had none at all.

She shut down, afraid she might pick up on whatever it was he desired most. He deserved to have some secrets. "I don't hate you," she said softly.

"How could you not?" he asked. He rubbed his eyes to hide the tears that threatened.

"You're a better guy than I've ever given you credit for," Heather admitted. "I looked at you and saw another version of Sebastian. Maybe that wasn't fair, but it wasn't far from wrong, either."

"Don't say that! I'm nothing like him."

"No, you aren't. You're everything he should have been." She sighed and handed him a tissue. "Stop pretending you aren't crying. Blow your nose, and let's go get some lunch."

"Really?" He had never looked more like a puppy.

She laughed. "Yes, but only if you promise to stop being pathetic."

"I don't know if I can," he admitted. "You aren't the only friend I expected to lose over this. I don't think Katie will talk to me again."

"Maybe not. You won't know unless you try."

He clenched the tissue in his hand. "Will you ask her for me?"

"No. You're going to have to do that on your own. I could tell her you're innocent, but she doesn't have to believe me, either."

"Could you maybe give me some advice about how to approach this? Because I really don't know how to say, 'Hi, I'm sorry my cousin is a nut job who assaulted you, but I'm not like that, honest.' I mean, where do I even start?"

"We'll talk about that over lunch." Heather turned to Jez, who had done a fairly bad job of pretending not to listen. "Are you coming with us?"

Jez shook her head. "I need to finish this. If you feel okay going alone, I'll stay here."

"I'm not a threat to you," Carter said.

"I know," Heather assured him. "Let me get my coat and we'll leave Jez in peace."

Despite his injuries, Carter made it to the door before she could and held it open for her, as she'd known he would.

CHAPTER TWENTY-SIX

Heather drove to a diner not far from the site. The coffee was decent and continually refreshed, which was all she required in an eating establishment. It took her a while to get Carter to stop expressing his gratitude and listen to her advice about Katie. The best she could do was offer him a female perspective. Being asked for relationship advice was more than a little weird, especially since she didn't even know what to do with her own, such as it was. She didn't bother to mention that. After a couple of hours, the waitress began to give them dirty looks. Heather left her a big tip to make up for hogging the table for so long.

On the way back, Carter started babbling about comic books. Heather teased him about his refusal to grow up and was treated to a lecture on the difference between comics and graphic novels and the growing market share of the latter, as well as the list of established authors who were writing them. She held up her hands in surrender and laughed when he expressed alarm over her driving with her knees.

The afternoon sun lit up the fall foliage until it practically glowed. She slowed the Jeep as they crossed the parking lot, so they could enjoy the show of colors over the faux castle of the front gate. She realized just how much she loved being there and how lucky she was to be allowed to call it home, if only for eight weeks at a time.

"Hey," Carter said, sitting up straighter, "what's that?" He pointed to a lump near the front gate. It looked like someone had dumped a pile of clothes.

"Some drunk probably changed in the parking lot and left his costume behind." She decided to take a closer look. As they approached, the lump moved.

He leaned forward. "That's a person!"

Heather's stomach flipped as she realized he was right. She pulled the Jeep up and left it idling as she jumped out. When she looked down, it took everything she had not to scream. Fox was curled into a ball, shivering and bleeding. He whimpered when she touched him.

"Take it easy, Fox. It's Heather. I'm not going to hurt you."

He sobbed, unable to speak.

Carter came up behind her. "Oh, man. This is bad. We need to get him back to camp." He bent down and picked up Fox, wincing at the extra weight on his foot.

"Let me help you," Heather said.

"No. I've got him." He cradled the young man to him as he limped back to the Jeep. "Just drive fast."

Heather sped across the site, careful to avoid the many potholes in the back lot. She pulled the Jeep as close to camp as she could. She ran ahead to clear a bench in the armory and laid a blanket over it before Carter laid Fox down. He was a mass of cuts and bruises. When they tried to remove his shirt, he screamed, a horrid, broken sound.

Lew rushed in from the stables. "What the hell?"

"I'm going to get Doc," Heather said.

Fox grabbed her coat. "Stay," he croaked.

"I'll go." Lew took off running.

Carter came back with a first aid kit. "I've never seen anything this bad." He handed a damp cloth to Heather. "See if you can clean him up a little."

"Help me," Fox whispered.

Heather knelt down by him. "We will, honey." She gently washed his face while he cried.

"My step-dad." He choked. It took him a few seconds to continue. "Drunk again. Said he didn't approve of my 'lifestyle choice.' Finally saw the show last weekend. I thought he'd be proud, you know? How much more manly can a job get?" He laughed, but it dissolved into coughing. "Guess it's a good thing I never told him I'm gay, huh? I'd probably be dead." He spit blood into the washcloth. "Maybe I am."

"Shhh, don't say that. Doc is on his way. You're going to be fine." Heather couldn't hold back her tears.

"Got nothing now. He destroyed it all. No home to go back to." The coughing resumed. Heather supported him while Carter put a folded blanket behind his head.

"Really wanted to finish school." Fox sighed and leaned back, closing his eyes. Within seconds, he had stopped breathing.

Carter moved Heather aside and bent over Fox. He pushed fast and firm on the squire's chest. Heather cried and sent up a prayer to any and every deity, offering anything they wanted if Fox would just start breathing again. One of them must have been listening, because Fox gasped. His breath was still too shallow.

"Where the hell is Doc?" Carter growled.

"It takes more than two minutes to get across the site, and he's all the way on the other side." A horrible thought struck her. "God, I hope he's home."

"It's okay," Fox whispered. "I just want . . . ." He couldn't finish.

Heather grit her teeth against fear, and opened herself to him. She dropped to her knees when the pain and sorrow washed over her. She pushed them aside, delving deeper than she ever had into anyone, deeper than she had any right to. When she found what she was looking for, she sobbed. All he wanted was to know that he had a home, some place he truly belonged, where people loved him for who he was.

"Okay," she whispered, leaning over him. "I can do that." She really didn't want to, didn't even know how she could, but she would never forgive herself if she failed him at the end. She cradled his head and gave him the Kiss. She filled him with love and acceptance and belief that he would survive. She gave him everything she had to give, wishing she could take away all of his suffering. Inside him, something changed. He shuddered and relaxed. As soon as he did, she drew back, taking with her all she had sought.

Everything was tinted red. Each breath brought a wave of pain. She reached out to Carter to steady herself, frightened and confused. He grabbed her hand to pull her up, but her legs wouldn't work. He lowered her to the floor, instead. From a great distance, she heard him call her name. She opened her mouth to speak but could only whimper. Her last thought before darkness closed over her was that she had done the right thing.

Soft light filtered through as Heather tried to open her eyes. It seemed too much effort. The pounding in her head was overwhelming. Breathing continued to hurt. She had no idea where she was, but she was quite sure it was not the jouster shack. For one thing, it was blissfully warm. A bed. Real sheets, too, and blankets. She managed to pry her eyes open, despite the stabbing pain caused by letting in the scant light in the room. She identified the fuzzy figure sitting in the chair, his head in his hands.

"Doc?" she rasped.

He jumped up, his movement a blur to her. He held up her head and placed a straw in her mouth. Water helped. She lay back on the pillows, dizzy.

"Fox?" Complete sentences were beyond her.

"Tended to and resting in the next room. You should do the same."

"What did I do?"

"You saved his life." Doc stroked her hair from her face. "Now sleep."

She closed her eyes and pretended, for his sake. The pain would not release her.

Jocko burst into the room. "What the hell happened?"

Like a sword, his voice sliced into her brain. She cracked her eyes, just enough to see him.

Doc bristled. "Calm down, or leave until you can contain yourself!" he hissed.

Jocko took several deep breaths. He was still quivering when he spoke. "I need to know exactly what went down."

"It seems our dear girl transfused Fox."

Color bled from Jocko's face. "That's not possible. She doesn't know how to do that."

"I don't believe she knew what she was doing. If she recovers, however, she will most certainly remember how it was done."

"What do you mean if?"

"From what I can tell, she absorbed his pain. All of it. I've given her what I can, but there's nothing more I can do."

"Then get her to a damned hospital," Jocko demanded.

"It will not help. There is nothing physically wrong with her that they could treat. Would you care to explain to them that she's had a psychic accident? I can tell you from experience, such a proclamation will not go over well."

"There has to be something we can do for her."

"Not we, my boy," Doc said gently. "You."

Jocko glared at him. "No."

"It is your decision, of course. We could send for someone else, but the nearest available Sword Breaker with Court sanction is in Texas. It would be at least a day before he could get here."

"You think I'd let him near her?"

"The only other option is to wait and hope she comes through it."

Jocko spun on him, fists clenched at his side. "Damn you!"

Darius strode in. "Watch your tone, Jocko. Doc is just telling you the facts. He didn't cause this situation. You will be polite, or you will leave."

Jocko closed his eyes and nodded. "My apologies, Doc."

"Your concern for her is admirable," Doc said. "Even if your conduct was not."

"The question remains," Darius said, "whether you'll do your duty. Think carefully about your answer."

"I won't cause her any harm," Jocko said.

"Yet you are doing just that by refusing to act. She needs you," Darius said.

"If she transfused Fox, she's a Sword Breaker. Is that why you want me to do this? To keep her from ending up like me?"

"God save me from idiots." Darius shook his head. "She's not a Sword Breaker, Jocko. She is a Queen."

Doc paled, grabbing the back of the chair for balance and lowering himself into it.

Jocko blinked several times. "And you're asking me to Break her?"

"No, you stupid boy, I am asking you to save her!" Darius bore down on Jocko, backing him into a corner. "You and I both know Sebastian is hunting her, and now you know why. We haven't found him yet, which you also know. He knows she's a Queen, and if he gets his hands on her, there will be war."

"I'll kill him before I let him touch her," Jocko growled. "Or die trying."

"Would it not be easier to Kiss her and take the opportunity from him?" Doc whispered.

"She could die."

"Is it for her you fear, or yourself?" Darius asked.

"What happens to me doesn't matter."

"It matters a great deal. If you save her, you could end up her Master at Arms—or more."

"You don't know that."

"Who the hell do you think you're talking to?" Darius roared.

Heather struggled to stay conscious through the waves of pain.

"I know what it takes to become what I am, boy. Now choose. You can fix her, or you can take your chances with the Court if you don't." The threat was implicit.

"That isn't a choice, Darius. It's a sentence, either way," Jocko said.

Passing out might have been a better option. Life with her would be the same as a death sentence.

"If you're going to do this, it has to be now," Doc said. "Give her the Kiss, and set her free."

"I don't know if I can." Jocko's voice shook. "I love her."

The older men fell silent, stunned.

Doc found his voice first. "Have you told her this?"

"Of course not. You know what I am."

"Your Talent does not preclude the ability to love," Doc pointed out.

"Just the likelihood of being loved in return. I knew the cost when I agreed to the job."

"So you take that choice from her, as well?" Dangerous amounts of anger spilled from Darius. Heather shuddered as it lashed against her.

"You say you love her. Prove it. Devote your life to her." Darius gave him a steady look. "Or get the hell out."

I am hallucinating. Heather's thought drifted, then dissipated. She took a shaky breath and let out a sigh, trying to remember how to speak. "Do I get a say in any of this?"

Doc rushed to her side, wan and troubled. "Easy, my dear. Don't strain yourself."

She wanted to laugh, but the pain was too strong. "I won't have any part of this if Jocko doesn't have a choice." Her voice was terrible, broken. "This is my fault, not his."

Jocko walked over to the bed. "It's no one's fault, sugar. It just is what it is. You did a good thing, saving that boy."

"Come closer," she croaked. Doc stepped away to give them what privacy the small room afforded.

Jocko leaned over, careful not to touch her.

"Did you mean it when you said you love me?" she whispered.

"I wouldn't lie about that."

"Then kindly tell the old men to get out of the room so you can Kiss me in private."

He opened his mouth then shut it again, shaking his head.

"That wasn't a question, Jocko. You don't want to make the decision, so let me. I promise I won't ask you to do anything you don't want to do after this." She wanted to say more but was too tired. There was no time, and everyone knew it.

"I can't."

"It's okay. I understand." She closed her eyes.

"No, darlin', you don't. If I Kiss you now, you'll Break. It could kill you. It's been too long since I fed. If I had something in reserve, I could try."

"Oh." She had no idea what he was talking about. "Just so you know, I love you, too." She sighed, and let the pain take her. Still, she could not go.

"Take me." Paula's voice drifted across the room. For a wonder, it hurt Heather not at all.

"You get the hell out of here," Jocko growled.

"Don't be more of an idiot than you already are," Paula retorted. "I'm offering you everything—one last time. Feed. Break me. Take what you need to save her."

"You can't be serious," Jocko said.

"Totally serious. I'm done with this life. I've done everything wrong since day one. I wanted so badly to be Queen when what I really should have wanted was to be like her. I can't be here, can't be this *thing* I've become, any longer. I've lost my place with the Queen, and no matter how hard the Court tries to keep things secret, people will figure out that I had a hand in Sebastian's stupid plan, so my social life will be shot, too. No one is going to hire me, even to work in the kitchens. My life with the Tribe is over. Unless you object to making the separation a little easier for me, then take my offer."

"Breaking is not easy."

"No, but I deserve a little pain for my part in this, even if I didn't fully understand what Sebastian planned. I knew he was going to hurt her, and I agreed to help him. I need to go back to my world, the one I never should have left. I need to remember who I was and figure out where it all went wrong. I can't do that if I'm part of the Tribe, because I'll have to come back to feed. Break me. Please."

Jocko turned to Darius. "Do you accept this?"

"She's offering freely. I can't object." Darius did not sound pleased.

"Nor I, though God save me for being a part of it," Doc said.

"If she's willing, I don't need a witness," Jocko said. "We can do this in the next room."

Heather forced herself to speak. "No. If she's going to sacrifice herself for me, I will bear witness to it." She shuddered. "Unless she objects."

"I don't know whether to be impressed or disgusted by that show of nobility," Paula said. "But knowing you, it was offered without acrimony."

"You don't have to do it here, if you don't want. You don't have to do it at all."

"I really do. Accept my offer, and I'll accept yours. You should know what he can do." She turned to Jocko. "You made me Tribe, and I made a hash of it. Unmake me so I can do a better job in the real world."

"Will you?" he asked.

"I can't do worse, and I'm not inclined to. So unless there's some elaborate ritual, can we please get this over with, so I can go pack?"

"No ritual." He stroked her cheek. "I'm sorry. For everything."

He held Paula close and lowered his mouth to hers. As the kiss deepened, she arched against him. His arm locked around her. He opened himself and gave her the last Kiss she would receive. Power flooded the room. Heather drew from it without thinking, and the pain receded.

Jocko cradled Paula's head as her eyes closed. She screamed into his mouth as a violent spasm took her, then she collapsed, unconscious. He broke away. As Darius carried Paula from the room, Jocko covered his face with his hands. Doc sat silently in the chair, eyes wide.

"Go," Jocko said softly.

Doc shuffled to the door with one last look at Heather. She had never seen him look old before.

Jocko closed the door and turned to regard her. "Now you know which one of us is the monster."

"Don't you dare," she hissed. "You will not demean her sacrifice like that. I won't let you. That was one of the most horrible and beautiful things I've ever seen. Don't make it small."

"You need to know what I am," he said.

"I knew already. What I don't know is if you can accept what I am. Or might be." She couldn't put it into words. "If giving me the Kiss could screw up your life in ways that you can't handle, then I don't want it."

"You don't understand," he growled. "I don't know what will happen. I could Break you anyway."

"That doesn't scare you as much as the idea that we might both get stronger or end up bonded for life."

He gaped at her. "Is that what you think?"

"It can happen."

"Of course it can, but that doesn't frighten me nearly as much as the idea that I could lose you."

"Despite what all the men who have tromped through this room believe, I am not about to die for a Kiss."

"No, you're stronger now. I can feel it." He sat down on the edge of the bed. "But if I do this wrong, you'll leave, and I'll never see you again."

"You really are a jackass sometimes, you know that? There's nothing to say I couldn't stay with you, just because I'm not Tribe."

He sighed. "Breaking doesn't take everything away, though I wish it did. You'll still feel the emotion of the crowd, still want to feed, but you won't be able to do it. From what I'm told, it's pure hell. That's what I do to people."

"Jocko?"

"Yeah, sugar?"

"Shut up and Kiss me."

Jocko pulled the covers back and stretched out beside her. "The more contact we have, the easier it will be."

She shifted then clenched her teeth.

"You don't need to move." He rolled onto his side, his arm touching hers from shoulder to hand. He threaded his fingers in hers as he lay his other hand on her cheek, turning her to face him. "Just relax."

He kissed her. There was no magic, no pull, just love. She closed her eyes, letting the scent of him fill her, lost in tenderness. He pulled back, searching her face. She smiled at him and nodded. He squeezed her hand.

She braced herself to receive the Kiss, eyes open. Warmth spread through her, smoothing away the hurt. Freed, she opened to him. Energy rolled off him until it suffused her. She stroked his back and pressed herself against him. He deepened the Kiss, exploring her mouth, fingers threading through her hair. Every nerve throbbed until she was sure light poured from them. There was nowhere he was not. The final barrier dropped as she finally let go of her fear and became what she was meant to be. She let him drink her in and responded in kind. His body shook as their power met, danced, entwined—and settled.

He lay atop her, trembling, his face buried in the crook of her neck. She ran her fingers through his silken hair and kissed his forehead. His eyes flew open and he rolled off her, panicked.

"It's okay. You took the pain away. All of it." She turned onto her side. "I will never be able to thank you enough."

"What did you do to me?" he whispered.

"I don't know who did what." She laid her head on his chest. "But it was lovely."

"Never doubt that." He held her to him. "No matter what happens next, know that I love you."

"That's good," she murmured and fell asleep.

When she awoke the next morning, he was gone.

CHAPTER TWENTY-SEVEN

oc insisted that Heather have a proper breakfast before letting her leave. She drank her coffee and watched the small displays of affection as Tansy moved around the kitchen—a touch on Doc's shoulder, a kiss in passing, the playful slap of Jasper's hand as he tried to snitch bacon, the smiles she gave them as she laid down each plate. They made a good family.

After breakfast, Tansy walked her home. She apologized for the ruined sweater. They'd cut it off her when they'd thought she was hurt, only to realize all the blood had come from Fox.

"Is he going to be okay?" Heather asked.

"It will take him some time to heal, more from the wounds of being rejected by his family than from the bruises, but I think he'll come out all right." Tansy tilted her head. "I'm almost more worried about you."

"I'm pretty sure I'm fine."

"Very convincing." Tansy gave her a soft smile. "I have faith you'll pull through all this, but take it easy for a while, huh? I don't think Doc can handle much more excitement this season."

"I'll do my best." Heather hugged her and went upstairs to tell Jez and Cami what had happened. What she could, anyway. They were mostly concerned for her well-being and happy Fox would recover. They didn't mention anything about Fox coming out on his death bed, so Carter must not have mentioned it, proving once again that he was a decent guy. Cami grudgingly accepted that, even without the last bit of information.

There was no sign of Jocko, but that wasn't surprising. He was probably recovering from having saved her life. Heather decided it would be rude to wake him up. Besides, she was still tired herself, and his room was all the way across the faire site.

Lew came over in the afternoon. He wrapped himself around Jezebel until she beat him back. He turned to Heather. "About the fight."

"I'm sorry we didn't run it today. I'll get Jocko, and we'll do it before sundown, I promise."

He fidgeted. "No, girl, you won't. Your fights are cut for the weekend. You're done."

"What? I'm fine! Doc said so."

"Doc did. Bob didn't, and Darius agrees with him. I have no idea what their problem is, but the big guy wants you to stop by after you get over your hissy fit."

"What fit?" Heather ground out.

"The one he expects you're going to have right about now. He's in the armory whenever you're ready to talk."

"Good. Plenty of weapons to hand."

"Which is why I'm going to stay here and keep your girlfriend company." Lew plopped on the couch.

Jez snorted. "Like hell. I have work to do. Go harass someone who might fall for your shtick."

"Aw, baby, that's so mean. I'm not all that cavalier with my stick."

"You go set Darius straight, while I evict another jouster." Jez advanced on Lew.

"Another? I guess the rumors were wrong about you feeling you were above us. Come to think of it, that has potential, too." He grinned.

As Heather walked down the stairs, she heard the distinct sound of a slap, followed by deep laughter. At least someone was having a good time.

Darius was polishing armor when Heather arrived. It was a job usually left for squires, but with Fox laid up and Tyler not due until morning, everyone was working a little harder. Brock took one look at her and left without a word. Darius called after him, but the big squire kept going. He knew a fight was brewing.

"What the hell are you doing, Darius?" Heather put her hands on her hips.

"Scut work, little sister." He looked up at her. "This won't play, you know. Stronger than you have attempted to browbeat me. I am sorry. I would rather have seen you fight this weekend. I think it would be good for you."

"Doesn't look that way," she huffed. "By keeping me out of it, you ruin three scenes."

"The first is filler. We've got apprentices lined up for the chess match. You're benched, and there's nothing I can do about it." He went back to polishing armor.

"Why?"

"Because you have no fight partner."

Heather managed to keep her feet by leaning on the edge of the weapons rack. "Where is he?"

"I believe he went home."

"I'm going to kill him."

"Then I suppose I shouldn't give you his address."

"I have a way to track him down," she growled. "Why did he do this to me?"

"You may want to ask him that when you see him." Darius remained calm. "If you assure me that you will go in unarmed and listen to what he has to say, I will tell you where to find him after the show."

"There is no show for me this weekend, remember? I'll take that address now, if you please." She held out her hand.

"You might want to give him time."

"Are you ordering me to stay?" she asked.

"I can't give you orders anymore, Heather. You should have realized that."

"I am not what you want me to be," she hissed. "I won't take that position."

He sighed. "It doesn't matter. I know what you are, even if you refuse to do anything about it."

She grit her teeth. If he was going to insist on adhering to the hierarchy, she would make it work for her. "Then do as I ask and tell me where to find him."

He shook his head. "I told them this would happen." He set the armor aside, reached into his pocket, and handed her a piece of paper.

"There are things you don't know, and it's not my place to tell you. Please listen to him before you pass judgment. It will all be clear soon enough."

She shoved the paper in her pocket. "I'll listen. And then I'll go see my parents and let my mom fall all over herself trying to get me to stay. I'll eat turkey and watch football and decorate the Christmas tree and, if I'm really lucky, find a way to deal with all this without ever setting foot on another faire site. I have had just about as much as I can take."

"Good luck." He wrapped his massive arms around her, kissed her on the forehead, and let her go. As she walked away, she heard him whisper. "See you next season, little sister."

She began packing as soon as she got back to the booth. All her exhaustion had burned away, replaced by anger and determination. Jez watched from the doorway for a few minutes, then sighed and helped her. They loaded up the Jeep and hugged each other while they cried. Cami refused to come. She hated good-byes. Michael walked up and gave Heather a sealed envelope with instructions to not open it until the first time she pulled over. She threw it on the passenger seat and got in.

When she reached into her jacket pocket for her keys, her hand closed around a loose one. She pulled it out, blinking away her tears. She drove the jeep to the side gate, left it idling, and walked to Jasper's booth to return his key. He wasn't there, and she didn't want to walk all the way across site to find him. She trudged up the stairs and let herself in.

Except for the refrigerator, there was no sign Jocko had been there. The room was perfectly clean and painfully empty. She put the key on the table where Jasper was sure to find it and turned around to leave. Tied to the doorknob, she found the black ribbon. Next to it, a note was affixed to the door. *I'm sorry.* That was it. He'd had no more to say to her. She tied her hair back with the ribbon, locked the door, and left.

Sorry was not good enough.

When she stopped to get coffee she ripped open Cami's note. *Don't be stupid.* She laughed. That covered so much and was patently impossible. She stuck the note in her visor and read it every time she stopped.

She had expected to drive through the night. Tears made it difficult. Her anger could only sustain her for so long so she finally relented and found a motel. In the morning, she took a long bath, braided her hair, and got back on the road. She imagined how the faire would be and wondered if anyone besides her close friends would realize she had gone. She gave a rueful laugh. Of course they would. The rumor mill would be wild with speculation, almost none of it right.

Another day on the road, alone with her thoughts, did nothing to improve her mood. She did take the time to stop in West Virginia and enjoy the mountain views. Despite her desire to find and throttle Jocko, she opted for another night in a motel. The effects of her ordeal lingered, so she slept much longer and more deeply than she'd expected.

As she neared her destination, late afternoon sun filtered through trees still sporting green leaves, the air heavy with the last remnants of a summer that would not let go. She pulled off the highway and, after a few miles, found the rural road she sought. Wisps of hair escaped the braid and stuck to her face. She shrugged out of her jacket and rolled down the windows. The breeze did little to cool her.

She turned onto a narrow lane of hard-packed clay, grateful again for her trusty little Jeep. After several sharp twists, the track straightened. At the end was a small house with a wrap-around porch. Two high-backed chairs were angled slightly to allow for both conversation and enjoyment of the view. A BMW sat off to the side, under a large tree. She slowed. One last look at Cami's note shored up her courage. She parked, walked up the steps, and knocked on the door.

An astonishingly beautiful woman opened the door. Long hair fell in dark waves to her waist. She had flawless skin the color of a latte, high cheekbones, and a delicate nose. No lipstick could have bettered the perfect mouth that formed her welcoming smile.

"Are you lost?" Her rich voice was full of concern.

"I may be," Heather said. "I'm looking for Jocko."

The woman pressed her hand to her chest, her hazel eyes wide. Gems flashed in the afternoon light. The diamond on her ring finger was particularly impressive. "I see. One moment." She took half a step back and called over her shoulder, "*Jacques? Vien ici.*"

"*Pas maintenant. Je suis occupé*," he answered from the back of the house.

"*Oui, maintenant. Je suis sérieuse!*"

His answer was lost in the clatter of pans.

Heather stood rooted to the spot. Their love was palpable. She pulled herself together. "I'm sorry. I should go."

"If you made it all the way out here, you must have a reason. He won't be but a minute." Footsteps behind her proved the assertion. The woman opened the door a bit further and stood aside.

He strode down the hallway, wiping his hands on a dish towel. When he looked up, he slowed. His gaze did not leave Heather as he approached. She could read nothing in it.

"What are you doing here?" he asked.

The small woman looked up at him and shook her head. "That is no way to greet a lady." She raised a perfectly manicured hand and slapped him in the back of the head. "Jackass."

"Heather, may I introduce you to my sister, Gabrielle?" He stepped out of her reach. "Gabrielle, this is Heather."

"Better, but you are still a lout." Gabrielle stepped onto the porch. "I'm delighted to meet you, Heather. Can I offer you a drink? You must be exhausted. I'll just go on in and fix us something." She disappeared.

Heather tried to recover her equilibrium. "I didn't get a chance to answer."

"No one does. Gaby assumes the answers will be the ones she expects."

"You said she lived in New Orleans."

"It doesn't matter where she is, the protocol is the same."

"So this is your house? How did you manage that?"

"My father did one good thing for me before he died. Of course, you wouldn't have much liked what he left me. I've been working on it during the off season for years. It's a decent place to spend a couple months, and it keeps me out of trouble. Mostly."

He fell silent as Gabrielle brought out a pitcher and glasses. She set them on the table and retreated into the house, closing the door behind her.

"She won't let us in until we work this out, you know. She can't abide fighting in the house." He poured two drinks and handed her one.

"When I first saw her, I thought . . ." She shook her head.

Jocko laughed. "Lost more dates that way in high school than I care to remember. All I had to do to get a girl to dump me was take a walk with my sister."

"She doesn't look like you." None of this was what she'd planned to say.

"We had different fathers. Hers stuck around." He shrugged. "You planning to tell me why you came all the way down here when you had a show to do?"

"Because my idiot partner bagged on me," she pointed out.

"I feel bad about that, but it was necessary. I figured you'd stay to sing, at least. They're going to miss you."

"I blew out my voice when my psycho stalker tried to abduct me, remember?" She rolled the cool glass in her hands.

"That's not a problem any longer."

"What, my voice or the whack job who tried to kidnap me?"

"Both, I'd say. Darius assures me the Court has Sebastian cornered. I'll know better about your voice as soon as you finish ramping up to holler at me."

"You deserve to be yelled at," she said. "Why did you leave like that, without even a word?"

"I had to."

She sipped lemonade and waited—until she realized he wasn't going to offer details. "Are you going to make this more difficult than it already is?"

He grinned at her. "Probably."

She set down her glass and walked down the steps.

"Hold on, sugar." He followed her.

She spun on him. "Don't you dare 'sugar' me! You save my life, tell me you love me, then run away. Explain that, or let me leave in peace."

"I don't know how."

"To do what, tell me the truth or let me go?"

"Either. Both." He ran his fingers through his hair. "Hell, I don't even know where to start."

"Anywhere will do. You talk in circles most of the time, anyway."

"Fine." He took a deep breath. "You Broke me."

She stared at him. "I don't . . . ." She swallowed. "How?"

"Wish I knew. But the fact is, I'm not a Sword Breaker anymore. I knew it as soon as the Kiss was over. I held you until they came for me. I'd have stayed until you woke up and told you myself, but they said I had to leave.

And they were right, for a whole lot of reasons."

"No!" she cried. Her legs gave out. She wished she could blame it on the long drive.

He caught her before she fell. He stroked her hair, unraveling her braid as she cried into his chest. "Hey, now. It's not a bad thing."

"How can you say that?" she hiccupped.

He brushed away her tears. "Because, you set me free. I don't have to do that ever again. I'm not a monster anymore."

"I am," she whispered.

"No, darlin', you aren't. I'm relieved to be done with it."

She pushed away from him. "Relieved?"

He nodded. "Very."

"Our relationship, whatever it was, is over, and you're relieved?" She wiped her face with her sleeve. "You son of a bitch. All that talk about how you loved me was just a line."

"No." He reached for her.

She pulled back. "Don't touch me!"

"As her majesty wishes, but it's gonna make it a hell of a lot harder for me to protect you night and day if you leave that order in place."

"It's going to be impossible for you to protect me if you aren't Tribe," she spat. "Not that it matters, since I am never going to be a Queen, no matter what they say."

He threw back his head and laughed. "You mean that?"

She glared at him. "You bet I do. I'll find some way to deal with the longing. Go back to school. Do theatre if it gets bad. I won't play by their rules. I am done." She stalked toward her truck.

"All right then." He caught up to her, grabbed her around the waist, and turned her back toward the house.

"Let me go." She struggled.

He kept his arms around her. "If you insist you aren't a Queen, then I don't have to follow your orders."

"You could respect my wishes," she spat.

"Yes, ma'am, and I will. If you'll let me kiss you good-bye."

"Fine, but make it quick. I have a long way to go."

"Yes," he said, "you do." He turned her in his arms, brushed her hair out of her face, and Kissed her.

The world spun. Her heartbeat quickened as he held her to him, devouring her mouth. He hardened. Her response was instant. All she wanted was this moment, the taste and feel of him, the strength of his arms, his blood pulsing in time with hers. Her fingers curled in his shirt, his tangled in her hair. There was no beginning or end, just the Kiss. He gently pulled away, stroking her back as she regained her balance.

"I thought you said . . ."

"I said you Broke me, and you did."

"Then how can you . . .? How could we . . .?" Words failed her.

"After you Broke me, you made me whole. I didn't understand it at first, not sure if I do now. The fact remains, you made me your Master at Arms. One way or another, you're stuck with me. They told me Ardyth was planning on inviting you to her place for a while, so you don't go into this part of your life blind, the way you did when you first got Kissed. I figured I'd come home to settle some things, so Gaby could sell the house."

"Why? It's lovely out here."

"Didn't think you'd want to live in the middle of nowhere, a city girl like you."

"I've been living on the road for over a year. At least you have indoor plumbing." She looked up at him. "You do, don't you?"

"Now." He chuckled. "But it might be a while before I can find you a deep, claw-footed tub."

"What made you think I'd want to stay with you anyway?" she challenged.

"Simple." He kissed her again, a normal one. "You love me."

"Oh." She leaned into him. "There is that."

"And I love you. It seems a good place to start." He nibbled her neck.

Gabrielle came onto the porch. "I won't have you rutting in the yard like animals," she said. "No time for that anyway, Jacques."

Heather grinned at him. "About that, Jacques." She purred his name.

He clenched his jaw. "Don't. Just don't."

Gabrielle put her hands on her hips. "You have dinner to prepare, and you need to tell me where the extra linens are. And guest towels. You do have some, yes? You can't be bringing guests here without proper supplies. I swear you were raised by wolves. I know you live with barbarians, but that's no excuse to forget your upbringing." She walked back into the house, muttering.

"Tell me she doesn't live here," Heather said.

"No, but she comes to visit often enough. Best get used to it."

"Only if you agree to come to my parents' house for Thanksgiving."

He raised one eyebrow. "Think that's a good idea, do you?"

"Oh, it should be very interesting."

"I suppose we ought to go in before she comes back out swinging something. She only acts the lady for company. Soon as she finds out you plan to stick around, she'll show you her true self. That's when the fun starts."

"I can't wait."

"If we kiss in the yard for five more minutes, you won't have to."

"I'll pass." Heather laughed. "For now."

"Knew you were a smart girl." He took her hand.

She let him lead her up the stairs. Hands on her waist, he pivoted and lifted her over the threshold. Then he stepped inside, closed the door, and wrapped his arms around her. She leaned into him as the rightness of it all settled into her bones.

She was safe. She was loved. She was home.

About the Author

Rebecca Kovar laments the loss of gloves and hats as social convention and the wearing of corsetry as a daily habit. She has been known to wield a wicked sword and a vicious red pen and is a champion of the proper use of commas. Many years ago, she ran away and joined the next best thing to a circus, which taught her how to survive in almost any environment and made clear the importance of asking the right questions. She likes her monsters monstrous, rather than angst-ridden, and doesn't mind if they aren't all that pretty. Given a choice between blood and treacle, she'll pick blood every time. She writes short, dark stories, longer urban fantasy, and the occasional steamy romance. She currently spends her days righting wrongs and her nights writing them .

www.ingramcontent.com/pod-product-compliance
Lightning Source LLC
Chambersburg PA
CBHW070842250626
47159CB00003B/890